Hailey held his hand up close to Gloster's face, pulled the trigger and blew half of Gloster's face away. Gloster flew backward as if he'd been hit by an invisible truck. His hands clawed high in the air. The glass shattered against the wall. Gloster hit the wall then crumbled sideways to the floor. His heels banged on the tiles. His body jerked. Hailey saw red and white muck from Gloster's head smeared on the wall behind Gloster's body. The towel in which Hailey had wrapped the gun smoldered. Black powder burns stained the white towel where the bullet had ripped through.

Hailey unwrapped the towel and slipped the gun under his belt, against the small of his back, and walked from the room quickly down the stairs into the tangle of Málaga's backstreets.

DARK DEEDS

Ken Welsh

PINNACLE BOOKS NEW YORK

DARK DEEDS

A Pinnacle Books edition, first published in Great Britain by
Methuen London Ltd.

First printing/September 1984

ISBN: 0-523-42178-8

Can. ISBN: 0-523-43166-X

Cover art by Paul Stinson

Printed in the United States of America

PINNACLE BOOKS, INC.
1430 Broadway
New York, New York 10018

9   8   7   6   5   4   3   2   1

DARK DEEDS

PART ONE

Hailey flew from Paris to Málaga with only a small army-style duffle bag which he could stow under the aircraft seat as luggage. That was the way he always travelled, no matter whether the trip was a short inter-city hop or an intercontinental marathon. The bag contained a change of clothes, nothing more. But the large alligator skin wallet he carried in a specially sewn pick proof pocket inside his tailored jeans held much more useful things. In that he carried an American passport, New York State and International driving licenses, an International Health Certificate proving he had received shots for cholera and yellow fever, a sheet of paper containing a dozen names, addresses, telephone, telex and cable numbers of banks around the world, 10,000 Swiss francs in 1000 franc notes and a thousand American dollars in assorted notes. Hailey could have forgotten the duffle bag and lived quite comfortably out of that wallet. It contained one other item. An impressive document. A banker's order for one hundred thousand dollars payable on demand in any currency at any correspondent bank in the world against a New York account. The banker's order was an indication of Zeller's absolute trust in him.

At the airport immigration counter Hailey handed his passport to the inspecting officer.

"How long will you be staying in Spain, señor?" the officer asked.

"Couple of months," Hailey answered in simple, but clear Spanish.

"And what is the purpose of your visit?"

"Tourism."

3

The stamp came down on a blank page and the officer handed Hailey back his passport. "Enjoy your stay in our country, señor."

Hailey nodded, slung his bag onto his shoulder, eased his way through the press of passengers waiting for their luggage and strolled through customs. No one stopped him. The visa was good for six months. What Hailey had to do would take only a couple of days.

He found the change desk and exchanged 1000 Swiss francs for 44,000 pesetas. As she handed him the money, the girl cashier smiled at him. Women noticed Hailey. They noticed his lean tallness; they noticed the casual yet obviously expensive way he dressed; they noticed the soft tone of his voice, but most of all they noticed his thick, long, golden hair which he brushed back over his ears and which rested below the level of his collar. Women loved Hailey's hair. And now, in mute recognition of the girl's smile, Hailey pocketed his money and then brushed his long, golden hair from his forehead.

Hailey paid off the cab outside the Málaga port. He looked around a moment to take his bearings. He stood on the edge of the Plaza Queipo de Llano with the docks and the sea behind him. Half a mile to his right, at the end of the famed sub-tropical Alameda gardens which lined the main thoroughfare leading east, stood the bullring and soaring above the ring and the city were the 3000 year old Gibralfaro fortifications built by the Phoenicians. Hailey began to remember his geography. He waited for the lights and walked across the square and into Calle Larios. After five minutes he turned right into a narrow street called Chinitos.

Chinitos is a passage full of bootblacks, bars, locksmiths and knife-grinders, one of a warren of alleys surrounding the nearby cathedral and diocesan palace. Hailey walked quickly and unerringly through this maze until he reached a near derilect three-story apartment building with weeds sprouting on the roof between its moss-covered tiles. Patches of damp blistered the whitewash inbetween a spaghetti-tangle of electrical cables pinioned up and across its crumbling facade. The ten-feet-high wrought-iron front gates hadn't been closed since

1937 when five Republican sympathizers barricaded themselves inside to await the arrival of Franco's Italian allies. They'd been routed in a brief fire-fight and summarily executed in the cobbled courtyard behind the gates where they'd made their heroic but tactically useless stand. A broad stairway, its steps worn to uneven curves during the passage of centuries, led to apartments on the second and third stories. An old, black-clad woman sat on a chair knitting in a pool of sunlight.

"*Que quieres, joven?*" she asked Hailey.

"I would like to speak to Gloster, the Englishman," Hailey said in Spanish. "Does he still live here?"

Distaste brushed the old woman's face. She jabbed upwards with one of her knitting needles. "*Primero piso, segunda derecha.*"

Hailey nodded and walked swiftly up the stairs. First floor, second on the right. A hand-written card held by a rusty drawing pin outside the door announced *Juan Gloster.* Spaniards have trouble pronouncing the name John. Hailey knocked and heard a surly voice inside demand, "*Quien es?*"

"Gloster?"

The door opened a crack and Gloster appeared, pulling at the zip of a pair of trousers he'd only just stepped into. He was as Hailey remembered him, big and flabby, but in even worse physical condition now, his gut bulging over his belt, his skin sallow, head balding. He stared at Hailey for a moment before recognizing him, and Hailey noted how Gloster's eyes narrowed for an instant as he realized it would be a busy day. He stepped outside and closed the door behind him. Down in the courtyard, the old woman turned her head back to her knitting as Gloster emerged.

"I didn't expect you," Gloster said. His breath stank of wine.

"Won't you invite me in?" Hailey asked.

"You've interrupted me."

"I apologize for the disturbance," Hailey said grandly, and nodded his head in a sarcastic bow.

"What do you want?"

"To talk to you."

"We can talk here."

Hailey shook his head.

"I'll get a shirt and we'll go to a bar."

"Inside," Hailey said, quietly. "It's a confidential matter."

Gloster's lips pressed together as if he was formulating an argument. Then he thought better of it. He opened the door and spoke rapidly in Spanish. A female voice protested. "*Fuera de aqui!*" he shouted.

Hailey glanced down into the courtyard. The old woman's needles clicked frantically as she strained her neck to see what was happening above her. A moment later, a young, busty girl, wearing only a clinging shift and high heels, opened the door and brushed by the two men without a word or a glance. The crone's eyes ducked again to her work as the girl strutted down the worn stairs.

Hailey followed Gloster into the dimly lit, dirty flat and dumped his bag on the floor. A double bed with rumpled sheets stood to one side under a window overlooking the courtyard. A sagging couch, a small desk laden with old *Sur* and *Sol de España* newspapers, two straight-backed chairs, a massive Braun color TV set on a stand, and a stained circular table were the only other furniture. The table was stacked with greasy dishes and empty *Savin* wine bottles. On the left of the room were two doors. Hailey saw that one led to a miniature kitchenette, the other to a bathroom. He could hear the wheezing cistern above the toilet. Gloster, Hailey decided, not only looked like a pig and talked like a pig, but lived like a pig. But Hailey had met Gloster before. He'd known what to expect.

Hailey nodded over his shoulder. "Latest player on the team? How do you survive, Gloster? How come the opposition don't castrate you? You must be the only English pimp in Spain."

"I get by," Gloster said.

Hailey hung his thumbs from his pockets and watched Gloster slouching against the wall. "Zeller told you to dump the girls and find another cover."

"Fuck Zeller."

"Zeller pays you."

"And I do my job. What I do on my own time is none of Zeller's business."

"Zeller doesn't agree."

Gloster pulled a crumpled pack of *Ducados* from his pocket, extracted a cigarette and lit it without offering Hailey one. "The girls are a perfect front. The police think I'm a crazy foreigner with more gall than brains. But I make sure my girls pass them enough information to keep them happy."

"Things are changing in Spain, Gloster."

"If the cops are pressured into moving against me, they'll warn me first. That's the arrangement."

"And where will you go? I doubt that her Majesty's Brittanic government will welcome you home. And if they did, that's no good to Zeller. He wants you in Spain."

Gloster pushed himself off the wall, picked up a shirt from the old couch, pulled it on and buttoned it over his flabby belly. "That's the trouble with you fucking Yanks. You think you own everyone. Well, Zeller doesn't own *me*."

"Zeller isn't a Yank," Hailey smiled. "But I'll tell Zeller what you said."

Gloster walked to the table and poured wine from a nearly empty bottle into an unwashed glass and drained it in me one go. He sniffed and wiped the back of his hand over his mouth. "So what do you want, sonny-jim?"

"Weapons," Hailey said.

"I guessed that," Gloster sneered. "How many, what type and where?"

Hailey walked away from where Gloster sat with one haunch on the table and leaned against the door. He smiled. "Take it easy, Gloster. We're associates. You should show me a little respect."

"Respect, my ass," Gloster said. "Zeller sends a kid like you out on a man's errand, and the *kid* tells *me* to show some respect." Gloster spat on his own living room floor.

Still leaning against the door, still with his thumbs hooked into his pockets and still smiling, Hailey said, "I want thirty sub-machine guns, same number of handguns. They must be old. Second-world war. Owens, Stens, Thompsons, something like that. If you've got Thompsons, then try and give me Colts; same caliber. I want about six thousand rounds."

"What the hell do you want that antiquated rubbish for?"

"None of your business, Gloster. Can you supply?"

Gloster dropped his cigarette butt into the dregs at the bottom of a coffee cup and fumbled in his pocket for his pack. It was empty. He crumpled it and tossed it into a corner. "From the Tangier warehouse," he said.

"Thompsons and Colts?"

"Cases of the bloody stuff gathering dust. No one wants those dinosaurs anymore. I warned Zeller when he bought them."

Hailey took a pack of *Winston* from his shirt pocket, carefully tapped one free and lit it with a gold, Dupont lighter. He watched Gloster's eyes following his hand as he slipped the pack back into his pocket. He didn't offer Gloster one.

"What model Thompsons?" Hailey demanded.

Gloster's face spread into the imitation of a grin. "Take your choice. MIs or MIAIs. Would you know the bloody difference, sonny-jim?"

Hailey drew on his cigarette, savoring the smoke, then exhaled toward the chipped, red-tile floor. Staring downward at the butts and mess on the floor, Hailey said quietly, "The MI928AI replaced the MI928AI. It was redesigned without the Blish piece or the Cutts Compensator and carried simple battle sights. The MIAI eliminated the hammer and was fitted with a fixed firing pin. As it contains less moving parts, I'd prefer you to supply me with the MIAI. I also want new barrels fitted and three twenty-round box magazines for each gun. The thirties tend to jam." He looked up. "Do I get full marks, Gloster?"

"Didn't like you the first time we met, sonny-jim," Gloster said. "Nothing's changed."

Hailey drew on his cigarette, then jammed it out under his heel. "How do you contact Tangier, Gloster?"

"Coded telex," Gloster pushed a pudgy finger through the butts in an over flowing ashtray and found one better than an inch long. He lit it. "The consignment will be arranged within four hours. Where's it going?"

"None of your business."

"It's my bloody *business*," Gloster exploded. "Get it in your head, sonny-jim, you're a fucking errand boy." He slammed the palm of his hand against his chest. "*I* buy and sell for Zeller. *I* set up deals. *I* handle Zeller's cash money. *You're* nothing but a snotty-nosed little messenger!"

Hailey took another cigarette from his shirt pocket and lit it. He didn't say anything.

"If I don't know where the consignment's going," Gloster yelled, "I can't do the bloody job. Which means I can't get *you* out of my fucking hair."

"You'll have the consignment sent to Asilah," Hailey said. "That's all you have to worry about. You'll have it there in forty-eight hours. Who's our man in Tangier?"

"Mohammed ben Ulan," Gloster snapped. "And he's *my* man, not *our* man."

"Tell Mohammend ben Ulan to wait for me in the Atlas Bar. I'll get to him forty-eight to sixty hours from now." Hailey hefted his duffle bag off the floor and slung it over his shoulder. "I want the telex confirmation from ben Ulan by six o'clock tonight. I'll be here then."

Hailey opened the door, then turned back to Gloster. "I also want a handgun for myself. Tonight. Something discreet. Twenty rounds."

"What about my commission for all this?"

"Tonight, Gloster, when I come by. When I see the confirmation you'll get your cash." Hailey smiled and turned again to close the door behind him.

"Hey!"

Hailey paused. "You shouting for me, Gloster?"

"How the hell is ben Ulan supposed to recognize you in Asilah?"

"Listen sonny-jim," Hailey said, "just stop asking questions and start doing as you're told. Just make sure ben Ulan's in the Atlas Bar." Hailey winked and closed the door against the rush of expletives.

Hailey made his way through the twisting maze of narrow streets back to Calle Larios. He came out of Pasaje Chinitos and into the crowded main street, then turned left and headed towards the sea. Halfway along the length of the street he turned into the old *Café Español* his favorite the last time he'd been in Málaga. It'd changed; it was only half as big as before; one part had been turned into a liquor store. Hailey sat at a corner table, well away from the groups of businessmen who argued noisily about *fulbol* and politics as they took their mid-morning break. He ordered a coffee from the elderly waiter and thought about Gloster.

Gloster was an obnoxious bastard, not that Hailey gave a damn. Hailey had been sent to Málaga to do what he had to do and Gloster was part of it and that was all. Hailey wouldn't get involved. Hailey never got involved. Hailey would return to Gloster's at six o'clock that evening and do what Zeller had told him. Zeller had told Hailey to arrange the small arms shipment from Gloster's inventory. Zeller hadn't said Hailey had to like Gloster. Zeller had said Gloster was a liability. Zeller said Gloster didn't do as he was told. He said Gloster was a drunkard. Drunkards talked about things they shouldn't; they talked in their sleep. Gloster slept with his own women; the women he pimped for; the women Zeller had told him to be rid of. One day he would talk in his sleep and the girl who heard it might decide she didn't like Gloster any more and tell the police what she had heard. That would mean trouble for Zeller.

"Also," Zeller had said, "Gloster is gross and I cannot stand grossness, and Gloster is unintelligent, another trait I despise. Gloster, I must admit, is an error. We shall correct that error." Zeller had smiled. "*You* will correct that error for me, dear boy," he had said to Hailey. "Kill him."

The waiter served Hailey's coffee. Hailey stared at the glass sitting on the saucer, at the white packet containing the two cubes of sugar, and at the teaspoon. Hailey saw his inverted, abstracted reflection in the shining spoon. Hailey could hear the voice in his head even now. Kill Gloster. Get rid of Gloster. Gloster is an error. The other part of Hailey could hear the voice too. But that confused Hailey. The other part of him? Someone inside him listening?

Hailey tore his eyes from the distorted reflection of himself in the spoon. The noise and chatter and laughter in the bar faded. The periphery of his vision dulled and drifted out of focus. He raised his eyes and stared at the big photograph of Málaga behind the bar. He seemed to be staring at it through a tunnel. One part of his mind recognized the photograph for what it was. Another part was still hearing Zeller's voice saying *Kill Gloster. Gloster is an error. Correct it, dear boy. Gloster is gross. Kill him.*

It's as if there's two of me, Hailey thought. He stared at the photograph and listened to himself think and to the other part of him hearing what Zeller had told him to do. Hailey and that other young man dwelling inside his head both knew what they had to do, but Hailey was the one who did it. Hailey always did what he was told. Hailey didn't know how to do anything else. When Hailey was told to do a job he just went right out and did it. No arguments. No ifs, buts or maybes. Hailey just did his job and kept right on doing his job. There was money, women, travel, adventure and the chance to kill. Could a man want more? Hailey did his job and he had all those things. Hailey didn't *know* why he did what he did, but that didn't worry him. The only thing that worried him—no, not worried, but confused him—was that young man, that other part of him, that thin shadow superimposed upon himself who sometimes slipped into focus in Hailey's mind and made himself known without allowing himself to be realized. Like a lonely vagabond, too shy to step forward and say hello.

Suddenly, the noise and conversation in the bar reached a momentarily higher pitch and Hailey snapped out of his trance. He stirred sugar into his coffee and sipped it. He'd forgotten the young man. Hailey only remembered the young man when he superimposed himself on Hailey's mind. It was then that Hailey knew that the young man had tried to visit before. But now, as he left fifty pesetas on the table and walked out of the *Cafe Español* and back out onto the crowded city pavements of Málaga, Hailey was once more in control, and the young man didn't exist, had never existed.

Hailey found a public phone booth and rang Block's apartment at Puerto Jose Banus. He told Block he was on his way.

* * *

Hailey hired a taxi driver to take him the fifty kilometers along the coastal road through the resort towns of Torremolinos, Fuengirola and Marbella to Puerto Jose Banus. He sat back and enjoyed the trip. The Costa del Sol was well named. Even though it was November the sun shined and, here and there, clutches of winter tourists sunned themselves on the gray sand. Some of the hardy paddled in the chilly waters. Outside Fuengirola, Hailey saw a circle of fishing boats working with nets to one side of the underwater reefs jutting out from the Punta de Calaburra below the white lighthouse. Then they were into El Chapporal and the square kilometers of Mediterranean pines which concealed hundreds of shining white villas, most of them owned by northern Europeans who had fled south to escape high taxes and low winter temperatures.

One day, Hailey, thought, I'll buy myself a villa like that. He imagined it. Big and white with cool, marble floors. And with a pool, and perhaps a tennis court. He'd have the money soon. A few more years with Zeller. A few more jobs. Then he'd have the rest of his life ahead of him to use as he wanted. What would he do? He hadn't thought too much about it; he didn't think too much about anything. Sometimes he was conscious of that fact. He'd be sitting in a bar watching people walk down the street and he'd realize he wasn't thinking about anything. His mind would be empty except for that one thought—that he was thinking about not thinking. That was a contradiction, and he knew it, but after a few seconds of struggling with the contradiction, of trying to pin it down and understand it, he would stop thinking about not thinking and watch the people some more. That contradictory thought was like the young man inside of him who never really stepped forward. The thought never defined itself properly.

Hailey wasn't an imbecile. Hailey *did think.* But only superficially, only in one part of his brain, that part which deals with simple gratification and primary accomplishment. Hailey would think of things like buying himself a big house, or taking an ocean cruise, or finding a girl to take to bed. And he thought about his work. When Zeller or Tristan gave him a job he thought about that. He'd consider every angle, every possibility, figure out exactly what to do and how to do it and then go ahead and accomplish the task. He could think on that level, alright; that was why Hailey was so dangerous. But Hailey couldn't think about the things normal people do. He was incapable of thinking in emotional terms. Emotions were alien impulses to him. He could consider them—on about the same level he would consider a caged tiger in a zoo—but he could not think in terms of love, hate, anger, revenge, happiness or satisfaction. He did not think of concepts like past, future, eternity or death. He never thought of moral problems like honesty, responsibility or whether one man should or should not kill another. And Hailey never felt uncertainty, remorse or fear.

There was something missing in Hailey. He was an automaton. Hailey just did what he had to do, what he was told to do. It was all he *could* do.

At Puerto Jose Banus, five kilometers west of Marbella, Hailey paid the taxi driver, tipped him generously and asked him to wait an hour. He strolled by the Customs post and into the vast rectangle of the port.

Puerto Jose Banus was named after the flamboyant Madrid businessman who had built it in the early Seventies. His friends warned him he'd go broke; his enemies hoped he would. But the massive investment paid off and now, particularly in high summer, it was often impossible to find an empty berth among the thousands offered by the company.

The port was bounded on the seaward side by a four hundred meter long breakwater and at the far end by dry docks and port facilities. Along the other two perimeters rose banks of apartments built in neo-Andaluz style. On street level the port offered the most expensive lineup of restaurants, boutiques, cafés and bars on the Spanish coastline.

At the *Shark Club*, the first bar on his right after entering the port, Hailey sat down to wait for Block. He ordered a red wine and sipped it slowly. At the *Shark Club* the service was friendly, the prices reasonable and the view of the moored boats perfect. It was the view that interested Hailey.

Hailey wanted a boat.

In Puerto Jose Banus, at any time, $50,000,000 worth of

craft lay at their moorings. If a couple of big 150-feet-plus ocean going motor yachts sailed in—toys of some Arabian playboys, or the prestige symbols of giant multi-national corporations, complete with swimming pools, helicopters and speed-boats—then that figure skyrocketed. You didn't look at one of those babies under twenty million dollars.

The boats in Puerto Banus were moored in a distinct and prestigious pecking order. On the first quay—the one in front of Hailey—and close-by the control tower, lay yachts and cruisers of twenty meters and up: the big, steel TSDYs and sleek, teak-decked deep-sea cruisers and the fast sloop and ketchrigged motor sailers, all capable of trans-Atlantic crossings; none of them worth less than $250,000, many worth a million.

Working down the quays the craft got progressively smaller: the fifty footers, the forty footers, the thirty footers and so on, until at the far end, at the quay, furthest away from the control tower and under the eye of the tradesmen working at the dry docks, the tiny day-sailers and even smaller four meter sailing dinghies and outboard speedboats and runarounds lazily dipped and bobbed under the influence of insignificant bow-wave turbulence from their big brothers entering the harbor mouth a half kilometer away.

Hailey wasn't interested in a seventy foot ketch-rigged motor sailer, nor in any stately 100 foot ocean going motor yacht and least of all in a four-meter sailing dinghy.

Hailey wanted something big enough to tackle coastal waters, but not so big that two men—or one in a pinch—couldn't handle it by themselves. Above all, Hailey wanted something fast. Very fast. With a long cruising range.

He was sipping his third wine before Block found him. They hadn't met before, but Block had been warned of Hailey's arrival ten days ago and told what he had to do. Hailey had told him on the phone that he'd wait at the *Shark Club* and that he'd have the army duffel bag at his feet.

Block stood six-two and carried arms and shoulders to match his height. He wasn't the sort of guy anyone played games with. He wore jeans and sneakers and a red and white striped matelot-style tee-shirt, and affected short-cropped black hair and a full, thick beard.

Block strolled down the quay with his eyes fixed on the *Shark Club* and scanned the ten or so customers drinking at the outside tables. He walked straight up to Hailey and touched the army duffel bag with his toe.

"Eh, man, you Tristan's friend?" he asked.

Hailey nodded and indicated the seat beside him. Block sat down and signaled the waiter to bring him the same as Hailey. He lit a thin, black cigar, leaned back and blew a stream of smoke into the air.

"Got a call a while back to hunt up something for you."

Hailey nodded and toyed with the stem of his glass.

"So what do I call you, man? What's you name?"

"No names," Hailey said.

"What's with the drama, man? We're just doing a little job."

"Call me man, man," Hailey said.

Block grunted a laugh. "Shee-it. A fuckin' live one. OK mister man, you got it."

He held out his hand and when Hailey held out his Block slapped it in a mock brothers salute.

"You doing good works for me, Block?" Hailey asked.

"The absolute best. The abso-fucking-lutely best."

Hailey stood and dropped two one hundred peseta notes on the table. "Then show me."

"My drink, man, what about my drink?"

"Later," Hailey said. "I want to see what you found."

Block shrugged and grinned. "You're the boss, man."

"Yes," Hailey said.

Hailey hefted his duffel bag and the two of them strolled down toward the second quay.

"You worked with Tristan long?" Hailey asked.

"About three years."

"Where?"

They heard a polite honk behind them and stepped to one side as a cream Mercedes sports-coupé glided past. The girl behind the wheel who smiled at Hailey as she drove by was special—blonde hair flowing, white tee-shirt showing off bronzed arms, and Hailey returned her glance—but the car wasn't worth a second look, not in Puerto Jose Banus. In Puerto Banus, Mercedes were a dime a dozen, lost in the thickets of Rolls Royces, Maseratis and Lamborghinis, some of them carried on the decks of their owners' massive yachts.

"Where?" Hailey asked again.

"All over, man," Block said. "Israel, Greece, did one out of Ibiza. Couple in Italy. South of France. Malta. This is my second in Banus."

Hailey stopped. Block flashed his big grin and spread his hands. "Don't get your balls in a knot, man. The first I did long hair, no beard on my first day in Spain two years back. Now I got short hair, long bread and no one remembers me." He turned and walked on. "Besides, the first ones, the ones I did that first day here, shit, man, they had bad luck." He grinned. "Lost at sea."

Hailey nodded, satisfied. "Did Tristan tell you about the job?"

Block shook his head. "He just said, find a boat."

"A fast boat."

"That's what he said."

"And . . . ?"

"So just keep on walkin' man."

They turned right and walked out to the end of the second quay, strolling along like a pair of tourists enjoying the sights. Real tourists were there, too. Kids ran up and down the quays. Couples wandered slowly, arm in arm. A plump German woman smoothed the wrinkles from her dress and posed herself sheepishly in front of a shining white fifty-foot Bagglieto while her stocky husband photographed her for the family album.

That was another great success of Puerto Jose Banus. The *hoi-polloi* could enter the magic world of the international yacht-set and fantasize for a few hours that they were part of it. And it was all free—a multi-million dollar spectacular laid on for everyman, and no one even asked an entrance fee.

Block pointed across to the third quay. From where they stood they could see the harbor stretching away from them. Way in the background, the 1217 meter mountain which protected Marbella from the hot *terral* wind, jutted proudly into the hard, blue, winter sky like a chunky, sculpted breast.

Hailey followed Block's pointing finger. The boat was

moored between a brace of forty-feet Bermuda ketches. Hailey nodded; a *Seawolf*. Hailey hadn't seen many—maybe two or three in English waters—but he knew their reputation for guts and he knew cruisers didn't come much faster.

"Tell me," Hailey said.

"She's called *Destry*. Thirty-six feet. Powered by a pair of 250 horsepower Ford Sabre diesels. They're tuned for 300 horsepower intermittent output. She goes like the powers of shit, man."

"How fast?"

"How's thirty knots sound?"

"Full throttle?"

"Cruising, man, cruising. This is a fucking thoroughbred, man. She'll top thirty-five knots if you let her go."

"Instrumentation?"

"The works. Seascan radar, Neco autopilot with remote control compass, you name it, she's got it."

"Depth scanner?"

Block tossed his cigar stub into the harbor. "Pressurized hot and cold water, as well."

"Auxiliary?"

"An Avon S300 inflatable powered by a twenty-five horse-power Penta."

"That's a big tender for a thirty-six footer."

"The owner's a skin-driving nut."

"What's the weight capacity of the S300?"

Block rocked his hand from side to side. "Around 1200 pounds."

"Speed?"

"With helmsman alone, maybe twenty knots. Fully laden you drop fast, say fifteen."

Fast enough, Hailey thought. She'll do. He lit a cigarette without offering one to Block.

Hailey turned his back on *Destry* and stared out toward the control tower. "Any ideas about how we get aboard?"

Block's face spilt into a broad grin. "That's the easy part, man. Done my homework, man." He slapped Hailey on the shoulder and squeezed as he laughed. Hailey flinched, glared at him and moved half a step away as Block's hand dropped and the laugh choked. "Sorry about that, man," Block said. "Like no offense, OK?"

"Just tell me how we board her," Hailey said softly.

"Owner's name is Quinn. Rich fucker. His old man owns half Manhattan. He bought *Destry* in England and cruised her down here. He's on a round-the-Med jaunt. He's sailing with his girl and one crew who captains for him. Big bearded guy named Teal." Block looked nervously at Hailey and lit another of his cigars. "I got friendly with Quinn. Told him I had this writer friend coming over from the States—that's you, man. Told him you were researching some book and wanted a day aboard a cruiser. He's sailing for Nerja tomorrow afternoon. He agreed to take us along. Idea is, we cruise to Nerja with him then bus back."

"That simple?"

"Quinn's real nice guy. Says it's no sweat for him to carry us a few hours."

"What time does he sail?"

"Two o'clock."

"Do you have a gun?"

"Naturally, man."

Hailey pointed to a bar at the end of the quay; the *Coco-Loco*. "I'll meet you there at one tomorrow afternoon." Hailey turned and walked away.

Block followed. "Hey, man, where you going?"

"What's it to you?"

"We gotta work up some ideas about how to do this thing."

"I'll work up the ideas, Block, you just do as you're told."

Block nodded his head gently, then flicked his cigar toward Hailey's feet. "O.K., boss, but what about my fucking drink?"

Hailey didn't break his stride. He didn't look back. "Do me a big favor, Block, don't swear in my presence. Foul language offends me."

In the taxi on the way back to Málaga, Hailey ran through in his mind what he had to do. Getting rid of Gloster would be easy, and he didn't expect any problem hijacking *Destry* or loading the arms in Morocco. But trouble might come when he handed the weapons over to a fishing boat off the Basque coast.

The problem was that Basque terrorist organizations infiltrated each other. The weapons Hailey would deliver had been bought by BEKA, but if ETA had a man inside BEKA and knew about the shipment, that was where the potential problem lay.

Hailey settled back deeper into the back seat of the SEAT 1430 Diesel. The taxi driver hadn't spoken a word to him since they'd left Marbella. He was playing flamenco cassettes with the volume turned down low. Hailey smoothed back his golden hair. He lit a cigarette and stared out the taxi window at a family of gypsies, complete with donkey-drawn cart and an assortment of scruffy kids, who were camped on a rubbish site opposite a beach outside Fuengirola. Hailey would worry about ETA and BEKA when the time came. It wasn't the kind of situation he could plan for.

The Basque situation was the type of political mess ready-made for a man like Zeller. The Basques had suffered unacceptable indignities throughout the Franco era, including the erasure of their *fueras*, or traditional laws dating from the Middle Ages, and the suppression of their language and customs. Guerrilla groups had risen to fight the oppression. After the death of General Franco, the arrival of democracy and the vote by Basques to create an autonomous state within the Spanish constitution satisfied most groups but cut no ice with the hard-liners who demanded nothing less than a Basque homeland completely independant of Spain. The guerrillas became terrorists. And Zeller moved in, as he'd moved in on a dozen other trouble-spots.

There remained perhaps a dozen would-be terrorist bands in Alava, Guipúzcoa, Vizcaya and Navarra, the four provinces of the *Euskaldunak*, or Basquelands. Most of them were bar-room philosophers who talked a lot and, if they'd drunk enough, occasionally attacked a cop on a street corner. There were three main groups, and it was with these that Zeller dealt.

Euskadi Ta Askatasuna, known as ETA, the Marxist inspired organization fighting for a Basque homeland independent of Spain, hit world headlines in 1973 when they detonated a land-mine under a car carrying Admiral Carrero Blanco, Franco's President of the Government. They blasted the Admiral, his driver and the two-ton car over a thirty-six feet high Madrid convent wall. Now, disregarding the democratic choice of a majority of their countrymen, they extracted financial support from Basque businessmen by threatening death to their families if they didn't pay a "revolutionary tax;" they assassinated police and public officials; they kidnapped industrialists and held them for ransom.

Ranged against this far-left ETA group was a splinter party called BEKA. BEKA had recently broken away from ETA after deciding that Marxism could not offer a viable future to an emerging European nation. BEKA promoted a contorted philosophy which it labeled "Basque Democratic Socialism." A submachine gun battle between ETA and BEKA had left eleven dead in the streets of San Sebastian, including three old-age pensioners, a housewife and her twin eight-year-old daughters.

The third group, fighting both ETA and BEKA, was a mysterious but well-organized cadre of killers calling themselves PECT, *Pueblo Español Contra Terrorismo* (Spaniards Against Terrorism) who claimed that their object was to defeat Basque terrorism and bring peace to *Euskaldunak*. Their true mission was to cause so much trouble in the Basquelands that Madrid would be forced to move in more and more police and, eventually, the army, thus gradually usurping the infant Basque autonomous state. To this end the PECT murdered police and blamed the killings on ETA. They killed ETA men and pointed the blame at BEKA. They assassinated BEKA men and blamed their deaths on the police.

Zeller sold weapons to all three groups. He sold the best to ETA. His thinking was very clear. ETA had existed the best part of twenty years. They were well organized. They had tremendous buying power derived not only from "revolutionary taxes," bank robberies and ransoms from within Spain, but also from sympathetic elements of the French Basques across the border. If Zeller didn't give them the guns they wanted, they'd buy elsewhere. It was as simple as that. On the other hand, BEKA was badly organized, poor, and had no other sources of weapons supply. Zeller didn't believe they could continue their three-front war against ETA, PECT and the police for more than another year. He wasn't about to waste good weapons on a group like that.

Weapons dealing, for Zeller, was more than just business. It was a political game, too. If arms dealers backed the right side, when that side came to power, the dealer found himself with a good friend—and huge contracts if he was asked to supply equipment for a national army, or a police force. For that reason, Zeller also supplied first-rate weapons to PECT. If a *coup d'état* ever toppled the Madrid government and the fascists moved in again, PECT would remember Zeller. Zeller didn't really believe that PECT or ETA would ever be powerful enough to change the course of the Spanish political thrust, but Zeller dealt with weapons like another man deals with cards. "Play discreetly," Zeller once told Hailey, "play carefully, play the odds, but take the occasional chance. One never knows when one will take the jackpot."

Hailey booked in for one night at the *Málaga Palacio* hotel. The desk clerk requested he leave his passport so he could fill in the obligatory police card; the *señor* could pick it up in the morning. The passport identified Hailey as Chales Montford Harrington. Every time Hailey set out on a new job for Zeller, Tristan supplied him with a new passport and a new banker's order matching the name on the passport. If Hailey unknowingly made an error on a job and returned to the same country it would be that much harder for authorities to pick him up. The $100,000 banker's order was what Zeller called Hailey's "trouble money." Wherever Hailey was in the world he could use the money to make a deposit or payment for Zeller on an arms shipment. Or, if Hailey found himself in trouble, he could use the money to buy or bribe his way out of it. Zeller thought a lot of Hailey. The truth was that Zeller had more than $100,000 invested in the man. Hailey was Zeller's right arm. And Hailey was Zeller's brain in the field.

Hailey spent five minutes relaxing on the balcony of his room. From there he could see out over the jigsaw of Málaga's traffic snarls, across the Alameda gardens and to the port. At the dock on his right, cars and passengers were boarding the Málaga-Tangier ferry ready for the evening run.

Hailey looked at his watch. Twenty to six. Time to finish his business with Gloster. Hailey walked out of the *Palacio*, turned right and strolled past the cathedral. He crossed the road, dodging traffic, and cut up an alley where several *bodegas* offered Málaga sweet wine by the liter if you brought your own bottle. He reached Gloster's apartment at ten to six. The old woman was still in the courtyard, sweeping the cobbles with a worn-out broom. She glanced once at Hailey mounting the stairs then bent back to her work muttering that she didn't understand these *extranjeros*, these foreigners with their strange ways.

Hailey knocked on Gloster's door.

"*Espera un momento*," Gloster called.

"Open the door!" Hailey demanded.

"Wait a minute, damn it!"

Gloster opened the door a crack. Hailey pushed it open and shoved by Gloster. A girl—a different girl—lay naked on the rumpled bed. She didn't bother trying to cover herself when she saw Hailey. She got off the bed and slipped into a pair of pants and skirt, and pulled a yellow T-shirt over small, high breasts. Gloster zipped up his trousers and nodded for the girl to leave. She kicked on a pair of high-heels and walked out the door smiling at Hailey.

"Auditioning again, Gloster?"

"You're a rude bastard, sonny-jim."

"You should watch it Gloster. You're getting old. Too much fornicating and you'll damage yourself."

"I'm just about sick of you busting in here, sonny."

"I said I'd come at six."

"It's ten *to* six."

"So I'm early."

Hailey shook his golden hair clear of his eyes, brushed past Gloster and sat on the edge of the bed. He lit a cigarette, inhaled deeply and tapped the ash onto the floor.

"Did you do as I told you?"

Gloster's lips compressed. "I did as you *asked*."

"And . . . ?"

"And ben Ulan will be waiting for you in Asilah, with the consignment."

"New barrels on the Thompsons?"

"He doesn't have time to change them. They're packed in a separate crate." Gloster scratched his belly. "My deal with Zeller calls for ten dollars commission on each weapon I handle for him, plus a dollar per hundred rounds. Two dollars on handguns."

"Did you get my handgun, Gloster?"

Gloster stepped past Hailey, flipped up the mattress and took out a rag wrapped bundle and tossed it onto Hailey's lap. Hailey unwrapped the bundle to reveal an 8-shot Llama XA.32 automatic with two spare magazines. Hailey released the magazine from the butt and checked it was loaded. He snapped it back, applied the safety and reached around and slipped the gun into his belt against the small of his back. He dropped the two spare magazines into his coat pocket.

"Happy?" Gloster asked.

"Oh, you're very efficient, Gloster, no doubt about it."

"You might try thanks, sonny-jim."

"Thanks," Hailey said, smiling.

"You can tell Zeller he can add a hundred and twenty-five dollars onto my next retainer check. I had to buy the Llama off the street."

"I'll tell him," Hailey said.

"Now what about the money?"

"Let me see the telex from Ulan."

"*Please,*" Gloster said, trying sarcasm.

"Please," Hailey said, quietly, as if it didn't matter anymore.

Gloster took a sheet of paper from his pocket and handed it to Hailey. Hailey scanned it and nodded. He put it in his own pocket.

"You owe me four hundred and twenty-two dollars," Gloster said. "Three hundred on the Thompsons, sixty-two on the Colts and Llama, sixty for the rounds. I won't charge you on the new barrels or the twenty-four rounds with the Llama." Gloster smiled. "Call it four-twenty. I'm feeling big-hearted."

"Call it five forty-five," Hailey said. "I'll pay for the Llama. Save Zeller worrying about it." Hailey took out his wallet. He sorted five hundred and forty-five dollars from his assorted American notes and handed them to Gloster. Gloster counted them, grunted, dropped them on the table and poured himself a water glass full of red wine.

"Zeller got any more work?" he asked.

"Sure," Hailey said, "but I'll use your toilet before I explain."

Gloster downed half the glass and watched Hailey as he went into the bathroom and shut the door. Hailey took out the Llama and wrapped a filthy towel which was laying on the floor right around the automatic and his hand. He waited a moment, then flushed the toilet. When Hailey walked back into the living room, Gloster had his back to him. Hailey walked over to the big color TV set and switched it on. He turned the volume up loud, so loud the speaker vibrated. Gloster swung around.

"What the hell are you doing?"

Hailey walked toward him with the towel wrapped around his hand.

"What the fuck's wrong with your hand?"

Hailey held his hand up close to Gloster's face, pulled the trigger and blew half of Gloster's face away. Gloster flew backward as if he'd been hit by a invisible truck. His hands clawed high in the air. The glass shattered against the wall. Gloster hit the wall then crumbled sideways to the floor. His heels banged on the tiles. His body jerked. Hailey saw red and white muck from Gloster's head smeared on the wall behind Gloster's body. The towel in which Hailey had wrapped the gun smoldered. Black powder burns stained the white towel where the bullet had ripped through.

Hailey strode quickly over to the TV set and turned it off. He unwrapped the towel and slipped the gun under his belt again, against the small of his back. He took the American dollars from the table where Gloster had left them and stuffed them into his pocket. He stood over Gloster's body assuring himself the man was dead, then knelt down and carefully covered the shattered head with the dirty, powder stained towel. He watched the red stain spreading through the fabric.

Hailey walked from the room, shut the door behind him and pushed. It only opened from the outside with a key. Hailey walked quickly down the stairs past the old lady who still worked at sweeping the cobbles and out into the tangle of Málaga's backstreets.

It'd be two, maybe three days before Gloster started stinking badly enough for someone to break in and find his body. By then, Hailey would be out of the country.

The girl moaned under Hailey. He dug his fingers deeper into her buttocks. She pushed at his shoulders and tried to twist away. Hailey thrust harder at her, slipped his hands from under her and grabbed at her wrists. She twisted again and jerked her hips, trying to free his penis from her. Hailey let the weight of his hips go dead against her so she couldn't disengage. He pushed her arms over her head and when she strained to free herself her breasts lifted toward him. Hailey saw her nipples were hard and erect. He bent his head to suck them, first one then the other. She stopped fighting him. Her legs lifted, clutching his hips, locking behind his back. Her hips started moving rhythmically to the thrust of his penis. He bit the side of her breast. She flinched with the pain. Her head tossed from side to side. Her eyes were closed, her mouth open, then as Hailey sucked hard on her nipples again, her teeth clenched and she thrust her hips hard into him, trying to get more of him.

Hailey had picked her up in the lobby two hours after he'd killed Gloster. He'd bought her a drink and they'd talked a while. She was Canadian, on a three month tour of Europe. She was nineteen. She said she was looking for experience. She said she loved Hailey's golden hair. Hailey gave her some experience. She shared his bed for two hours. He'd been rough with her from the moment he closed the door behind them. He'd stabbed into her so hard he'd hurt her. He'd bitten her, scratched her, slapped her buttocks with stinging blows. At first she hadn't minded at all; she'd felt excited; Hailey was different to her fumbling high school lovers back in Toronto; she'd entered into the spirit of the thing. But he proved insatiable and he rammed at her desperately and the bites and scratches and slaps got harder and weren't any fun. He'd scared her. She wanted to leave, to get the hell out of that room, but the wouldn't let her, he held her down and in spite of herself she found herself silently begging for the roughness, as if the pain excused her for enjoying the copulation. And he seemed to know that.

When finally he finished using her, Hailey flopped on his back and stared at the ceiling. She lay looking at him. He didn't seem to know she was there anymore. She went into the bathroom and examined herself in the mirror. Her buttocks were red and wealed from the slaps and scratches. Bite marks adorned her breasts and stomach. Her vagina ached dully. She saw bruises darkening high up on the inside of her thighs.

Hailey dumped her. When she'd dressed he got up naked from the bed and walked to the door and opened it. She stared at him, noting the thin scar coming out of the golden hair and tracing itself down over his eye. There was another scar, a heavy one, coming out of his pubic hair and curving up to just above his navel. She said something to him, but he didn't answer. His eyes were vacant, distant; they didn't acknowledge her presence beside him at the door. She felt a shudder go through her as she stepped out into the carpeted corridor.

When she'd gone, Hailey took the Llama from the bedside drawer where he'd secreted it. He lay on the bed, staring trancelike at the ceiling, his hands caressing the gun, his fingers tracing its outline; caressing the high-polish blue finish of the barrel, the finely machined cavities of the ventilated slide, the checkered surface of the tough plastic on the butt. And his fingers stroked the solid curve of the target style trigger nestling within its guard. Still staring wide-eyed at the ceiling, Hailey pressed the magazine release button and slid out the fresh, fully-loaded magazine he'd inserted after killing Gloster. He rested the automatic on his bare chest and, staring at the white ceiling, let his fingers unload the eight .32 caliber cartridges. He clicked them in his hand, feeling their weight, then, still without looking, slipped them back into the magazine one by one. He slid the magazine back into the butt of the automatic, slapping it home with the palm of his hand. He raised the weapon and sighted at a figure in a picture of old Málaga which hung on the wall. Hailey always had a friend on the job. He liked the Llama.

Hailey lowered the gun and leaned over and turned off the bedside light. He stared into the darkness. He still held the gun. Outside the traffic was quieter, a low background hum. He heard a jet crossing the city. He stared toward the now unseen wall where the picture of old Málaga hung. He could feel himself relaxing as his pupils expanded and he tried to make out shapes. He coudl feel himself drifting deep within himself to that other part of his mind where his friend lived, the friend who was etched like a black shadow around the intricate outline of his brain. Hailey fell asleep.

At midnight, Peter Quinn sat in the *Coco-Loco* nursing a last brandy and *café solo*. Only a handful of customers remained, yacht people mostly, and they huddled in intimate groups talking quietly among themselves. Outside, a rising wind rattled stays and wind indicators on the masts of moored yachts in the quiet and darkened harbor.

From where he sat, Quinn could see the outline of *Destry*. He experienced a near erotic pleasure every time he looked at her. *Destry* was his dream, his sleek promise of freedom and adventure. And more: *Destry* was his hard-earned prize after five frustrating years at Harvard Business School suffered in deference to his father's insistence that he prepare himself for the future, and a two-month gut-wrenching gamble with the thirty thousand dollar trust fund his late mother had left him.

Quinn swirled the brandy in his glass and barely suppressed a grin. The gamble had paid off. And how! If it hadn't, he wouldn't be sitting in a bar, in a Spanish port, gazing out at his own boat and contemplating the year ahead during which he and Jenny and his captain, Bob Teal, would explore the Western Mediterranean port by port and cove by cove and, if Teal had his way, bar by bar.

Quinn had met Teal two months ago at Port Vauban in Antibes, on France's Côte d'Azur, when he was looking for his boat and Teal was hunting a job. The tough, heavily bearded, forty-year-old adventurer had just signed off from a sixty-foot ketch which he'd captained across the Atlantic for its owner. Quinn took an immediate liking to the good humored, profane American, and that night, after an extended tour of the bars in neighboring Juan-Les-Pins, had signed Teal on to captain the boat he didn't yet own.

Together they spent a boozy, boisterous three weeks touring harbors and talking with yacht-brokers, hunting the boat which would suit Quinn's purposes. Three times Teal saved Quinn thousands of dollars by advising him to turn down offers which at first looked exceptional. After listening to Teal's careful explanations as to why the boats they were examining were potential money eaters, Quinn was left with a healthy respect for Teal's encyclopaedic knowledge of seamanship and boat construction. No one could put one over on Teal.

They finally arrived in England, and, answering an ad in a yachting magazine, traveled to the great harbor in Poole, Dorset. There they found *Destry*. Quinn took one and knew he had to have her. In the back of his mind he prayed Teal would find nothing wrong with her. He waited ten agonizing hours while Teal crawled over her from stem to stern checking every bolt and bulwark before declaring her not only seaworthy, but the best goddamned bargain afloat. The bargain cost Quinn $150,000 and he didn't begrudge a cent of it. *Destry* was his; his dream was becoming a reality.

Quinn sipped his brandy. That'd been one hell of a day when he put the cash on the table for *Destry*, because that same day he'd met Jenny. While Teal arranged for an overhaul on the powerful twin Ford Sabre diesels, Quinn took the train up to London to arrange insurance. He arrived at Paddington Station after dark and taxied directly to the Savoy Hotel on the Strand. He first saw her in the lobby as he checked in, and admired her lithe good looks and long, blonde hair. When she'd caught him looking at her he'd politely averted his gaze. Half an hour later while waiting for a cab to take him to a Chinese restaurant in Soho, he saw her in the street. This time he smiled and she smiled back. At eleven o'clock when he returned to the hotel bar for a nightcap she was sitting alone at a table. He asked her to join him in a drink. She accepted.

She was twenty-two years old, daughter of a Boston dentist, and fresh from a Swiss finishing school. Her parents, she said, insisted she have the best of everything. She shrugged apologetically. She was traveling Europe for a year, but she hadn't bothered buying Arthur Frommer's *Europe on $20 a Day*. She stayed in the *Savoy* in London, the *Crillon* in Paris, and no doubt she'd book into the *Palacio* in Madrid and stay in the *Ambasciatori* in Rome. Jenny spoke fluent German, French, Italian and Spanish. She played tennis and skied. She'd met Woody Allen and Princess Margaret of England. She would study sculpture when she returned to Boston.

She was bored, she said, and dissatisfied. She wanted to *do* something with her life. Her parents were super, she said, there was no problem there. But they didn't understand her. She'd had to fight for the year traveling around Europe. She had to make the most of it, find out what made the world tick. She didn't want to be a Boston Society belle who dabbled in art.

Quinn had melted. Jesus, he'd understood everything she was saying. God, wasn't he facing the same thing, in another form, himself? They talked long after the bar closed, and it'd gone from there.

Far too fast, Quinn thought. What was it? Five weeks? And already marriage had crept into the bedroom conversations. He pinched the bridge of his nose between his fingers and shook his head. Always a sucker for the ladies, he thought. Always been the same. It seemed his adult life had been a series of passionate involvements that ignited like brushfires and burned out just as quick; leaving, like brushfires, scarred ground and trouble in their wake. Quinn had been the butt of his freewheeling friends in Harvard. While they exhausted themselves on a merry-go-round of one-night stands, Quinn was always plodding on with the process of extricating himself from the complex aftermath of some tempestuous romance. Quinn was emotionally incapable of taking a woman to bed and then walking away from her the next morning with a smile, a thank you and a bunch of roses. Quinn always got involved. Jesus Christ, how many times had he been engaged in Harvard? Three times? Three times in five years? Women, Quinn thought, ruefully, have an uncanny way of taking advantage of men with monagamous tendencies.

Quinn drained his glass at a gulp and listened to the laughter of the groups at the bar. Outside, the wind had lifted and he knew it would be whipping up white-tops beyond the breakwater. He hoped it'd settle so they'd have calm seas for tomorrow's hop along the coast to Nerja.

Quinn lit a cigarette and rubbed his gold lighter. When he'd met Jenny, he'd fallen for her like a rock, told her within days that he loved her, told her that after the cruise he wanted to marry her. Yes, *he'd* started the bedroom marriage talk! As usual. And three weeks later recognized that he'd gotten himself in too deep again. And now he was cooped up in a 40 foot cruiser with her, not just sleeping with her every night, but living with her all day, too. So, how did he get out of this one without really hurting her?

That was the thing; he didn't want to hurt her. Jenny was something special, a girl in a million. He fiddled with the cigarette, watching the smoke curling up past his fingers. Perhaps if he left it alone he'd find he didn't *want* to break it off with her. Maybe. Perhaps. So maybe he was right with what he'd decided to do. Just leave it alone. Enjoy the trip with her. See how things unfolded during the year. It was certainly no hardship being with her. The only difficulty was his damned conscience. Having concluded that he might not love her after all, his strait-jacket sense of morality was making him squirm because he was still taking her to bed and encouraging her with scenarios for the future.

Quinn stubbed the cigarette and lit another. Twenty-six years old, he thought, and you still approach women like a moonstruck kid on his first date.

How uncomplicated life would be if he was capable of following Teal's credo. "Love 'em and leave 'em," Teal said. "Love 'em well, sailor, and leave 'em fast." Teal's attitude was enough to give any feminist an apoplectic fit, but women flipped for him. Like the one he'd met right here in the bar just three hours ago. If the show was running on schedule, Teal would be loving her about now—and leaving her about ten the next morning.

Quinn contemplated his empty glass. He'd promised Jenny he would return to *Destry* around midnight. She'd stayed aboard to wash her hair and iron clothes. Ten minutes more wouldn't make a difference. What the hell. He wandered to the bar for a refill.

While he waited for the barman to open a new bottle of *Soberano*, he listened to two sailors yarning as they leaned against the bar beside him. One had hit trouble between Sardinia and the Balearics when both his diesels had packed up and he'd lost his auxiliary outboard over the side. He'd jerry-rigged a mast made out of desk railings, sewn four blankets together for a sail, managed to maneuver himself into the south-westerly currents, then drifted for three days, using the sail whenever he had favorable winds. He'd struggled to within twenty miles of Formentera before he spotted a yacht. It answered his distress flare and towed him into La Sabina.

Quinn carried his brandy back to his table. He sat and sipped contentedly, letting his eyes wander over the darkened scene of the harbor outside the window. Mediterranean ports were a universe away from Harvard and the years he'd spent attending dull lectures, reading dry books and analyzing ambiguous statistics. And sailors were a wildly different breed from the club of accountants and financial decision-makers his father wanted him to join. He'd taken his degree to placate the old man, but he wasn't about to step onto the first rung of the corporate ladder at Quinn Estates and bury himself in the back-stabbing intricacies of practical business administration—not just yet. He had to fulfill a few of his own ambitions before he started realizing his *father's* ambitions for him.

Quinn didn't hold anything against the old man. On the contrary, he respected him; more than that, he loved him. The core of the problem was that the old man had made it the hard way, a route which didn't allow frivolity, and he saw his son's attiude to life as *pure* frivolity. *If you don't get on when you're young, you don't get on. Finish!*

James P. Quinn was one of a kind. He'd arrived in New York City from Ireland during the Thirties as a penniless fourteen year old orphan. Within twenty years of stepping off the rust-bucket on which he'd worked his way across the Atlantic, he'd made a million dollars out of real estate. Yet, he wasn't a man slavishly bound to the crossbars of the dollar. When Peter's mother died when he was only twelve years old, James P. Quinn had given the same attention to his son's life as he did to his business. He'd become mother *and* father to Peter, setting aside the time necessary to give Peter the love and attention a growing boy needed.

There were no complaints there, Quinn thought. No man could have done more for his son during that time of loss which had coincided with the emotional confusion of puberty. It was just that the old man was a damned hard act to follow.

James P. Quinn was a practical creature who saw life as a rigidly structured game; you played standard moves at specific times and in recognized ways, and life yielded to your demands. But Peter was the quintessential romantic who considered life a great swirling maelstrom of possibility; you took a deep breath, jumped into the whirlpool and waited to see what would happen. How the hell did you explain an attitude like *that* to a man who'd once fought a wild dog for a stale half loaf of bread on the New York docks?

That was the crux of the conflict which Quinn knew was breaking the old man's heart. But what could he do? Sacrifice his life to his father's dream that he'd step into his shoes? One day perhaps he would. But it needed this year of freedom, this year's sabbatical from the battle of succession, for him to make a decision.

Quinn played the gamble which had given him this precious year six months previously. At twenty-one he received the capital and interest from the trust fund his mother had established for him. He'd bought a five year old Mustang and then, against his father's expert advice, had allowed the money to languish for years in a fixed deposit bank account. Then, while he fumed and fought his way toward his business degree, he conceived the idea of the Mediterranean trip. He lived in the idea, let it gain form, used it as a lifebuoy to save himself from drowning in the accumulation of trivia he absorbed each day. It took on magnitude in his mind; he would create a truly Ulyssean adventure, a voyage of self-discovery. But he wouldn't do it on the cheap. That was one thing he'd learned from the old man—if you want to do something, do it right.

Quinn visited the bank. He found he had nearly $100,000. It wasn't enough, not even near enough; he figured his boat would cost that and more.

Quinn withdrew his money and bought gold at $180 per

ounce. It was 1979, that crazy year when the gold market was a see-saw of financial adventure. Fortunes were won and lost in days, even hours. It took Quinn two months. During that time gold slipped back under $150, then leapt by mind-boggling increments to over $300. Quinn hung on. On the terms he'd set himself, salvation only manifested itself if he won in a big way.

Gold hit $400. Quinn gritted his teeth. It topped $425 and he knew he was getting somewhere. He made his calculations for the tenth time. Gold skyrocketed to a touch over $500 and Quinn made his decision. He'd play the odds for three more days. He ordered his broker to sell—come what may—in exactly 72 hours. Then Quinn gassed up his ancient Mustang and drove down to Florida. He booked into a hotel. He didn't read a paper or watch television. When the time was up he called his broker. He'd sold at $457. Quinn grunted his thanks and replaced the receiver. He was worth over $250,000. He'd won his year. He slept fifteen hours straight.

Two months later, Peter took his degree. James P. Quinn hugged his son with pride, wiped tears of joy from his eyes and joked about Irishmen crying at weddings and dancing at wakes. That night, after a celebration dinner at *Lugano's*, Peter told his father about the money he'd made in gold and the plans he had for that money. The old man listened quietly. Peter told him that within the next week he would fly to Europe to begin hunting his boat. The old man said nothing against him. He only nodded and wished him well. Later in the evening he toasted Peter and thanked him for finishing his degree.

The next morning at three o'clock, James P. Quinn was so drunk Peter had to help him undress and get into bed. He'd gazed up at Peter and said, "Jesus, but my own son made one hundred and fifty grand on the gold market before he even finished college!" Then he smiled and instantly fell asleep. During the whole evening he'd never once mentioned Quinn Estates.

Quinn finished his brandy and paid his bill. Outside the wind gusted and he turned up his coat collar and jammed his hands deep into his trousers pockets as he strolled along the quay between the double rows of silent, moored yachts toward

between the double rows of silent, moored yachts towards
Destry. Well before he reached her he saw that all her lights
were out. Jenny must have turned in already.

He couldn't get the old man out of his mind, hadn't been
able to for a long time, ever since he'd made the decision to
give himself this year. A classic situation. Torn on the one hand
by the genuine wish to be the good son and prove his worth to
his father, and on the other by a desperate fear that to do so,
now, before he'd faced the world on his own terms, would be a
self-imposed sentence to a lifetime of bitterness that he'd never
had the guts to say "no" to someone he loved.

He paused at *Destry's* gangway, and in the back of his mind
continued the adoration of her structural harmony that had
begun the day he'd first seen her in Poole.

Was the problem that simple?

Perhaps it all got down to commitment. He'd been able to
commit himself to the idea of the trip. He'd been able to
commit himself to the ownership of the boat. Unequivocally!
But they were the only two commitments he'd ever made: to an
idea and to an inanimate object. Commitment to people came
harder. The old man sure missed out on commitment. And so
did all those women he'd been so enthusiastic for and then
ditched. And Jenny; she wasn't getting much in the way of
commitment.

He boarded *Destry*, his rubber-soled shoes silent on the
spotless, teak deck. He made his way below. He turned on the
light above the chart-table just in case Teal came home early
from his tryst. He used the head, then slipped off his shoes and
padded forward across the carpeted salon to the master cabin.

When he opened the door he saw Jenny's form on the double
bed, huddled beneath the feather continental quilt they slept
under. The big bed didn't leave much room in the small cabin.
Jenny had goaded Quinn to have it installed. "If you're the
master of a ship," she joked, "then you should *live* like the
master!"

Quinn undressed and slipped beneath the cover. Jenny was
naked. Carefully, so as not to disturb her, he eased himself up
against her warm buttocks. He felt her stir. He lay still.

"It's OK," she whispered, "I'm not asleep." She reached back with one hand and stroked his thigh.

"I woke you."

"I was waiting for you." Her fingertips drifted up his thigh to his hip. She eased her hand between them and twisted his pubic hair between her fingers.

Involuntarily, he pushed in hard against her hand. When he relaxed the pressure her hand grasped at his growing erection. Then she turned over to face him, one long leg flung over his hips, opening her crotch to his exploring fingers.

They played with each other for a minute, then she whispered, "Kiss my breasts," her signal that she was ready. Quinn rolled on top of her. She kicked off the quilt and lifted her legs high up around his waist. Quinn pushed her arms above her head and trapped them there. He nuzzled the soft hair under her armpits, then slowly lowered his face, first to one springy breast, then the other, gently scraping his beard stubble over them.

Her crotch started lifting at him, grinding against his penis, but he didn't enter her. She struggled to release her arms from his grasp, but he kept them pinned above her head. It was the game they played. She was powerless to take what she wanted until he let her.

"My nipples," she whispered, "my nipples." Pinning her down even harder, meeting her grinding pubis with his own pressure, he drew them first one then the other, into his mouth, sucking gently until he felt them stiffen, then, when she arched her back, seeking his penis, he let her arms free, transferred his hands beneath her straining buttocks and let himself slip into her. Her arms snaked around his neck, gripping him to her in a desperate embrace. It didn't take them long.

Later, they lay quietly, Jenny with her head on Quinn's shoulder, their bodies drained by the love-making, and cosseted by *Destry's* slow, lulling, nearly imperceptible rocking. They talked for perhaps an hour.

At one time Jenny said, "You know, I've had it made since the day I was born. Best schools, rich parents, privileged future. None if it meant anything, or made any sense until I met you. You've made a life for me, you know that?"

Later, she said, "Are we going to *do* something with this trip? I mean, is there any way we can *make* it into something other than just a year roaming around? A trip like this should be creative in some way." She kissed his chest. "And I don't mean just physically."

Then, as she turned over and pushed her bottom back into him, just before she went to sleep, she drowsily asked him to tell her he loved her.

"I love you," he'd said quietly, and then silently repeated the words in his mind, analyzing them, wondering bitterly why, whenever he said those words, they hung over him like Damocles' sword suspended by a hair, as if waiting to skewer him with his own half-truth.

Nothing was simple in life, he thought, and then cursed himself for having allowed such a mundane cliché escape from what was supposed to have been such a finely educated mind.

But look at it, he told himself. You build toward something like this trip, and now it's happening you should be ecstatic: but you're not, not really, even though you pretend to be.

You say you have to stand on your own feet, out of the reach of your old man, just for a year, till you sort things out: but you know damned well the trip isn't going to sort anything out and that it's nothing really to do with the old man.

And you have this woman here who adores you, who wants to marry you, who thinks you're putting her life in perspective for her: but you're not doing that; you've already admitted you probably won't marry her; you don't really care for the love she offers you; and in the end, if you toss her out of your life, you might destroy her.

When he was sure she was asleep, Quinn dressed and went up top. He walked to *Destry*'s bow and contemplated the sight before him. He gazed across the hundreds of boats laying quietly at their moorings and beyond the harbor to the black mass of La Concha mountain rearing into a clean, star-specked sky, faintly illuminated by a great, bone-colored moon. He listened to the lonely, beautiful sound of harbors the world over: the gentle slop of wavelets on hulls; the friendly creak of straining mooring ropes; the soft rattle and hum of stays, rhythmic in the wind.

A dream for a dreamer, Quinn thought disparagingly. That's the bottom line. I'm a fucking dreamer.

But whatever the motives that had brought him here, a man only had one time like this in a lifetime. Jenny was right, they had to create something tangible out of the dream. For himself it would have to be a sense of reality which could sustain him for the rest of his life.

And Quinn knew that if he didn't give it his best try there might be nothing left for him in all the years to come.

At twelve-thirty the next day, a waiter at the *Coco-Loco* served Hailey a glass of chilled Montilla *fino* and a *tapa* of olives. Block hadn't arrived.

From where he sat at an outside table Hailey could see most of the port. A pair of blue-uniformed customs men, members of the national *Guardia Civil*, strolled along the quays checking yachts newly arrived that morning. Hailey watched them as they sought permission to board a motor-sailer. He noted how one of the pair lagged behind the other, the thumb of his right hand casually hooked over his holstered pistol, as his partner spoke with the captain. That was how the *Guardia* operated in public; politely, but always one covering the other. The system didn't always work. In the Basquelands the *Guardia* were losing a man a month to ETA and BEKA. Hailey edged forward in his chair, leaning one elbow on the table to relieve the pressure of his own automatic which was digging into his back.

Hailey could see *Destry* from where he sat and noted the challenging sweep of her bow riding high above the glass-smooth sheen of the harbor waters. Soon she'd be up on her haunches, cutting through the Mediterranean like an arrow, the Ford Sabre diesels vibrating the reinforced GRP hull, spray scything from the bow and shooting high amid-ships as she bounded along her course. One day Hailey wanted a boat like that. One hundred thousand dollars if you could find one second-hand. Hailey thought of the one hundred thousand dollar banker's draft in his wallet. He smiled to himself. Sure, he could buy a boat with the draft. But Hailey wouldn't cheet Zeller. That was unthinkable. That was impossible. Zeller was part of Hailey. Hailey was part of Zeller. Hailey wouldn't cheat Zeller. Hailey couldn't cheat Zeller if he tried to. The thought left Hailey as soon as it had made itself known. He looked again at *Destry*. The ultimate rich-boy's toy. But today, Hailey would be using the sleek craft not as a toy, but a tool. And when he'd done the job, he'd sink her.

At one-fifteen Block arrived and signaled the waiter for a beer.

"You're late," Hailey said.

"Sorry about that, man," Block said as he slid into a chair beside Hailey. "I was saying *adios* to a fine piece of ass. She didn't want me to go."

"When you're working with me, keep on schedule."

Block opened his mouth to protest, thought better of it and lit a cigar instead. The waiter brought his beer. Hailey waited until he'd gone before he spoke.

"We're taking *Destry* to Asilah. We're loading merchandise and running it up the Spanish northern Atlantic coast."

"What sort of merchandise, man?"

"What's it got to do with you, Block?"

Block spread his big hands in surrender, and grinned. "Forget it, man. Idle question. I apologize."

Hailey sipped his *fino*. He stared out at *Destry*. "We off-load the merchandise, scuttle the boat and get out of Spain. This is your last job in Spain. Go to Paris, cable Tristan, and wait further orders."

"Gotta come back here, man." He indicated with his thumb the apartments above him. "I got a contract on the apartment."

"So forget it."

"I got good stuff up there, man."

"You'll be paid for it." Hailey stared at Block until Block looked away.

"Got the girl, man," Block said, softly.

"You can get women wherever you are," Hailey said.

Block played with the moisture on the side of the cold beer glass. "Sure," Block said, "there're plenty of women."

"You knew how it'd be when you signed up, Block."

Block nodded. "Sure, sure, sure," he said. He gulped at his

beer. "They're expecting us," he said. "What do you want me to do?"

Hailey could see two men working on *Destry*'s deck. He saw a girl in a red bikini climb atop the cabin housing, spread a towel and stretch out to catch some afternoon sun.

"We'll take them an hour out of port, until everyone's relaxed and used to us. When I give you the nod act immediately and do exactly as I say."

"We gonna do them straight off?"

Hailey shook his head. "Not right away."

"But we're gonna do them."

Hailey nodded.

Block smiled. "I like that."

"You're not supposed to like it," Hailey said. "You're just supposed to do it."

"Yeah, sure," Block grinned. "But it's the next best thing to 'Nam, right?"

"In 'Nam," Hailey said, "we didn't get paid so much." Hailey downed the last drops of his *fino* and tossed a hundred peseta note on the table beside the glasses. He slung his bag on his shoulder and walked down the quay toward *Destry*.

Block glanced once toward his apartment, then shoved his hands in his pockets and followed.

A mile offshore, *Destry* bounded westward like a greyhound loosed from its leash. Two phosphorus topped waves gushed from her bows. They turned and flattened, uselessly racing to catch the frothing wake which ran like ploughed snow tossed from beneath her stern.

To port, the Andalusian coast spread in a panorama of white seaside resorts backed by tawny mountain ranges. Westward, a hundred miles beyond Málaga, the snow-covered Sierra Nevada carved its image into the deep blue, winter sky. Nerja lay fifty sea-miles ahead, Puerto Jose Banus fifteen astern.

Topside, Teal sat at the wheel. Hailey leaned against a window to one side of him, noting the control panel layout and assessing Teal. The man was trouble, Hailey decided. He stood six feet and was built like a tank. The muscles in his thick arms bulged as he guided *Destry* through the light swells. A long scar sloped along his left cheek and disappeared into his thick, black beard. Teal was over forty, but Hailey knew he was the fittest man aboard. Block was big, but he wouldn't last a minute in a stand-up brawl with Teal. The guns were the great equalizers; the guns and the speed with which he and Block would move.

"Want to take her?" Teal asked.

Hailey cupped his hand around his ear. He'd hardly heard a word. Teal had said over the growl of the big engines.

"I said, want to take her!" Teal said loudly.

"Wouldn't know how," Hailey said.

"You want to write a book about boats, you should try handling one."

Hailey grinned as Teal vacated the chair. Hailey slipped in behind the wheel. Teal held the wheel until Hailey got it.

"We're heading sixty-nine degrees," Teal said, pointing to the compass. "Anything between sixty-eight and seventy is fine. Turn her gently; she responds like a Chevy on an oil-slick. That's it. Don't over-correct." He tapped the inter-com. "You spot any traffic within four hundred yards, call me. I'm going below for a beer with Quinn and your friend. Attaboy, sailor." He slapped Hailey on the shoulder and swung down the gang-way to the salon.

Hailey settled in the chair, one foot on the rung, the other on the deck for support. He held the wheel lightly, expertly, letting *Destry* swing off course a few degrees, then gently hauled her back to a dead sixty-nine. She responded beautifully. Then, because he knew Teal would be watching his progress on the salon compass, he let *Destry* slide away to seventy-two degrees and then jerked her back suddenly so she slid through sixty-nine and sat on sixty-seven. Hailey smiled to himself. He had to stay the amateur for a while yet. He corrected, clumsily, oscillating the leaping bow wildly through six or seven degrees. The intercom buzzed. Hailey lifted the hand-set.

Teal's voice rasped into his ear. "You're doing fine, sailor, but you're costing me fuel. Correct slowly. Just before she reaches her heading haul back the wheel a fraction, otherwise her weight and power take her over the center. Attaboy."

"Like this?" Hailey asked, as he eased her back on course.

"Attaboy. Be with you in five, soon as I chug this San Miguel."

The receiver clicked in his ear and Hailey replaced the set. He settled back into the chair, feeling the vibration of five hundred horsepower coming up through the deck. He held *Destry* within a touch of her course. His eyes automatically scanned a hundred and eighty degrees in front of him, port to starboard and back again. At twenty-seven knots there was no point in looking astern. Nothing would be overtaking.

One of the big engines suddenly touched a fake note, and Hailey's hand immediately reached for the starboard throttle control. With his hand actually on the black knob he stopped the instinctive movement. an amateur wouldn't have heard the slight lessening of revs, much less know how to tune the engine.

Hailey's eyes scanned the horizon and then flicked back to the compass. The rose was oscillating between sixty-nine and seventy-one. He brought the bow back to sixty-nine and left it there. He tried to figure the course. Quinn had taken *Destry* out of Banus and turned onto a heading of ninety-seven degrees. Then, at Punta de Calaburras he'd changed course to sixty-nine degrees which Hailey figured would take them in a straight line across the Bay of Málaga to Nerja. Thing was, neither Quinn, Teal, the cute little blonde down there, nor *Destry* would get anywhere near Nerja. Hailey was going to swing *Destry* around onto a reciprocal bearing to head her back toward Punto de Calaburras. Then he'd plot a course into the Straits of Gibraltar.

A minute later, Teal climed back up the gangway and took the wheel from Hailey.

"Not bad," he said. "If that was your first go, you're OK." His rough, sun-ravaged face broke into a grin. "You could be a natural-born helmsman."

"It's difficult," Hailey said. "I'm surprised at how difficult it is."

Teal nodded toward the salon. "Quinn says go get a drink."

Hailey descended into the salon. With Teal up top and the four of them below, now was the time to take the cruiser.

The salon layout was a triumphant example of maximum comfort and utility built into minimum space. A well-padded sofa which doubled as a single bunk ran down one side of the length of the cabin behind a collapsible table. On the other side a stove, washing-up basin, refrigerator and miniature deep-freeze competed for the space allotted the galley. A fold-down chart table with its own swivel chair and a handy tubfull of charts stood forward of the galley. Fixed to the bulkhead above the table was the compass on which Teal had checked Hailey's course, an inter-com hand-set, shelves containing books and maps, and a row of tapes to supply the VHF stereo cassette-radio which sat tucked into an open space between rows of food storage cupboards which claimed every other available wall space in the salon.

Through the gangway leading forward, Hailey saw three doors; one on either side which he guessed led to toilet and shower compartments, and one directly forward which would open into a double cabin. Aft, was another door which would lead to a second cabin and an access hatch to the Ford Sabre diesels.

Hailey nodded his thanks as Quinn handed him an uncapped bottle of San Miguel. He squeezed in behind the table beside Block and the blonde who'd been introduced to him as Quinn's girlfriend, Jenny. Hailey sipped the beer and watched as Quinn spread a British Admiralty Chart on the chart table and ran his finger along their course. The man was under thirty, a stocky five-feet-ten. His sandy-hair was expensively barbered and his skin was burned; it didn't have the fine, leathery patina of someone who'd spent years at sea. Block's description of him was accurate; a rich boy playing sailor.

Jenny tossed aside the magazine she'd been skimming and smiled at Hailey. "What sort of books do you write, Mr. Mann?"

Hailey smiled, and when he answered he looked straight into her eyes. "I'm not being flippant," he said, "but I write anything which I think will sell." He saw her smile in return and wondered just how long it would have taken him to get her into bed if, in other circumstances, he'd decided to compete for her with Quinn. Two days, he thought, three days maximum.

"It must be so interesting being a writer," she said.

"Much like any other job," Hailey said, "it gets boring if you can't get away from it now and again."

Jenny smiled again, and Hailey revised his original estimate. One day, he thought. I could take her off Quinn in one day. He let his eyes wander over her firm, brown breasts which were slung precariously in the tiny bikini top. Perhaps I *will* take her, he thought. Perhaps after I take the boat I'll take her. Victor's spoils. I might do that, he thought, I might do that.

Hailey lifted his eyes back to her face and noted that her lips had pursed in a light-hearted challenge at his boldness. She stroked a finger of her left hand over her throat. Hailey still smiled and he knew that the moment had gone on too long, but still he stared, and for one flashing second he felt the other young man emerging and Hailey fought to push him under, then took a deep breath and blinked his eyes fast several times and squeezed his hand around the cold beer bottle and raised it to his mouth.

He saw Block frowning at him. Block knew the moment had gone on too long, as well, and was confused as to why Hailey would risk a scene with her or Quinn at this moment. Hailey wondered why Block was frowning at him. Now that the younger man had submerged into his mind again he'd forgotten him.

Quinn turned from his chart, swiveling the padded chair so he faced the three behind the table.

"I figure another three hours," Quinn said. "We should reach Nerja just before dark. There's no harbor, so we'll anchor and go ashore in the tender. Perhaps crawl through a few bars together."

"Sounds a good idea," Hailey said, amicably.

"Will you stay there overnight?"

"It's up to my friend," Hailey said. He looked at Block. Block shrugged. "Sure, man, why not. Maybe tomorrow we'll see the sights."

"What's this book about, Mr. Mann?" Quinn asked.

"I'm calling it *Lifestyles*," Hailey said. "I've picked a dozen different ways that people live—yachtsmen, actors, politicians—and am preparing a chapter on each. My publisher is very interested."

"Have you had success with previous books?" Quinn asked. He grinned. "I mean, should I recognize your name?"

Hailey stood and stretched. He nodded nearly imperceptibly at Block. He saw Block's jaw clench and his hand fall below the level of the table.

Hailey smiled. "Don't worry. You're not supposed to know me." He stepped across the salon and leaned against the refrigerator. "Frankly, I'm better at other things." Hailey's hand was behind his back. He saw Block was ready to move. He pointed the Llama XA at Quinn. "Please don't move," he said quietly.

Quinn moved instinctively, fear and shock propelling him toward Hailey. Hailey took one quick step backward and held the automatic out at full reach in front of him. "That's your first and last chance," he said.

Block had his gun in his right hand, a snub-nosed Smith and Wesson five shot .38 Centennial. The moment Hailey made his move, Block clamped his left hand around Jenny's mouth, stifling the gasp which had threatened to turn into a scream.

"Cover the gangway in case Teal comes down," Hailey said. "If he does, kill him."

"Don't scream, babe," Block told Jenny. "You got that now?"

Jenny nodded and Block released his hand from her mouth. Block's fingerprints were on her cheek. A tiny dribble of blood etched itself down her chin where he'd jammed her lip against her teeth. She touched her fingers to her bruised mouth. Hailey heard her jerky, frightened breathing; it didn't sound so different to the breathing of that Canadian humping beneath him last night.

Block balanced one hand on the table and vaulted over it into the middle of the cabin. He leaned against the closed door of the aft cabin so his gun covered Quinn, Jenny and the gangway. If Teal came down, he'd come down backwards. He wouldn't even know what hit him.

"OK," Quinn breathed. "OK, you bastard." Hailey could hardly hear his voice above the muffled roar of the engines. Quinn was scared, but Quinn was also itching to do something. To manly. To be a cowboy. To jump me, Hailey thought, and smash me in front of his girlfriend. Hailey kept the Llama pointed right at the middle of Quinn's chest.

"What the hell is this?" Quinn breathed. His eyes flicked from Hailey to Block and back again.

"Sit down," Hailey said, nodding to the chart chair. Quinn sat. "Sit on your hands," Hailey said. Quinn did as he was told. "Don't move," Hailey said.

"You want to steal a boat, you've picked the wrong one," Quinn said. "You can't disguise a boat like this, you can't sell it."

"Where do you keep your weapons?" Hailey asked.

"I don't carry weapons," Quinn said.

"All yachtsmen carry weapons," Hailey said. He permitted himself a smile. "They carry them to try and prevent this sort of thing. Where are they?"

Quinn hesitated. "There's an old Beretta automatic in the wheelhouse tool locker," he said.

"And?" Hailey paused. "I'll tear the boat apart if you don't tell me, Quinn."

Quinn nodded at the forward cabin. "A Garand carbine under the bunk."

Hailey jerked his thumb over his shoulder. "Get it," he snapped at Block.

Block darted towards the cabin. He returned a moment later with a beat-up Garand short-barrelled MIE5 tucked under his arm.

"Get rid of it," Hailey told him.

Block reached over the table, unhooked a porthole latch and tugged against the seal. A syphon of needle-fine spray shot into the cabin and the noise from the engines suddenly magnified. Block eased the barrel of the rifle out the porthole and shoved the weapon out into the sea. He clipped the porthole closed.

Jenny had begun to sob uncontrollably. "Go sit with her," Hailey told Quinn. "I want her to stop the theatricals."

Both Hailey and Block kept Quinn covered while he slid into the seat beside Jenny. "Search the fore and aft cabins," Hailey told Block. "Anything which can be used as a weapon, bring it here."

Block nodded and moved forward. Hailey took Block's

place so he could cover Quinn and Jenny and the gangway. Quinn put one arm around Jenny, trying to comfort her.

"Put your hands on the table where I can see them," Hailey said, "and leave them there."

Quinn laid his hands flat on the table. "You going to tell us what you're doing?"

"Taking you to Gibraltar."

"Why?"

"No more questions," Hailey said.

The inter-com buzzed. Hailey reached for the handset beside the compass.

"Quinn there?" Teal's voice rasped from the set, mixed with the dull throb of the diesels.

"In the toilet," Hailey said.

"The *head*," Teal said, "The *head*." He laughed. "O.K., sailor, just tell him his captain called because he's dying of thirst."

"I'll bring up a bottle right away."

"Make it two. Attaboy!"

Hailey replaced the handset. Jenny still sobbed. Quinn stared at Hailey as if in Hailey's face he could find an answer to his problem.

"Listen," Quinn said. "You going to kill us? Throw us overboard? Give us the life-raft? What the hell are you going to do?"

"I said no more questions."

"Or are you gonna make us walk the fucking plank?"

"I sort of need you, Quinn," Hailey said softly, "but I could probably learn to get by without you."

Block returned with a handful of screwdrivers and wrenches and a hammer. "This is the lot."

"Shove them in a locker, then take Teal up two beers. Tell him Quinn said I could have another steering lesson. I'll be up there in a couple of minutes."

Block opened the nearest locker and pushed the tools in among a supply of canned food. Then he slipped the Smith and Wesson under his shirt and around the back where Teal wouldn't see it and took two San Miguels from the refrigerator.

He flipped the caps with an opener hanging by a string from a bulkhead and went up top.

"Get into the forward cabin," Hailey told Quinn.

Quinn slid out from behind the table. He touched Jenny briefly on the arm. "Do as he tells you," he said, "and we'll be O.K."

Jenny nodded. Hailey stepped back as Quinn passed him.

"Get into the cabin," Hailey said. "Put the key in the keyhole on the outside of the door."

Quinn moved forward. He turned as he opened the cabin door. "Don't hurt her," he said. "Just don't hurt her."

"Get inside," Hailey said.

Quinn took the key from inside and slipped it into the outside keyhole. He stepped inside and closed the door.

Block came below.

"No problems?"

"Nothing, man," Block said. "He said he's ready when you are. He says get a move on. He's gotta take a piss."

Hailey nodded at the closed door of the forward cabin. "Quinn's in there. Go lock the door. Then search the aft cabin."

Block locked the door, then strode back through the salon to the aft cabin. He closed the door after him. Hailey lowered the Llama and picked up his nearly full bottle of San Miguel. He took a deep swig, then took out his handkerchief and carefully wiped his mouth. He shook his head to clear his long, golden hair from his eyes.

"What are you going to do with us?" Jenny asked him.

"What's your name? Jenny, right? Well, Jenny, does it really *matter* what happens to you?"

Jenny shook her head. Her face screwed up as if she was going to start crying again. She kept shaking her head.

"I mean, what's it matter what happens to anyone, Jenny?" Hailey swigged again from the beer. "A year here, a year there. It's all the same, right?"

"It matters what happens to *me*," she said.

"But the others don't matter?"

"I didn't say that," she sobbed.

Hailey smiled. "No, you didn't say that," he agreed. His gaze scourged her body again. "You're a lovely girl, Jenny."

She stared at him with wide eyes.

"That's good," Hailey said. "Now you're not crying."

Block pushed out of the aft cabin door. He carried a black, metal toolbox. "It's clean," he said. "Only the toolbox and this." He showed Hailey a clasp knife, a marvellously engineered tool with a stag-horn handle. He opened the blade; it was hand-etched in an oak-leaf design. "A Puma," he said. "Reckon I'll keep it for a souvenir." He snapped it closed.

"No souvenirs," Hailey said. "Dump the lot on the deck." He nodded at the aft cabin door. "Then put the key outside the door. We'll keep Teal in there."

Block grunted and pushed the toolbox into a corner, but when he went back to the aft cabin to change over the key, he had the Puma concealed in the palm of his hand. You didn't find a knife like that every day. German knife. Solingen steel. And fuck you, Mr. Mann. Goddamned knife like that was worth a hundred, a hundred-fifty bucks. Block slipped the Puma into his jeans pocket. He walked back into the salon grinning. "You want me to get Teal?"

"I'll bring him down."

"He's a tough mother, man. I'm bigger than you."

Hailey rested cold, blue eyes on Block. "I said, I'll bring him down," Hailey said.

Block kept on grinning. "Sure, man, sure."

"Watch her." Hailey looked straight into Jenny's eyes. "But don't touch. She's special."

Jenny's mouth opened as if she wanted to say something. She raised her hand to cover the cleavage between her breasts. She watched Hailey head up the gangway.

With the Llama concealed, Hailey stepped into the wheel-house. Teal stood, feet braced against *Destry*'s occasional pitch and roll as she slapped through a wave, his thighs leaning back on the helmsman's chair. He held the wheel in one hand, and when he saw Hailey saluted him with the bottle of San Miguel he held in the other.

"You're just in time," he said. "Gotta go to the head."

He put down the bottle and moved aside so Hailey could step

in and take his place. "Same course," he said. "Hold her steady, sailor."

He watched as Hailey took the wheel and the bow slipped to starboard a few degrees. "Correct her gently, that's it. You got it." At the gangway he turned to go down backwards. "Back in five," he said.

As Teal started to descend, Hailey knew he had only seconds before Teal turned into the salon, saw the weeping girl and then Block with his gun. He hadn't worked with Block before. He didn't know how he reacted. Hailey suspected Block was indecisive and made mistakes.

Hailey flicked the self-steering lever to automatic, grabbed the twin throttle controls and hauled them back to below half power. The Ford Sabres moaned and *Destry*'s bow sank a fraction as the twin props slowed and lost their traction.

Teal sprang back into the wheelhouse. "Sailor, for Chrissake don't play with the throttles."

Hailey's Llama was pointing at him.

Teal didn't speak, didn't think. Hailey saw the big arms rising as Teal launched himself in spontaneous reaction.

Hailey side-stepped with one leg stuck out. Teal tripped, crashing sideways, catching his hip on the helmsman's chair, the back of his shoulder thumping into Hailey's chest. Hailey brough the butt of the automatic down on Teal's head. The metal grazed him, opening a long gash along his scalp.

Teal grunted in pain, but tried to take the advantage by shoving his weight in harder against Hailey, forcing him backwards. Hailey slugged him again, catching his shoulder with the butt. Teal sagged, then scrambled on all fours, trying to regain his feet. Hailey slipped away from him, got free by half a meter, then launched a kick which caught Teal full in the face.

Teal shouted with pain as blood poured from his nose and split lips, but still he tried to get Hailey, the sheer momentum of his anger spurring him forward. Hailey kicked him in the arm, throwing Teal off balance so that he crashed onto the deck.

Hailey stepped back a pace and leveled the Llama directly at Teal's head. Teal stopped fighting. He spat blood onto the teak deck and held a hand to his shattered face. His voice was muffled by the hand and the blood. "O.K., you bastard," he said. "O.K., you cunt."

"Get on your feet," Hailey said.

"Fuck you," Teal said.

Hailey moved the automatic fractionally so it aimed away from Teal's head. "I'll put a bullet in your left arm," Hailey said quietly. "Then I'll put a bullet in your right arm."

Teal struggled to his feet and slumped against the bulkhead. He still held one hand to his face. His other arm hung limply. Hailey watched him slowly turning it, testing it for damage. He could see a bruise spreading from where he'd kicked Teal in the face.

"Turn around and lean on the bulkhead," Hailey said.

Teal turned slowly until his face was against the bulkhead. Hailey unlocked the automatic pilot, then spun the wheel, taking *Destry* around in a wide, slow circle. He watched the wake and when he'd completed the circle, and *Destry* was cruising back along her own tracks, Hailey checked the compass. The reciprocal bearing of sixty-nine degrees was two hundred forty-nine. Hailey saw the rose steadying at two hundred forty-six and turned the wheel a touch more to coax the bow further to starboard. As the bow settled on the exact heading, he locked in the self-steering, grasped the black, plastic knobs of the twin throttle levers and slowly eased them forward until the big diesels were at full revs and *Destry*'s bow rode high out of the water. The Ford Sabres screamed. As the big boat crossed a swell, she nearly planed, dumping back into the trough with a thump like a mortar shot heard in the distance. *Destry* was touching thirty-nine knots.

Teal turned sideways from the bulkhead. "You'll burn her out," he grunted.

"What's her safest top?"

"Thirty-six knots."

"Sustained cruising?"

"Thirty-two."

"Engine condition?"

"Overhauled in Dorset six weeks back." Blood from Teal's

nose smeared down the wall. "For Christ's sake don't fuck her up. This is no toy."

Hailey said nothing. He eased the throttles back until *Destry* slowed to thirty-six knots. He listened to the engines. The scream had gone; now they sang with an excited, punching throb.

On the deck to one side of the wheel, Hailey saw the toolbox locker. He flipped open the lid and found the old Beretta. Teal watched as he threw it overboard. It bounced once off the wake and was gone.

"Get below," Hailey said.

Hailey kept well back as Teal pushed himself away from the bulkhead, turned and descended the gangway backwards. He didn't take his eyes off Hailey. Hailey followed him down, bracing his back against the wooden ladder, one hand on the rail for support, the other keeping the Llama trained precisely on Teal's chest.

In the salon, Teal looked at Jenny and at Block.

"Where's Quinn?" he demanded.

"Get into the aft cabin," Hailey said.

Jenny came to her feet. "He's hurt. Let me help him."

Block dragged her back down.

Hailey indicated with the gun for Teal to start moving.

"He's *hurt*!" Jenny screamed. Block raised his fist as if to backhand her. She flinched from him. *"Leave her!"* Teal shouted, then, softly, to Jenny, "Forget it, kid. I'm O.K."

Hailey shoved Teal toward the aft cabin. Teal stumbled to the door. Hailey told him to open it and get inside. When Teal was in Hailey turned the key in the lock.

"Get topside," Hailey ordered Block. "Get her off self-steering and hold her steady on 249 degrees. I'll give you a new course in a minute."

Block nodded and sprang lightly up the gangway.

Hailey put the Llama on Admiralty Chart 773, *Strait of Gibraltar to Adra and Cabo Tres Forcas*, which lay spread on the chart table. He glanced out the starboard porthole. A touch astern he could just recognize the white stack of the eighteen meter high Punta de Calaburras lighthouse perched atop its cliff a few kilometers southwest of Fuengirola. Hailey estimated

Destry cruised six kilometers offshore. He took the Brown and Perring parallel rule and a pencil and ruled a direct line between his estimated position and Europa Point on the tip of Gibraltar. Then he opened the rule and stepped it across the chart until it was centered on the nearest compass rose. He marked the point. He added four degrees for compass deviation which was posted on the graph by the salon compass and deducted another six degrees for magnetic variation. He didn't bother allowing for tides and currents.

He buzzed Block on the intercom. "Turn her to 236 and hold her," he said. "Correct visually when you see Gibraltar; aim her at Europa Point."

"Is that where we're picking up the stuff?" Block asked.

"We're going into the Bay, to the fuel bunkers," Hailey told him. "That's why we've kept these people aboard. We'll need them."

"Eh, man," Block said. "How's about bringing up a beer?"

"No booze until we've finished," Hailey said. He replaced the receiver, cutting off Block's mutter. He opened the dividers and stepped them off along his course. He estimated they'd be rounding Europa Point in less than two hours.

"You're going to kill us," Jenny said.

Hailey looked at her as if suddenly remembering her presence.

"You're going to use us somehow to get the fuel and then kill us."

Hailey said nothing.

Her face was damp from weeping. The dried blood from her cut lip traced a thin line down her chin. She held a tissue which she twisted between her fingers. She sniffled, then took a deep breath, trying to compose herself. "You don't have to kill us." She tried to say it softly, but her voice betrayed her fear and the words came out huskily. "You can let us off in Gibraltar. At the fuel bunkers. We won't say anything."

Hailey lit a cigarette and sucked at the smoke greedily. He ignored Jenny and rummaged on a shelf above the chart table. He found a cardboard bank wallet, opened it and saw a wad of bills. He riffled through them, estimating over $5000 in various currencies. He closed the wallet and slapped it in his hand.

Zeller had told him that any money he found on a job was his to keep. A bonus, he'd said, think of it as a bonus. Hailey unzipped his duffle bag and dropped in the wallet. Spoils of the victor, he thought.

He looked at the girl.

Her wide, red-rimmed eyes pleaded with him. "The life raft," she said. "You could put us in the life raft. It'd be days before we were found. You'd be safe. You'd never be caught."

Hailey lifted the Llama from the chart table and stared at it. "That's right," he said, softly. "I'd never be caught."

Hailey turned the gun slowly in his hand, hefting its weight, caressing it lovingly. He concentrated on the gun. Hailey forgot the girl. The gun hypnotized him. He concentrated on some dim memory of something someone had told him. The excited punch of the diesels mingled with his thoughts. He felt his body relaxing, felt the tension of the last fifteen minutes lifting, felt the sharp bounce and buffeting of the hull as *Destry* raced towards Gibraltar, the Atlantic and his Moroccan destination. *You'd never be caught.* Is that what they'd told him? Had they told *him* that, or that other part of him?

Hailey saw an inverted silhouette of himself reflected in the gun-metal blue of the automatic's barrel. He stared at the reversed and upside-down image and concentrated hard, sensing again that other part of himself, the young man who dwelled within him. Perhaps *he* knew what they'd been told. *You'd never be caught . . . never be caught.* He'd heard them say that, heard them explain, and he'd listened but now he couldn't remember, couldn't remember anything, not what they'd said, nor who they were, nor where he'd been when they'd told him. It was like a black hole in Hailey's brain, a vacuum which contained just one thing, a pulsing memory of something that had happened, and every so often something slid out of the memory and into his mind, and around the diffused edges of the hole was the occasional formless knowledge of his friend who lived within him.

Ever so slowly, Hailey turned the gun and watched the black, upside down, mirror image of himself creep around the convex shape of the barrel and disappear.

Hailey snapped out of it and stared at the girl.

" . . . the money," she was telling him. "But I have some. You can take it. and the boat, the boat's worth a fortune." She was crying again. "Christ," she wept, "we're on a holiday and this happens. Quinn and I are getting *married* and *this* happens. Take what you want, but let us go. *Please!*"

Hailey looked at the cigarette in his hand. It had burned right down and ash had fallen on the charts. He stubbed the butt and flicked the ash away. He lit another with his gold Dunhill.

"You're marrying Quinn," he said, matter-of-factly.

She rested her forehead in both hands. Her breasts heaved as she sobbed. "I love him."

"You love him."

She nodded.

"That must be very nice for you both."

She lifted her head and looked at him.

"I mean, how do you arrive at that conclusion?" Hailey asked seriously. "How do you decide that you are in love?" He drew on the fresh cigarette and slowly blew out smoke. "How do you *know* you're in love?"

Jenny stared straight at him. "Look," she said. "I'll do anything you want. I'll make love with you. Just let us go."

"You'll make *love* with me?" Hailey asked.

She nodded.

"Then you're in *love* with *me*, too?"

"You know what I mean," she said. Her voice was cracking again. She tried to say something else but she couldn't make the words come. She stopped. She closed her eyes and swallowed. "I'll fuck with you," she said. "Promise to let the three of us go and I'll fuck with you. You know what *that* means."

Hailey nodded. "Sure," he said. "Fucking I know all about. But love is the big mystery. That's what I want you to tell me, Jenny. I want you to tell me what love is."

Hailey looked at her, waiting. He saw her Adam's apple moving as she swallowed. And her right hand covered the cleavage of her breasts, like an old lady walking down the street of a Spanish mountain village—except old Spanish ladies didn't wear bikinis and talk about fucking. Hailey flicked his head, shifting the long, golden locks away from his eyes. He drew on his cigarette and waited. Perhaps she did know something about love, and would tell him. Love *was* the mystery for Hailey, a strange, cabalistic word, yet tossed into the air like confetti. Women had often told Hailey they loved him, but they'd never explained what they meant, and whenever he asked all he'd got was giggles and gropes. And now, as Block held *Destry* locked on an arrow straight course for Gibraltar, Hailey waited.

He watched Jenny. She was approaching hysteria now, fighting to control herself, and her hand had moved from her brown breasts to her throat, and she rubbed her throat as if that would hold the tears back.

Hailey waited to learn about love.

Block eased the twin throttles forward so that the big diesels gurgled throatily just a touch above idling speed. In the aft cabin, Teal felt *Destry* settling in the water and he rolled across the double bunk to look out the starboard porthole.

Destry was heading into Gibraltar Bay, slowly edging by the docks and waterfront loading bays rimming the base of the thousand feet high Rock. The great green and white bulk of the ancient Pillar of Hercules stretched a full four miles, shaped like a massive, crouching lion ready to spring across the narrow connecting isthmus into Spain.

Now Teal knew what was happening. Mann, or whatever he called himself, wanted to refuel *Destry*. That's why he'd kept the three of them alive—in case someone at the fule bunker recognized *Destry* and wondered about the strangers aboard her.

As if on cue, Teal heard Mann talking on the inter-com. Teal stood and tried to walk to the door. A deep, throbbing pain pulsed through his head. he felt his knees go, and clasped both hands to his forehead. That golden-haired bastard had really thumped him. Teal grunted, fighting back the nausea which made him want to vomit. A minute after he'd been shoved into the cabin he'd fainted. The last two hours he'd spent laying quietly on the bunk, marshaling his strength, trying to figure how to get them all out of this mess. Christ, there'd been enough warnings about taking strangers aboard. There'd been enough yacht-jackings in the Mediterranean these last two years to make a man wary of taking his god-damned mother-in-law aboard! But those guys had seemed genuine enough. Oh yeah, and one of those genuine guys had kicked his face in, and now here he was kneeling in the middle of the cabin, trying not to spew up on Quinn's lovely carpet, and holding his face and trying to get to the door to hear what that bastard was saying.

O.K., you big tough fucker, Teal said to himself, get your ass moving.

He tried to stand. His legs wouldn't let him. His leg muscles had turned to jelly. His stomach heaved as the throbbing pain pulsed like a jack-hammer in his head and he gave in to it and retched. A stream of liquid spurted from his mouth over Quinn's beautiful, thick-pile carpet.

That's the beer out, Teal said to himself. You drink too much beer, ass-hole. Now get on your feet.

The vomiting helped. The dull ache still boomed away in his head, but at least his stomach wasn't churning anymore, and he'd found the use of his legs again.

Teal tested himself with two tentative steps and when he found his muscles responding, knelt by the door with his ear pressed to it.

The Golden-Haired Boy wasn't on the phone anymore. He had Quinn in the salon with him.

"What's your maximum range?"

"Around six hundred," Teal heard Quinn answer.

"What if she's held down to twenty-five knots?"

"You might get six-fifty." Good, Teal thought, the boy isn't playing smart-ass. Nothing to be gained doing that. Just go along with the bastards until we get out chance.

"You got any spare fuel cans?"

"There's three five gallon cans lashed down forward by the life raft cannister."

"We're docking at the bunkers to refuel. You're coming up top with me. If anyone asks about Teal, you say he's sick down below and the girl's looking after him. You do or say anything stupid, Quinn, and my friend will kill her."

"You're going to kill us anyway, so why should I cooperate?"

"Because you're an optimist, Quinn. Because you think you might just get out of this." There was a pause. "You may, Quinn, you never know. Now, let's go . . ."

It has to be soon, Teal told himself. It has to be soon. Mann's going up top with Quinn. That leaves the other one down below with Jenny. Mann's the dangerous one. The other one's just a kid. He's big, but he's only a kid. I can take him if I can get at him. I have to get him while Mann's still up top. And I have to get this thing done within half an hour. As soon as we've cleared the Bay he's going to kill us. How the hell do I get out of this damned cabin?

Teal breathed deeply, hyperventilating, trying to force extra oxygen into his bloodstream, trying to forget the nagging thump in his head. He looked under the bunk, pulled open drawers and lockers. He could tell by the disarray of clothes and personal effects that one of those bastards and been through everthing before him. No tools, no weapons. Nothing to help him get out, nothing to help him if he *did* get out.

The chair. If he could force apart the back legs he could remove the crossbar. He picked it up and cursed the fine craftsmanship which had gone into every last detail of *Destry's* fittings. The chair was built of mahogany, heavy and strong. Teal grabbed the two legs like a man trying to bend the bars of a prison, and applied every ounce of his strength, the huge biceps on his scarred, brown arms bulging, the sinews and veins in his forearms pushing to the surface of his skin as if they wanted to escape his body. The legs moved. He heard them creaking. Teal kept the pressure on. He heard the glue in the joints crack and then a snap as one end broke free. He released the pressure and felt the blood flooding the arteries in his temples. He relaxed a moment, gasping for breath, then prized the crossbar free of the legs. It was about fifteen inches long, and solid. If he could swipe the bastard across the ear with that he wouldn't get up in a hurry. The leg would've been better, but it was too long to wield in the confines of the salon.

O.K., so now he had a weapon. All he had to do was get out of the goddamned cabin so he could use the fucking thing.

Teal sat on the floor with his back to the door and approached the problem logically.

The portholes: he could open them, but they were too small for a man to squeeze through. If he opened one and yelled for help to the guys at the bunker he ran the risk of getting Quinn or Jenny killed.

The walls: forget it. The only way you could get through those was with a drill or an axe.

The ceiling: no go. Teal could remove the paneling, but then he'd be presented with caulked, inch-thick teak planks. He'd need a box full of tools and an hour to get through.

The deck: no way. There was a hatch to the engines, but when he got to the engines, then what did he do?

The inkling of an idea formed itself in Teal's mind. Perhaps he could seize up the engines and, while the Golden Haired Wonder held a gun at his head in an attempt to make him repair them, try to figure a way to take him. But he dismissed the idea immediately. Their only chance was within the next twenty minutes or half hour while Mann was up top and the other one down below. While they were spilt up.

The door: he changed his position, leaned against a locker and examined it. The hinges? They were on the outside. The lock? It was locked. Could he pick it? Sure, if he had some tools and a little experience in safe-breaking. Could he break straight through it, smash straight through with his shoulder? Teal dismissed the idea. You didn't put your shoulder through solid mahogany doors fitted with expensive brass locks.

Teal slumped. Those two bastards had them sewn up. They hadn't missed a trick: removed tools and weapons from the cabins; kept them separated; kept Jenny under the gun so they'd think twice about trying anything.

So what do you do, Teal? he asked himself. Lay like a chicken with a headache and wait for the guy with the axe to knock off your head?

Teal heard the note of the diesels lower even further. He looked out the starboard porthole and saw that *Destry* lay snug against the oil-stained face of a cement dock. They were at the fuel bunkers. He crossed the cabin. Out the other side the animal shape of Gibraltar filled the horizon. He saw the new marina and the jumble of buildings sprawling up to the castle and the wooded slopes above. The engines stopped, and he heard good-natured yells and orders as the dock hands secured *Destry* fore and aft. Then he heard feet scuffing the deck above him and knew the fuel cap was being unscrewed and the big hose being inserted. He could hear conversation and laughter, but couldn't make out the words.

Teal stood, gripping his club. He swung it through the air in frustration. Jenny and the big guy were still talking, but now the engines had stopped he could detect the fear in Jenny's voice. The poor kid. What was she, twenty? Her big holiday with Quinn before Quinn flew her back to the States to meet his old man and explain their marriage plans. She was all set to be a millionaire's wife. And here she was in the middle of this cute little situation. Cute, alright.

Teal knelt at the door to look through the keyhole and try and see what was happening in the salon. He couldn't see anything. The key was in the lock.

The key!

Jesus Christ! Teal came to his feet, aches, pains and throbbing head forgotten, and wrenched open the clothes locker. There was a way out of this, Jesus Christ, yes, there *was* a way out. He hurled clothes aside, praying as he hunted that he'd find what he needed. Two wire coathangers! there they were, jammed up one end of the locker!

Two wire coat hangers! Christ, how long ago had he learned this stunt? In the comics, when he was ten? In the Saturday afternoon movies, in Brooklyn, all those years back, when he'd managed to scrounge fifteen cents for fare and a ticket?

His hands shook as he held the hangers in his hands, and he breathed deep again, trying to calm himself. A goddamned kid trick for Christ's sake, but it'd get him out of there and at least give them all a chance. If he could pull it off; if they were lucky.

And what do you do when you get out? You worry about that *when* you get out, he told himself. You sock that big bastard and put him out of action, and you worry about the Golden Haired Wonder later. And you hope Quinn's on the ball. But Quinn was O.K. He was a rich kid, a playboy, a kid chasing dreams, but he was O.K. He was no slob. And he was tough, he could handle himself. No match for those two up there maybe, but Quinn'd do what he had to do as well as he could. The girl was the problem. Little Jenny. She was the one he had to worry about. She'd probably never seen a gun or a bleeding man before. In Swiss finishing schools, and English horse-riding schools, and ballet acadamies, and first class restaurants and chintzy bars and flash discoteques you didn't get much chance to see blood and guts. Jenny was the problem.

Worry about it when you come to it, Teal told himself. Just get that door open.

He'd pulled one wire coathanger open into a near circle, and straightened the handle of the other. He ran his hand along the rubber weather seal at the base of the door. It had to come off so he could slide the hanger underneath. It wasn't screwed on, just glued. He grabbed another hanger from the locker and with the hook handle, pried free one end of the rubber strip. It came loose. He took it in his stubby fingers and ripped it away. Now he had maybe a three-quarters of a centimeter gap between the base of the door and the floor.

They'd finished refuelling up top. He heard the cap being screwed back in place, heard someone walking forward and dumping the spare jerry cans up by the bow. Now he heard voices again and a moment later the hull vibrated as Quinn or Mann punched the starter button and the twin Sabres sparked into life. Teal felt a slight roll as the boat began moving. He glanced out the staroard porthole. *Destry* was creeping beyond the quays, heading out of the harbor toward the center of the Bay. Astern he could just see the high, white apartment buildings of Algeciras strung around the broad reach of the Spanish side of the Bay, reflecting the dying sunlight.

Slowly, inexorably, the big diesels changed their note and *Destry* surged forward, lifting her bow, heading for the Straits. Teal figured Mann would stay up top with Quinn until they were clear of the Bay and well into the shipping channel. He didn't know if Mann intended heading up the coast toward Portugal, or across the shipping separation zone and south towards Africa. It didn't matter. He, Quinn and Jenny had only two possibilities: overpower both of their unwelcome passengers and regain control of *Destry*, or jump overboard and take their chances in the sea. If it was the latter, Teal knew their chance of survival was one in a hundred. But if it came to that it'd be one chance better than waiting for a bullet in the head.

Swiftly, he slipped the opened up coathanger under the door, then he took the other with the straightened handle and inserted it into the keyhole. As gently as he could, he pushed at the key, feeling it move millimeter by millimeter. If he shoved too hard it would bounce out of the encircling trap of wire and he'd never snare it. Sweat beaded Teal's forehead as he inched the key forward.

Destry was moving at over twenty knots now, sitting on the haunches of her stern, kicking the choppy sea at the entrance of the Bay. She bucked as she slapped a breaking white-top and slowed fractionally to port. Teal cursed under his breath and steadied his hand, waiting for *Destry* to settle into her rhythm again.

Slowly, forcing himself to be patient, Teal eased the key forward. He felt it give, then felt the slight pressure on the end of the wire stop, and heard, or rather sensed, the faintest thump as the key fell out of the hole and onto the deck on the other side of the door.

Teal tossed his makeshift tool aside and lay flat on the floor trying to look under the door. He could see part of his circle of wire, but not enough to know if he had the key. Taking the handle of the opened-up hanger, he slowly eased it back under the door.

Hailey leaned against the emergency locker at the back of the wheelhouse watching Quinn at the wheel, his feet braced against *Destry's* pitching as she raced diagonally across the Inshore Traffic Zone towards Morocco. The sun was well gone now. A smear of orange cloud on the horizon slowly turned black.

There'd been no problem from Quinn at the Gibraltar fuel bunker. Quinn had done what he was told, acted the part of the playboy sea-captain to perfection, answered questions smoothly, joked a little. Quinn was no fool, Hailey decided, and that was why Quinn was dangerous. More dangerous, perhaps, than Teal who was safely locked below in the aft cabin.

Hailey had already decided what he would do with Quinn. When they were half way across the Straits he would simply shoot Quinn in the back, right where he stood at the wheel. Quinn wouldn't know a thing. He'd put the bullet in between the shoulder blades, just at the level of the heart. Quinn would die instantly. Then Hailey would lock *Destry* onto automatic and throw Quinn's body overboard. That'd be Quinn out of the way. That'd be the most dangerous one done with. Then he'd lock the girl in the forward cabin and leave her there. He'd leave Teal where he was, in the aft cabin. He was safe there, he couldn't do anything. Try and get Teal out of there and he'd put up a fight. He was too strong to mess with. So he'd leave the girl forward, and Teal aft, and when he'd delivered the guns to these BEKA boys he'd sink *Destry* and the girl and Teal with her. That was the simplest thing, the cleanest thing, the thing with the least risk to it.

Hailey had no remorse about killing the girl, no more than he'd had about killing Gloster. For a moment he'd thought she would turn out different from the rest of them, that she'd have something intelligent to say to him. But she'd just sat and stared at him with her hands clasped across her breasts and tears running down her face like some virginal schoolgirl who thought she was about to be raped. Sat and stared at him and stuttered and begged him not to hurt her. A fool, like all the others. And like all the others, Hailey had looked at her and listened and felt no more toward her than if he'd addressed his attention to a side of beef. Tristan had been right when he'd told him never to get involved with women. "Women," Tristan had said, "are a convenience." So for this one, this Jenny, it was all over for her and that was that.

But Hailey felt a twinge as he thought of *Destry* going to the bottom. He could see Block and himself racing away from *Destry* in the Avon raft and *Destry* with her cocks open and a couple of holes in her side slowly settling stern first because of the weight of the big diesels and he thought it a hell of a thing that it was necessary to kill a boat like *Destry*.

* * *

Slowly, Teal told himself, slowly you son-of-bitch. If it's sitting on the wire and you pull it in too fast and the key will slip over the edge.

Teal felt his throat going dry. He swallowed, forcing himself to coax the wire slowly and methodically, centimeter by centimeter. He felt himself panicking, felt the urge to yank the wire in under the door fast and take his chances. He let the wire go, stood up and stretched his muscles. He forced himself to stand for a full ten seconds and deep-breathed again, trying to make himself relax. He had to do this right. It was the only chance he or the others would ever get.

He sprawled on the carpeted deck again and resumed gently pulling the wire toward him, forcing his hand to move steadily, smoothly, and then he had it. He had it! The tiny piece of machined brass that meant the difference between life and death sat in the palm of his big hand.

Teal knelt and pushed his face against the door, closing one eye and squinting through the keyhole with the other. He saw Jenny sitting behind the table, her elbows on the table, her head bowed and both hands covering her face. The black-bearded kid sat with one haunch resting on the side of the chart table. If the bastard would stay like that, Teal would have him. He'd never hear the door being opened above the vibrating moan of *Destry*'s engines.

The kid stood and stretched. He had his gun in hand. Now he faced Teal. Teal cursed. He'd have to wait until the kid turned around again. Clutching the key like a lifeline, Teal checked the portholes. He could just see Europa Point to port. On the starboard side he could see the lighthouse on Punto Carnero on the Spanish coast, its revolving beam cutting a golden swathe across the dark waters, highlighting the white-tops. *Destry* was running south west across the Inshore Traffic Zone lane. They were more than a mile offshore and heading further seaward all the time. The bastard was running *Destry* across to Morocco. Teal figured Mann would stay topside with Quinn another few minutes until they'd settled onto their course. Then he'd come below and put the kid on the wheel. Now he'd got his fuel he might kill them at any time.

Teal knelt to the keyhole again. The big bastard was saying

something to Jenny, saying it quietly. Teal couldn't hear a word above the throb of the diesels. Then the kid lifted the automatic and playfully pointed it at Jenny and Teal saw Jenny cringe back from the table and the kid lowered the gun and started laughing.

You bastard, thought Teal, you bastard, you'll get yours.

Now the kid tucked the revolver under his belt and went and sat on the table in front of Jenny. He was laughing at her again, then stood up. He glanced at the gangway, then stepped across to the mini-fridge and took out a bottle of San Miguel. He flipped off the cap with the opener hanging on the wall and again settled himself with one haunch resting on the chart table.

With his back to Teal.

Teal breathed deeply. Got to do it quick, he told himself. Hit him, get the gun, then get topsides after the other one. Don't think anymore, he told himself. Just do it!

Destry still headed southwest, away from Spain, bucking a little as she butted the occasional whitetop. Hailey still leaned against the locker, watching Quinn at the wheel. Night had claimed the sky now, only the merest touch of orange tinting the western horizon. Over *Destry's* stern her bubbling wake trailed a glittering track back toward. Andalusia's darkening shore. Off the port bow, a full moon rose like a cannonball shot from the indigo sky, a dull, brass skull that subtly lit the choppy waves and the peaks and valleys of the Riff Mountains on the African mainland.

Quinn stood stoically at the wheel making minute adjustments to send *Destry* along the new course Hailey had ordered. Twice, three times he had glanced back at Hailey, trying to judge if he had a chance to jump him. But the thin glow of the instrument lights didn't illuminate him; he remained an expressionless silhouette against the western sky. And Quinn knew he held the automatic in his hand. There was no point in taking a ridiculous chance. Not now. Later perhaps, when there were no other chances left, but not now.

"We heading for Tangier?" Quinn asked.

Hailey didn't answer.

Quinn glanced at the compass, then half turned to look toward Hailey.

"Watch the course," Hailey said.

"I'm curious," Quinn said.

"Why?" Hailey asked. "What difference does it make?"

Quinn shrugged and turned back to the wheel. "You're stealing my boat, you've attacked Teal, you've terrified my girl. What's the purpose? You can't sell a boat like this; you'd be picked up the moment you tried." Quinn forced himself to speak evenly, to control his voice, keep the fear from it. He didn't need fear polluting his brain now; he had to keep his mind clear, keep himself ready to move. "You running gold? Illegals? Drugs? Weapons?"

"What difference does it make?" Hailey asked again.

Quinn forced lightness into his voice. "If you're going to kill us, mister, I'd like to die with my curiosity satisfied."

"Tell you what," Hailey said, "If I'm going to kill you, I'll satisfy your curiosity first."

"That's one I owe you," Quinn said. He settled back to the wheel, his eyes canvassing the sea ahead, then checking the compass, then the sea again. He steered the boat automatically, his mind churning to discover just one possibiltiy, just one way of getting his hands on that bastard behind him.

Teal inserted the key into the lock and slowly turned it. The well-oiled tongue slipped silently out of its catch. He changed the club from his left hand to his right. He gently pushed the door until it was open wide enough for him to see the kid. The kid still sucked on his beer. He muttered something to Jenny. Jenny stared at him, her face a mixture of distaste and horror, her eyes wide, as if hypnotized by what he was saying. She hadn't seen the door opening.

Hailey watched Quinn at the wheel. Quinn's face was lit by the dull, green glow from the instrument panel. Hailey hefted the Llama in his hand, changing his grip. He'd put the bullet into him soon, when they were just a little further out from the coast and there was less chance of the body floating into the beaches, or coastal fishermen snagging him in their nets. Not that it mattered too much. Within thirty-six hours *Destry* would rest on the bottom off the northern Spanish coast, and Hailey and Block would be out of Spain.

One day, Hailey thought, I'm going to have a boat like *Destry*; one day when I've made my money and I leave Tristan and Zeller. I have to talk to Zeller about that next time Tristan takes me to see him. I'll explain it all to Tristan so Tristan understands and then he'll help me explain it to Zeller. And I have to talk to Zeller about the injections, and the box. I don't need them anymore. I'm O.K. now.

Tristan gave him the injections and then helped him into the box, and he lay there suspended and dreaming while Tristan softly spoke to him. It was for the headaches he got because of the wound he'd picked up in Vietnam when the grenade had exploded and the tiny fragment of metal had become embedded in his head. The army doctors had opted to leave the shrapnel fragment where it was. The head wound got him back to the States and earned him promotion to sergeant, a Purple Heart and an honorable discharge after two months in a hospital. He'd had no problems with the wound for over a year. Then the fragment had shifted minutely, putting pressure onto an optic nerve, and blinding headaches had driven him nearly crazy.

He'd already been working for Zeller then, had done three simple jobs for him. When the headaches started, Zeller had admitted him to a private clinic where they'd started with the injections and the box.

He'd met Tristan there. Tristan was a doctor. Tristan worked for Zeller, too. He'd explained that Zeller had a particular interest in him. Tristan had become his good friend. Tristan talked to him in the box when he was suspended and dreaming, spoke to him softly and soothingly. He could never remember what Tristan spoke to him about. But the injections and the eerie world within the box and Tristan's quiet voice cured him . . .

Teal slipped out of the open cabin door, club poised ready to slug the kid. Jenny saw him. She tired to control her reaction, but her eyes instinctively flickered and widened and signaled what she'd seen.

Block got the message. At the very instant Teal stepped forward and brought the club down, Block dropped the beer, ducked and spun to face Teal, all in one fluid, dangerous movement. The swinging club missed Block's head and glanced off his shoulder. Block's forward motion propelled him into Teal. Teal grunted and jolted Block under the chin with his forearm. Block's head snapped back, but the blow didn't stop him. He grabbed for the .38 Centennial under his belt. Teal poked the end of the club straight at his face, like a lunging swordfighter. Block dodged. The splintered end of the club ripped across his ear, tearing the lobe. Blood welled from the wound. Block tuggd again at the butt of the revolver, but the hammer was caught under his belt. Teal kicked at Block, catching him on the kneecap. Block grunted and tumbled, his hand forgetting the gun. Teal brought the club down over Block's back and booted at his face.

Block was down but still fighting. Teal kicked desperately again at Block, but Block got his hands around Teal's foot and jerked. Teal crashed back against the chart table. The chart-table broke away from its hinges and Teal landed in a half-sitting sprawl on the deck.

Through blurring vision, Teal saw Jenny moving slow motion toward him, her mouth wide open but with no sound coming from it, her hands clenched into fists. Suddenly Block was on top of him. He had the San Miguel bottle. It was broken. Block held the bottle by the neck and jabbed the jagged end at Teal. Teal blocked with his right forearm and fist, saw great red gashes opening along the length of his arm, but didn't feel a thing. He shoved his open hand into Block's face and heaved with his hips, twisting at the same time, trying to force Block from him.

Block lost his balance, toppled, rolled away from Teal, crashing into furniture in the tiny confines of the cabin. He came to his feet, tugging again at the .38 in his belt. Jenny leaped onto his back, hanging around his neck with one arm and pummeling him with her free fist. Teal tried to get up, slipped, fell onto his side, pinning his wounded arm beneath him. Pain cloaked him like a shroud. He grunted, grabbed at his fallen club, started scrambling to his feet.

Block hauled the revolver free of his belt and at the same time jabbed back with his elbow into Jenny's stomach. She gasped as pain tore through her solar plexus and the wind left her, but she hung on. Block pivoted, hurling Jenny like a stone from a slingshot. She crashed into Teal.

Teal saw the whole thing coming before it happened. Frantically he tried to disentangle himself from Jenny. He tried to yell a warning, but his gasping breath betrayed his voice. He saw Block stumble and raise the revolver. With his wounded hand, Teal raised the club and hurled it. But even as the club flew from his hand, Block took one step back and fired. The shot exploded like a thunder clap within the confines of the tiny cabin, the .38 slug ploughing into Jenny's head, and Teal felt the hot mush and sharp slithers of brain and skull gushing over him.

The club caught Block in the face. He yelled as it gouged into his cheek. He lost his balance and crashed to the deck, grabbing at his face, the revolver spinning from his hand and sliding down the carpeted forward passageway.

Teal acted without thinking. One part of his brain shrieked that Jenny was dead, another that he had to go get up top. Like an automation, he stumbled over Jenny's dead body, booted at Block's head and scrambled toward the gangway. He didn't wait to see if Block was unconscious, nor did he try to retrieve the revolver. It would cost him precious seconds to do so. The golden-haired bastard up top would have made his move the instant the shot boomed above the drone of the diesels.

Quinn was faster! The moment he heard the shot, he rammed the twin throttles forward, cutting the power of the massive diesels, and at the same time launched himself low and backwards in the direction of Hailey.

Hailey fired instantly, but *Destry's* bow lurched seawards as her power was suddenly reduced. The shot chopped into the instrument panel on Quinn's right, showering the steering cabin with glass.

Quinn grappled at Hailey's spinning him, one hand grabbing Hailey's gun arm, his free forearm clamping itself around Hailey's neck. Hailey twisted once, ramming his leg between

Quinn's thighs. He dropped the gun and snatched at Quinn's up-raised arm. With one smooth movement, he hauled down on Quinn's arm and at the same time twisted his hip into Quinn's stomach and hooked the calf of his leg up into Quinn's testicles. Quinn gagged at the sudden pain; felt himself flying through the air. He landed doubled over the guard-rail outside the enclosed steering cabin, frantically fought for his balance, then slid down *Destry's* hull, plummeting head first into the ocean.

As Teal bounded up the gangway, *Destry* suddenly lurched. Teal stumbled, grabbed at a railing, fell, hauled himself to his feet and scrambled up the remaining steps.

As he came to the top he heard a cry of pain, saw Quinn head down over the guard-rail and Hailey on his knees grabbing at the Llama.

In a flash, Teal computed the situation: Jenny dead; Quinn overboard; the kid behind him perhaps out to it, perhaps not; this bastard in front of him with a gun in his hands. No chance. No chance.

Teal launched himself toward the side. At the instant he moved, Hailey fired. The Llama's bullet caught him high in the left arm, but Teal's weight kept him going. Hailey fired again, but missed, and by the time he'd pulled the trigger a third time, Teal was in the air, a massive silhouette against the dark sky, knifing downward into the embracing, concealing depths.

For long minutes Teal was unconscious. He came to in a cold and dark world, the black tent of the sky above him and the inky gloom of the ocean beneath. In the cave-like darkness the only visible thing was the eerie light highlighting the white-tops which sloshed over him and carried him back and forth as they swelled and troughed.

As he realized he was still alive a searing pain charged through his lungs. He coughed and choked, then vomited, feeling and tasting warm, salty sea-water heaving itself out of his stomach.

The only sound apart from the suck and slop of the sea was the retreating moan of high-powered diesels.

"Teal? Teal?"

Only then, at the sound of Quinn's voice did Teal realize that a supporting hand was grasping him by the shirt, keeping him from drowning as the incessant waves buffeted over him.

"Jesus, oh Jesus Christ, they killed her," he moaned.

"I know," Quinn said. "Don't talk. Don't waste energy. Just stay afloat." He coughed and spat out water as another wave broke over them.

Teal vomited another mess of salt water out of his gut, tried to tell him again about Jenny.

"Don't talk," Quinn said. "If we stay afloat until dawn, we've got a chance."

"Let me go now," Teal said. "I'm O.K. now."

Quinn released his grip, then splashed two or three strokes away from Teal so they'd both have room to float. He kicked off his shoes to make it easier to move, and loosened his belt to make it easier to breathe. He decided to leave on his clothes in the hope that they'd give his skin some protection against the salt. He floated, trying to keep one eye on Teal, and another on the rhythm of the waves, so he could close his eyes and hold his breath as they broke over him. He stretched out, spreading his arms and legs. He checked Teal. Teal had done the same, except he'd folded his wounded arm across his chest. Quinn wondered if the *poniente*, the sharp west wind driving in from the Atlantic and kicking up the white-tops, would drop, or if it would whip up the sea even further. If that happened, Quinn knew that he and Teal would be drowned within an hour. They couldn't survive cubic meters of water slopping over them minute after minute; each breaking wave would take its toll of strength and will, seeping into ears and nostrils, forcing its biting saltiness into lungs and stomach until finally they would be retching uncontrollably and gasping with opened mouths for the life-giving air. But there would be none—only more water and salt.

Teal coughed as another white-top rolled over him. Quinn paddled himself closer in case he needed help. He could hear Teal gasping for breath. Teal had seen what had happened to Jenny; Quinn knew he'd seen her killed. He knew Teal would never have dived overboard if Jenny was still alive. Quinn had heard the shot. He hadn't thought about it then, he'd just acted, made his play, taken his chance against that bastard behind him with the gun. But when, from the black trough of the Atlantic he'd seen Teal lunge for the side, seen Mann, or whatever his name was, firing at him, seen Teal's dark shape launching itself and the muzzle flashes of the automatic splitting the blackness, he'd known. If Jenny had been alive Teal would have stayed and fought. Jenny was dead.

Quinn had got to Teal within minutes. He'd been floating only half conscious, his arms spread, his face dipping into the sea and jerking out with a reflex action as even in his unknowing state his body had demanded air. Quinn had grabbed him by the hair and forced his head out of the water, then clenched his shirt to support him.

Then, suddenly, beautiful *Destry* had become a predator. With her white hull shining in the moonlight she'd hunted them in slow, wide, circular sweeps, the Ford Sabre diesels gurgling in protest as they were leashed back to a near standstill. Quinn had hung onto Teal and watched. There was nothing else he could do. Then those bastards aboard had found the switch to the emergency swivel light mounted on the side of the wheelhouse and the powerful 500 watt beam had skimmed across the wavetops hunting, darting between the troughs, searching for them, stabbing like a golden knife through the blackness.

At times *Destry* was so close to them—no more than sixty or seventy yards—that Quinn heard their voices carrying on the breeze, mixed with the throaty rumble of the diesels. Quinn clung to Teal, keeping his head clear of the water, trying to protect him as each wave broke across their shoulders; and had prayed that the search-light never found them.

Then five, ten minutes later, they'd given up the search. While the bearded one stayed at the wheel, the one who had thrown Quinn overboard went below. Quinn saw it all. Moments later he came back up the gangway with Jenny's body over his shoulder. Quinn had stifled an insane impulse to scream at him, to roar obscenities across the short distance separating them. With horror and disgust and tearing, ripping rage he watched him raise Jenny's body over his head. He'd stood like a heathen offering a sacrifice. For one instant, as *Destry* dipped in the sea, the emergency light seemed to explode behind his head, outlining that flowing golden hair. Then he heaved Jenny's lifeless body into the ocean.

Quinn had seen that. Quinn had stared at the black hole in the night where *Destry* had been, then watched the tiny pinpricks of her navigation lights as she put on power and disappeared toward the horizon. Then the night closed around them, and the spray whipped them, and the waves clawed them, and Quinn felt no desperation nor fear—only the certainty that he would survive and hunt the man with the golden hair to the ends of the earth.

PART TWO

Quinn lay on top of the hotel bed, still in his clothes, staring at the angle where the wall met the ceiling. His eyes stung grittily from lack of sleep. The suffused grayness of the early London morning barely lit the room. Out on the Strand traffic hummed as the city gathered momentum.

He'd walked back to the hotel at midnight after a nearby club closed and drank all the half bottle of Johnny Walker he'd bought at the Málaga airport duty free shop when he'd flown out of Spain yesterday. He'd lain there drinking and trying to fully comprehend that this was the same hotel where'd he'd met Jenny just weeks before.

He felt bad; his throat raw from cigarettes, his bowels vaguely loose from the whisky. His head ached; he felt dirty: he had to take a shower, get himself moving. The curtain billowed as the winter wind blew through the barely opened window and stirred ash in the butt-filled tray on the coffee table beside the easy chair. Quinn closed his eyes, then slowly raised his hands and covered his face. Red motes of tiredness and tension danced behind his heavy lids. What the hell could a man do now?

It was his fault. Quinn couldn't escape that fact. There were precautions you took before inviting strangers aboard when you owned a boat. You checked them out some way. Casual visitors came recommended by someone you knew, or not at all. If they were new crew you took their passport details— better, you took their photographs as well—and left them safe ashore with your marine insurance company representative, or posted them to him, or left them with some competent friend. Then if you were murdered or marooned, or your boat was hi-jacked, someone had hard facts to take to the coastguard or the police. What you didn't do was allow any Tom, Dick or Harry come aboard without taking steps to protect yourself, your crew, your passengers and your boat. Those were the ground rules. But who ever followed rules? And now this.

Fishermen picked them up.

A dirty, broad-beamed thirty footer out of Algeciras, with an eye to ward off evil spirits painted on its high, gaudily decorated bow, had spotted them in the first light of dawn after they'd been in the water all night.

Quinn and Teal were hanging onto a lump of driftwood pushed by the currents over from the east. They were both frozen to the marrow, with Teal delirious from his wound, which the salt water had crinkled like the moldering rind of an orange.

Their rescue boat was called *Maria de los Dolores*. She'd been the tenth boat to pass them, one of scores out of Gibraltar, Spain and Morocco that fished the Straights every night. When the other boats had passed Quinn screamed himself hoarse, knowing even as he did that he'd never be heard above the noise of their engines. When the *Maria* appeared, Quinn was too exhausted to yell. He'd watched her ghostly silhouette emerging from the great shimmering ball of the rising sun, heard her cut her engines, heard the shouts, saw men rowing in her tiny auxilliary toward them, and found himself chattering to Teal like a little boy:

"It's O.K., Bob, hang on, they're coming, Bob, they've got us, it's O.K. now, it's O.K. now, Bob."

When the fishermen hauled them into the rowboat Quinn fainted. When he awoke he and Teal lay side by side on an old mattress in the wheelhouse, and *Maria's* grimy-faced, unshaven captain was trying to make him sip from a brandy bottle while the mate swabbed antiseptic onto Teal's wounded arm. When the feeling started returning to Quinn's numbed limbs the pain was so intense he'd screamed in agony.

The telephone by the bed rang. Without sitting up, Quinn reached for it. He heard reception tell the caller to go ahead. He recognized Johnny James's voice, the investigator at

Marine Insurance Limited who Quinn had telegrammed from Spain.

"I'm available all day," Johnny said. "Any idea when you can make it into the office?"

"About an hour," Quinn said.

"Fine. Look . . ." Johnny cleared his throat. "I received a report from our agent in Marbella. He spoke with Teal before he left hospital. I didn't realize it was so bad."

Quinn said nothing, just held the receiver to his ear and stared at the ceiling. James would offer his condolences and he would listen. It wouldn't help.

"I'm sorry about the girl, old man."

"Thanks, Johnny."

"See you in an hour or so."

Quinn replaced the receiver. He closed his eyes as if the simple physical act could cancel everything, destroy the mental turmoil. Perhaps condolences were all that was left. During those twelve hours in the water, he'd been sustained by a sense of rage, by searing fantasies of the vengeance he would visit on those two bastards who'd murdered Jenny. Particularly the man with the golden hair. He held more hatred for him than the other one who had actually shot her. Seeing her thrown overboard had raised an atavistic fury in him. Junking her like that. Tossing her to some voracious sea-god who would feast on her bones. It had been a primeval act, the act of a sub-human.

Quinn swung his feet to the mat by the side of the bed, rested his elbows on his knees and buried his face in his hands. What could sustain him now that he'd returned to the world of polite society where well-intentioned friends and acquaintances tried to dismiss his sorrow with a simple condolence?

Teal was no stranger to violence.

As he walked slowly along the quays of Puerto Jose Banus, hunting the port for any sign of those two bastards who'd killed Jenny and taken *Destry*, he, like Quinn, found himself filled with the need to commit an act of revenge. Unlike Quinn, Teal had seen violence before, participated in it, suffered from it, and sometimes, during mad, illogical moments, even enjoyed it.

In his twenty-five years of wandering the world, first as a deckhand on any tub that would take him, then as an officer in the Merchant Marine, and during the last ten years as an articled captain working on the million dollar yachts of the rich and privileged, Teal had had occasion to use his physical strength many times. He'd contested fist fights on ship's decks and survived terrifying bar-room brawls which had left even tougher men than him crippled for life. And three times, Teal had killed to save himself: once with a clasp knife when he'd slit the throat of a thug who'd attacked him in Jakarta; twice with a firearm when a pair of crooked cops had visited his hotel room in Bangkok and tried to rob him. He'd wrestled an automatic from one and shot them both. Friends had smuggled him out of the country.

Teal walked by the outdoor tables at *Cristian's* and the *Shark Club*, past the *Salduba* and *Sinatra's Bar* and down to the *Coco-Loco*. He didn't seriously expect to find them, but nothing else remained to do. He had no lead. He had to look, to do something, go through the motions while he tried to figure a plan. It was his second day scouring the port. He'd spoken with over thirty people; barmen, waiters, quay hands, boat owners, crew. No one could help him.

He stepped aside to allow a group of tourists by, then took the table they'd vacated outside the *Coco-Loco* and waited to order. He gazed down the quay to where *Destry* had lain only two short weeks before. Unconsciously he stroked the bandage covering the wound in his left upper arm. The bullet from the Llama had smashed through flesh and muscle, but miraculously exited without touching bone. It hurt still, was bruised and stiff, and he couldn't use the arm or even flex the muscles, but the wound had closed and the doctors at the Algeciras hospital, where Teal had spent twelve days, told him it would heal within a couple of weeks.

His arm. Jesus, he thought, my arm is the least of the fatalities in this tragedy. Jenny dead; Quinn mentally shattered; *Destry* gone. And, according to the Spanish police, nothing to be done about it.

When the captain of the *Maria de las Dolores* landed them in Algeciras port, the immigration police called an ambulance to speed them to the provincial hospital. They were attended in a private ward under discreet guard. On the second day when he and Quinn had recovered enough to be interviewed, the police questioned them separately and, a couple of days later, grilled them again. The story they told obviously coincided with details of the police investigation. They weren't worried again.

The day Quinn left hospital, seven days after their rescue, an inspector from the Algeciras force visited. He told them that Moroccan and Spanish coastguards were alerted to apprehend *Destry* if she was sighted, and that fishermen on both sides of the Straits were watching for Jenny's body. So far, it hadn't been sighted. The inspector, who spoke broken, but carefully enunciated English, lowered his head in respect. He feared her body would now never be found.

"What about the hi-jackers?" Quinn asked.

"We have no luck," the inspector said.

"What the hell have you *done*?"

The inspector ignored the unreasonably directed anger in Quinn's voice. "We have spoken with many people in the port of Jose Banus," he said, "more than one hundred, but we have found nothing. Understand that the descriptions of the criminals is the descriptions of many people. One is tall with the black beard which is the same as you, Señor Teal. One is tall with long gold hair." He shrugged. "We have checked also the records of immigration in major cities for the arrival of Mister Mann, also the hotel registration cards of the week before the crime in a one hundred kilometer radius of Málaga, but they, too, do not have the name of Mann. We continue to work, Señor, but I fear little is to be done."

Quinn lit a cigarette and stared out the window. Laid out like that, Teal saw the inspector was right. The cops didn't have much to work on.

"You are free to go when the doctors permit," the inspector said. "I ask only that you give us addresses where we can contact you if we get the luck with this case." He nodded, walked to he door, then paused and turned. "I wish to offer my personal sorrow for this thing that has passed." He lowered his head again and closed the door behind him. So there wasn't much chance of the police finding anything. Nor the insurance people.

When Quinn left the hospital he'd spent five days scouring the bars, clubs and discoteques in the ports and tourist resorts between Estepona and Nerja on the off-chance that he'd spot them. During that time the local representative of Marine Insurance Limited interviewed him, and Teal gathered from the rep's attitude that he'd heard it all before and there wasn't much to be done. So that left him and Quinn.

In hospital Quinn swore to Teal that he would find the killers himself. He didn't know how, or where, or how long it would take, but he would make the effort. It was the most positive thing Teal had ever heard Quinn say. Quinn asked him point-blank if he would stay on the pay-roll and help him. Teal accepted immediately. He owed Quinn a big one. Quinn had saved his life. But more than that, he'd liked Jenny. She'd been a typical screwed-up rich kid, but she'd had style, and in quiet conversations she'd treated him as a father figure, divulging everything to him: her dissatisfaction with her life before she'd met Quinn; her excitement about the trip; her plans for the future. Teal had felt deep affection for her, found that, surprisingly, he enjoyed simply yarning with her. He called her daughter. And those bastards had left him with a nightmare. He'd seen her head explode, felt her brains splash over him. Teal had never told Quinn that part of it.

So, sure, he'd help Quinn hunt the bastards. And if luck ever brought them together, he'd help Quinn do what had to be done. Quinn was angry, but didn't possess the killer instinct. Teal had seen enough of the darkness in his own soul to know he could shove a grenade up their asses and pull the pin without thinking twice.

Teal ordered *café solo* from Jesús, the waiter. Teal knew him from when *Destry* was berthed down the quay.

When Jesús served the coffee, he said: "How's the arm?"

"You heard what happened?" Teal asked.

"*La policia* questioned every bar in the *puerto*. Then your friend asked questions and then a man from the insurance company. Everyone is asking questions, man, it's a big deal, this thing." Jesús accepted a cigarette from Teal and lit them both with a plastic lighter. "The *señorita* Jenny got killed, right?"

"Right."

"That's the shits, man."

"Right." Teal asked Jesús to sit down a moment. "What did the police ask?"

"They looking for a big guy with a black beard and this other guy with the long hair. Him I never see."

"And the one with the black beard?"

Jesús sighed and rocked his hand back and forth in the Mediterranean sign-language for perhaps, maybe and who knows. "All these sailors, man, they all got black beards, like you got the black beard, right?"

"Right."

"And you get coupla hundred *clientes* each day. You don't look so much at the faces. You take the order and you think, gotta take this order to table six, or table seven. Just some special people you get to know. *Simpáticos*, you know? Like your friend and the *señorita* Jenny and you, man."

Teal sipped his coffee and nodded. His cigarette pack was empty. He asked Jesús if he'd bring him another pack. "Sure, man," Jesús said, "no problem."

He was wasting his time, Teal thought. Those guys would be crazy to return to the port. He idly stirred his coffee and took another sip, listening to the laughter of the group at the table opposite him. Then again, he thought, perhaps not. They know the girl's dead. The golden haired wonder must know he put a slug in me before I went overboard. They hunted us with the lights but never found us. Maybe they presumed we went straight under. And who survives a night in the Straits with a moderate sea running? Just sheer luck we're alive, that and Quinn's guts in *keeping* us alive. They might've come back. He sighed. Yeah, sure, until they got wind of the investigation, then they would have pissed off.

Jesús brought teal a pack of *Ducados* and sat down again. "Tell you what, man," he said, "Any way I can help, you just ask. I like that *señorita* Jenny a lot; she some doll, man."

"So what did you tell the cops, Jesús?"

Jesús shrugged. "That I never see this guy with the long hair. Maybe he here one day, but I don't remember him."

"And the guy with the black beard?"

"Everyone got black beards, man."

"He's real tall."

"Like you, man."

"You been to America, Jesús?"

"'Merica? I got no money for that."

"Where'd you learn English?"

"I start at school. Then I learn here, in the *puerto*. You gotta speak English, man, nobody speak Spanish in this country no more. All these *extranjeros*, how you say, these tourists. I speak some French, little German. Man, I take orders in eight languages. Fucking genius, man."

Teal slowly tore the cellophane from the pack of *Ducados*. He tapped one out for each of them, then accepted a light from Jesús. "You speak good English, Jesús. You even speak slang."

Jesús's eyes clouded blankly. "Slang? What's that, man?"

Teal hunted for the word among his meager command of Spanish and couldn't find it. "You know, Jesús, you say things like, what's that, *man*? I gotta go now, *man*."

"*Ah, si,*" Jesús said, "The bad habits in speaking, yes?"

Teal nodded. "You learn that stuff here?"

"I got this 'Merican friend, a *cliente*, he come here all the time. He always say, man this, and man that, you know? He's a good guy . . ." Jesús trailed off and looked at the ash on his cigarette and then at Teal.

Teal slowly drained the rest of his coffee. "Another American," Teal said. "How about that. Maybe I'd like to meet him, have a drink. What's his name?"

"He's a big guy," Jesús said quietly. "He got a black beard, like you."

"Shit, that doesn't mean anything," Teal said. "Lots of us black beards around."

"Didn't think of him when *la policia* asked, man," Jesús said. "But you got no problem with him, he's an O.K. guy."

"How long's he been in the port?"

"Charlie Block?"

"That his name? Charlie Block?"

"*Si*. Charlie. Carlos. He been around maybe a month."

"You seen him today, Jesús?"

Jesús shook his head. "Not for a while. He was here maybe two weeks, then gone a week, then he come back a few days and now he gone again. That's how it is in the port. People come and go."

"Any idea where he is?"

Jesús shrugged. "He say he's looking for a boat. Maybe he got a job now. Or maybe he's outa town. His girl still here." Jesús made a voluptuous figure in the air with his hands. "She really something, man. *Madre de dios*, really something. A *sueca*."

"Swedish?"

"The best *chicas*, man." He winked. "I know them *suecas*."

"She and Charlie together long?"

"Since I first saw him. Charlie and Briggette. They got the second floor apartment there. She works somewhere in the port." He pointed to an apartment block entrance beside the bar. "But look *señor* Teal, you got no problem with Charlie, he not the one you're after. He's real nice, you know?"

"Sure," Teal said, "no problems there." He stood and stretched, then took a thousand peseta note from his shirt pocket and passed it to Jesús. "You think of anything interesting, Jesús, you leave a message for me at the Hotel Don Pepé."

Jesús dug in his pocket for change. Teal held up his hand. "Have a couple drinks on me."

"Hey, man, you don't have to do that."

"That's O.K. You just remember me if something comes up."

Teal pocketed his pack of *Ducados* and strolled away from the *Coco-Loco*. He walked down the quay to where *Destry* had been moored. He shoved his hands in his pockets and checked the sky. Cloud skudded in from the southwest. That usually brought rain from the Atlantic. An angry, shifting sheet of grayness obscured La Concha's summit. The chilly wind cut through Teal's light jacket and he shrugged deeper into it. From one of the boats he heard pop music drifting out of an enclosed cabin. He heard laughter. Teal turned so he faced down the quay toward the white apartment blocks with the shops, bars and restaurants beneath. Beside the *Coco-Loco* he could see the entrance to the apartments were Jesús said Charlie Block's girlfriend lived. He'd think about it first, then he'd go and see Briggette, have a word with her.

Big coincidence here, Teal thought. Waiter who talks like the guy who blew the brains out of your friend's girl. Except the guy fits a description.

A man with a black beard was walking down the quay toward Teal. Teal felt his heart jump. Big guy, six-one, six-two, broad shoulders. The guy saw Teal staring at him. He smiled. *"Bonjour, monsieur,"* he said, and walked a gangway and boarded a thirty-six foot ketch tied up at *Destry's* old mooring.

"Bonjour," Teal responded.

Teal had an uncomfortable feeling about this Block who lived with the Swedish girl. He had the strange, nagging feeling that this Block was the one he was after. He stared at the apartment building. From where he stood he could see there were at least two apartments on the second floor, left and right, and maybe two more at the back. Jesús hadn't said which belonged to Briggette. But he wasn't going to knock on the door, not yet. If this Block was the man, and he saw Teal, Teal knew he had a good chance of getting killed. Jesús said Block hadn't been around for a few days. But if he'd heard about the police investigation and realized Teal and Quinn were alive, he might be hiding in the apartment.

Teal turned and wandered down to the end of the quay. He turned and faced the apartments again. He had plenty of time. He'd just work this out, nice and slow.

"Well, old man," Johnny James said, "to me you look like a chap who needs a strong cup of tea."

"Make that coffee," Quinn said, "black, no sugar." He couldn't help but grin as Johnny pumped his hand and indicated a chair for him in front of his desk. He'd immediately liked James when he'd met him a couple of months back. His opinion hadn't changed.

While James hunted up his secretary to prepare coffee, Quinn glanced around the spartan office. It didn't fit in with the image of one of England's biggest marine insurance companies. Wooden parquetry floors with two or three scatter rugs, and handsome velvet curtains framing the windows which looked out onto the historic city of London were the only touch of luxury. Quinn guessed the rugs and curtains hadn't been chosen by James. For the rest, the office contained James's plain wooden desk and chair, two chairs for visitors in front, a typewriter on a stand, a bank of six chest-high filing cabinets and a door which led to a private bathroom—the only status symbol which suggested the high regard in which James was held by Marine Insurance Limited. His secretary's office was equally as workmanlike: typewriter, desk, two chairs, filing cabinet and telex machine. Efficiency didn't require expensive trappings.

Short, broad-shouldered and tough, James looked like a rugby player and talked like a public school boy who'd spent his youth fighting the Battle of Britain in Spitfires. In fact, he was only thirty-five years old. He'd spent twelve years in the London Metropolitan Police Force, reaching the rank of Detective-Inspector, and the last five as an investigator with Marine Insurance.

When he returned with coffee for Quinn and tea for himself, he didn't waste time emphasizing how sorry he was for what had happened. He'd offered his condolences over the phone and that was it. Johnny James wasn't given to repeating himself. He flicked open a file on his desk.

"Right," he said, "our chappie in southern Spain interviewed your captain, Teal. Read through that . . ." he slid the file over to Quinn, ". . . and tell me if it's substantially correct."

Quinn read through a six page statement signed by Teal and a half-page summing-up by the insurance agent. "That's about it," he agreed.

James closed the file and put it aside. "Right, Peter, a few questions. You'll be claiming something in the vicinity of

seventy-five thousand quid from us. It's a fair old whack."
James leaned back in his chair and put his feet on the desk.
"We don't give the stuff away."

Quinn sipped his coffee. "Shoot," he said.

"You didn't contact our insurance agent until three days
after the incident. Why?"

Quinn frowned. "Because I was in hospital recovering from
the effects of exposure."

"You're sure of that?"

"The police will verify the fact."

James nodded. "How much money was aboard *Destry*?"

"Around five thousand dollars."

"Other valuables, apart from instrumentation and personal
belongings?"

"No."

"No jewelry? No gold, silver, diamonds, or other precious
stones?"

Quinn shook his head.

"Drugs?"

"No."

"Not even marijuana?"

"No."

"Anything which, if you'd entered a port and attempted to
take it ashore, could be classified as contraband?"

"No."

"Booze, perfume, photographic gear, video tapes, pornogra-
phy?"

Quinn shook his head.

"You ran a clean boat, old chap."

"I was on a holiday. I wasn't in business. Money was no
problem."

"How much are your worth? Cash bank accounts, convert-
ible stocks, real estate, the lot."

"Around eighty, a hundred thousand dollars."

"Mind if we check that?"

"It's no secret. I'll get you bank certificates if you want."

James smiled and reached forward for his tea-cup and
saucer. "We'll do our own checking." He sipped tea. "What

debts do you have? To anyone. Business acquaintances. Friends. Family."

"I owe nothing."

"No gambling debts?"

Quinn shook his head.

"Horses, cards, casinos?"

"No."

"You don't gamble?"

"No."

Johnny slipped his feet off the desk, put down his cup and saucer and leaned forward. "You were in the casino beside Jose Banus port two nights before the incident."

Quinn angrily reached for a cigarette. "That's true."

"Then you *do* gamble."

"I've been to casinos or racetracks maybe five, six times in my life."

"So you have a flutter now and again. How much did you drop at the Banus casino?"

"I won fifty bucks."

Johnny grinned again. "Perhaps you should do it more often, old chap." He reached into his pocket for a lighter, leaned forward and lit Quinn's cigarette. "After you phoned our agent in Marbella, he went to Algeciras to see you. You'd left hospital. No one knew where you were. Not even Teal. He said you were on private business. What did he mean by that? What business?"

Quinn drew on his cigarette and averted his eyes.

Again, Johnny said, "What business? What business would be so pressing that a chap just out of hospital, a chap who's lost his girl, a chap who's waiting to put in a claim for one hundred and fifty thousand dollars, would disappear for three, four days, without telling his only friend in the area where he was going?"

"Is this relevant to your investigation?"

"Everything is relevant when this amount of money is at stake."

"It's a private matter."

"Then it won't go beyond the company."

Quinn reached forward and angrily stubbed out his cigarette

in the glass ashtray on Johnny's desk. "I was looking for the two men who did this thing."

Johnny nodded. "And . . ?"

"And nothing. The police had no luck and made it clear that they didn't think they would. I felt . . ." Quinn shrugged.

"You felt you'd do something yourself." Johnny nodded in sympathy. "The police rarely do have any luck in these matters. Once in a while they make an arrest and get a conviction. We even recover the odd boat." Johnny stood and paced the confines of the small office. "But the majority of these crimes are committed on the high seas, in international waters. Police and coast guards go through the motions of investigation, but as long as the crime hasn't physically taken place in *their* waters, in *their* ports, they're not too concerned. And there's practically no international cooperation in these matters."

Johnny stopped pacing and leaned straight-armed on the desk. "I might add that most owners and crew don't survive these attacks. They end up the way Jenny did. The way you and Teal would have if it hadn't been for that fishing boat."

He sat down again. "Look, old chap, sorry about the cross-examination. We're obliged to continue a personal investigation into your affairs, but I can tell you that everything you've told me ties in with what we already know.

"We put on the tough front because we're considered fair game by every sea-going crook in the damned world. Some of the things people do to get money out of us would make your short and curlies shrivel. Case just last month of a chappie who said he'd lost his yacht off the Cyclades Islands and banged in a claim for sixty thousand quid. Said he was rescued by a Greek fisherman under similar circumstances to you. We poked around and turned up one or two interesting facts. First, no fisherman picked him up. He'd come ashore at midday, calm as you please, in the yacht's boat, outboard and all, loaded to the gunwhales with instrumentation and everything of value he could unscrew. He started selling if off the same day. That sort of thing soon gets around in Greek *tabernas*! So we looked further and discovered that he'd *sold* the yacht he was claiming against two months previously and that the boat he sank was a bucket he'd bought in Yugoslavia for under five thousand. If we'd paid out he would've come away over one hundred thousand pounds in the black—nearly a quarter of a million dollars. Chap in question is back in England facing fraud charges."

Johnny lit a cigarette and inhaled deeply. "But cases like that, well, you can't really hold it against the chappie. Simple fraud. Perhaps he had pressing debts—hence my nasty questions about your gambling habits. Or perhaps he was broke and knew he could never sell his boat for what it was worth. Anyway, no one gets hurt, except my board of directors, and the company's reputation on the stock market."

Johnny James paused and looked down at his desk. "Then we have cases like yours," he said quietly. "When people get killed. Yours is the tenth to come through this company this year."

Quinn looked up, surprised.

"Through *this* company! Twenty-three cases through all British companies. But you and Teal are the only survivors off those twenty-three boats, all of which disappeared with their crews."

Quinn opened his mouth to say something, but didn't find the words.

"I know," Johnny said. "It's unbelievable. Twenty-three British registered boats gone *with* their crews. It adds up to one hundred and three people, all almost certainly dead. That's just during this year. And there will be more. We only find out when relatives of the missing people contact us."

Johnny stubbed out his cigarette and rested his feet on the table again.

"Then there's the continental figures. There's no international cooperation between companies, police or coast guards on this thing, in fact that's one of my jobs, to instigate an inter-company cross-referencing system and, also, to create an international boat registry. But, from the continental companies I'm in touch with, I know that this year at *least* another fifty-eight boats have disappeared. So now we have a total of eighty-one craft missing with three hundred and seventy people."

"But surely you can't pull all these cases down to piracy."

"The boats missing were, without exception, seaworthy craft equipped with sophisticated instrumentation. All carried experienced crew or captains. None, to the best of our knowledge, put out S.O.S.'s. We've projected percentages based on past experience and the best we can come up with is around point-one percent of boats and crews of this caliber going down in storms, and one-point-three percent of boats which are cruising distant islands, say in the Pacific, which will eventually turn up safely. And, yes, we have one single-handed yacht sailed by a chappie who we know was having family trouble; he may have disappeared on purpose. So, that works out as one-point-three-four percent of eight-one. And on our possible drop-out and you have a maximum of, say, two boats which we reckon we'll one day hear from."

Johnny lit another cigarette. "Our conclusion is inescapable. Yacht-jacking in the Mediterranean area is now endemic. We put the figures on a graph, and found that the crime is rising by a steady eighteen percent each year." He jabbed the air in front of him with the cigarette. "And it will almost certainly get worse. As more people find themselves well-enough off to indulge in what was once only a rich-man's sport, and the more boats are bought, the more piracy there'll be. Damn it, it's such an easy thing to do. You gain access to a man's boat and when it's fifty miles into international waters, you pull a gun and force the crew overboard. How do you fight that sort of thing?"

Johnny came to his feet and nervously began pacing again. "You can't. That's the short answer to it, _unless_ people are warned about the dangers. And the only people who can do that are the insurance companies who simply don't cooperate enough, the police who are too busy doing other things and the coast guards who are under-staffed, under-equipped and more concerned with territorial incursion than crimes which invariably take place outside their patch of national waters."

Johnny sat with one haunch on the window-sill and stared down into the street as he spoke. "You Americans are the only ones I know of who _are_ doing something, but even so you're working so slowly that in the meantime the problem is mushrooming to inconceivable proportions.

"Back in 1974 a joint Coast guard and Congressional study of the years 1971–1973 came up with the extraordinary fact that twenty thousand boats belonging to U.S. citizens had disappeared in the South-eastern Atlantic, the Gulf of Mexico, along the Pacific coast and around the Hawaiian Islands. Now most of those boats were later recovered, or their disappearance satisfactorily explained. Savage storms with subsequent capsizes through incompetent handling claimed quite a few. Kids stealing boats for joyrides and then grounding or scuttling them in out of the way places was high on the list. There were thousands of cases of boats stolen for resale. And that's one reason, by the way, that we need this international register I spoke of. Yachts are stamped out like saucepans, now. Boat builders crank out fifty, a hundred, even two hundred fiber hulls, and each is identical. If a man's yacht is stolen, he can't recognize the damned thing after it's been tarted up by the thieves."

Johnny returned to the desk to light yet another cigarette and began pacing again. The more he talked, the more excited and angry he became. Quinn listened to the catalogue of disaster, realizing that Johnny James was obsessed with the yacht-jacking problem way beyond the call of his job.

"But in the end," Johnny said, "when the investigating committee had eliminated every conceivable possibility, they were left with a total of six hundred and ten vessels which had vanished in what they euphemistically called 'mysterious circumstances'—that is, during perfectly calm weather conditions—and which have never been recovered, or, indeed, sighted again. Over two thousand owners and crew disappeared with those boats, and none have been seen nor heard of since. No bodies have been found."

Johnny began pacing the perimeter of the room. Quinn found himself following his movements.

"Lovely stuff, isn't it, old man. Well, there's more. Projecting those American figures, which are the latest we have, into the mid-1980s and combining them with our up-to-date English figures and only the continental cases we *know* about, we can assume that this year, around the world, between 1300 and 1700 craft will disappear. If you allow four people per craft, we're talking of a loss of life in the vicinity of six thousand eight hundred souls."

"Jesus Christ," Quinn whispered.

"Yes," James said, "Jesus Christ Almighty, and may he watch over sailors at sea. And if you'll excuse my purely mercenary bent of mind, insurance companies are currently taking it in the neck for about sixty million pounds sterling per year."

"A hundred and twenty billion bucks?"

James stopped pacing and leaned on the desk, staring not so much at Quinn as beyond him.

"Yes, old chap. It's a pretty penny, isn't it!"

At three-thirty that afternoon, Teal still paced the quay from where he could see the entrance to the apartments. He'd left his post only twice—and then for not more than five minutes at a time—once to drink a cognac to warm him against the nippy wind, and once to buy a pack of cigarettes and a sandwich. In all the hours he'd waited there'd been no sign of anyone fitting Briggette's description entering the apartments.

Teal was tempted to inquire more about her, but he knew that would be stupid, perhaps dangerous. In the port's small, closed community centered around the bars, restaurants and boutiques, word would get back to her, and if she *was* connected with Block, and Block was still around, he'd know that someone was after him.

A stake-out was the answer. Nothing could be done quickly. Everything must unfold in its own time without any pressure from an observer. And Teal had all the time in the world. He'd wait until Judgement Day if it gave him a chance to even the score for Jenny and for Quinn. And for himself.

Teal hunched down into his jacket, lit a *Ducado* and sat on one of the service boxes which supplied water and electricity to the moored yachts. The apartment entrance lay maybe eighty yards away up the quay and across the road which skirted the periphery of the northern face of the port. His eyes wandered along the waterfront, checking strolling couples, noting who came out of bars, watching automobiles and motorbikes.

Teal watched, and waited.

At four-thirty Quinn threaded his way along Fleet Street's crowded pavements, walked around Aldwych's stately curve and entered the busy, arrow-straight thoroughfare of the Strand, heading back toward his hotel.

Johnny James had devoted most of his day to Quinn. They'd talked in his office until one, then lunched in *The Wine Bar* in Chancery Lane before depositing themselves in a secluded corner of *The Punch*, the old Fleet Street journalists' pub.

There, in the unlikely atmosphere of old London, with light glancing through stained-glass doors and cigrette smoke drifting to cloud the ceiling, they sat on worn leather couches, and James continued reciting the facts he'd uncovered during years of research about modern day piracy in the Mediterranean. Each tale he told hammered another nail in the fanciful dream of the peace and solitude a searching man could find by cruising Homer's legendy sea.

Piracy, James explained, took many forms. Sometimes the act was simple robbery. A drunken yacht owner talked too much in a bar and revealed that he carried valuables aboard his boat. During his next absence from port his boat was boarded and robbed. Or, if the valuables were bulky, the boat itself would be stolen, sailed to an isolated beach or cove, the valuables transferred ashore in the ship's boat and the yacht left at anchor. In these cases the owner could consider himself lucky. He still had a boat, and he was still alive.

Sailors rarely survived other forms of piracy.

A trick used since men first sailed the seas, was still popular off the north African coast. A cruising yacht would be signaled by a rowboat drifting miles from shore with no apparent means of locomotion. Bound by the laws of the sea, the yacht would heave-to to give aid. The men in the rowboat would explain that they were fishermen, stranded when their boat capsized and sunk. They would beg a tow to the nearest land. What sailor worth his salt could refuse such a reasonable request? With lines secured the yacht would change course for land.

Within moments the "fishermen" would haul themselves to the stern of the yacht, cover the crew with weapons, board, murder the crew, change course to rendezvous with their own boat, waiting over the horizon, strip the captured boat of valuables and sink it. Instruments, sails, engines, tools, metal fittings, ropes, chains, food, liquor, fuel and personal belongings on the average well-equipped yacht could result in a haul worth thirty or forty thousand dollars to these scavengers.

But this, James said, was a well-known ruse. Several crews had shot it out with their would-be murderers and lived to tell the tale. Consequently, fishermen genuinely in trouble often stayed in trouble unless they managed to rescue themselves. Yacht owners in northern African waters now preferred to batten down their consciences as a guarantee to their own safety.

The most terrifying story James told happened over a period of years in the early sixties. During 1961–63 many boats disappeared in Sicilian waters—no one knew exactly how many. Only in 1963 when a survivor rescued by a passing Coast Guard boat told the story did the facts emerge, and even then they were scarcely believed.

The sailor, one of a crew of four on a forty foot ketch, told how his yacht had been pursued by a fast, ex-British navy torpedo boat. With the ketch under full sail, the TP boat had come alongside, slowed to the yacht's speed, and edged within five meters. Then, without warning, a crewman emerged from below with a flame-thrower and fired a stream of burning petroleum jelly directly into the mainsail and jib. As flames roared through the rigging and the yacht's helmsman desperately tried to ram the torpedo boat in a useless gesture of self-defense, two more crewmen raked the yacht with automatic weapons, strafing backward and forward along the deck until they thought everyone was dead. Everyone was, except for the survivor who had been knocked overboard by the swinging main boom after a freak shot ripped apart the boom sheet. From the sea, the sailor watched as the crew on the torpedo boat waited until the yacht's sails burned themselves out, then came alongside and grappled the two boats together. The pirates spent two hours stripping everything of value from the

yacht and siphoning fuel from her tanks. Then the two boats
separated and the yacht was sunk by bazooka fire, three shots
carefully placed along her waterline. The pirate boat waited
until the sea completely swallowed the evidence, then headed
full speed back toward Sicily. Perhaps because of the survivor's
well publicized story, the pirates ceased their operations,
because as far as authorities knew, the ketch was the last boat to
disappear in their waters for several years. By then, anyway,
the pirates would have been rich beyond caring.

But these were the dramatic tales, the stuff of fiction and
rousing adventure movies. The common reality of piracy, or
yacht-jacking in the Mediterranean was equally as deadly to
the victims, but considerably more mundane in operation.

As happened to Quinn, Teal and Jenny, guests insinuated
themselves aboard for a day cruise and took over the boat. A
crewman suddenly produced a weapon. That's all. That, a few
shots, and it was over. Quinn could still feel the fear pulsing
through him when he realized the only reason the three of them
hadn't been killed immediately was because the man with the
golden hair needed him to show his face at the Gibraltar fuel
docks, and that he couldn't risk killing Teal and Jenny straight
away and having Quinn put up a fight in Gibraltar. And in the
end Jenny had got it. And in the end, he knew it was Jenny's
death which had caused the confusion which had saved him
and Teal.

James explained that hi-jacked yachts which weren't face-
lifted and sold, were used in four different ways. To smuggle
contraband, run drugs, deliver arms and ship illegal immi-
grants.

Both James and Quinn agreed that with *Destry* heading
across the Straits toward Morocco, the yacht-jackers planned
using her to run a boat-load of hash back to Europe. Then, if
they'd followed form, they would have scuttled her. The odds
of find her here were practically zero.

Quinn waited at a pedestrian light, then hurried across the
street into his hotel, a womb of quietness after the frenetic,
ceaseless noise of traffic on the Strand. The desk clerk handed
Quinn an envelope along with his key.

Quinn walked through to the bar and ordered himself a

double Scotch. It was the first time he'd visited the bar since the night he'd met Jenny.

Involuntarily he turned and looked at the table where they'd sat. They'd talked that night until after the bar closed, until after the barman had set them up with one last drink, raised his eyebrows, shook his head and gone home. And they'd kept talking until three, when the night-cleaners moved in and started vacuuming, mopping and polishing. They'd picked up their keys from the half-asleep night-clerk and Quinn had escorted Jenny to her door. He'd kissed her gently; she'd responded. They'd kissed again, deeply, satisfyingly, pressing in against each other, expression a physical yearning for each other. Quinn's gallantry and Jenny's breeding kept them apart that night. Quinn kissed her once more and, as if cued by a director, he whispered goodnight at the same instant Jenny turned the key to open her door. Quinn hadn't slept. He tossed and turned beneath the blankets in the dark room disturbed by flashing images of the girl and tortured by a hard, painful erection which refused to abate. Sometime after six in the morning, he slipped on his robe and padded down the carpeted corridor to the elevator and rode up to Jenny's floor. He tapped timidly on her door, afraid as he did so that she'd be angry at him and rebuff him for his boldness and stupidity. But she'd opened the door within seconds, stood there in a long, silk nightgown, illuminated warmly by the soft glow of the hall light. She took his hand, led him in and closed the door. In the dark, in the coziness of the carpeted, heated room, they kissed, undressed each other, kissed again and fell onto the bed, her legs high around his waist hauling his hardness into her, and they'd fought with their bodies to force themselves closer, and parted moments later, both finished, giggling like children in the darkness and shushing each other, and then, miraculously Quinn had found himself erect again. It was a wild, sweet beginning to whatever it was they'd had.

Quinn looked back to his Scotch. He felt anger throbbing in his veins. No, not really anger anymore. Frustration. The knowledge that nothing had been done, nothing would be done, nothing *could* be done. Jenny's bones would lay on the ocean floor forever, yet her death would remain unrevenged. Jesus, it was too much to take.

He sipped his drink, tried to control himself. There were some things you had to learn to live with. Fuck it and damn it! He sank the double and ordered the same again. He remembered the envelope and tore it open. It contained a telex from his father. He was flying in to Heathrow Airport in—Quinn glanced at his watch—two hours.

Teal's wounded arm throbbed and he massaged it gently. Then the girl arrived and he forgot the pain.

She slipped out of a battered SEAT 124 Sports Coupé. Teal checked the time. Six-thirty. The sun was setting, its rays reflecting a panorama of colors off the cloudy sky, turning the harbor water into a subtle blend of orange and pink. It had to be her, Briggette, young, beautiful, blonde, the way Jesús had described her.

The girl locked the car door and quickly walked to the apartment entrance. Teal tried to imagine her timing. Across the tiny lobby, up the first flight of stairs to the landing, turn, up the second flight, fumble for keys, insert the key, open the door, switch on the light.

She switched on the light. Front left, Teal noted, or front right as you faced the harbor. O.K., so now, at least, he knew that. A moment later another light came on, bathroom, probably, and now off again. And now the first light was turned off, too. She was leaving already. Good. And if she'd walked into a dark apartment, and left the apartment dark that meant no one else was in there.

The girl emerged at the apartment entrance moments later. She was shrugging into a cardigan and tossing back her long blonde hair to clear it off the collar. She left the SEAT Sports where it was and hurried along the waterfront. She's late for a date. Teal thought. For a date with whom? With Block? But without the car? Block wouldn't still be in the port knowing that the police had been investigating. Would he?

Teal followed her. She had a sixty or eighty yard start on him. He let her keep it. She walked swiftly toward the far end of the port, toward a cluster of bars. She turned into one called

El Marinero Feliz. Teal saw her greet a waiter at the door and disappear inside. Teal approached the bar slowly. He stayed across the road, right on the edge of the wharf. From inside no one would be able to recognize him even if they noticed him. When he came level with the bar he stopped, turned, hunched over and lit a cigarette and took a five second look inside. The girl was behind the bar, chatting with a customer sitting on a high stool in front.

She works there, Teal realized. She starts at six-thirty and she was late. She hurried up to the apartment to go to the bathroom and grab a sweater. So where had she come from in such a hurry and late for work? From seeing her boyfriend, Block? And is Block the bastard I'm after? The one who shot Jenny? We'll see, thought Teal, we'll fucking well see.

Teal crossed the road and took a table on the patio in front of *El Marinero Feliz.* From where he sat he could glance in through the window and see the bar. The girl still talked to the customer, laughing. He couldn't hear what they were saying. Boy, Jesús was right, she really was something.

A white-shirted waiter asked Teal what he wanted. Teal ordered cognac. The waiter asked if Teal wouldn't rather sit inside where it was warmer. Teal shrugged and grinned. Hell no, he said, he liked looking at the boats.

When the waiter brought the drink, Teal gave him a hundred pesetas. "Just a quick one," he said. He looked at his watch. "Got to go somewhere. Might come on back later. When do you guys close?"

The waiter shrugged his shoulders. "Twelve-thirty. One o'clock. Maybe later."

"Shit," Teal grinned. "They make you work all night! Still," he nodded back toward the bar, "that's not so bad if you're working with a *chica* like that, right? What is she, German?"

"She's a *sueca*," the waiter said. "How do you say . . . Swedish."

"She's *muy guapa*," Teal said in his broad Spanish. "What's her name?"

"Briggette," the waiter said. "We been doin' the night shift together a month now. She's real nice."

"I should be so lucky," Teal said. He drained the cognac, made a show of looking at his watch then stood and clapped the waiter on the shoulder. "Gotta go. See you in a coupla hours *amigo.*"

Teal walked quickly back to Briggette's apartment block. He'd just pulled the oldest burglar trick in the world. Observe a dwelling, wait for the occupants to leave, follow them, establish how long they will be absent, return to the dwelling and knock it over.

As Teal approached the apartment block two couples carrying armfuls of bottles entered the foyer ahead of him. Teal slowed down until they were up the first flight of stairs, then followed. He paused outside Briggette's door. A name tag read *Briggette Bjerstedt*. He heard the couples laughing as they continued up to the next floor. Then he heard a door slam.

There were four apartments on the first floor. He knew there were no lights on in the one opposite Briggette's. He swiftly checked the other two by kneeling down and looking through the cracks at the bottom of the doors. No lights. As he walked back to Briggette's apartment the couples above turned on music. Loud rock. Great, he thought. No one would hear what he was going to do.

He leaned his weight against Briggette's door top, then bottom. No catches. Only the lock at the center of the door. Teal glanced over the stairwell to assure himself no one was coming up, then squared himself in front of Briggette's door and kicked with the flat of his foot against the lock. He gasped as pain jarred through his wounded arm, but he'd felt the wood in the jamb give. He kicked twice more, each time screwing up his face as the shock shot through his body and bit at his wound. Once more, he thought. He quickly checked the stairwell again, then launched his final kick. Teal lost his balance and crashed against the wall beside the frame as the door burst open and slapped against the inside wall. He recovered himself and listened for any sounds of opening doors. No way, he thought, no way anyone would have heard me above that music. He slipped inside, closed the door, and jammed a chair under the knob to keep it shut.

Teal closed the curtains on the window facing the port and

switched on the light. He moved quickly through the apartment, checking its layout. Living room, two small bedrooms, kitchenette, bathroom.

He started with the bedrooms. The smaller, with a single bed, was empty, except for a pile of clothes on the floor waiting to be washed. Teal quickly examined each item. Bras, panties, panty-hose, stockings, blouses, two skirts. No men's clothes. He opened the wardrobe. Empty, except for a line of coathangers. He looked under the mattress. Nothing.

In the master bedroom, the double-bed was neatly made. The beside table was bare except for an unopened pack of tissues. The table drawer was empty. Teal looked under the bed. Under one side he found a couple of two week old Swedish newspapers. Under the other a copy of *Penthouse*, folded back on a nude spread. Both the papers and the magazine were dusty. Teal checked the bedside table again. Dust.

He opened the three drawers in the small dresser. All women's underclothes, two scarves, stockings. Not much. He moved to the wardrobe. No men's clothes. A few skirts, blouses, one pair of slacks, one pair of jeans. Somehow the place seemed bare, unused. No cosmetics on the dresser top in front of the mirror.

Teal moved into the bathroom. Nothing of interest. No toilet paper. He checked the bathroom cupboard. None there, either.

In the living room, he found a framed photograph of Briggette with a clean-cut blonde young man. A Scandinavian, he guessed. Certainly not that bastard from the boat. The man held Briggette's hand in a way that showed she wore an engagement ring. Teal replaced the photo. He could guess what had happened. Briggette had come to Spain on a holiday, been seduced by the lifestyle, found herself another guy and decided to stay. Beside the photograph he saw a stack of letters. He checked them. All written in Swedish, all in the same handwriting, all post-marked Stockholm. He wondered if she answered them anymore. Stiff shit, buddy, Teal thought.

He found nothing in the living room to link Briggette with the man on the boat, or with any other man except the Swedish boyfriend. Perhaps Jesús had guessed correctly, perhaps

Briggette's boyfriend had found a boat and sailed. He moved into the kitchen, opening cupboards and drawers. Nothing, apart from cutlery and crockery. The refrigerator was empty, the door ajar, the plug pulled out. Briggette definitely wasn't living in this apartment. So where *was* she living? And why did she keep this place on? Was she in the midst of an affair she knew would end soon? Living-in with a sick friend for a couple of weeks, helping out with household chores?

Teal felt faintly disgusted with himself. Now that the search had yielded nothing he felt like a back alley snoop checking through a girl's dirty underwear and her love letters. Shit, and there *was* worse to come. To make it look like a genuine breaking and entry job, he had to mess the place up a bit. He took a knife from the kitchen and walked back into the living room ready to rip open the easy chairs. He couldn't bring himself to do it. He tossed the knife onto the low coffee table. He'd caused this girl enough anguish already—she'd feel violated when she found the smashed open door and knew someone had pawed through her personal belongings. Leave it Teal, he told himself, get the fuck out.

He turned off the lights, slipped through the door and hurried downstairs into the fresh, cold air of the port. Nothing, he thought, I'm right back where I started.

He sighed, lit a cigarette and inhaled deeply, suddenly feeling depressed. A whole, wasted day. And tomorrow he'd be back on the prowl again, chatting to bar-owners, waiters and boutique salesgirls, sailors and maintenance men. For one long instant, he thought of forgetting the whole damned thing, of flying to join Quinn in London tomorrow, of holding the kid's hand until he'd gotten over this whole stinking mess, then saying *adios* and heading back to southern France to find himself a new boat. Yeah, sure, Teal, he told himself, you do that, you chicken-shit out on Quinn. Make you feel real good.

Angry at himself, he tossed away the cigarette and thrust his hands deep into his pockets. He'd head back to *El Marinero Feliz* and start chatting up that friendly waiter. Someone, somewhere had to know something about those two bastards. The cops hadn't discovered anything, but the cops had other things to do. Teal had nothing else to do.

He started wandering back toward the bar. He walked by Briggette's SEAT sports. He stopped and looked it over. He knew the model. Young guys around town favored them. Neat lines, fast and powerful. Not the sort of automobile young girls usually bought. Certainly not in this beat-up condition. He peered in through the driver's window and saw a large box of groceries on the back seat.

Teal looked at the box for maybe five full seconds then turned and walked in the opposite direction toward the car park, got into his rented Renault 5, drove it back into the port, U-turned and parked fifty yards behind Briggette's sports and faced in the same direction.

He wound down the window, lit a cigarette and stretched out his bulk as best he could within the confines of the compact car.

Teal would wait for Briggette to finish work and follow her and he wouldn't leave that damned Renault for five minutes, just in case she unexpectedly left work early.

The box had contained bread, canned food, fresh fruit, a jar of coffee, a pack of long-life milk, half a dozen half bottles of beer and half a bottle of *Johnny Walker*.

The groceries sure as hell weren't for any sick girlfriend. And, laying by the box was a copy of the *Herald-Tribune* and a copy of *Penthouse*. There was an American male still lurking somewhere in Briggette Bjerstedt's life, and tonight Teal had the feeling he would find out where. And who.

In Heathrow Airport's transit lounge, James P. Quinn embraced his son, hugging him with both arms. For a long moment they said nothing and Quinn felt a strange release of tension as his father held him, a sensation reminiscent of childhood, when the old man would put his arms around him to comfort him and the troubles of the day were dissipated by affection. Then, when he was a kid, it was like the old man could pour strength into him, transfer some of that crochety old Irish steel into his body. He'd loved it when the old man held him.

They parted and looked at each other. Loudspeakers crackled and called passengers to flights. People jostled as they picked up luggage and moved to exit gates. The old man looked older to Quinn, but somehow stronger.

"Thanks for coming," Quinn said. "But I didn't want you to travel all this way."

"Six hours isn't far to come," James P. Quinn said, softly. "Buy why the bejesus did you wait two weeks to tell me what had happened?"

"I got into this mess. I figured I should clean up as far as possible before worrying you."

"And have you?"

"As far as possible, yes."

They sat beside each other in a corner away from the crowd. Peter lit a cigarette and Quinn Sr. noted the nervous way he played with it in his fingers. "Your telex only mentioned the bare bones," he said. "Tell me the rest."

The telling took fifteen minutes. He started with the two men boarding for a day trip with them and finished with him and Teal in hospital. His father knew he'd bought the boat. He knew about Jenny. Quinn had made a point of writing regularly, feeling that if he laid out episode by episode what he was doing with his life, the old man would come to understand his motives. Quinn finished the story and pinched the bridge of his nose with thumb and forefinger. God knew what his father thought now.

"What can I do for you?" Quinn Sr. asked.

Peter breathed deeply and looked at his father. There was no triumph in the lined old face, no bitterness, no sarcasm; only concern. Peter felt a stab of guilt that he had even considered his father might exhibit pettiness at this moment. He never had; they'd had their arguments, their battle royals, their family squabbles, but the old man never held anything against his only son. Whatever their disagreements about Peter ignoring a career to go galavanting around the world, they were forgotten. Someone in the family had been hurt. The family was back to back now. Jesus Christ, even the Sicilians could learn a thing or two about family from the Irish.

"Jenny's parents," he said. "The Spanish police informed the American Consulate in Seville of her death and they passed the word to the Boston police who told them. I wrote a long letter, trying to explain. I'd appreciate it if you would visit them."

"I think you should do that," Quinn Sr. said quietly.

"I can't. I'm busy."

Quinn Sr. raised his shaggy eyebrows in an unspoken question that demanded an answer.

Peter hesitated. "Dad, I don't expect you to understand." He didn't say it belligerently, but as a matter of fact.

"Try me, at least," his father said.

"Teal and I, we've decided . . . The truth is, that *I've* decided, and Teal has agreed, that we're going to look for these people."

"That's a police matter, surely."

"The thing happened in international waters. The police made an investigation and got nowhere. They made it clear they wouldn't be spending much more time on the case."

"We can hire professional investigators."

Quinn looked at his father in appreciation. He may have underestimated the old man a moment ago, but he hadn't expected this amount of committment. "Thanks, Dad," he said, "but I want to do it myself."

"For Jenny," his father said flatly.

Quinn nodded.

"Because you loved her," his father probed.

Quinn looked away.

"Money's no problem," Quinn Sr. said evenly. "If you need it, I've got it. Telex me, and I can have it with you within fifteen, twenty hours."

"Thanks, Dad. I'll remember. Look," he said, "now you're here stay on a day or two. Get a good night's sleep, at least."

Quinn Sr. shook his head. "If there was something I could do for you here, I would. I can sleep on the plane as well as in a hotel bed." He paused. "If you need me, telephone and I'll hop a flight back." He put his arm around Peter's shoulder. "Come on, son, let's get a drink. Bejesus, you look like you need one."

Two hours after he'd greeted his son, James P. Quinn lay stretched out in a first class seat on the Pan-Am London–New York night flight. His eyes were closed and he'd plugged himself into the classical music program, listening to a pianist playing soothing Chopin melodies.

But Jesus, Peter had looked a wreck. And no wonder after what he'd been through. And perhaps he was heading for worse with this story of chasing down the buggers who'd killed his girl and stolen his boat. But what could a father do about that? Tell his son to forget he was a man and to come home and sell real estate? What a thing life is; what a damned rotten thing. The violence, and the pain, and the confusion. He understood how the lad felt. He felt guilt because he'd never loved that girl. Jesus, Jesus, Jesus, his own son was up to his arse in a melodrama, off to chase the villains and not even knowing why. And how was an old doddering Irishman to tell his son that even if he caught the buggers and got them jailed, or killed them without getting himself killed, that he'd be haunted by this ridiculous, punishing guilt for the rest of his life? So he'd been playing around with a lassie and telling her things he hadn't meant and the girl had been murdered believing he loved her. Well you didn't chase those murderers because you felt guilty. God in heaven, no. You chased them for revenge! An eye for an eye, a life for a life. *Two* lives for a life if necessary. That was something the old Irish understood. And the English, too, when the Irish had finished with them. But that knowledge didn't help Peter. Peter had to come to understand that for himself.

James P. Quinn switched off the music program and removed his earphones. He pressed his service button and had the stewardess bring him a double whisky. He sipped it, feeling tautness in his shoulders and in his gut. He recognized the symptoms from long ago when he'd been Peter's age and fighting to survive. He was frightend, shit bloody scared. Frightened for his only son who soon might face physical danger. And nothing that he, the wise old man, could do for him but hope and pray.

Later, he slept, but nightmares weaved in and out of his mind. He saw Peter with blood on his hands and hopeless anguish on his face. And saw his dear, dead, beautiful wife walking in the park with the sun flashing through the trees backlighting her long, black hair. And saw her son laying writhing on a hillside, his hands clutched to bloody guts.

The stewardess gently shook him awake and smiled at him

and gave him a sedative with a glass of water, but the hateful image persisted in his mind.

He felt useless, impotent, because he knew there was nothing he could do for his son.

At a little after one-thirty Teal jerked awake. A car door had slammed. He shook his head to clear the grogginess of sleep. The battered SEAT Sports fifty yards in front of him was pulling out from the curb. Teal could just make out Briggette's long, blonde hair reflecting from street lamps.

Teal turned the key and the Renault engine fired and started. He let Briggette go until she'd pulled a hundred and fifty yards ahead, then followed her with only his parking lights lit. She slowed for three couples straggling across the road from a still open bar toward a yacht moored on the second quay. Teal slowed to keep his distance behind her.

Once away from the port, Teal switched on his headlights. He kept well back from her. Briggette turned right on the double-laned coastal highway. Traffic at this hour was light, and she raised her speed to over one hundred kilometers per hour. Teal cursed and jammed his foot down, feeling the nippy little Renault respond. He accelerated until he was a safe hundred yards behind her. As they entered Marabella they caught a light. Teal saw it changing from green to caution five hundred yards back and slowed, letting two cars pass him and fill in the gap between Briggette and himself.

On the Málaga side of town she turned left and drove up past the bullring. Teal still had one car between him and the SEAT, a Citröen that had slipped out of a side-street after they'd made the left turn. There'd been enough traffic shuffling behind her that even if she'd looked he doubted she would suspect she was being followed.

On the outskirts of Marbella, as they began climbing into the hills behind the town, the Citröen peeled off up a farm track and Teal was left alone with the SEAT. He still lay a hundred yards behind, but he decided to increase the gap and slowed down until Briggette had a two hundred and fifty yards lead.

The road wound around mountain-sides, becoming steeper with each kilometer. Most of the time, the SEAT was out of sight and Teal was following its lights which reflected off hillsides as the two cars climbed higher into the sierras. They were driving toward the farming village of Ojen which Teal vaguely remembered from an excursion years before. Before and beyond Ojen was desolate hill country dotted with deserted farmhouses, which could be hired cheaply from owners who now lived in the village. Writers and artists seeking the quiet life rented them. Teal guessed Briggette was heading for one of these. If her friend lived in a village she wouldn't have to carry groceries to him.

Teal was right.

Two kilometers before Ojen, he rounded a bend onto a straight stretch of road, and saw the SEAT parked in a layby chopped out of the hillside. Briggette was reaching into the back of the Sports for the grocery box. Teal didn't slow down. He zipped by her and continued for half a kilometer, around the bend and into the next straight stretch. There he maneuvered the Renault through a tight three-point turn, switched out his lights, turned off the engine and coasted slowly and quietly back down the mountain.

He braked the Renault before turning the bend. He silently opened the door, got out and walked down the road until he saw the SEAT. Briggette had gone. Teal got back in the Renault and without closing the door or starting the engine, released the handbrake and rolled down until he was safely parked off the road and in the layby behind Briggette's car.

He left the Renault door open and crossed the road, which had been carved into the mountainside, and looked down the slope. She was a hundred yards away, with the grocery box balanced on one arm and a torch in her other hand, gingerly threading her way down a mule track which wound through stunted olive trees. As a scudding cloud briefly uncovered the moon, Teal saw her black, moving shape faintly illuminated, and as his eyes adjusted to the darkness he saw that the track terminated two hundred yards distant in a broad, raised plateau on which stood a tiny, single-storyed farmhouse, glowing whitely in the eerie light.

As the girl walked the last few yards to the farm, Teal squatted by the side of the road to keep his silhouette low. He watched as she paused in front of the closed door. The windows were dark; no lights shone inside. From where he was he couldn't tell if she knocked or called a name. Then, at the instant the door opened, the shifting cloud curtained the moon's meager light. Teal cursed silently, strained forward uselessly from his crouched position and peered at the figure in the open door. He couldn't tell if it was male or female, only that it stood a head higher than the girl.

Anyone that tall has to be a man, Teal reasoned. But it doesn't have to be *my* man. Get your ass down there Teal and find out.

He was already moving, picking his way down the steep trail, ducking overhanging olive branches, trying to place each foot before taking a step to avoid sending shale slipping down the slope. He stopped every ten yards, staring into the pitch blackness, trying to take his bearings for the next short assault on the mule track, wishing to Christ that the moon would appear again.

Twice, despite his caution, dirt and shale gave beneath his feet, rolling down with an unholy clatter which split the perfect stillness of the night. And once, he walked into the sharp tendrils of an olive-tree branch which tangled in his hair, scratched his cheek and made him mutter again against the stygian darkness.

Then he was clear of the olive grove and walking up the slope to the top of the plateau where the farmhouse stood. Suddenly light flared. Teal stopped, lowered himself silently until he was laying face down in the dirt. He hadn't been able to tell if the light had come from inside or outside the house. He lay motionless, staring at the ground in front of him, separating the tiny sounds of the night from his own nervous breathing, analyzing them, discarding them in his mind, working down to the core of his senses to discover the one noise that might represent danger. He heard nothing except insects, the rustle of leaves in the grove behind him, the occasional noise of a bird or nocturnal animal. He let five more minutes pass, then, still laying on the ground, raised his head until he could see the farmhouse. Through a window he saw the soft flickering of what could only be a candle.

Teal knelt on the trail. He permitted himself ten seconds in which to gently massage around the aching wound in his arm. At the same time he considered his foolishness in approaching the farmhouse without a weapon or any sort. Dumb bastard, he told himself, fucking dumb.

He stretched to full height, once, to relieve his cramped muscles and continued up the slope. He was only twenty yards from the house. He kept the candle-lit window in the periphery of his vision so as not to destroy his night sight. He reached the small, cobbled terrace which fronted the house, crossed it with three silent steps and flattened himself against the ancient white-washed wall between the window and the studded front door.

One look was all he needed. But not yet.

He listened.

From inside he heard the mumble of voices, one male, one female. He couldn't hear what was being said. Once or twice he heard soft, intimate laughter, then another sound which he strained to recognize before realizing it was liquid being poured into glasses. The voices started again, softly, more urgently, as if something serious was under discussion, then rose to an argumentative pitch and quickly softened again as if a truce had been reached. The soft laughter; the intimate mumble. Teal listened, fine-tuning his ears to catch even a snatch of the conversation, but he understood nothing.

The conversation continued for nearly fifteen minutes. Teal fought back the temptation to snatch a look through the window and have done with it. But he made himself wait. He didn't know where they were. If they faced the window and saw him, then he would blow it. Calm down Teal, he told himself; you've got all night, you've got nowhere to go, no one's pining in her bed waiting for you to come home.

Then the voices lowered, and the steady candle-glow against the window beside Teal flickered and shifted and dimmed, as if it had been moved to another place in the room further from the window. Teal glanced at the window, trying to judge from the aura of light reflecting on it where in the room the candle was, and tried to judge from that the layout of the room. He could not hear the voices anymore. He waited three, four minutes, searching for clues of sound of movement which would reveal to him what was happening in the tiny farmhouse. They're reading, he thought. Or they've gone to bed and left the candle lit.

He knelt on the hard, rounded cobbles, feeling them bite at his knees, and on all fours eased himself beneath the window. Moving slowly, almost imperceptibly, he raised his head until his eyes were just above the level of the window sill.

They were in bed, alright, but they weren't reading and they weren't sleeping. Far from it. Teal's eyes widened involuntarily as he saw them. They were on a mattress on the floor at the back of the room, both naked. Her back was to Teal as she straddled the man, her buttocks humping down on him, the top of her body bent forward. His face was obscured by her body, buried in the plump mounds of her breasts.

Teal remained motionless. His eyes scanned the room. It was maybe five meters wide by eight long with both a front and back door. There were no furnishings apart from a table, two chairs and the mattress. To the left another door led to the only other room which Teal guessed to be a tiny kitchen.

Briggette rolled on her side, keeping the man between her legs. Teal squinted into the dim light. He still couldn't see the man's face. Briggette rolled onto her back, her arms encircling the man. Teal watched as she caressed his waist and hips and then clawed her fingernails across his buttocks. The man twisted and pumped into her harder, then suddenly came to his knees and patted Briggette's thigh. Teal watched her raise herself, turn and kneel with her legs spread wide, her head down on the pillow and her back arched so that her bottom pushed back at the man. She reached between her legs, grasped the man's erection and slid it into herself and then cupped his balls while he drove in and out of her, his fingers pulling at the nipples on her full, swaying breasts.

Teal watched coldly, with as much involvement as if he'd been at a Reeperbahn live fucking show. He idly wondered if he'd ever intruded on a person's privacy as much as he had on this girl's today.

Suddenly, the man came. Teal heard his gasp of pleasure from outside the window. He leaned over Briggette's still kneeling figure, one hand fondling her breasts, the other working between her legs. Briggette stiffened, her head lifted, her long hair obscuring her face. Then they both collapsed on their backs beside each other on the mattress.

Teal expelled a long sigh, turned, still on his knees, crawled across the cobbled patio and as silently as he could scrambled down the incline into the olive grove.

It took him five minutes to quietly pick his way along the mule-trail back up to his car. He slid into the Renault, held the door closed with one hand, released the handbrake and let the car roll downhill well away from Briggette's Sports before slamming the door closed, switching on his lights and turning over the motor.

Back in his room in the 5-star Melia Don Pepé, Teal glanced at his watch as he reached for the phone. Two forty-five in the morning. Well, that was just bad luck for Quinn. The night clerk dialed him straight through to the London Savoy. He had Quinn on the line less than a minute later. He didn't waste time with long explanations.

"I've found one of them. The one with the black beard. His name is Block."

"Alone?"

"He's shacked up with a girl, but she's no problem. Just get yourself down here tomorrow. Hijack a fucking plane if you have to."

Teal replaced the phone and stretched out on the bed. He closed his eyes and gloated over the image in his brain of Block with his black beard laying back on the mattress, his chest heaving from his sexual exertions, not knowing that he'd been tracked, watched and identified. It was the most pleasant thing he'd had in his mind since the day those two pricks had ruined their lives. And Teal felt a deadening, stone-cold rage in his heart as he considered what had to be done to Block to encourage him to tell the whereabouts of his pal—the golden-haired wonder.

Quinn got the last standby seat on the Iberia Heathrow-Málaga flight and made it to Teal's hotel by three that afternoon. Teal drove them to the port, staying in the inside lane, cruising at a sedate seventy kilometers per hour.

"Is the girl involved?" Quinn asked.

Teal shook his head. "I reckon she's just having a fling with Block. Now she finds him on the run so she's helping out. My guess is he's spun her some cock-and-bull story. I don't think she knows what's happened."

"And what about Block?"

Teal shrugged. "After taking *Destry* he came back here thinking we were dead. The police started investigating, he got scared and ran. He's probably waiting for things to quiet down before he sneaks out of the country."

Quinn nodded. "When do we get him?"

"The girl will be down tonight to work in the bar. We take Block then. No need to involve her."

"Who do we contact?" Quinn asked. "The *Guardia civil* of the *policia armada*?"

Teal glanced at Quinn, then ran the Renault out of the lane and onto the shoulder of the road. He sat looking straight ahead, his hands still resting in driving position on the wheel.

"Listen, boyo," he said evenly, "let's sort of get this straight between us. The object of the exercise is to even the score."

He looked at Quinn and waited for him to nod agreement. Then, his voice flat, emotionless, he continued. "To do that, we talk with Block and encourage him to tell us where his friend is."

Quinn looked at Teal and forced himself to hold his gaze when Teal's cold eyes met him. "And then?"

"And then," Teal said, "we kill Block."

"Just like that?"

"You've got it," Teal said. "And my guess is we'll have to rough him up pretty bad to make him talk."

"Jesus *Christ*," Quinn said.

"Well what did you think?" Teal asked. "That we'd let the cops take him? You think the cops would tell us where the other one was after they made Block talk? Or did you think we'd ask Block to sit down and say, please Mr. Block, tell us where that sonofabitch of a friend of yours is? Or perhaps you thought we should bash this bastard around a bit, make him talk and *then* give him to the cops? They'd have you out of Spain so fast your head'd be spinning. You don't fuck around with police business anywhere, least of all in Spain."

"So we torture Block, then murder him."

"If you feel like working up a little guilt you could state it in those terms. I'd prefer to say we're going to force him to help us, and then get rid of him."

"I don't like it."

"I don't blame you. But let me tell you this. There are no heroes anymore, nor are there gentlemanly villains. You want Block, he has to be done away in the night, quietly and efficiently, with the same compassion you show when you crack a cockroach under your heel."

Teal reached into his shirt pocket for his *Ducados* and lit two. He passed one to Quinn. "I'm a shitty speech-maker, Peter, but it gets down to this. Do it properly, or don't do it. Hand that bastard over to the cops and any half-baked lawyer will have him free within weeks."

Teal stopped talking, angrily jammed the Renault into gear and took off fast. They didn't speak again until he stopped in the car park behind the port. Quinn got out of the car and walked alone through to the port. When Teal caught him up a half minute later, Quinn was standing, legs apart, hands deep in his pockets, staring out across the galaxy of moored yachts and cruisers, his gaze fixed on some distant point beyond the harbor. A hard sun etched his shadow on the quay beside him, then, as he turned to face Teal, a galleon of gray cloud obscured the sun and his shadow smeared into oblivion.

"O.K.," Quinn said. "O.K. We do it properly. We go the whole way."

Teal nodded, understanding completely the fear and distaste he saw glazing Quinn's eyes. "Tonight," he said.

Within an hour, and for two hundred dollars, Teal had bought two .38 revolvers with twelve rounds apiece from the captain of a sixty foot cruiser. Teal had met the captain a half dozen times during the last ten years, each time at different points which spanned the face of the globe. For the captain, selling the guns didn't mean anything. He had others, and he made a hundred and twenty-five bucks on the deal. He was discreet and the guns were untraceable. He'd bought them two years ago in a bar in Papeete from a down-and-out Japanese sailor.

Later, Quinn and Teal sat at a quiet table at the back of a bar and ordered toasted sandwiches and coffee. On a napkin, Teal drew a rough sketch of the trail leading from the road up to the farmhouse, and beside it another sketch of the house's simple layout.

They would approach the house after dark. Teal would conceal himself at the back, Quinn at the front. Quinn would throw a handful of stones onto the terrace. Teal was betting Block would come out to investigate. Whichever door he came out, front or back, they would wait their chance and have him.

"And then?" Quinn asked.

Teal pushed his coffee cup aside, folded the paper napkin and slipped it into his pocket. "Then," he said, "we play it by ear."

At six-thirty, after the winter sun had slipped below the horizon, Quinn and Teal strolled by Briggette's apartment and along to *El Marinero Feliz*. The battered SEAT Sports was parked out front. They crossed the road and walked by the bar to make sure the girl had started work. She stood behind the bar, polishing glasses as she chatted with two men who sat in front of her drinking beer from glass mugs.

"O.K.," Teal said, "let's go. The party's on."

The doubled back toward the car park.

Somewhere among the olive groves a pair of cicadas chirped their ear-splitting trill into the darkness. Banks of cloud swelled from the sierras, blotting all suggestion of moon or stars.

Quinn lay on his stomach behind the huge, gnarled trunk of an ancient carob tree whose umbrella-like branches offered the farmhouse its only relief from summer heat. He glanced at his watch again. Four minutes to go. Teal had told him to wait ten minutes before he threw the stones, time for him to make his way slowly and silently around the back of the house and find cover.

Quinn clutched the revolver in his right hand. His hand sweated. The wood and metal butt of the gun felt warm and wet in his hand. He tried to control his breathing. Stay under cover, Teal had told him. Don't show yourself if he comes out your side. You can bet your balls this bastard knows how to shoot.

He looked at the house again, at the soft glow in the window. If Block moved in there he'd see shadows flickering across the window. There were no shadows. Block would be sitting, perhaps reading, or laying on the mattress, sleeping.

Quinn felt around for stones. He scraped together a handful of six or eight, each about half the size of a matchbox.

He looked at his watch. Thirty seconds to go. He came into a kneeling position behind the tree, shifting the gun to his left hand, picking up the stones in his right.

Just keep under cover. Don't show yourself. Just do what you have to do. No heroics. He could feel his heart bashing against his chest cavity. He felt breathless. He wished he could walk away from all this, forget it, forget what had happened to him, to Teal and to *Destry* and forget what had happened to Jenny. A sudden image flashed into his brain of that other one holding her above his head, hurling her like a broken doll into the dark sea. He felt physically ill, felt he might vomit. He breathed deeply, willing strength and purpose into his body and mind.

He moved half a yard from behind the cover of the tree and tossed the stones with a soft under-armed chuck and stepped back behind the tree, transferring the revolver from his left hand to his right as they landed on the cobbles with a scattered bouncing sound. He watched the lit window.

For a moment, nothing. Then he saw a giant black shadow stream across that part of the room he could see through the window and knew that after hearing the sound and listening, Block had stood up and headed for the door. No, not the door, the candle; the window pane went as black as the night sky, became a black square against the still visible white-washed wall as Block snuffed the flame.

Quinn listened. No sound. He stared at the door, waiting to see if it would open. He felt sweat coursing down the small of his back beneath his thick jacket. Safe behind the tree, he reached into his pocket for his handkerchief and wiped the butt of the revolver and then rubbed his open right hand against the leg of his trousers. His temples throbbed. His eyes blurred from the strain of peering into the darkness.

The door opened half way. Oh, Jesus, he thought, he's coming out *my* side! They hadn't planned on this. Christ, they'd been so sure he'd slip out the back and work his way around to the front and that Teal would get him from behind.

Quinn stared at the door, straining his eyes wide in the darkness, willing his retinas to open even further so he could see more. I won't be able to move, he told himself. Christ, I'm scared! I can't do this sort of thing! I can't do this!

Block slipped out the door, his extended arm sweeping a gun in an arc from one side of the patio to the other.

And suddenly Quinn found himself shouting. "*Don't move you bastard, don't move!*"

And Block hurled himself to the cobbles, his automatic spitting three fast rounds that shattered the night and hissed and hummed angrily off the shale on either side of the carob.

Quinn shoved his gunhand out from behind the tree and loosed a shot toward Block. The muzzle flash exploded like a sun in his eyes. His hand jerked high in the air from the recoil. His ears rang from the blast of the shot.

"*Coming through!*" he heard Teal yell, then heard the crash of the back door and a moment later the smash of breaking glass as Teal wrenched open the window shutters.

Yelling, Block scrambled around and fired twice into the window. And, propelled by some warrior's sense for the main chance, Quinn found himself sprinting forward from behind the cover of his tree, his gunhand rigid in front of him. He felt his finger squeezing on the trigger, was conscious of his shot spinning off the cobbles and burying itself into the wall.

Block turned, fired again, the bullet cracking the air beside Quinn's ear. At the same moment Teal burst through the front door like a tornado. Before Block could twist around Teal kicked at his wrist, sending his gun slithering across the cobbles, then grabbed Block's hair, wrenched his head back and shoved his own gun against his ear. Block's big hands lunged for Teal. Teal slapped him behind the ear with the barrel of the revolver. Block slumped, half stunned.

"You O.K.?"

Quinn swallowed and nodded. His ears rang. Now that the sudden burst of action was over, he felt the same as he had before it started; weak and scared. "I'm O.K."

"You did fine," Teal said. "Couldn't say you did it neat, but you sure as hell did it noisy." Block was on his knees, groaning; Teal still held him by the hair. "Let's get this prick inside."

They hauled Block into the farmhouse and sat him on a chair. Quinn lit a candle with his cigarette lighter. Teal bound Block's hands behind the back of the chair with a length of rope he'd bought at the port chandlers. Block groaned, still groggy from the blow to his head. Quinn looked at him in the candlelight. The last time he'd seen him he'd had a gun pointed at Jenny. Now he was moaning and his head flopped down on his chest and he had spittle on his black beard. In a little while, Quinn thought evenly, he'll be dead. We're going to kill him. He thought of all the nightmares he'd had about Block and his friend, all the murderous daydreams about what he'd do if he caught them. Well, now he'd caught one, and he felt no anger, no rage. He was a calm as a judge, and like a judge he would pursue the process of justice to its logical end.

Teal searched Block's pockets, putting everything on the table. He tossed Block's wallet to Teal. "Check that," Teal lit another candle and moved around the house searching Block's belongings.

Quinn opened the wallet, pulled out the cash. "Around a thousand bucks," he said. "Twenty thousand pesetas. French francs, Swiss francs. Maybe fifteen hundred dollars total."

"Shove it in your pocket," Teal said, as he went through Block's spare cothes by the bed. "It won't buy another boat, but it'll help cover expenses." Teal grunted in surprise. "Look at this! Never thought I'd see this again." He tossed aside a pair of trousers, came back and put his candle on the table. "Found my knife." He opened the Puma and the hand-etched blade glinted in the candlelight. "Won this beauty ten years ago in a card game."

"Who are you?" Block mumbled. His chin still rested on his

chest and his head rolled from side to side. "You're not police. Who are you?"

Teal grunted. "Worse than the cops, boyo, worse than the cops."

He flicked the knife toward the table. It thunked into the wood beside the candle, vibrating from the force of the throw. Block's eyes lifted toward the sound, then slowly he raised his head and saw Quinn in front of him, the revolver hanging loose in his hands. Quinn watched the truth of recognition transform his features, saw the eyes widen, the lips part. Then Block turned his head and peered up at the black shape behind him. He closed his eyes.

"What was your friend's name?" Teal asked softly.

Block didn't answer.

"Where is he?"

Block's eyes were still closed.

"What did you do with the boat?"

Block opened his eyes and stared at the candles on the table.

Teal stepped from behind the chair so Block could see him in the flickering candle-light. "Tell you something," he whispered. "I'm gonna kill you, mister. Cooperate and I'll do it quick and you won't know a thing. Fuck around with me and you'll still be crawling around the floor with your guts hanging out when the girl arrives." Teal said it reasonably, like he was discussing the price of a boat.

"I don't like you," Teal said, still reasonably. "You shot my friend's girl, you played with her. You pointed your gun at her, scared her, laughed at her when she got scared."

Teal raised his revolver and held it three inches from Block's forehead. Then he lowered it across his face, down his chest, over his stomach and held it pointed at his genitals. Suddenly he jammed the barrel of the gun right into Block's balls. Block jerked in the chair and kicked his legs, only his hands tied to the back of the chair stopping him from doubling over onto the floor. He dry-retched, then moaned then dry-retched again.

Quinn watched the candle-lit tableau, saw the dark shadows flowing and abstracting themselves on the walls as the candle flames flickered from the draft of movement. Teal had never told him that Block had terrorized Jenny with a gun. He felt nothing. He watched Block squirming in agony on the chair, his legs crossing and uncrossing trying to find relief from the excruciating pain.

"What I'm going to do next," Teal said, reasonably, "is pour whisky on your hair and light it." He took the half-finished bottle of Johnny Walker from the food box by the table and uncapped it. He took a swig and offered the bottle to Quinn. Quinn shook his head. The scene was already unreal enough.

"You should believe me," Teal quietly told Block. "But I don't think you do."

He grasped Block's hair and forced his head back. He splashed the whisky on Block's face and Block gasped as it stung his eyes and nostrils. Then Teal splashed the rest over his beard and hair. He took a candle from the table and held it in front of Block's face. "You'll go up like a Christmas pudding," Teal said, "in about five seconds from now."

Block's head slumped onto his chest again, but his eyes stared at the candle. Quinn saw the candle-flame reflected in his retinas.

"I don't know his name," Block said.

"You called him Mann," Teal said.

"I call everyone man. He wouldn't tell me his name. So I called him Mister Mann."

"You don't know the name of the guy you work with?"

"I never worked with him before," Block breathed. *"For Christ's sake get that thing away from me!"*

Teal stood the candle on the table and moved behind Block. The room stunk of whisky.

"Did he hire you in the port to do the job?"

Block shook his head. "Tristan hired me."

"Who the fuck's Tristan?"

"He works with Zeller."

Teal paused, considering how to ask his questions. Already, this had gone deeper than he'd anticipated. There were more than two involved. More than Block and his friend. He nodded to Quinn. "Scribble down those names and anything else that's useful."

Quinn put his revolver down beside the candles and the

Puma which was still stuck into the tabletop. He found a biro, hunted for a scrap of paper and couldn't find one. He took a one hundred dollar note from the money he'd taken from Block's wallet and resting the paper on the table, wrote, "*Tristan. Zeller.*"

"O.K.," Teal said, "Tristan hired you and Tristan works for Zeller. Who's Zeller?"

Block shook his head. "I don't know."

"Hell of a lot you don't know, boyo."

"The other guy knew Zeller. He talked about him."

"What did he say?"

"Nothing much."

"What the fuck does that mean?"

"He mentioned Zeller, man, he mentioned him, that's all. Zeller this, and Zeller that."

"You've never met Zeller."

"No."

"But you work for him."

"Indirectly. Tristan's my boss."

"You've met Tristan?"

"Once."

"Where?"

"Paris."

"When?"

"Three years back, when I joined the organization."

"What *is* the organization, Block?"

"I don't know anything about it."

"You been with it three years, Block. How come you know nothing about it? You're *shitting* me!" He reached toward the candle.

"*I'm straight, man, I'm being straight with you.* Jesus! We get boats, that's all."

"And?"

"And use them."

"For what?"

"Smuggling. You know, man."

"Tell me about *Destry*. What did you use her for?"

"*Destry* . . . yeah, well, man, great boat. Christ. We ran guns up to the Basque coast. Little town up there, don't remember the name, fishing port, Coupla sardine boats or some damned thing came out and took them off us."

"Who were the guns for?"

"Shit, man, who knows? One of them crazy Basque terrorist groups."

"Where did you pick up the guns?"

"Asilah, Morocco. Down south of Tangier."

"Who gave them to you?"

"Some guy, I dunno. Took us over to this little cove. We ran 'em out in the tender."

"What did you do with *Destry* after you'd made delivery?"

"We scuttled her, man. Ran ourselves ashore in the Avon raft. Like, sorry about that, man."

"You're sorry, are you?" Teal said.

"Sure, man. Great boat."

"You sorry about the girl, too, Block?"

Block didn't answer.

"Great girl, that, Block." Teal paused. "How many other yachts you hi-jacked, Block?"

"Some."

"How many?"

"Maybe a half dozen."

"You don't count so well."

"O.K., eight in all. O.K.?"

"With your pal, Mr. Mann?"

"Told you I'd never worked with him before."

"Who with, then?"

"Various guys."

"Who?"

"Doesn't matter, man. They're dead."

"You killed them?"

"You got it."

"And the crews?"

"Yeah."

"What did you use the other yachts for?"

"Did a gold run out of Malta to Sicily. Ran heroin from Greece into Israel. Rest were all arms runs. Greece to Lebanon. South of France to north Africa. Like that."

"You take the boats, kill the crews, run the stuff, then kill your partners. Why?"

"Because that's what Tristan wants."

"But you didn't kill that golden-haired freak."

"Tristan didn't tell me to."

"He must be something special. You, too, Block, you must be special if Tristan's never ordered you knocked over."

"I'm efficient, man."

"You were," Teal said, "until you forgot to kill us."

"That was Mann. I would've killed you right off." He spat on the floor as he said it. Teal walked around in front of him and backhanded him across the face. Quinn saw blood on Block's lips.

"If you've only seen Tristan once, how does he give you orders?"

Block didn't answer. He rolled his head and sucked at the blood running out of his mouth. Teal hit him again, this time full in the face with his closed fist, knocking Block over backward in the chair so his head smacked onto the tiled floor. He leaned over, grabbed Block by his hair and hauled him and the chair upright. "Try again," Teal said, softly. "How does he give you orders?"

"Paris," Block whispered. His eyes were closed, his mouth open. From the way he spoke, Quinn guessed his nose was broken. Blood smeared over his face and into his beard. "Flat 11, Rue Plisson 3, 14th arrondissement. He always knows where I am, I contact him after each job. I got a key to the apartment. When there's a job I go to the apartment. I get instructions. And a bank draft."

Quinn scribbled the address on the one hundred dollar note.

"Where's the key?" Teal asked.

Block nodded to his things on the table which Teal had taken from his pocket. Quinn picked up the keyring with the single key and slipped it into his own pocket.

"How did Tristan hire you?"

"I was on the run from the French cops. I was selling dope. Killed a coupla guys. The cops were onto me. Tristan heard about me from the guys who were looking after me. He's some sort of crazy doctor."

"Just how many men have you killed, Block?"

"You mean like in 'Nam or in real life?"

"Forget it," Teal said. "Forget I ever asked. When's your next call in Paris?"

"I've checked out on them guys, man. Sick of that shit, all that moving around. Got the girl," he said. "Jesus."

"You said Tristan is a doctor. What sort of doctor?"

"Shit, man, I don't know. A doctor. Who knows? Maybe Zeller is sick or something."

"Where is Zeller based?" Teal asked. "Paris?"

"They say he lives aboard a yacht."

"But where? France? Spain? England?"

"Afloat. They say he never comes ashore."

"Who told you this?"

"Rumors, man. You know? You hear a word here, a word there."

"Tell me about Mr. Mann."

"A weirdo. A real killer."

"That's something coming from you, Block."

"Hardly human, man. Eyes like fucking ice."

Teal moved around behind Block again. He leaned both hands on the back of the chair, one hand on either side of Block's shoulders. He kept on with the questions, spitting them out, probing, examining every aspect of Block's answers. Quinn listened, his pen poised over the hundred dollar bill, waiting to draw information from Block's laconic answers. He wasn't getting much. Two names and an address.

Then Block moved.

Quinn saw everything; would later see it in his mind split-second by split-second with all the clarity of a slow-motion film on a screen in his brain.

Block moved massively upward, driving down against the floor with his legs, launching himself and the chair off the floor. Teal was still leaning on the chair. Block's head caught Teal under the chin and Quinn saw blood spurt from between Teal's lips as his jaw snapped closed and his teeth clamped down on his tongue. Teal's head snapped back. Block was on his feet, the chair incongruously attached to his back. He swung around, booting at Teal, catching him in the stomach. Teal folded, gasped for breath, crashed onto his side on the floor, rolled in agony.

Quinn saw it, felt rooted to the spot, unable to move. Block roared, hunched his shoulders, strained, and the rope tying him to the chair floated snake-like across the room and the chair crashed to the floor and then Block came at him, hands outstretched, both wrists bloodied where the rope had been.

Block's hands encircled him, lifting him off the ground. Quinn felt something was breaking in his gut. He gasped frantically for air as it was forced out of him. He tried to grab at Block, but his arms were pinned to his sides. Block's forehead butted him in the face, once, twice. Flashes of light exploded in Quinn's head. Quinn kicked, desperately, knowing that if Block butted him another time he'd lose consciousness. His kicks caught solid flesh. Block's grip loosened. Quinn drove a fist into Block's stomach. Block roared again and slung him by one arm across the room. Quinn landed belly down across the table, crushing out the candles. His gun was there! His fingers scrambled across the table. He had something in his hand. Not the gun; the knife. The Puma. Block was on top of him, hauling him up by the hair. In the sudden darkness, Quinn could see nothing. He twisted out of Block's clutch, slipped, crashed onto his knees. Block's ankle caught the table leg in the darkness, tipping it over. Quinn rolled away, the knife held out front in the dark. Block's black shadow loomed over him, kicking, connecting against his thigh. Quinn kicked back, catching Block in the ankle. Block stumbled, fell, his hands reaching out for Quinn. Quinn slashed with the knife, heard a shriek of pain as the Solingen steel blade opened up the length of Block's arm. Quinn rolled in between the two great arms and sank the knife into Block's chest. The arms encircled him, squeezing. Block made strange, whimpering sounds. The arms still squeezed. Quinn twisted the knife, feeling the strength go out of the arms. The arms let go. Quinn pulled out the knife, heard a gurgling sound in Block's throat. Quinn rolled over so he straddled Block, deliberately raised the knife and plunged it into Block's chest, then ripped it down. Block arched his back once. Quinn felt a shudder in Block's legs. Then Block was still.

Quinn rolled away and lay a long moment staring into the darkness. He felt weak. He breathed deeply, sucking oxygen into his lungs and mentally checked himself over. Bruised mostly, he decided. I'm O.K. He made the analysis in a detached way, like a doctor examining a patient he'd never met.

"Quinn?" Quinn heard Teal moving in the darkness. "Quinn? Are you O.K.?"

"I'm O.K.," Quinn said. "I'm going to light a candle."

He came to his knees, took his cigarette lighter from his pocket, flicked it, found a candle by the upturned table and lit it. The wick sputtered, blossomed orange light around the room. Teal was on his knees, his revolver held in a two-handed grip, pointing directly at Quinn.

Teal lowered the gun, came to his feet clutching his stomach, half bent over. "Some ballgame." He saw Block lying dead with blood over the front of his shirt, saw the blood all over Quinn and the knife in his hand. "You hurt?"

Quinn shook his head, picked up his revolver and the hundred dollar bill with the names and address on it. "Let's get out of here," he said. He lent Teal a supporting arm and helped him out of the farmhouse, across the cobbled patio and down the mule-track. They paused before attempting the upward section of the track, both breathing heavily. Quinn sat with his arms hunched over his knees, deep breathing, looking back through the darkness toward the house. They'd left the candle burning. The faint, glowing rectangle of the window punctuated the darkness.

At the hotel they reached Teal's room without anyone noticing the mess they were in. They checked themselves over. Bruises for Quinn, bruises and a split tongue for Teal. Teal swilled water in his mouth, spat it in the bathroom basin then took a bottle of whisky from his bag. He took a long swallow straight from the bottle. "Antiseptic," he grunted and passed the bottle to Quinn.

Quinn took a sip then slumped in an easy chair. He found the hundred dollar bill in his pocket and unfolded it. "Zeller and

Tristan," he read. "Rue Plisson 3, 14th arondissement. I'll book tickets first thing tomorrow morning."

"We're going to Paris?"

Quinn nodded.

Teal shrugged and picked up the whisky bottle. "Thought you might have had enough."

"I have," Quinn said.

"So, why Paris?"

"'We do it properly, or we don't do it,'" Quinn said. "Unquote."

Teal smiled, nodded and took another pull on the bottle. First blood, he thought. And now the kid ain't a kid anymore.

While the Air France jet circled in a stack over Charles de Gualle airport, Teal worked on making his last whisky of the flight last as long as humanly possible. Quinn lay back with his eyes closed, trying to force himself to relax. The events of the previous night had left him tired and aching. His ribs gave him pain every time he moved. His forehead was swollen and a dirty, brown bruise spread from his right eyebrow up into his hairline, the result of Block butting him. But Block had come off worse. Block was dead. Quinn had gone over the fight several times in his mind. He was surprised how little that death worried him. Block had tried to kill him and he'd killed Block. He felt no moral pang. If anything, he only felt exultant that he, Peter Quinn, graduate from Harvard Business School, had emerged victorious from a fight to the death—and with honorable wounds which would remind him of his triumph for a few days to come.

After cleaning themselves up in the hotel room, he and Teal had examined their every move that night. They agreed that they'd left no physical evidence which could connect them to Block's death. When his body was finally found, the police might realize he was one of the men involved in the *Destry's* disappearance, and might guess who was responsible for Block's death, but if no physical evidence existed which obliged them to act officially, and the two suspects were out of the country anyway, they would probably file Block away

under "unsolved" and consider themselves fortunate they
didn't have to worry about him anymore.

But there remained the matter of Briggette. Teal felt bad
about the girl. He'd ransacked her apartment, followed her,
spied on her. Yet she wasn't responsible for anything that had
happened. Teal didn't want her to find Block's body, firstly
because she'd go to the police, and secondly because of the
shock it would give her. Quinn and Teal had decided that Block
would drift out of her life forever, the same way Teal was sure
he had recently drifted into it.

So, last night, Teal had written a note, taken it to the port
and paid a Spanish boy five hundred pesetas to deliver it to her
at the bar.

The note read:

*"Decided to get moving. Should be in France Tomorrow.
Will write. Don't go to farm. Think it's being watched."*

And Teal had another note in his pocket which he would post
at the airport when they landed in a few minutes:

*"Am safe. Have ticket to U.S.A. Cannot return to Europe.
Keep or sell anything of mine you have. You're a great kid.
Sorry it ends like this."*

Enclosed in the envelope with the note were five one
hundred dollar bills.

Teal figured that when she'd recovered from her broken
heart she might use the money to go home to Stockholm, to the
young man in the photo who had written her all those letters.

Quinn and Teal walked along the Quai St. Michel, dodging
flocks of rowdy Left Bank students crowding the stands of the
bouquinistes, the second-hand booksellers. At the Pont au
Double, which led off from their left across the river Seine to
the Ile de la Cité, they stopped to check the fold-out Paris city
map they'd bought at the airport.

Using the bulk of Nôtre Dame cathedral looming behind
them on the stern end of the ship-shaped island as a landmark,
Quinn traced their route and fixed their position. After a
moment's hesitation he nodded to their right and they turned
into Rue Lagrange and a couple of blocks later took another

right, plunging into the rabbit-warren of narrow twisting streets of the Quartier Latin.

Rue Plisson was no more than a lane, a cobbled, dead-end street hardly wider than a truck. Filth from up-ended dustbins was strewn down its length. Ancient warehouses with split, wooden doors lined one side, while on the other stood a row of decrepit five-story apartment blocks. Number three, Rue Plisson, was one of the latter.

Quinn and Teal stopped, contemplating the entrance. They looked at each other. Quinn shrugged and led the way into a dank lobby which smelled like it was used by every passing drunk who felt the need to relieve himself. A flight of iron-balustraded wooden stairs wound upward into the gloom. As they climbed, Quinn wished they still had their weapons—any weapons—but because of airline security they'd left the revolvers, wrapped in an old towel, behind a toilet bowl in the Málaga airport.

Number eleven was on the third floor. Teal flicked his lighter to illuminate the door and check the number. They both listened with their ears flat against the flaking paint. They heard nothing from inside.

"I'll check next door," Quinn whispered. He walked across the hall to number twelve. He knocked gently and stepped back a pace. A fat man wearing a singlet and baggy trousers supported by wide suspenders opened the door.

"*Ah, bon jour, monsieur,*" Quinn said in his college French. "I have knocked, but my friend next door does not answer."

"That is because he is not there," rasped the fat man.

"I thought he might be sleeping."

"He may be sleeping," the fat man said, "but if he is not there, then he is not sleeping there. And if he was there, and sleeping, and you knocked, then you would have woken him, as you have woken me."

The door slammed in Quinn's face. He turned back to Teal and shrugged. "You heard the man. He's not there."

Quinn dug in his pocket for the key they'd taken from Block, and inserted it in the lock.

"I'll go first," Teal said. "Keep away from the door."

Teal turned the key in the lock as quietly as he could. Then, when the tongue was free, he pushed open the door hard and stepped aside out of the possible line of fire. Nothing happened.

Quinn and Teal entered, closing the door behind them. Number eleven was one large room with an alcove for a kitchen and a small bathroom with toilet, shower and basin.

While Teal checked the kitchen and bathroom, Quinn started on the living room. The table was littered with newspapers in English and French and several old copies of *Paris Match*. A cupboard in the corner was empty except for a battered suitcase. Quinn opened it. Nothing. A shelf along one wall held a few dog-eared *Serie Noire* paperbacks, two full packs of *Gauloise* cigarettes and a broken pocket-knife. He turned to the bed sitting beside the wall opposite the dusty window. It was neatly made, the linen fresh.

Teal stood in the door of the kitchen alcove and made an empty-handed gesture. "No one's stayed in a long time," he said. "Loaf of bread on the sideboard. Mold all over."

"Newspapers are a couple of weeks old," Quinn said. "Nothing here."

Hands on hips, he looked around the room one more time, double checking if he could have missed anything in so small a space. He walked to the bed. He knelt and glanced underneath. Concealed by the shadows so it was barely visible was a black box, a cube, perhaps two feet on either side. Quinn glanced back at Teal.

"What is it?" Teal asked.

"I don't know," Quinn said. He reached under the bed, slid out the box, lifted it, grunting from its weight and carried it to the table.

Quinn released two metal catches so that the top of the box lifted and the front fell forward.

"What the hell is it?" Teal asked. "A typewriter? God-damned big for a typewriter."

"It's a telex," Quinn said. "A portable telex."

"What would that be doing here?" Teal asked. "Why the hell would there be a portable telex in a slum like this?"

Quinn ran his fingers along the keyboard. "I don't know. Except Block said he came here to receive instructions."

Quinn looked under the bed again and found a shoebox containing a roll of paper and several fresh tapes.

Teal experimentally pressed a key. "Instructions from whom," he mused. "And from where?"

"Good question," Quinn said. "Tristan? Zeller?"

Teal walked to the window, looked out through the caked dust to the dirty, cobbled street below, thinking, wondering just what they'd got themselves into and whether they were capable of following through any further.

Through the machine's keyboard, Quinn saw something yellow against the matt-black of the box's floor. He took a pen from his pocket, poked through the keys, trying to spear it out, but he couldn't maneuver the pen between the arms of the keys. He unclipped the retaining catches on the baseboard and lifted the hefty machine from its box.

"What are you up to?" Teal asked. He walked back to the table.

"There might be some answers on this."

Quinn held up a two foot length of bent yellow paper tape punctuated with the distinctive spindlings of a telex code.

Teal fingered the tape. "Maybe," he said quietly. "We sure as hell have nothing else to go on."

Through a crack in one of the broken warehouse doors opposite Rue Plisson 3, Hailey stared up at the window of apartment number eleven.

He'd walked back from the Right Bank after an appointment in a worker's café on the Rue du Temple, feeling very pleased with himself. Zeller was having trouble taking delivery of a large shipment of used FN rifles. The Belgain government agency had played particularly hard-to-get. Even the offer of a substantial bribe from Zeller's man in Brussels had failed to sway the head of the agency in his thinking. Now, under Zeller's instructions, Hailey had placed the bribe in a different sector entirely. A Libyan merchant, dealing in the import and export of fine porcelain could fix everything. For ten thousand dollars "expenses" and another five thousand dollars "fee," he could approach a friend of his brother-in-law's who was highly placed in the Libyan department of defense. A buyer, designated by Hailey, would be supplied with a Libyan "end certificate," a guarantee that the FNs would be bought by, paid by and, finally, used by the Libyan armed forces for a period of at least seven years. With the bought piece of paper in his files the head of the Brussels agency would feel safe in releasing the weapons to the buyer. If he followed the usual form used by bureaucrats in the sale of second-hand weapons, the government receipt would be understated by at least five percent of the total involved—a useful amount of cash which the official would discreetly channel into his numbered Swiss bank account. The official would be happy, and Zeller would make another massive profit when he resold the weapons to any one of twenty terrorists, mercenary or revolutionary customers who continually clamored for fine guns.

It had been a good day for Hailey. But now this.

Walking up Rue Plisson to the apartment which he hadn't used since the day after he and Block had taken the fast little boat out of Jose Banus harbor in Spain, he had glanced up at the window of number eleven and seen the suggestion of movement behind the dirty glass.

He'd slipped into the deserted warehouse and waited, and watched. Once, someone had come to the window and stared out but Hailey hadn't been able to make out if it was a man or woman, a friend or foe. Quite possibly the person in the room was a member of Zeller's organization, but Tristan had been in touch with him during the last two weeks while he moved between Brussels and Paris, and hadn't mentioned that anyone would be staying at Rue Plisson.

Suddenly, Hailey stepped back a pace, deeper into the shadows behind the warehouse door. A man, no, two men, were stepping out of the lobby into the street.

For one brief second, their faces didn't register in Hailey's mind. Then he recognized them, and knew he had trouble on his hands. They were the two men from *Destry*! The two men who should have been dead!

In an instant, he analyzed what had happened. There was only one way they could have discovered the room on rue Plisson. Block must have told them. Which meant that Block had disobeyed orders and returned to Spain after the job.

Hailey did not feel any anger toward Block, because it was not in his nature to do so. He only knew that Block would be executed—if those two hadn't already done the job for him.

The two men walked quickly down the lane and turned right, leaving his view. Hailey followed, keeping eighty yards behind as they wound their way through the quiet back streets, then closed the gap to thirty yards when they reached the busier streets leading into Boulevard Saint Michel. They stopped. Hailey ducked into a bookshop doorway, knowing that what he was doing was dangerous, that his golden hair would give him away immediately if they saw him. But he had to know where they were going. Zeller would want to know. Zeller would be angry. He'd have instructions about these two.

They were after a cab. Hailey watched them signal one already carrying a fare, then another, but it, too, was occupied. If they got into a cab, he'd lose them, they'd be a mile away before he could hail one for himself. He looked up and down the crowded street trying to figure what he could do. He felt the faintest tension behind his eyes, as if a headache was starting. He'd suffered from headaches these last two weeks that had left him writhing in agony on his bed with both hands jammed across his eyes to keep out the light. No medicine helped. Only Tristan could stop the headaches. He had to get to Tristan soon. But he had to do this first. Because Zeller would want to know about this. He had to do this for Zeller before he worried about anything as trivial as a headache.

He tried to ignore the vague pulsing in his temples, and concentrated on the problem. Quinn and Teal still waved at cabs, but so far they were all full. The next one, or the one after wouldn't be.

Then, the answer presented itself. A young man, a student probably, bumped into him, excused himself and smiled as Hailey stood aside to allow him to enter the bookshop. As Hailey had watched Quinn and Teal he'd seen the young man on the very periphery of his vision running across the pavement toward the bookshop. Now, two things happened: Hailey saw Quinn and Teal wave at another cab and saw it slow down; and he realized why the young man had entered the bookshop in such a rush; his girlfriend had double-parked on the Boulevard while he dashed in to make his purchase.

Hailey moved instantly. He reached the little blue Dyane 6 with the girl at the wheel at the same time Quinn and Teal climbed into the cab. Hailey wrenched open the passenger side door of the Dyane and slipped into the seat, an automatic in his hand, pointing straight at the girl.

"Police business," Hailey said. "Follow the cab in front."

The girl's eyes widened. "*Merde!*" she breathed.

"Do it!" Hailey hissed, ramming the gun into her ribs.

The girl cursed again, hauled the dash-mounted lever into gear and pulled out after the cab.

"You're a sensible girl," Hailey said. "That's good." He tucked the gun back into his waist-band, under his jacket.

"You're no *flic*," the girl said. "You speak French like a Bulgarian peasant."

"American peasant," Hailey said. "I'm with Interpol." He reached into his jacket for his wallet and extracted a 1000 franc note. "Keep up with that cab and this is yours." Hailey reached over and tucked the note high up between the girl's slender, jean-covered thighs.

The girl lightly clenched Hailey's fingers with her thighs as he withdrew his hand and flashed him a smile. "Another one of those and you can *have* the car," she said. She steered deftly left to avoid the wing of a big Peugeot which braked in front of her, hop-scotched forward through the city traffic and placed herself two cars behind the taxi. "And me, too," she added.

"Think of your boyfriend," Hailey said. "He'll be waiting for you."

"Pfu!" the girl said. "He's a child. A philosophy student." She smiled at the beautiful man with the golden hair seated beside her. Her brow creased as she kept her place in the traffic behind the cab. He was staring trance-like through the windscreen of the Dyane, his eyes wide and vacant. As if he wasn't really there.

Hailey paid off his cab in Rue Lagrange and walked to Rue Plisson 3, trying to ignore the throbbing pain which had spread from his temples right through his head, burning like a drop of molten lava in the middle of his brain and constricting his forehead like a taut iron band.

The girl in the Dyane had followed Quinn and Teal to Charles de Gaulle airport. Hailey watched them book in at the British Airways counter for the 7 pm flight to London. Then, after they'd passed through immigration, made change at the bank, he slipped into a public phone booth and dialed straight through to a London-based Zeller employee. Quinn and Teal would be watched from the moment they came through Customs at Gatwick airport until they reached their destination. If Zeller told Hailey to follow them to England, he'd know exactly where they were.

In number eleven Hailey glanced around the room. Everything seemed in place. There was nothing of interest to snoopers anyway. Tristan insisted that each temporary tenant take or destroy any evidence which could tie in with the organization.

Hailey knelt to pull the telex box out from under the bed. He gasped as a sudden rush of blood pounded through his head. He opened the box, ran the lead to the special wall plug, fitted the paper roll and fresh tape, and swiftly tapped out a message.

Hailey lay on the bed, lit a cigarette and waited, trying to ignore the rhythmic waves of pain flooding his brain. He knew what would be happening. The communications officer would deliver the message to Zeller. Zeller—and Tristan, if he was there—would consider its implications, then Zeller would dictate an answer to the communications officer who would rush it back to the telex room for transmission.

The answer came ten minutes later, just as Hailey lit his second cigarette. He walked unsteadily from the bed to the table and watched the flashing keys as they clacked out their message, inscribing it on the fresh, white paper. When the machine was silent, Hailey ripped the paper from the machine.

The message read:

RECTIFY INCOMPETENCE. ELIMINATE BOTH PROBLEMS.

Hailey crumpled the message into a ball, tore off the used piece of coding tape and walked slowly into the kitchen alcove. With his cigarette lighter he lit the message and the tape, dropped them into the sink, waited until they had burned and flushed the ashes down the drain.

Then he lay down on the bed, stared at the ceiling and listened to the demons in his head as they waged a battle he was sure would destroy his sanity.

PART THREE

"We found this in the Paris apartment," Quinn said. He took the length of tape from an envelope and handed it to Johnny James. "We found it jammed under a portable telex machine. Can we make a print-out from it?"

"If it's in good enough condition, yes." Johnny examined the coding holes. "Seems alright. I'll run it through our machine. It may contain something useful."

"If it doesn't," Teal said, "we've reached the end of the line."

Quinn and Teal had gone straight to Johnny James's City office the morning after their arrival from Paris. Quinn outlined to Johnny everything that had happened since he'd received Teal's message to return to Spain. Everything except Block's death; he'd skipped that, saying that Block had escaped after questioning. Johnny's response to the lie had been a raised eyebrow and the faintest of smiles. Johnny James was no fool.

Johnny called his secretary, gave her the length of tape and asked her to run it through the investigation department's telex.

"Later," he said, "I'll run a check through our files and see if Block's name has cropped up before." He paused, lit a cigarette. "Anything else?"

"Nothing," Teal said. "Well, a couple more names. Guess they can't mean much at this stage."

"What names?" James asked.

Quinn dug into his shirt pocket for the hundred dollar bill on which he'd scribbled the names and the Paris address while Teal had interrogated Block in the farmhouse. He passed it to James.

"Expensive scratchpad," James said as he unfolded the

139

note. He scanned Quinn's scribble, then pursed his lips. He stubbed out his cigarette and leaned back in his chair. "Zeller," he said softly. "Block worked for *Zeller*!"

"You know him?" Quinn demanded.

"Know *of* him, old chap, know *of* him. You say Block escaped?"

Quinn nodded.

"I'd give my eye teeth to chat with him for half an hour."

"Who is Zeller?" Quinn asked.

Johnny James dropped the hundred dollar bill on the desk, stood, stretched, and walked to his window. He looked down on the street below. "Zeller is a mystery man," he said. "Zeller is an arms dealer." He turned to face them, leaning against the window frame, his hands pushed deep into his pockets. "You chaps are risking your necks, you know that?"

Quinn and Teal glanced at each other but said nothing.

Johnny nodded his head and smiled. "Laconic Yankees, eh? Well, I'm with you all the way, and I'll help however I can, both personally and in my capacity as an officer of Marine Insurance. But don't ever underestimate the danger of what you're doing."

He walked to his chair and sat down again. "We know Zeller deals in arms. We've suspected his involvement in organized yacht-jacking. But until you linked his name with Block we never had any proof."

James sighed, lifted his hands off the desk then let them come gently to rest again. "We *still* don't have any proof. Block is the first person I've heard of to directly admit his connection with Zeller. And you say Block has 'disappeared'— if that's the euphemism we've agreed upon."

Johnny lit a cigarette and inhaled deeply. "I first heard of Zeller two years ago at a conference in Rome. A few of us investigators and security chappies attended as a private police force to protect the nobs. Naturally we chatted about cases we'd been involved in."

Johnny picked up the hundred dollar bill and briefly examined it as if reassuring himself that Zeller's name was still there. "One Italian chap, name of Ferracuti, was investigating a half million pound claim against his company for a burned out toy factory. The police had proof the fire had been started with a plastic explosives bomb."

"A toy factory bombed?" Quinn asked. "Why?"

"Ah, well," Johnny smiled. "People think insurance companies are fair game, don't they? This particular company was verging on bankruptcy. The owner had liquidated machinery and supplies and decided he could turn financial disaster into quick profit by burning the factory and claiming insurance. Ferracuti decided the factory owner had used the bomb to make it look like an outside job. A fraud was involved. But to find enough evidence to bring the man to court, the police and the insurance company needed hard facts—like where he'd bought the explosives."

Johnny stubbed his cigarette. "As it happens, Ferracuti never found out and the toy manufacturer was never charged. But during his inquiries Ferracuti went underground and discovered horrifying facts about the availability of weapons in Italy. Money buys you anything over there, including land-mines and heavy machine guns. They're all available from criminal sources.

"Ferracuti decided to see exactly how the buying chain worked from a customer's point of view, and dropped the word in a certain bar in the Trastevere that he was in the market for an automatic pistol. Within an hour he was taken to see a local hoodlum, called Rossi, who laid out a dozen brand new automatics for him on a kitchen table. Ferracuti picked himself a .32 HSc Mauser, and paid the equivalent of two hundred pounds sterling for the gun and twenty cartridges.

"As a matter of course, Ferracuti phoned Mauser in Germany and found the gun had been sold, along with forty-nine other HScs plus one hundred Mauser Parabellums, to an American sporting arms importer. The importer bought them personally, while on holiday, and had them shipped aboard his own personal yacht which was lying in Bremen harbor."

Johnny James glanced first at Quinn, then at Teal, as if to emphasize what he would say next.

"That yacht was never seen again, nor the arms dealer, nor his crew. The family subsequently claimed successfully against an American insurance company and this fact was in Ferracuti's files.

"About a week after buying the Mauser, Ferracuti met Rossi again, in a bar, and bought him a drink. Ferracuti said he had thirty or forty million *lira* to invest and he wouldn't mind working with a man like Rossi. Rossi took the bait. The problem with his business, he said, was that he didn't have cash to break into the bigtime. There was big money to be made selling weapons in Rome, but his profit margins were cut because he had to buy from middlemen. But if he could buy from source and be a middleman himself, then fortunes were to be made. With forty million *lira*, some twenty-five or thirty thousand pounds, he could buy from source.

"And where was source? Ferracuti asked. Rossi explained that there were several, but the source with the best and most up-to-date weapons, the source which he knew had supplied his middleman with the Mauser that Ferracuti had bought, was a man called Zeller!"

Quinn sat forward in his chair. "And Zeller could only have got those Mausers from the American's yacht."

James shrugged. "Zeller could have got them from someone else who stole them from the American yacht. But after what Block told you about running weapons from Morocco to Spain, I think that would be giving Mr. Zeller too much benefit of the doubt."

"Did Ferracuti find out anything more?" Teal asked.

"No," Johnny James said. "Two days after talking with Rossi, he was shot dead in the Via del Condotti, in broad daylight, on his way to work."

"And Rossi?"

"Rossi was found a week later. In the Tiber. His hands had been cut off and his tongue cut out. He died very slowly." He paused, traced a finger on his desk. "Not to labor the point, chaps, but I repeat my warning about you risking your necks. These people play rough and they know what's happening within their area of interest. Zeller—or someone—obviously discovered within hours that Rossi had talked with Ferracuti and had Ferracuti followed to establish exactly who he was. When they discovered he was an insurance investigator he was executed." Johnny chopped his hand through the air. "Just like that! Then Rossi was picked up and tortured to death, either to squeeze extra information out of him, or simply as a warning to other small-time hoods to take care whom they associate with."

Johnny was interrupted by his secretary, who knocked on the half open door and walked straight in. "I've got the print-out, Mr. James, but it doesn't seem to make much sense." She handed James the length of yellow tape and a sheet of white print-out paper and left the office.

Johnny glanced at the print-out, shook his head and handed it to Quinn. "What do you make of that?"

Quinn read the print-out twice and frowned. It made no sense at all. He showed it to Teal, who handed it back to Johnny James.

The message read:

ESRAM	DELLI	POPMU	CSEDR
DACSA	OWTSE	ASLLA	
SSSEL	OW		

"Great help," Quinn said.

"Cypher-text," James explained.

"Any way of making sense of it?" Teal asked.

"Depends how complicated the code is," James said. "If it's difficult, I wouldn't fancy your chances because there isn't much text to analyze. But I have an old friend who owes me a favor or two. He worked in an army cryptology office before he became a copper. I'll let him see this."

James slipped open a drawer in his desk and rummaged around. He found a paper covered book and started flipping its pages. "In the meantime we can check the call-up numbers in the Telex Directory. They *can't* be in code."

He was less than two minutes finding both references. "Here we are," James said. "The message was sent from 998137, Trans-Europe Trading, 3 Rue Plisson, Paris. It was sent to 8619580, Trans-Europe Trading, Via dei Mille, Rome." He scribbled both addresses on a scrap of paper. "I'll have out people in Paris and Rome check the business registry offices. At least we'll find out who the front men are at these addresses."

Quinn grunted his thanks, then fidgeted in his seat and leaned forward. "What more can you tell us about Zeller?"

James hesitated. "Quite a bit," he said, "but nothing else first hand." He paused again. "There's a man, a chap named Sanderson. I've talked to him about Zeller several times. He's had a file open on Zeller since 1972. I think you should meet him."

"He's been investigating Zeller?"

Johnny nodded.

"Why?"

"I'd prefer it if he told you."

"Who is Sanderson?" Teal asked.

"A colonel. They call him 'Red.' Colonel Red Sanderson."

Quinn knew the name. It was buried somewhere in the back of his mind. A name he'd heard before. A face? A face he'd seen on TV, in magazines? Then he remembered.

"Sanderson," he said. "The mercenary!"

"Yes," Johnny said. "That's him."

"How the hell does a mercenary fit into this?"

"Do you want to meet him?" Johnny reached for the phone.

"Of course. But why is a man like Colonel Red Sanderson interested in Zeller?"

Johnny dialed the number. While he waited for Sanderson to answer his phone he looked at Quinn and said, "Because he wants to kill Zeller."

At 5:45 p.m., Quinn paid off his cab at the Muswell Hill roundabout and walked through the typical suburban London shopping center in the direction of Colonel Red Sanderson's house in Roberts Road.

The Colonel had refused to see both Quinn and Teal together. James explained that two attempts had been made against Sanderson's life in the last three years. The Colonel didn't know who had made them. The attempts had turned him into an ultra-cautious man.

While Teal stayed with James to help him prepare the final report on the loss of *Destry*, Quinn had taxied to the *Daily Telegraph* offices in Fleet Street and, with the introduction of one of Johnny's journalist friends, gained access to the newspaper's huge research and clippings library where he drew out their file on Sanderson.

Now, as he walked toward the Colonel's house, shoulders hunched and hands deep in his pockets against the biting cold of London's winter, he reviewed what he had learned.

The two inch thick file had contained hundreds of articles in half a dozen languages from a score of countries. Quinn concentrated on two long biographical pieces from the *Daily Telegraph* and *The New York Times*.

The Colonel had been born in London in 1924, the son of a seamstress and a coal merchant. The inauspicious beginning hadn't stopped him entering Officer School and emerging in 1942 as a Second Lieutenant of infantry. In his first action at the first battle of El Alamein in July that year he earned a Mention in Despatches for risking his life to save a wounded platoon sergeant. In October, at the second battle of Alamein, he won a Military Cross after leading his men against a machine-gun post. He also won his Lieutenancy. By the end of the war he was a Captain.

In 1950, after a stint with the occupation forces in Germany, Sanderson was in action again, this time in Korea, and no sooner was the armistice signed at Panmunjon than the now twenty-nine year old Major volunteered for his third war, the operation against communist insurgents in the jungles of Malaya.

In 1957, after three years of jungle patrols and more decorations, Sanderson earned his promotion to Colonel. But at the end of his tour of duty he resigned his commission, an act which surprised his superiors who had him ear-marked as a career man who would go far. Sanderson knew what he wanted to do. During the next three years he used his Army back-pay to help support himself while he indulged in the interest which had consumed his off-duty hours during his five years of inactivity in Germany during the occupation: military scholarship.

The result of his labors was a 600-page manual called *Counter-Insurgency Technique on the Third World Battlefront*. The British used it in the Middle East, the Americans in

Vietnam, the French in North Africa, the Belgians in the Congo.

But it was the second part of the *Telegraph* article which had fascinated Quinn. It had been sub-headed *The White Knight Commando*.

After the publication of his book in 1961, Sanderson met an Israeli girl in London and married her. Together, they went to live in Israel. The newspaper articles were vague about his activities during the next three years, though the *Daily Telegraph* hinted at reliable but unsubstantiated evidence linking him with MOSSAD.

Then, in 1964, for no understandable reason, Sanderson flew to South Africa and enlisted with one of the foreign mercenary commandos hired by Tshombe in his effort to put backbone into his government forces and conclude the debilitating Congo Civil War. *The New York Times* reported that his action was inexplicable to all who knew him. He had left a wife with whom he was apparently deeply in love, and his two year old daughter, Lena, to fight in one of the dirtiest wars to ever scar humanity's history. The *Telegraph* suggested he had enlisted to escape his involvement with MOSSAD. Whatever his reasons, it was at the relief of Stanleyville that Sanderson earned his name as *The White Knight Commando*, the name upon which scores of newspapers and magazines worldwide had hung tens of thousands of words.

In Stanleyville, rebels held two thousand white hostages whom they threatened to kill if government forces approached the city. In a controversial tactic, Belgian troops parachuted into Stanleyville from U.S. Army Air Force planes while government and white mercenary columns force-marched against the city. The rebels slaughtered over fifty hostages before the Belgians were able to fight their way through and rescue the rest, and during their advance and in vicious street by street fighting, government forces killed more than six hundred rebels. Then the city was looted, women raped, men tortured, children nailed to shop doors, rebel officials disemboweled. Before government army leaders could restore order, their men had murdered eight hundred innocent civilians and pillaged every shop in the city center which contained anything remotely valuable.

That night, as order was slowly restored, rebel units in the European center and the three Congolese suburbs were rounded up and trucked to the city stadium where they faced a jury of twenty thousand Stanleyville citizens. Each rebel was presented to the mob on a flood-lit platform. If the mob acclaimed him he was set free; if they jeered, he was dragged away and executed. No one knew how many rebels were shot that night; few were spared.

At three o'clock in the morning of that long night, Sanderson was woken by his Sergeant and told that he and five men had been ordered to drive a truck to a farmhouse twenty miles outside Stanleyville where rebels were thought to hold five Belgian nuns, taken there from the Isangi Mission. A strong mercenary force had already set out to rescue the rest of the Isangi missionaries ninety miles from the city.

Sanderson's taskforce located the farmhouse an hour after dawn. Apart from his Sergeant and four soldiers he had with him a young freelance newspaper photographer, an Australian named Burlington, who hounded Sanderson for permission to accompany him as they loaded the truck with weapons and ammunition, medical supplies, food and spare gasoline cans.

Sanderson concealed the truck three hundred yards away, fanned out his men and advanced on the farmhouse by foot. Burlington snapped photographs all the way, and continued photographing when they walked into an ambush a hundred yards from the farm. Three men died instantly in the deadly crossfire, a fourth was wounded in the arm and a grenade shattered the Sergeant's right foot.

Sanderson didn't hesitate. Followed by Burlington and the wounded soldier, he zig-zagged for the truck. A hundred yards away, the soldier took a burst in the back which somersaulted him forward, and tore out his chest. Fifty yards away a bullet nicked Burlington's shoulder. Sanderson grabbed at him as he stumbled, kept him on his feet, half dragging him to the truck. Once in the cabin, he thrust his FN rifle at him and yelled at him to fire for his life. Sanderson rammed the truck into gear and in a display of sheer, fanatical courage drove straight through the advancing ambushers and into the farmhouse compound. Racing the huge truck in a circle around the compound, Sanderson smashed three rebels beneath the wheels and killed another two with a grenade while Burlington shot two more.

Three of the nuns still lived. All had been raped. The two dead had been tortured, their breasts hacked off. While the ambushers were advancing cautiously across the scrubby ground in front of the farm, Burlington photographed the carnage in the room.

With the three surviving nuns lying on the truck tray, safe behind its steel sides, Sanderson ordered Burlington to drive straight through the advancing rebels and stop by the wounded Sergeant. Burlington did as he was told, trying to ignore the whine of bullets richocheting off the truck's body work, praying that no stray bullet would hit the engine, disabling them, or worse, hit him or Sanderson. The Sergeant was dead when they reached him, hacked to pieces by the rebels when they'd found him wounded in the grass.

Safely back in Stanleyville, Burlington followed Sanderson's directions and drove to a building near Lumumba Square being used as an emergency hospital. It was here, as the Colonel helped one of the nuns off the truck, that Burlington took the picture of Sanderson that earned him his name, *The White Knight Commando*.

As he walked along the quiet suburban streets, Quinn could see the picture in his mind's eye. It had been printed over four columns in the *Telegraph*. The tall blood-stained Colonel, his left arm supporting the weeping nun with her clothes torn half from her and her hands shielding her face in shame, his right brandishing his FN rifle, his face a mask of fury as he shouted at someone to help him. It was the stuff of legends, and Burlington had helped create the legend. For millions of people around the world, that photograph still defined the terrors of war in Africa.

Quinn turned into Roberts Road and checked the numbers. Sanderson's house stood at the other end, a good half mile along. He wondered just what this man would be like, this strange man who thrived on war and disaster and who understood the dark side of human nature so well he could write books about it for the guidance of others. There'd been three more books. The most famous of them even Quinn had heard about, *Contained Action Against Urban Terrorism*, a handbook used by security forces throughout the Western World.

After the Congo, Sanderson had set up as a freelance, moving to neighboring Angola with a team of specialists charged with search and destroy missions against guerrilla bases over the border within Congolese territory. And after Angola his dangerous trade took him on a nightmare tour of the 20th century with terrifying whistle-stops in Vietnam, Central America and the Lebanon. In thirty years, Sanderson fought in eight wars seeing, by choice, the very worst that man could conjure against himself.

But there was worse to come. In 1972, Red Army guerrillas slaughtered his Israeli wife during their attack at Lod Airport. That year Sanderson finally came home from the wars, to bury his wife and take his young daughter, Lena, away from the Middle East, and back to his native land, unseen, except for fleeting visits, for over ten years. *"The White Knight Commando,"* one of the articles concluded, *"has finally said a farewell to arms."*

It was dark now, the wind blowing, leaves on the plane trees rustling, the street lights glowing with halos in the faintly misty air. A woman carrying a bulging shopping bag walked briskly towards Quinn, pushed open a garden gate and walked up the path to the entrance of her house. Inside, a soft light lit a front room window. The occasional car slipped by him and parked among rows of other cars in the streets, their drivers hurrying from vehicle to house. Quinn watched the rhythms of normality as he walked, and experienced a sadness which lingered on the periphery of his consciousness.

Quinn pushed open the gate of Sanderson's house and walked through the apron-sized front garden to the door. The house looked identical to all others in Roberts Road, red brick, double-storyed and with a high gabled slate roof. Quinn rapped a brass door knocker shaped like a dolphin, and waited.

He heard voices inside, a woman's and a man's, then a door closing and approaching footsteps. A silhouette appeared through the leaded stained-glass of the front door and he heard the rattle of a safety chain being released.

"Can I help you?"

Quinn's mind, full of the information he'd read at the library, registered who she was before he really saw her. Lena. It had to be Lena.

"I have an appointment with Colonel Sanderson," he said.

She nodded and stepped back for him to enter, and only when he stood inside as she closed the door did he realize what a stunningly beautiful young woman she was. Tall and lithely strong, gracious, almost catlike the way she moved. She was faintly olive-skinned—her mother's blood, Quinn thought— her long black hair, her dark eyes, her cheekbones full and high, signaling her part membership of the Middle Eastern races.

She smiled. "What's your name?" she asked.

"Quinn. Peter Quinn."

"Of course, My father mentioned you were coming. I'm Lena Sanderson." She held out her hand, and Quinn shook it, surprised at the strength of her grip. "Would you like to wait in here?"

Quinn followed her to a sitting room on the left of the small entrance hall. She stood aside and ushered him in.

"Make yourself comfortable. I'll call my father."

She closed the door behind her, leaving Quinn alone. Quinn pushed his hands into his pockets and glanced around the room. Nothing in it hinted at the Colonel's profession: comfortable settee and two armchairs, a telephone on a coffee table, an old pine dresser displaying half a dozen antique plates, and a bookcase. Quinn walked to the bookcase and scanned the titles it held. Hardbacked popular novels from a book club, a handful of cooking books, back issues of *The National Geographic*. Two prints in fancy gilt frames, a Monet and a Pissaro, decorated the walls. It unreasonably crossed Quinn's mind that he had come to the wrong house, that he'd unwittingly entered the safe, comfortable home of a bank manager or a supermarket director.

"Who are you?"

Quinn turned from the bookcase towards the deep, well-modulated voice. It came from a tall, wide-shouldered, slightly stooped man wearing carpet slippers, baggy cords and a thick, handknitted cardigan open all the way down to reveal an incongruously bright red shirt. The man stood at the door with his hands behind his back and his feet slightly apart, the army's "at ease" position. But it was Sanderson's face that made Quinn hesitate a moment before answering. The face that stared out of the newspaper articles had been young, dashingly handsome, a face to fit the image. This face was ravaged beyond the Colonel's years, savaged by time and experience, wrecked and recreated by plastic surgery. Both of his cheeks, Quinn saw, were cross-hatched with scars which disappeared into the unnatural smoothness of a plastic surgeon's handi-work. Another scar ploughed its way from above one shaggy eyebrow to disappear into the remains of the ruddy hair which had earned Sanderson the nickname "Red." But the face remained strong, retained vestiges of a classic profile, with deep blue eyes computing unerringly the movements of the young man they saw before them.

"My name's Quinn. Johnny James from Marine Insurance arranged for me to see you." Quinn hesitated, unsure of himself, sensing a calm hostility in Sanderson's attitude. "I believe he spoke to you about me . . ."

"We'll see."

"I beg your pardon?"

"I said, We'll see. We'll *see* if you are Peter Quinn or not."

Sanderson took his arms from behind his back. His right hand held a Colt .45 automatic which he pointed at Quinn.

Quinn's hands started out of his pockets. "Look . . . !"

Sanderson raised the automatic a fraction. "Hands back in pockets, please. We'll only be a moment. Turn around. Feet eighteen inches from the wall. Open your legs wide. Rest your forehead against the wall. Put your weight on your forehead."

"For Christ's sake . . ."

"Do it."

"What the fuck is this?"

"It'll only take a moment."

Quinn turned, did as he was told, feeling the blood pulsing through his forehead as he stretched out, balancing against the wall. Strangely, he felt no fear, experienced only an over-whelming feeling of ridiculousness at his contorted, painful position. He felt Sanderson's hands running up his legs, brushing his crotch, patting his back and shoulders, then each of his pockets.

"Nearly done," Sanderson said softly. "Nearly done. Excuse me one moment while I check your wallet."

Quinn felt Sanderson slip his wallet from inside his jacket pocket and heard the soft shuffle of his slippers on the carpet as he backed away.

"Stay exactly like that, please. Just a moment more. Let's see. International driving license, security card. Names match. Good. At least that's something. Relax now, please, but keep your hands in your pockets. Turn around and face me, but keep your hands in your pockets and spread your legs three feet apart."

Quinn did as he was told, realizing the impossibility of even beginning to move quickly from the position he'd been ordered to hold. Sanderson sat on an easy chair with the wallet open and its contents spread on the coffee table. He took the phone off the rocker, laid it beside the wallet and dialed a number. The automatic pointed directly at Quinn's chest.

Sanderson held the receiver to his ear and waited patiently.

"Johnny? Sanderson. My visitor has arrived. He would appear to be Mr. Quinn. Would you be so kind as to describe the physical appearance of the Mr. Quinn you know?"

Sanderson listened, nodding, running his eyes over Quinn. Then, "Thanks," he said, and replaced the receiver. He stood, walked over to Quinn, the gun still in his hand, reached up and brushed back the hair from Quinn's forehead, revealing the bruises, now yellowing, which Block had inflicted on him during the death fight in the farmhouse.

"Your friend Teal was with James. He mentioned the bruising. Sorry to put you through that, Mr. Quinn. It was necessary." He slid the Colt behind some volumes in the bookcase and held out his hand.

Quinn relaxed, letting out a long breath, and shook the Colonel's hand. "Do you do that to all your guests?" he asked.

"All the ones I don't know personally. I don't encourage visitors. I have a reputation in the street for being a crochety old bastard. Neighbors *never* drop by to borrow a cup of sugar." He turned to the door. "Lena?"

Lena came through the door from the entrance hall. Quinn's eyes widened, then he smiled and shook his head. Lena, too, held a Colt automatic, the black gun seeming huge in her tiny white fist.

"She knows how to use it," Sanderson said. "Most kids brought up on a *kibbutz* do. Lena, darling, would you make coffee? We'll take it in the study."

Lena nodded and walked ahead of them toward the kitchen. As Sanderson led the way toward the back of the house to his room, Quinn glanced into the kitchen and saw Lena slip the automatic into a cupboard behind an earthenware pot with the word *Flour* blazoned across it. She caught Quinn's look, smiled sheepishly, and Quinn found himself returning the smile as he followed the Colonel down the short passageway.

The small room, no more than twelve feet by twelve, contained a desk, two chairs, a filing cabinet and upwards of two thousand books. One whole wall of shelving bulged with books; books lay piled atop the filing cabinet; a column of books rose behind the door from the floor half way to the ceiling; stacks of books two and three feet high offered a tottering obstacle course between the door and the desk which itself was covered with sheaths of newspaper and magazine clippings and more books. Even the small portable typewriter which sat on a moveable stand beside the desk played host to another half dozen books. The busy, untidy workroom offered a nearly humorous contrast to the prim, suburban neatness of the front sitting room. It offered no suggestion that the man who worked there managed a bank or a supermarket.

"Quite a mess, eh?" Sanderson said. He waved an arm about the room. "This is probably the best library, on military history in Britain. Not the biggest, but the best." Sanderson indicated that Quinn should take the chair in front of the desk, then rolled out the bottom drawer of the filing cabinet. "Whisky suit you?"

Quinn nodded and scanned the desk as Sanderson poured out generous measures of Scotch. Among the piles of newspapers and clippings he saw a folder stacked with manuscript pages. He ran his fingers over it. Momentarily, he remembered those frustrating, but uncomplicated days when he'd worked on his business doctorate.

"The latest one," Sanderson said, handing him a glass. "At a standstill, I'm afraid." He chuckled. "Even pedantic old military historians suffer from writer's block."

Sanderson settled into the comfortable swivel chair behind his desk, leaned back, sipped his whisky and talked about his books. Quinn studied him, trying to relate the stories of violence and war he'd read, and his reception at gunpoint moments ago, with this quiet, well-mannered man who exuded a professorial air and the implication that he'd led a life devoted to scholarship and research. He wondered how many men in the last forty years had underrated Sanderson and paid for their stupidity with their lives.

"You're the only writer I've ever met," Quinn said, "who practices what he preaches."

Sanderson's look told Quinn he didn't find the remark amusing. "Less and less. War is a young man's business, Quinn. I'm fifty-eight. You don't fight battles at my age, except from the safety of an operations room. The odd brief engagement, perhaps, if it's worthwhile."

"Worthwhile?"

The deep, blue eyes riveted onto Quinn's face. "I've never fought a war, or supported a cause I didn't believe in, Quinn. I don't kill for fun. I wouldn't find that becoming."

Quinn felt himself flush and wrenched his brain to find an answer which would cover his idiocy in assuming that this man fitted any preconceived conclusions he'd reached about a mercenary's motives.

Sanderson waved a finger as if to cancel Quinn's embarrassment. "Don't worry about it. No reason why you should think differently of mercenaries than anyone else. For centuries we've been ready made villains and scapegoats and, I might add, rarely unemployed. Yet the same societies which hire us, condemn us when we've helped them win their cause. For some reason a different morality is applied to professionals who choose their own wars than to regular soldiers who blithely follow their country's politics whether they believe in them or not. And if you say the mercenary most likely fights for money and not for ideals, well, I'll answer that most likely a soldier fighting under his own flag also fights for money. Most certainly don't fight for patriotic motives. In Vietnam, for instance, I saw few allied troops fighting for any cause they could define. Most fought to survive after being press-ganged into service by their governments."

Sanderson lit a cigarette and blew smoke toward the high ceiling. "Society has used mercenaries since the earliest days of organized warfare and condemned them just as long. The Greek writers refer to mercenaries, the Byzantines hired Spanish mercenaries during the fourteenth century, and during the fifteenth century Europe's nobility was delighted to buy the services of any professional soldier who would wield a sword or fire a musket for them. In the eighteenth century Frederick the Great's Prussian army was fifty percent foreign, and Britain had no compunction about using Hessian mercenaries to try and halt the American Revolution. For that matter you Americans didn't hesitate to hire Indians to fight the British and the Hessians."

Sanderson spread his hands and smiled and Quinn saw how the light reflected from the shiny patches of plastic surgery on his cheeks. "It goes on and on. Fully two-thirds of Wellington's 67,000 troops at Waterloo were employed foreigners; mercenaries, including Americans, fought on both sides during the Spanish Civil War; mercenaries fought for Chiang Kai-shek in 1937; they've fought in the Congo, in Angola, in Vietnam and just about any other area of conflict you care to name. And let's not forget the most famous mercenary force in history, the French Foreign Legion, most of them foreigners employed to fight under the French flag. Luckily for the French, the Legion has been sufficiently romanticized in story and film to escape moral judgment by the world at large."

Sanderson stood, stretched and walked to the double French

doors which led out to a small patio and back garden. "Anyway, Mr. Quinn, as you know, that is what I am, a mercenary. A man who fights for money. You are not required to believe that I have ever lifted a weapon out of sheer moral outrage or any sense of idealism, misconstrued or otherwise." He turned from the window. "Johnny James told me that you are interested in Zeller. What do you know about him?"

For a moment the sudden change in the course of conversation threw Quinn, then he, too, stood and began pacing the room with a contained restless energy and for the fifth or sixth time since it had happened related the sequence of events which had shattered the framework of his life. A moment after he began speaking, Lena walked quietly into the room, placed the coffee tray on top of papers on the desk, then sat in her father's chair and listened intently as Quinn unfolded his tale of death, disaster and detection.

"And this Block mentioned Zeller's name?"

"Yes."

"You're not mistaken about that?"

"I wrote it down as he said it." Quinn showed Sanderson and Lena the hundred dollar bill.

Sanderson nodded. "And you want Zeller?"

"Yes."

"How badly?"

"I want him," Quinn said. "I want him dead."

"I thought you wanted Block and this golden haired fellow."

"I got Block and I still want the other one. But I want Zeller, because ultimately Zeller is responsible for everything that happened. Him and this Tristan."

Lena poured coffee for Quinn and Sanderson. Sanderson took his cup and turned to stare out the window into the darkness again.

"Johnny told me you have a file on Zeller," Quinn said, "but he wouldn't tell me why. Said he preferred you to tell me. Who is Zeller? Why would you have a file on him?"

Sanderson didn't answer, but stood rock-like, staring into the blackness beyond the window.

Then Lena spoke, softly, privately, directly to Quinn, as if sparing her father the telling. "Zeller," she said, "killed my father's wife, my mother. Not directly, any more than he directly killed your fiancée. Zeller didn't pull any triggers, but he killed my mother."

Lena paused, her dark eyes hesitating between her father's immobile figure and Quinn's questioning face. "I was with my mother when it happened," she said. "I was twelve years old. It was in May 1972, in Lod airport, when the Japanese Red Army attacked."

Her eyes met his, questioning, gauging whether or not Quinn understood the significance of the date and the place. Quinn averted his eyes. He knew. He'd read about it that same afternoon. "But Zeller," he asked softly. "How does Zeller fit into all this?"

Sanderson turned from the window. He walked over, put his whisky glass on the desk and stood behind Lena, his hands resting gently on her shoulders. "I had friends in the Mossad who kept me in touch with the Israeli investigation into the attack. They discovered that Zeller supplied the weapons used by the Japanese Red Army terrorists.

"At the time, that didn't interest me. My first reaction, and that of Mossad, was to go after the Red Army. In fact we did. I accompanied an Israeli commando unit on a raid into the Lebanon where we attacked a PLO camp, destroyed a weapons dump, killed half a dozen *fedayin* and three Japanese terrorists who we knew were planning another raid, this time against a primary school in one of the border *kibbutzim*.

"For a while I felt as if I'd taken my revenge, but during the following years as I worked on my books, and researched terrorism and counter-terrorism, using information gathered from security men in Mediterranean and northern African countries, I found Zeller's name cropping up regularly as one of the main suppliers of weapons to terrorist groups—but not only to terrorists. This man will sell anything to anyone in any quantity. Ten automatic weapons to a terrorist commando, a single pistol to a thief, a complete inventory of handguns, rifles, machine guns, mortars, grenades and tens of thousands of round of ammunition to a company sized invasion force. It's all the same to Zeller."

"And now you want to kill Zeller."

Sanderson nodded. "Eradicate is the word. I want to eradicate him." Sanderson squeezed Lena's shoulders affectionately, moved away from behind her and leaned against the window frame. "Zeller is an animal. A man who lives off death and suffering. He's amoral. A predator preying off a confused world; a man offering allegiance to no one and nothing except the bottom line of his accounts book."

Sanderson folded his arms and Quinn noted the bulge of muscle under the old cardigan. Even as he approached his sixtieth year, a time when most men are well on their way into physical decline, Sanderson remained strong. His physical fitness, coupled with a sharp, analytical military mind honed during forty years of theoretical and practical application of warfare, added up to a formidable opponent for any man he chose to move against.

"The easiest way to understand Zeller," Sanderson said, "is if I tell you a story. You know there have been several attempts to invade Libya and overthrow Colonel Qadhafi. The most recent—one not reported in the press—occurred in 1975. A group of businessmen and politicians within Libya bankrolled two hundred and fifty mercenaries to land on the Libyan coastline, create a diversion, and march towards Tripoli while a force of insurgents within the city moved against key installations. I don't know what chance of success the revolution had, but that is beside the point. The mercenary commander, a Frenchman, bought his weapons from Zeller's organization. He paid over a quarter of a million dollars cash for them.

"Somehow, during the negotiations, Zeller's operatives concluded how the weapons would be used. Zeller betrayed the insurgent leaders to the Libyan government and they were rounded up and tortured until they revealed complete details of the coup attempt. So, when the mercenaries landed on the beaches they were slaughtered to a man in a prepared ambush. Very few of the insurgents escaped with their lives. Most were shot. The Libyans rewarded Zeller with half a million dollars in gold for his information."

Sanderson walked to his desk and splashed more whisky into his and Quinn's glasses. "That's the sort of man we're dealing with," he said. "A man who works only for reward. A man who betrays his own clients, even when the betrayal means their certain death." He turned and stared out the window into the darkness. In the distance, the orange glow of millions of city and suburban lights reflected from low clouds.

Quinn glanced at Lena, catching her staring at him, gauging his reaction to her father's story. She acknowledged his glance with a half smile and, again, he found himself returning the smile. For a moment he couldn't take his eyes from her, from the pure, clean beauty of that Mediterranean face with its cascading frame of long black hair.

"You might think me a strange old man," Sanderson said, without turning from his vigil at the window. "You might find my motives confused. You might consider it unusual that I have *grown* to hate the man involved in my wife's death. But I'm a complicated chap, Mr. Quinn. My initial reaction was to move against the Japanese Red Army, which I did—that was my revenge. When I found out about Zeller's involvement, I didn't think too much about it. Another weapons dealer. So what? I've met many weapons dealers. They're not necessarily bad men. As a group they're no worse than grocers or any other traders. I grew to hate Zeller much later when I discovered his attitude to his fellow man, his propensity for betrayal for mere cash. That is unforgivable.

"Zeller is responsible for the deaths of friends of mine; some were tortured to death because of him. And, yes, he sold the weapons which murdered my wife. But that's not why I want to kill him. I want him dead because he doesn't deserve to live." Sanderson turned to face Quinn. "Excuse me if I don't make much sense."

"I don't understand why someone else hasn't killed him," Quinn said. "The Israelis for instance."

Sanderson shrugged. "Why should they? He supplies weapons to their enemies, but no doubt he supplies weapons to their operatives in various parts of the world, too. To the Israelis, one weapons dealer more or less is of no importance. If Zeller doesn't sell weapons to the PLO, someone else will. And if the Israelis can occasionally use Zeller for their own purposes, why should they move against him?"

"And the police?"

"You answered that question yourself when you told me about police reaction to Block and his friend. There's not much the police can do when a crime occurs outside their jurisdiction and, as in Zeller's case, not much they can do when a criminal resides beyond their borders."

Quinn frowned. "I don't understand."

"Zeller is your modern day version of the flying Dutchman. He lives on a boat called *Shadow*. He's condemned himself to international waters the rest of his life. He hasn't set foot on land since 1969, after a near successful attempt to kill him by a group of Corsicans he'd double crossed in some minor deal."

"I still don't quite see the problem."

"There are quite a few problems, old chap. The principal one is money."

"I have money."

Sanderson smiled for the first time since Quinn's arrival. A weary smile, a resigned smile, a smile which said he'd heard it all before. "Not a thousand pounds, Mr. Quinn, or even five. If ten's your limit, I'll offer you another drink, solicit your promise not to mention our conversation and send you on your way."

"How much?"

Sanderson walked to his desk, pulled a pad and pencil in front of him and scrawled a figure. "I don't know you Mr. Quinn, don't know who you are or what you're worth, so I don't hold you at a disadvantage. That's how much." He held up the pad so Quinn could see it.

"A hundred and seventy-five thousand pounds!"

"Let's call if four hundred thousand dollars American. Give or take ten or twenty percent."

"Four hundred thousand dollars!"

Sanderson nodded. "Now you know why no one's ever got him. I've had hundred thousand pound contracts, *two* hundred thousand pound contracts in my time, but they've been from governments. And as we've discussed, no government is interested in Zeller because even though he's a dirty, nasty bastard, he's useful on occasion, so they leave him alone as long as he doesn't tread on their toes, and he's too clever to do that. Quite a few individuals want Zeller—you'd be the fifth I know of—but none of them had one hundred and seventy-five thousand pounds to spare, or wanted him that badly.'' Sanderson paused. ''How about you, Mr. Quinn. Do you want Zeller that badly?''

''I want him that bad,'' Quinn said, and as he said it he saw Sanderson's eyebrows raising; questioningly, hopefully, almost desperately. ''But why so much?'' Quinn asked.

''I told you Zeller lived on a boat. That boat is escorted by two fast cruisers equipped with radar and missiles. On the three boats he controls a force of some thirty crewmen, all armed.''

Sanderson turned and stared into the night yet again. ''If you choose to go against Zeller, Mr. Quinn, you're committing yourself to fight a small-scale war. A lot of people will be killed. You must consider that before you make your final decision.''

''I take it you have an attack plan?''

''I've had it for a long time, Mr. Quinn.''

''And you want to lead the attack?''

Sanderson turned and looked directly at Quinn, his blue eyes, set like bright stones in the scarred face, cutting the distance between them. ''Oh yes, Mr. Quinn, I will lead the attack. It would make a fitting finale to my career.''

When Quinn left the study, the colonel still stared into the darkness, whisky glass firmly in hand. Quinn sensed a brimming tension about him and knew that the next twenty-four hours, during which he had agreed to make his decision, would be long ones for a man who had been living a dream of revenge for ten years.

Quinn decided to walk the half mile to Muswell Hill to find a taxi to take him back into the city. As he stepped into Sanderson's garden, into the heavy coldness of the suburban night, Lena slipped out behind him, pulling on a duffle coat.

''May I walk with you, Mr. Quinn?''

Quinn stood aside at the gate to allow her to pass. ''Call me Peter,'' he said.

She nodded. ''Peter.''

She pulled the coat more tightly around her and pushed her hands into the pockets. They walked half the first block without speaking. Quinn sensed she wanted to say something to him, but didn't prompt her.

Finally, she said, "Will you go through with this thing?"

"I think so. I want to."

"Why?"

Quinn stopped walking, forcing her to turn and face him. Gusts of wind rolled leaves down the street towards them. In the background the never-ceasing hum of London's traffic teased the periphery of their hearing.

"I'm surprised you ask," Quinn said softly. "I want revenge. It's an old-fashioned motive, but there you are."

"It's a poor motive."

Quinn stared at the beautiful face half concealed in shadow by the duffle-coat hood. "And your mother? Don't you feel the need to avenge her?"

"I felt anger, I was twelve years old and I felt anger. And frustration because there was nothing I could do to bring her back. But revenge won't bring her back either."

They turned and started walking again. Quinn, involuntarily and quite naturally, put his arm through hers. She didn't object.

"What are you trying to tell me?" Quinn asked.

She was silent for a long moment and Quinn listened to the sound of their footsteps on the pavement. Then she said, "I'm frightened for my father. He's obsessed with Zeller, with the idea of killing him, destroying his organization. Whatever he tells you, he wants to kill Zeller because of what happened to my mother. But my father is fifty-eight years old. Men that old don't *do* that sort of thing. And if you come up with the money, he'll go ahead."

"I realize that."

"If you don't, odds are he'll not get another chance."

"You're frightened of losing him."

"Desperately frightened."

"Don't underestimate your father. If I don't go ahead, he will. Somehow."

She sighed wearily, an admission that she knew he was right, that any argument to the contrary would be only a repetition of fashionable attitudes bearing no resemblance to life's emotional realities. "Revenge is a kind of wild justice" someone had written, and an Israeli, especially an Israeli, understood that.

At the Muswell Hill shopping center an empty red double-decker bus stood silently within the roundabout, a huge sentinel, eerie in the orange glow of night.

Quinn wished her good night.

She nodded. "Peter," she said, "if you go ahead, I'll understand."

"Thanks," he said. He squeezed her arm briefly and, seeing an approaching cab, stepped onto the road.

"Peter."

He turned and looked back at her. She'd removed the coat hood and pulled her long hair loose from behind the collar.

"I'm sorry about what happened," she said. "To Jenny."

She turned and Quinn watched her walk into the night, her outline a haunting shape appearing and disappearing among the shadows of the trees and the glowing pools cast by street lights.

Quinn rode in the taxi back into the city brooding on the events of the evening; on Sanderson and his plan and on Lena, the exquisite Lena, so beautiful, so petite, so sensitive. And he remembered her with the big .45 in her hand and realized she would have used it if she'd had to.

Hailey waited.

He waited on The Strand in front of the *Savoy Hotel*, his coat collar turned up against the cold, concealing much of his long, golden hair. He stared in shop windows, waiting, watching pedestrians who turned into the hotel, watching taxis arriving, watching people leave the taxis and walk into the lobby. He waited for Quinn and Teal, the two men from *Destry. Eliminate both problems*, that had been Zeller's order, and that was what he would do. The London operative had tracked them from the airport to the *Savoy* and now, when they appeared again, somehow they would be eliminated. Hailey would personally rectify the incompetence of that fool Block who hopefully was now dead and in hell shaking hands with Gloster. Two fools.

Hailey glanced at his watch. Eight fifty-five. Neither of them had appeared. But it was still early. He hoped they'd come singly. It'd be easier that way. Take one, then the other. Teal first. He was the tough one, the problem. But Quinn had surprised him on the boat. The way he'd moved so fast. Hailey wouldn't underestimate Quinn. He never underestimated anyone. Or anything. That was why he was still alive. Why he'd got out of Vietnam. Out of the stinking jungle. Survived the ambushes and the booby-trapped huts and the pits on the trails, the pits with sharpened bamboo that left men who fell into them screaming in agony if they weren't lucky enough to get a stake straight through the heart, or through the eye and into the brain, or through the neck so they bled to death quickly. And never underestimating anybody or anything was why he'd survived working for Zeller and Tristan, why he'd been able to kill and live. You had no second chances when you had a gun in your hand. You killed or you got killed. That was all. Not that the idea of dying worried Hailey. He wanted to live but he wasn't scared of dying. Tristan had fixed that for him. Living was so much easier when you had no fear of death. You could do things that . . . you could do things that . . . you could do things . . . you could do things that . . .

Hailey rubbed his forehead with his hand, rubbed hard as if trying to remove a stain. The pain throbbed behind his eyes again. Not too bad, but it was there. Not as bad as in Paris when it had actually made him vomit, but it was there again and if he wasn't creful it'd get bad and there'd be that . . . strange . . . that strange sense of . . . the feeling . . .

He breathed deeply and stamped his feet on the ground to keep his blood circulating. He started humming tunelessly, forcing himself to ignore the tiny aching burr building behind his eyes. He had a job to do and he owed it to Zeller and Tristan to get it done.

Hailey took a cigarette from his pocket and lit it with his gold lighter, then stood watching the *Savoy* with the cigarette between his lips and his hands deep in his pockets, his right hand caressing the warm butt of the revolver.

It'll be done soon enough, he told himself. Tonight or tomorrow or the next day, maybe next week. But soon it'd be done and then he could contact Tristan and ask him to fix things, a nice, quiet time in the dark and the warmth and

Tristan talking softly, soothingly, brushing away the pain and explaining everything, fixing everything so that his head felt better and he felt relaxed and ready to work again. Soon, maybe even tomorrow he could go.

The pain still picked at him.

A taxi stopped in front of the hotel. Instantly, Hailey was alert. He dropped the half smoked cigarette and ground it under his heel. He stared at the cab, saw a shadowy figure lean forward to pay the driver through the safety window. The door opened. A trim young woman wearing an expensive fur strode confidently towards the hotel door. Someone else on the street stepped straight into the cab and it pulled out into the still heavy traffic on the Strand.

Hailey lit another cigarette and tried to ignore the pain in his head, a tiny pinpoint of pain which jabbed like a red-hot needle and which he knew would expand, blossom like a flower, until the inside of his head was boiling, seared with agony.

Someone brushed against him. He turned. A middle-aged man muttered an apology. The man's wife, well-groomed, hopelessly unattractive, caught his eye and held it for half a second too long. A half second which gave her time to smile and offer a reflexive invitation. Hailey was used to that. Younger women liked him, older women adored him. Younger women told him about his hair. Older women spoke of his cold, cruel eyes. They liked those eyes and they liked the cruel things he did to them. The older ones weren't scared of him, only scared of their husbands seeing the marks on their bodies. For the older ones, who knew all about love and romance and flowers and champagne in bed, Hailey was a breath of fresh, dangerous air, a beautiful, intricate, perverted sexual fantasy come true.

Hailey drew on his cigarette and waited. He wasn't thinking of women, he was thinking of the pain, wondering if it would stay away long enough to allow him to do what had to be done. He had to return to Tristan soon, to Tristan and the beautiful, warm darkness. He should have returned to Tristan after what happened in Paris, but he had to do what Zeller wanted. Tristan had *told* him that. He *had* to do what Zeller wanted.

Hailey closed his eyes, squeezed them tight together, saw an explosion of red behind the lids and opened them again.

He saw Quinn.

Quinn paid the cab driver, walked into the hotel lobby and asked at the desk if there were any messages for him. The clerk handed him an envelope from his keyhole. It contained a message sheet typed by the hotel switchboard.

> *To: Mr. P. Quinn, Room 247. Mr. Teal called at 8:30 p.m. to say he would be with Mr. James until after midnight and that he will breakfast with you at 8 a.m.*

Quinn thanked the clerk, pushed the message into his pocket and walked out into the street. He glanced at his watch. Nine o'clock. Still time for a Chinese meal in Soho. It took him less than fifteen minutes to walk to Lisle Street with its line-up of Chinese restaurants. He wandered from window to window checking atmosphere and menu cards, then finally chose one and stepped into a carpeted interior out of the cold.

He never noticed the man with the golden hair who had tracked him the whole way.

The street seethed with the overflow of crowds from Leicester Square who moved singly, in pairs, in groups, some hunting a good meal or a coffee house, some a last drink in a pub, some slipping guiltily into the maws of the sex shops to watch porno films in private booths or naked women invitingly gyrating in coin-in-the-slot peep shows. Some checked cards thumb-tacked to door frames—*Model Upstairs, French Mistress, Riding Instruction, Erections Demolished, Corporal Relaxation, Complete Massage*—glanced once around as if expecting wives or girlfriends to suddenly appear, and ascended to their particular pleasure.

Hailey leaned against a wall and watched the restaurant. So easy. He'd kill Quinn when he came out. Follow him back toward the hotel and in a dark street shoot him. Or why not right here? He looked around and considered the possibility. Wait by the restaurant door and when Quinn came out, pull the trigger, then cross the road into Leicester Place and melt into the crowds in the Square. Among the noise in the street no one would hear the crack of the silenced revolver, and in a city street like this no on would notice a man reeling against a wall and falling to the pavement. Not until Hailey was well away. Into the Square, into a taxi and gone. Simple. Yes.

Neon flashed. Red, green, garish. *Chinese Eats, Coffee Inn, Sex Shop*. On, off. On, off. Reflecting in wet asphalt as a steady drizzle fell from the tungsten smeared sky. Hailey pulled his coat collar higher.

Take him at the restaurant door, push the gun in against his heart. It's dark by the door. Two shots. He'll die instantly. Then that'll leave Teal. Get Teal out of the way and he could go back to Tristan.

The pain in his head was expanding like an exploding universe. Colors filled his brain, colors to match the neon. *Sex Shop, Hot Films, Nudes*. Red. Green. Red. Green. The street noise flattened in Hailey's ears, blurred into a thick dull monotone. He could hear his own breathing above everything, a gasping breath in his throat. And his head ached, throbbed with the rhythm of the neon. *Sex Shop, Hot Films, Nudes*. Red. Green. Red. He felt his vision blurring. Have to get to Tristan. Have to get Tristan to fix me. Blurring. His vision blurring like his hearing.

"You look lonely."

Hailey opened his mouth and sucked the chill night air deep into his lungs, forcing himself to snap out of it, willing himself to ignore the pain in his head. Someone was talking to him.

"Perhaps I can help you."

She was young, blowsy, extravagantly dressed in a sequined low-cut dress that clung to wide hips. She held back a thick, artificial fur coat so Hailey could see the goods.

"Fifteen quid," she said. "Twenty if you want something special. Got a nice bag of tricks," she smiled.

Hailey shook his head. "No," he said.

He tried to concentrate on the restaurant door across the street, tried to ignore the pain in his head and the neon and this woman in front of him.

"You a Yank?" She pushed the fur coat back further and put

her hands on her hips and swayed them gently. "I like Yanks. Gentlemen. You're a good looking fella. Like to buy me a drink? My name's June."

"Go away," Hailey said softly, trying to control the pain.

"Just a drink. Nothing else. You never know. A fella like you . . ." Then she looked into the cold, blue eyes and stopped talking. "O.K.," she said, "that's all right, mister, no offense."

Hailey breathed deep again. He felt in his pocket for a cigarette and lit it, drawing the smoke deep into his lungs. It tasted foul. He threw the cigarette onto the wet street. The pain in his head was bad now. He was beginning to feel ill. But there couldn't be any of that. No vomiting. Not here in the street. He had a job to do. He had to kill Quinn. That was orders.

He saw a pub a few doors down across the street. A couple of whiskies might steady him, tide him over, get him through the short time until Quinn appeared.

No. No drinking. Not now. No leaving his post. Quinn might have just gone in for a snack, one course, maybe only a pot of Chinese tea. He might be out any minute. Stick with it. Keep on the job. Do what you have to do. For Zeller. For Tristan. You owe them that. The way they fixed you. When those army doctors didn't. The shrapnel in your head. From the grenade. Thrown by the gook. In 'Nam. Ambush. Only survivor. Because you used your brains. Played dead. Everyone else dead. Fourteen. Choppers. Stacked in among the dead men. Blood all over you. Their blood. With the dead men all the way back to base. Shrapnel in your head. Pain. Headaches. You'll have headaches all your life. Intermittently. Uncomfortable. Not dangerous. Unfortunate. If we touch the shrapnel we might cause brain damage. Tristan fixed it. Zeller paid. Owe them. Gooks. Nearly got me. Not quite. No one can ever get me. No one can ever get me. No one can ever get me. No one can ever get me.

Quinn had ordered a crispy spring roll for starters, and now he was finishing a plate of sweet and sour pork with fried rice on the side. He poured a delicate porcelain cup full of steaming hot green tea and sipped. He glanced out the restaurant window. Raining. Well, it was London. What could you expect? Directly opposite, a blood red neon sign flashed rhythmically on and off, on and off, *Sex Shop, Sex Shop*. A group of young men stared into the window, slapping each other on the back, laughing, jostling, as they checked the merchandise. Soho, London's square mile of sin, didn't hold a dildo to good old Times Square, but it tried. Quinn watched the youths a moment, saw a man with his collar turned up high walk uncertainly across the road, then turned back to his sweet and sour. He glanced at his watch. Ten o'clock. He felt tired. He'd get moving soon. Get a good night's rest. Sleep on this thing. Decide just how far he wanted to go with Sanderson. Sanderson and his daughter.

Hailey leaned back in the darkened doorway of a radio and TV parts shop right beside the Chinese restaurant. The restaurant door was equipped with a bell on a steel spring so that when anyone entered or left the bell rang. He knew exactly what he would do. When the bell rang and Quinn stepped out, Hailey would walk behind him a few paces then speak to him, and as Quinn turned he'd jam the pistol into his chest and fire point blank two times.

That's what he'd do.

If he could do it.

If the pain in his head let him. The pain, painting the inside of his skull with molten lava. The pain, destroying him. And the neon. *Live Show, Sex Shop, Live Show, Sex Shop*, red green, red, green, the colors melting in the rain-wet pavement. Hailey stared at them, the rich greens and reds, and saw a universe within them, a shifting panorama of subtle, abstracted shapes. He concentrated on the liquid colors, tried to force his whole being into them, tried to catch them in his mind to let them fight the pain. He breathed shallowly, gaspingly, trying to force oxygen deep into his body. A couple walked by him, then a group of youths, talking, laughing, the sounds of their voices blurred and indistinct. Hailey concentrated, ignored the searing pain, clutched tightly on the revolver butt in his pocket, waited for the bell on the restaurant door which would signal someone's exit. Someone's. Quinn's. Ready. Ready. Get ready.

Do the job, this one and Teal, then find Tristan, and the deep coolness, the ever warmness, the soft voice, the soothing cure; lie in the box and dream, in the dark box, in the dreaming dark.

The bell rang.

Hailey tore his eyes from the melting, changing colors on the road as the sound of the bell registered on the periphery of his consciousness. Hailey pushed himself from his slumped, drunken-like position against the door and stepped out onto the street.

A man.

It was him. Turning up his collar against the drizzle and hurrying across the road. Three paces in front of Hailey. Hailey stepped out after him, staring at Quinn's back, his hand in his pocket curled around the revolver butt.

Now, miraculously, the pain was gone, replaced by a dazed sense of gentle giddiness. But Hailey could live with that. With only the giddiness he could do what he had to do. Get close to him, draw the gun, speak to him and as he turned, shoot. Then straight into Leicester Square, into a taxi and away. Back to the Savoy to wait for Teal.

They were across the road now, heading into Leicester Place, the short street leading into the Square. Hailey strode one pace behind Quinn, Quinn oblivious to his presence. Hailey looked quickly from side to side. No one close. Once in the passage he'd do it. He fixed his eyes on Quinn's back. His breathing came heavily. No pain in his head, but his breath came in gasps so loud he feared Quinn would hear him, turn, recognize him, run, or worse, fight. They reached the passage. Now. Pull the gun, kill him now, do it quick, before you lose control. *They can't get me. They can't get me.* They'd told him that. *They can't get me.* Do it!

Hailey stared at Quinn's back. Hailey had slowed down. Quinn strode six feet ahead of him now. Quinn's back, broad in its tweed jacket, moving up and down as he walked, rising and descending slowly, as if suspended from an invisible spring, a slowly bouncing marionette buried in the deep shadows of the poorly lit lane.

Hailey stared, his hand pulling at the revolver in his pocket, a hand without strength pulling at a fat object deep within the confines of a massive pocket, the bouncing puppet small in the distance now, not a shadow now, now a silhouette against bright lights glaring from cinema facades in the Square.

And Hailey was not alone.

In the ragged edges of his mind a friend was emerging to try and comfort him, a friend he couldn't define, a friend.

And Quinn was gone.

Merged with crowds in the Square.

Safely gone.

And Hailey stood, staring, the revolver in his pocket heavy and hot under his hand, his head dizzy, conscious that the other one within him had come again. The presence. The one who was but never spoke. The comfortable one. The confusing one. The other one who was also a part of him, but who never fully revealed himself, who only floated ethereally on the outer limits of his consciousness, waiting, as it were, for the right moment in which to declare himself.

I must, I must go, I must do, I must create opportunity to perform what is required of me. Hailey shook his head, forcing himself to clear his mind of the now unwelcome presence. *I must create opportunity to perform what is required of me.* A litany of purpose. Given to him by Tristan. To help him. A gift.

The other one—the other young man—retreated back into the confused depths of Hailey's mind and was forgotten.

And in his place came the headaches again.

Mushrooming like an explosion.

Spreading through his consciousness with the rampaging force of a typhoon.

Ripping.

Pummelling.

Defeating.

Hailey slumped against a wall, his head turned to one side, his face resting against the cold, wet, red bricks.

Quinn tried to look at the thing logically. He tried to question himself about reasons and motives. Why did he want to kill the golden-haired one? Why did he want to hunt Zeller? Was it because Jenny had been murdered, or was there another reason? Was there some deep seated sense of justice lurking within him of which he had never known the existence? Was this urge for revenge an extension of his yearning for adventure? Or was there some atavistic core within him, a warrior's instinct for the looming fight?

Quinn lay on his bed, comfortably propped up by pillows, sipping a long Scotch and soda delivered by room service. Outside, the drizzle had been replaced by sheets of solid rain shining in the glow of street lighting, and a keen wind was building, eddying around the hotel, rattling windows.

Lots of questions, Quinn thought, all posed by my finely educated business school brain. And the answer, the truthful answer, he'd decided, was most unphilosophical, completely free of the restraining parameters of logic, ethics and morals.

The answer was, yes he was going to do it, and he would do it because in these 1980's not one man in ten million got a chance like this. He would fulfill childhood fantasies. At the head of a troop of brave men, he would pit himself against a perverse villain, a villain responsible for the death of a beautiful damsel, and in a holocaust of retribution he would destroy that villain and all he stood for.

Try explaining that to a pipe-puffing college professor. Or to anyone.

To Lena, for instance.

Hailey sat at a corner table in the pub in Lisle Street, drinking his second double Scotch. The headache was disappearing again, as if the alcohol was melting it away. He'd vomited three times in the street from the pain of it. Now it was going. It only came when he was working, or about to work. He had to get back to Tristan. He'd failed. He'd missed Quinn. Had him six feet in front of him. Had only to draw the gun and fire. Hadn't been able to. Tristan and Zeller would be angry, but he had to get back to them for help before he continued with the job. He couldn't perform properly the way he felt now. He might make a mistake and a mistake could cause repercussions which might damage Zeller and Tristan. He had to be put right first, before he returned to the job. A day to reach Zeller, a day for treatment, a day to return. Then he'd be right. In the meantime he'd order the London operative to track Quinn and Teal.

Hailey gulped the remains of the second Scotch, left his table and pushed his way through the crowd at the bar to order a refill. One more long one would relax him completely, then he'd return to the Ladbroke Grove flat, telex Tristan for permission to leave the field for three days, contact the London operative, taxi to the airport and try and book a late night flight to Rome. Then, in the morning he could connect to Malta, and from there it would be only a quick helicopter ride to the darkness and the peacefulness.

"What's it to be?" the harried barman asked, reaching for Hailey's glass.

"Double Scotch and water," Hailey said.

"Want to make that two?"

Hailey glanced over his shoulder toward the voice and saw the girl in the fur coat who'd spoken to him in the street. June.

The barman raised his eyes questioningly and Hailey nodded. He paid with three one-pound notes and left the change on the counter. He took both glasses and walked to his corner table, knowing the girl was following. He sat down and watched June as she removed her fake fur coat to reveal the sequined dress, cut low so that all the world could see the two ample globes of her breasts. She took a cigarette from her handbag and leaned forward to Hailey's offered light. Hailey saw everything she had.

"What's your name?" she asked.

"Hailey."

She smiled. "Who Hailey, or Hailey what?"

"Just Hailey."

"That's a nice name, Hailey." She lifted her Scotch and toasted him. "Thanks for the drink."

Hailey nodded, sipped his, and stared at her. She concentrated on her glass.

"You're in a better mood now," she said.

Hailey lit himself a cigarette.

"You interested now?" she asked coyly. "We could have a good time."

Hailey blew smoke across the table above her head.

"I got my own place five minutes from here. You could stay the night if you want. Still only fifteen quid." She leaned forward so Hailey could see all of her breasts again. "Except you could have a midnight snack *and* a morning glory. I hate spending cold nights alone. What do you say, Yank?"

Without taking his eyes from her, Hailey reached into a pocket and took out a twenty pound note. He slid it across the table toward her.

June smiled, took the note, folded it and tucked it into her handbag. "A gentleman," she said. "But I bet you get your money's worth."

Hailey drained his Scotch in one long swallow, stood and walked toward the door. He didn't stop to help June put on her coat and he didn't look back to see if she was following. He knew she would be. The women always followed. Always.

Quinn and Teal breakfasted in a working-man's café near Covent Garden. They found themselves a table by the window where they could eat and talk and watch the armies of commuters running through the rain, rushing to meet nine o'clock deadlines.

Quinn explained to Teal every detail of his meeting with Sanderson the previous evening.

Teal mopped up egg yolk with a piece of toast and washed it down with coffee. "Sounds like a good old fashioned vendetta."

"Sanderson described it as a small scale war."

"And the girl—this Lena—is she as worked up as her old man?"

"Hard to say," Quinn said. "She claims not, but I think otherwise."

"And you?"

Quinn pushed his coffee cup aside, lit a *Winston* and stared out at the wet, busy streets. "I'm committed," he said quietly. "I'm going after him."

"You made up your mind quick on that one."

Quinn smiled. "Quick for me, you mean."

"Let's just say you're no longer an indecisive youth."

Quinn didn't respond to the tongue in cheek sarcasm. They

sat silently for a moment. Then Quinn said, "I don't expect you to get in any deeper in this. I can pay up your contract today."

Teal waved Quinn's words away. "My contract's at the bottom of the fucking ocean with *Destry*."

"It's getting rough," Quinn said.

"Rough's never worried me, boyo."

"Sanderson's talking about a military operation. Wholesale killing."

"Wholesale killing is too good for this lot. I'm in, Peter, for personal and humanitarian reasons. Let's leave it at that."

Quinn expelled a long breath and couldn't help grinning. He nodded his head. "Thanks."

"Let's get down to practicalities. Before we involve ourselves further, just where the hell is the money coming from? Four hundred thousand bucks is big bread."

"I'm worth maybe a hundred grand."

"Great. Only three hundred thou to find. I'm worth about ten which is as useful as pissing into the wind. But you're welcome to it."

Quinn dismissed the idea. "My party, so you don't get to pay."

"So what about the rest?"

"I guess Sanderson's got some."

"And . . . ?"

"And my old man."

Teal shook his head slowly from side to side. "If I know your old man, he ain't gonna like it."

"I'll make him an offer he can't refuse." Quinn looked at his watch. "Johnny James is waiting. Let's go."

June lay naked on her bed, too bruised and sick to move. The girls said it eventually happened to everyone who worked the streets. You met a weirdo, and he beat the shit out of you or maybe killed you. The man with the golden hair had nearly killed her. She lay staring at the filthy ceiling faintly illuminated by the dull morning light filtering through the dirty, curtainless window, and knew she was lucky to be alive.

He'd seemed O.K. Distant, introverted, tight-up, but basically O.K. And certainly not shy like some of the handsome ones she'd known during her years on the streets who'd turned out to be mama's boys or queers, men who'd never had a woman and who'd plucked up courage to buy their first time, a first time which often ended in a fiasco with her having to help them off with her hand. She'd met plenty of them, but this one was no mama's boy.

He'd walked into the room, looked around and stripped straight away, without waiting to be asked, and lay on the bed staring at the ceiling. He hadn't even watched June undress. And when she went to kneel over him on the bed he was already erect. She'd congratulated herself when she saw the hard-on, thinking she could bring this lovely looking lad off quick, then enjoy a good night's sleep, using his body to keep her warm. Not that she'd hurry it too much. He was beautiful, exceptional. He had a perfect body except for the scars. She wondered where he'd got those. She'd seen thousands of naked men, but never one with a body as beautiful as his. So perhaps she'd mix a little pleasure with her work and enjoy this perfect body for a while before finishing the job and getting some sleep. Maybe even work herself up with him. She liked to orgasm before sleeping. She nearly always masturbated at night before sleeping. It drained the tension from her, wound her down after the night's work. It was only fair, she'd think, as she started touching herself. A girl helps four or five men come then she's entitled to one nice come herself. She'd only let herself come with maybe six or seven clients of all the thousands she'd had over the years. Somehow it didn't seem right to involve herself so deeply with paying clients. She was doing a job, after all. The ones she'd let herself come with were all repeats, men she'd known for months. Like old friends, some of them. But the beautiful animal lying on her bed was different. She'd never seen him before, knew she'd never see him again, and she was cold, lonely and pissed off after a night that had hardly paid the rent. She needed a little comfort.

She didn't get any.

She lowered herself onto his penis, then leaned forward so her big breasts brushed his face. The few times she'd decided to allow clients to touch her breasts they'd started in on her nipples like children sucking lollipops. She had beautiful breasts, all her personal lovers and half her clients told her that. She wanted this one to play with them, help her on her way, but the man with the golden hair hadn't shown any interest. He'd closed his eyes and kept his hips moving under her. Boobs, she decided, didn't turn him on.

For the rest of it, he was expert. He rolled her through half a dozen different positions working only for himself, she knew, but with such intensity that it worked for her as well, a good solid fuck that not one man in a hundred could give, and she returned the compliment to the best of her professional abilities, feeling herself starting, slowly, ever so slowly, then building, faster and faster, until finally she buried her face in his neck and exploded her groin into him as she came.

"Oh," she whispered, as he kept at her, chasing his own orgasm, "oh Mr. America, I *love* you."

And he stopped. He withdrew from her and she saw that his erection had failed him. She reached for his cock, to massage it a little, see if she could get it back up for him so he could finish. He slapped her hand away and knelt between her legs.

"What do you mean?"

"Nothing," she said, not understanding him and reaching for his penis again. "Let's get this soldier standing at attention again. No problem. Happens all the time . . ."

He slapped her hand away again. "What do you mean? I love you. What's that mean?"

"Nothing, darling, come on, now . . ."

"What did you mean?"

She could sense it now, some sort of madness, and she felt afraid and rolled away from him and off the bed and stood up. "Nothing," she said, "I meant you are just fantastic."

"You don't say things like that."

"O.K.," she crooned, "O.K. handsome. Now you lay back and I'll get some lotion and finish that little job for you."

Then he was on his feet and he backhanded her across the face so she stumbled back over the bed. He grabbed her by the hair and hauled her up.

"*Love!*" he said.

And hit her again.

"*Love?*"

And split her lip open.

"There *is* no love!"

And punched her in the belly so she doubled up and crashed onto the bed.

And the thing she noticed, the thing that scared her more than anything, as he punched her and slapped her and clawed at her, as he bruised her and cracked her up so bad she'd need to go to the doctor today and wouldn't be working again for a month, the thing she noticed was that he did it without anger.

Coldly.

Like an automaton that had been trained to unemotionally react with violence to the use of the word "love"

But he'd been beautiful.

Johnny James doodled on a pad, listening carefully as Quinn told him about his meeting with Sanderson. When Quinn finished he sat for a long moment staring at the doodle— a mesh of interlocking three-dimensional cubes—and then looked up and gazed at a point mid-distant between Quinn and Teal.

"So," he said, slowly, "for four hundred thousand dollars we can rid ourselves of Mr. Zeller."

"That's it," Quinn said. "For the price of one decent boat."

"How will you get the money?" Johnny asked. He looked directly at Quinn, blandly, as if the question was posed in all innocence.

Quinn smiled. "I thought you might offer some ideas, Johnny. Marine Insurance Limited isn't exactly bankrupt. Figure how much Zeller costs you a year and then tell me if four hundred thousand wouldn't make a good investment."

"If you sank Zeller, old chap, it'd be a marvellous investment. But if Zeller sank you . . ." He didn't finish, but picked up his pen and started doodling again. "I'm embarrassed," he said finally. "Marine Insurance stands to benefit from the operation, but we're responsible to a chairman, a board of directors and several thousand stockholders. You can't put in the annual report that you spent four hundred thousand dollars fighting pirates. It's just not on. And there *are* certain illegalities involved . . ."

"Bullshit, Johnny," Teal said. "You guys have slush funds to cover stuff like this."

"I agree, there is a contingency fund for . . . for certain emergencies. But it doesn't stretch to four hundred thousand."

"How far?" Teal asked.

"Twenty thousand pounds. That's around fifty thousand dollars. Maximum."

"We'll take it," Teal grinned.

Johnny shook his head in mock disgust. "You American chappies certainly take the cake for forthrightness. But unfortunately you can't just 'take it' until I've talked the problem around a few directors. I'll make sure they agree; I'll take a bloody accountant with me to show what yacht jacking is costing us. But there'll be two provisos."

"Name them."

"The company's not involved, in any shape or form. In fact we'll simply deny involvement if there's any media leak."

"No problem," Quinn said. "And the next?"

"I'll be along to keep an eye on the company's investment."

"Welcome aboard," Teal said. He leaned forward and slapped Quinn on the shoulder. "A quarter of a million buckaroos to go, kid, and we're on our way."

"Next item," Johnny said. He took an envelope from his desk drawer. "The code. My friend cracked it." He slid a sheet of paper from the envelope and laid it on the desk so that they could all see it. "It's simple enough. I'll run you through. This is what we took from the tape . . ."

Johnny pointed to the first lines of letters:

ESRAM	DELLI	POPMU	CSEDR
DACSA	OWTSE	ASLLA	SSSEL
OW			

"Now, we reverse these groups . . ."

MARSE	ILLED	UMPOP	RDESC
ASCAD	ESTWO	ALLSA	LESSS
WO			

"And now run them together . . ."

MARSEILLEDUMPOPRDESCASCADESTWOALLSAL-
ESSSWO

"And here's the message . . ." He pointed to the last line on the paper:

MARSEILLE/DUMP/OP/R/DES/CASCADES/TWO/ALL/
SALES/SSWO

"Not really a code," Johnny said, "merely a jumble to confuse eyes which accidentally see it. The message is typed out without any break between words, then broken into five letter groups for easy transmission, and then those groups are reversed."

"What's this last bit mean?" Quinn asked.

"Can't help you with that bit, old chap, because we're missing the following letters. Could be some abbreviation, could be part abbreviation and part of a word. Frankly, I think we've done rather well as it is. *Marseilles dump operational, Rue des Cascades number two.* If anyone ever doubted Zeller's connection with arms dealing they could always toddle along to Marseilles and check for themselves."

Johnny took another sheet of paper from his drawer. "Our people in Paris and Rome checked the business registry offices. Trans-Europe Trading in both cities is registered under the same name. John Edward Smith."

Teal snorted.

"Well," Johnny said, "you can't win them all."

Quinn phoned Sanderson from his hotel room. "If I can raise the cash we're in business," he said.

There was the slightest pause at the other end of the line. "You're sure?" Sanderson said.

"I'm sure."

"You know what you're letting yourself in for? There's no guarantee the project will succeed."

"I understand that."

"And it's a lot of cash."

"I have a hundred thousand in personal funds. A mutual friend can find fifty. That leaves two hundred and fifty to find."

"Two hundred," Sanderson said quietly. "I have fifty. What about the rest?"

"That's my business," Quinn said. "With luck I can raise it in forty-eight hours."

"Quinn," Sanderson said. "How do you know I won't take your money and run?"

Quinn smiled as he spoke into the mouthpiece. "Because I'll be right by your side the whole way, Colonel." He replaced the receiver and looked at Teal who was staring out the window to the Strand and sipping his first drink of the day. "Now it's up to my old man," Quinn said.

"You're really jumping into this one, boyo. You haven't even seen the plans."

"I've done my homework on Sanderson. That's enough."

Quinn flew to New York that night. He reached his father's Manhatten offices at 10 a.m. New York time and over a ham and eggs breakfast, served at his father's desk, and washed down by a shared pot of fresh brewed American coffee, he explained to Quinn Sr. as undramatically as possible what he wanted to do.

"And where do I fit in?" Quinn Sr. asked.

Quinn smiled as his father tucked his wide Irish jaw into his shirt collar and steepled his fingers together. "The job will cost four hundred thousand dollars," he said quietly.

The wide Irish jaw dropped a half inch. "Jesus, Joseph and Mary, it's a god-damned war you're talking of starting."

"I've raised half. I'm here to ask if you'll loan me the rest."

Quinn Sr. stared at his son for a long moment, then abruptly rose from his desk and paced nervously around the room. He paused once, to glance at a fading photograph of his wife which he'd mounted on his office wall the week after she'd died and had carried with him to each subsequent office during his rise to bountiful prosperity. Then he sat on the edge of his desk, close to Peter.

"Money's no problem, son. Two hundred thousand, two million, it's all the same. I have money and I can raise money. But you said you intend accompanying this Colonel."

"Yes."

"You're talking about guns, about killing. About, perhaps, being killed. You can't ask a father to lend his own son money to do a thing like that. You want money to start a business, buy another boat, Jesus, anything, it's yours. But you can't expect me to give you money for *this*."

Quinn looked his father right in the eye. "I don't expect you to give it to me. I expect you to loan it to me."

"Same thing; with the money you can go out there and get yourself killed."

"I want to do it."

"Why? What will it prove? What will it solve?"

"It'll prove that some individuals are willing to do something for themselves, something governments don't seem prepared to do either for political reasons or because of sheer expediency. And it will solve, to some extent, the problem of yacht-jacking and arms running in the Mediterranean."

"That's quite a speech coming from you. But are those the real reasons why you want to get involved?"

Peter looked away from his father. "No."

"What are they?"

"I don't know."

Quinn Sr. smiled and poured them both more coffee. "You're an honest lad, I'll give you that." He sipped his coffee. "I saw Jenny's parents. It wasn't a nice task you gave me."

"I'm sorry. Thanks for going."

"How serious were you with her?"

"Not too serious. In the end, I don't think it would've worked out. She was a great kid." Quinn stared into his cup.

"Listen," Quinn Sr. said softly. "You're not blaming yourself for that, are you?"

"For a couple of weeks it was pretty rough, but I'm O.K. now. *Destry* was my boat so I'm responsible for whatever happened aboard, but I've faced the fact that I was tricked by the bastards. I was stupid enough to let them aboard, but it wasn't me who killed Jenny." Quinn averted his eyes from his father. "It took me a long time to convince myself."

"But now you're convinced."

Quinn nodded.

"But you're still willing to risk your life in some gesture of revenge.

"That's what I want to do. If you won't help me with the money I'll find it elsewhere. Time isn't important. This year, next year. It's all the same." Quinn walked to the window and looked out over the city and all it represented, the commercial jungle he'd worked so hard to avoid until he'd had at least a year during which to taste the possibilities of his youth.

He turned abruptly and faced his father. "Dad, if you lend me the money I guarantee to return to New York after the job's done and work for you for five years or until I manage to pay back the debt."

For a moment Quinn Sr. didn't answer. He felt something close to embarrassment at what his son had said. "Bejesus," he said at last, "you really *do* want to do this."

"Yes."

Peter's father took a deep breath and expelled it slowly. "What can I say?"

"That you'll loan me the money. I've never asked you for money before and I'll never ask you again."

Quinn Sr. turned so he didn't have to look at his only son. He bit his lower lip. "I'll have a draft at our London bank within twenty-four hours." Then he walked over to his boy and put his arm around him. "Now go and sleep and then get yourself back here and buy an old man his lunch."

Late that evening, when Peter had gone, Quinn Sr. sat staring down on the great multi-faceted jewel that was New York at night. From the deep canyons of the city rose the never ceasing grumble of traffic, proof that all was well, that the wheels still turned, the money multiplied, that the subtle rhythms of coercion and change still existed at the center of the world, that ideas still clashed, that men still battled for their ten cents worth.

And where was his son going?

James P. Quinn walked to the wall where the photograph of his wife hung. He stared at the old print, at the fine, beautiful face of the girl he still loved. He could see Peter in there, could see the Irishness of her reflecting from Peter's face every time he looked at the boy.

And now his boy was driven to pit himself against dark forces of which he had no knowledge.

And even if the lad survived, Quinn Sr. knew he could never hold his son to his promise. He wanted the boy beside him in the office, wanted to prepare him to lead the great enterprise he had built, wanted to hand Peter a slice of the American dream on a platter. But not under these circumstances. The boy had to come of his own free will. He must not come to serve out years of servitude to repay family dollars.

In his mind James P. Quinn bid his wife goodnight then walked through the offices of his empire hardly hearing the greetings of cleaning staff. He stood waiting for the lift, his shoulders stooped, feeling very old, very alone and very afraid.

Hailey rested naked in darkness and peace, the only sound that of his own breathing, deep and rhythmic. Soon Tristan would talk to him, soothe him, explain things to him, and he would be well, and he'd return to work again.

Hailey floated, suspended in an enclosed steel tank, in two feet of buoyant salt water heated to coincide exactly with his body temperature. He felt nothing, no sensation of touch or abrasion. The dark, black walled, black ceilinged tank formed a total womb, complete with amniotic fluid, recreating for Hailey the tranquil abode of a fetus, stimulating from the deepest layers of his mind long buried memories of prebirth existence.

Hailey had floated in the tank for fifteen minutes now. The helicopter flew him from Malta's Luqa airport to *Shadow*, which cruised at a sedate five knots eighty miles off the Malta group and on course for Sicily. He'd been taken straight below where he'd undressed and then stepped into the beautiful box and closed the lid. He hadn't seen Tristan or Zeller.

It took him the fifteen minutes to calm down, to prepare to empty his mind, to find the most comfortable floating position. And now he felt ready to enter the blackness of his being within the equal blackness of the box, and when he found the core of darkness the way Tristan had taught him, then Tristan would come and speak with him.

Hailey closed his eyes and saw faint color behind his lids. He opened them to blackness absolute and pure. His muscles felt relaxed now, his body harbored no tension. He felt no tactile sensation in the blood temperature solution, saw nothing, thought no definable thought, realized only the jagged remnant of a recent incident, a slightly confused image of a flapping coat as someone walked a city street and of a man leaning on a wall, his face resting on wet bricks. And now it all dissipated into the darkness and Hailey was empty, staring unseeing into the welcoming, infinite darkness of his second womb.

"Hailey."

Hailey heard, but did not hear.

"I am here."

The voice, soft and persuasive, filled the tank, emanating from a small speaker above Hailey's head.

"Are you quiet?"

"Yes." Hailey spoke, but did not know.

"I am in the darkness with you, Hailey, we are together, as always. You wanted me and I am here. I am always here when you want me. Do you want to talk?"

"Yes."

For ten minutes the voice was silent, but for Hailey the time passed in a heartbeat as he lay deep in the darkness listening to Tristan, waiting for his soothing, healing words.

"Has your head been hurting?"

"Yes."

"That's the wound. You served them in their war and when you were hurt they never had the decency to repair your wound. That was their thanks for your sacrifice. But we helped you; we did what we could for you."

"Yes," Hailey said, softly.

"And we will help you now, and always. Whenever you need help we will be here."

"Yes."

"We appreciate what you do for us. Without you we couldn't accomplish our work. You are the key to our success and we are pleased to admit that. So, naturally, we will always do anything to help you. You know that, don't you, Hailey. We work together, you and I and Zeller." The voice glided as gently as a swooping bird around Hailey in the darkness.

"You and I and Zeller," Hailey repeated.

"We understand each other."

"You and I and Zeller."

"We appreciate each other's talents, and work together." Hailey heard without listening.

"We know things, you and I and Zeller, and that's why we are successful. We know about good and evil, right and wrong, love and hate, ambition and authority. What is good and evil?"

"There is no good; there is no evil," Hailey intoned.

"What is right and wrong?"

"There is no right; there is no wrong."

"What is love and hate?"

"There is no love; there is no hate."

"What is ambition?"

"Ambition is ridiculous."

"What is authority?"

"Authority is a posture, a word used by lesser men to convince others of their invincibility." Hailey spoke mechanically repeating a litany learned long ago.

"Are they invincible?"

"No."

"Why not?"

"Because a single bullet can kill."

"Would you kill?"

"Yes."

"Under what circumstances?"

"If you or Zeller required the death."

"How would you kill, Hailey?"

"I would create opportunity to perform what is asked of me."

"And then?"

"And then kill."

"You would not feel fear?"

"There is no fear."

"You would not hesitate?"

"If there is no fear there is no hesitation."

"And when you had done what was asked of you, you would feel no shame?"

"If there is no good, nor evil, then there is no shame."

"And if you were caught?"

"I can never be caught."

"But *if* you were caught?"

"I can never be caught."

"But if you *were* caught, Hailey?"

"I can never be caught."

"Why will you never be caught?"

"Because I will never permit myself to be captured."

"If you are surrounded and outnumbered, how could you avoid capture?"

"I would kill myself."

"How?"

"By whatever means were at hand."

"There may be no means."

"There are always means."

"Tell me."

"By shooting, by stabbing, by hanging, by fire, by falling, by poison, by gassing, by vehicular impact."

"And if none of those methods were available?"

"By bleeding."

"Tell me."

"Veins may be opened with a pencil, with a sharp stone, with a piece of wood, with a key, or cut with the edge of a piece of paper."

"And what does all this mean?"

"It means that I am never alone in an emergency. I always have a friend."

"That's right, Hailey. You always have a friend, you are never alone You have your friend and you have Zeller and I, and together we can do what has to be done. Now let's talk about your headaches and I will tell you what to do so you don't suffer. Zeller and I don't want you to suffer, Hailey, ever . . ."

* * *

Two hours later Hailey emerged from the tank. After he'd showered to remove salt from the saline solution from his skin, two sailors accompanied him to the galley where he was given a light meal of scrambled eggs and toast washed down with a glass of red wine. Mixed with the eggs was a moderate dose of fast-acting sedative. The wine caused the barbiturate to act quickly, so that minutes later, when Hailey was taken aboard the helicopter which sat waiting on *Shadow*'s pad, he felt pleasantly relaxed, his mind still assimilating Tristan's instructions.

The chopper lifted from its pad, circled *Shadow* once and then headed back toward the horizon where the triple outlines of Malta, Comino and Gozo etched their flat profiles where the sea met the sky.

Hailey looked down at *Shadow*, black and sleek, cutting the sparkling sea, two escorts latched to her wake like pilot fish to a shark.

And he felt content within himself.

PART FOUR

Sanderson took two buff colored folders from his drawer and slid them across his cluttered desk to Quinn and Teal. One was titled ZELLER, the other OPERATION FLYING DUTCH-MAN. "Read these later," he said. "For now the most important thing is to understand where the money's going."

Three days after Quinn returned to London from the meeting in New York with his father his bank account stood at two hundred and eighty-nine thousand dollars. His father's two hundred thousand dollar loan had arrived and the hurried liquidation of his own assets had yielded the rest. As well, Johnny James had convinced his chairman that a fifty thousand dollar contribution to the project was an investment, not a donation. The destruction of Zeller's organization could save Marina Insurance hundreds of thousands of dollars annually. With the fifty thousand dollars pledged by Sanderson, the group counted on a working fund of three hundred and eighty-nine thousand dollars.

Sanderson pushed his hands deep in his pockets and stood at his favorite spot in front of the French windows, staring out into the dark suburban night. A gusting wind drove rain squalls against the windows.

"I've told you Zeller lives on a boat guarded by two fast cruisers which I believe are armed with missile systems. Zeller never sets foot on land. When his boat *Shadow* needs to dock for refueling or repairs, he transfers to one of the escorts. The escorts take it in turn to enter port for repairs and refueling. *Shadow* carries huge fuel reserves, enough to keep herself *and* her escorts at sea for over five thousand miles."

Sanderson turned to face them and leaned back against the windows. "So the problem is, you can't get Zeller on land and you can't really hunt him at sea. But his route is predictable. He moves from Cyprus to Crete to Malta to Ibiza and then works his way back again, with occasional stops in Tripoli or Benghazi when he's carrying arms to those Libyan madmen. The *only* way to get Zeller is when *Shadow* is in port and Zeller is aboard an escort."

"Why not bomb the fucker at sea?" Teal asked.

"Too expensive."

"You could pick up an old DC3 and a load of bombs real cheap," Teal said.

Sanderson smiled. "You forget the missiles. A DC3 wouldn't stand a chance. It'd be knocked out on its first pass. A faster plane is simply out of the question. A converted Lear jet, for instance, armed with sufficient weaponry would cost over a million dollars and even if we had that sort of money we couldn't guarantee the mission's success. What I'm suggesting is cheaper, simpler and surer."

Lena entered with a tray laden with coffee and thick toasted sandwiches. She handed them around then took the free seat beside Quinn. Quinn glanced at her and noted the strain in her face as she listened to her father speaking. For a moment Sanderson's words blurred and he missed an exchange between him and Teal. There was something so incredibly pensive about Lena's expression that he had to control an impulse to reach out and take her hand. It was a guilt reaction, he realized. Hadn't she told him that she feared for her father? And now he'd supplied money, the missing ingredient which would propel Sanderson into action and plunge him into the danger she feared so much.

"I've been into this thing," Sanderson was saying. "I've collated information on Zeller and his movements from dozens of sources during the best part of a decade. Believe me, I've considered half a dozen ways of attacking him. There are several *better* ways than the one I've chosen, but circumstances make them impractical."

Sanderson rose from his chair and began restlessly pacing as he outlined his plan of action. Quinn listened, mesmerized by the Colonel's intensity.

"I've chosen to attack Zeller in Ibizan waters. Ibiza is the second largest of Spain's Balearic islands, laying some sixty miles off the mainland. Ibiza has excellent air connections with most European capitals so we can get out quick when we've done the job.

"My plan calls for a fast cruiser. We buy it somewhere in Italy or France and in the same country arrange the purchase of the weapons we need. The cruiser carries them to Ibiza. Because of possible customs searches the cruiser never docks in a Spanish port, but heaves-to in the shelter of one of the small islands off the Ibizan coast.

"When *Shadow* docks in Ibiza for refueling, we knock out the crew and take over the boat. At gunpoint, we force the captain to follow his normal schedule. When he sets sail to rendezvous with the escorts our cruiser joins us, hugging the lee of *Shadow*'s Hull."

Teal waved his hand to interrupt. "Why's that?"

"Because both escorts carry radar. If Zeller sees two boats coming out to meet him, he'll know something's wrong. If the cruiser keeps close to *Shadow* both boats will register as only one signal on the radar screens."

Teal nodded. "And when we get within striking distance, *Shadow* and the cruiser split and each goes after an escort."

"We do better than that. *Shadow* carries a helicopter. A thousand yards from the escorts we launch the chopper armed with a light machine gun and a bazooka. The escorts will see the chopper go up, but if they still haven't seen our cruiser in the lee of *Shadow* they won't suspect anything. At the right moment the chopper attacks one of the escorts while *Shadow* and the launch attacks the other."

"You think the helicopter can sink the first escort?" Quinn asked.

Sanderson poured himself coffee and lit a cigarette, inhaling deeply, before answering. "I doubt it. But I'm banking on *Shadow* and the cruiser neutralizing her quarry while the helicopter keeps the other one engaged. Then we can turn our combined force against the remaining escort."

"And *Shadow*?" Quinn asked. "What do we do with her?"

"We sink her and go home in our cruiser."

"The crews?"

"As far as I'm concerned," Sanderson said, "they're hired thugs."

"You can't just murder them," Lena said, softly.

Quinn saw anger cloud Sanderson's face, then just as quickly dissipate before he answered his daughter. "There'll be no murder," he said evenly. "There'll be a firefight. Every man for himself."

Lena began to speak again, but Quinn gently pressed her thigh with his knee and said, "I think Lena means, what about those left alive after the attack."

"*Shadow* and the two escorts will be sunk. Any crew left alive choose between staying with their boats or going into the sea. We'll give them life rafts. From there they're on their own."

"They won't have much chance," Quinn said.

"They'll have more chance than any terrorist ever gave an innocent victim," Sanderson said. He stubbed out his cigarette and avoiding Lena's eyes, he said, "Under *all* circumstances, Zeller dies. If he survives our attack, he'll be executed. I will personally take the responsibility of pulling the trigger."

"If Zeller survives," Quinn said, "why not hand him over to the police?"

Sanderson expelled a long, frustrated breath. "Peter, for some reason you're clouding the issue. One moment you agree this bastard has to be exterminated because no one else will do it, and the next you suggest we hand him over to the very people who have never done anything about him. Hand him to which police? The Spanish? The Italians? The Israelis? They would all be delighted to have him. He supplies weapons to terrorists in all their countries. He's indirectly responsible for the deaths of countless apolitical noncombatants, including women and children, who died never understanding why they were being killed. But if they got him, they'd have to let him go. Democratic judcial systems are like that. They not only protect the innocent, but the guilty too when direct evidence is lacking. It's the only way the system can work, and people like Zeller take advantage of the system. To use a good American term, they *screw* it. So, finally, it gets down to frustrated individuals—like us—who are forced into the paradoxical situation of breaking laws to defend the law." Sanderson wagged his finger at Quinn. "And have no doubts, if we are caught the law will destroy us for taking things into our own hands."

Teal shifted uneasily in his seat. "Peter, we've been through all this."

"Hand Zeller over," Sanderson continued, "and the court will spit him out through lack of evidence and devour us for piracy, destruction of private property, murder, using unlicensed weapons and a dozen other crimes which we will have committed."

Quinn nodded. He tried to smile. "I guess I want it both ways. I want Zeller and his gang, but I don't want any more blood on my hands." He felt the faintest pressure on his leg. Lena's hand was resting on his thigh. He covered it with his and squeezed gently, hardly realizing what he was doing.

Sanderson sat behind his desk and offered Quinn a cigarette. Quinn lifted his hand from Lena's and took it, and then leaned forward for the offered light. Lena hadn't moved her hand.

"I'm glad you said that," Sanderson said, quietly. "I hate fighting beside men who kill without a second thought. In the end they are less than men. Any man who kills another, for whatever reason, accepts personal responsibility for the act. But taking responsibility doesn't necessarily mean he has to accept guilt."

There was an awkward silence for a moment, then Sanderson pulled the OPERATION FLYING DUTCHMAN file across the table and flicked it open. "Let's run through this budget. The minimum number of men with which we can accomplish the mission is thirteen. That's us three and ten more. And Johnny James says he's coming—that's fourteen. I'd prefer to use twenty, but with that number security becomes sloppy."

Sanderson folded back the file and turned it so Quinn and Teal could see.

MINIMUM ESTIMATE

Fast boat, twin engines, capable of 30 knots.	£100,000	$220,000
10 men × £4000 (£2000 per week for guaranteed two weeks.)	£40,000	$88,000
10 days training period. Lodgings, food, clothing, incidentals. At approximately £40 per man per day. (£400 × 13)	£5,200	$11,440
Weapons to arm 13 men	£5,000	$11,000
Airfares (approx)	£3,000	$6,600
Living expenses during op at approx £40 per day for 4 days	£2,080	$4,576
Medical	£25,000	$55,000
TOTAL	£180,280	$396,616

"Presumably we can sell the cruiser later," Quinn suggested. "Recover some money there."

Sanderson pursed his lips. "Perhaps, but I doubt it. The cruiser will be chopped around in the attack. If she's too much of a mess we'll be obliged to scuttle her when we get close to Ibiza and come home in tenders. I don't want to try explaining bullet holes to police."

"You've got these men down at two thousand pounds a week," Teal said. "Four thousand four hundred bucks. That's a lot of money for a heavy."

Sanderson smiled. "These men aren't 'heavies.' They're professional soldiers who will put their lives on the line. There'll be casualties. Perhaps twenty percent dead, plus wounded."

A long silence filled the room as Quinn and Teal absorbed exactly what Sanderson meant. If Sanderson expected three dead out of their force of thirteen, then he must also be anticipating another three or four wounded. From what he was saying, only half, or less, of the group could expect to leave the battlefield unscathed.

Lena broke the silence. "Excuse me," she said huskily. "I'm going to take some air. I'll make more coffee when I get back." Quinn turned and watched the slim figure cross the room. She closed the door after her. A moment later he heard the front door clicking shut. He felt a compulsive urge to follow her, then was brought back to the business at hand by Teal's question to Sanderson.

"What do we do with our wounded?"

Sanderson pointed to the budget sheet. "We have a medical reserve of twenty-five thousand pounds. With this money we rent a secluded villa in Ibiza and set it up as an emergency hospital. Basic operating equipment, drugs, bandages, instruments etcetera. We staff it with a doctor and two nurses. We patch up the wounded and leave them there to convalesce as long as necessary. Any money left from the reserve is divided among the wounded as a bonus."

"Agreed," Quinn said. He lit a *Winston*. "Where do we find our ten men?"

Sanderson smiled. "They're already found. I had a feeling you'd come through with the money, so I got straight to work. Eight are here in England; two Americans, a Scot and five Englishmen. The others are a pair of very tough Corsicans working in Paris. They'll fly in tomorrow."

"You know these men?"

"I've fought beside all of them. They're handpicked. I guarantee them among the best professional freelance soldiers in the world today."

Quinn pointed at the budget sheet. "You've budgeted to pay the men for only two weeks. Why have you called the Corsicans over already?"

"Because in two weeks we hit Zeller."

"Jesus Christ," Teal breathed. "So soon."

"Your timing in coming to me was perfect," Sanderson told Quinn. "*Shadow* left Grand Harbour in Valletta, Malta, three days ago. Zeller operates like clockwork. *Shadow* will dock in Ibiza harbor in twelve days time. We get Zeller then. If we don't, we have to wait another four months until he returns to the western Mediterranean."

Quinn felt his heart race, and a sudden shiver course through his body. "Can we prepare everything in time?"

"If we work sixteen hours a day, yes. We start tomorrow. Work through the plans detail by detail. Start arranging airfares. Assign someone to Ibiza to arrange a hotel and rent a villa. And tomorrow evening you, Bob and myself are meeting Johnny James at his flat to explain how we'll be using his company's money. I'll pick you up at your hotel around eight."

Sanderson stood and stretched. "Guess that's it for now, gentlemen."

Quinn pointed to the files. "I'd like to read those through. I'll return them tomorrow."

Sanderson shook his head. "You'll have to read them here. I can't let them out of the house. Stay the night if you like. Sleep on the couch."

Quinn shrugged. "All the same to me."

Teal reached for his coat. "I'll take a cab back to the hotel. See you there tomorrow around ten."

When Teal left Sanderson found a pair of blankets and a pillow and tossed them onto the couch in the front room. He stood at the door and looked at the young man settled into the easy chair with the two thick files on his lap.

"You've put up the money, lad, and I thank you for that. But you don't have to come on the op. It's a job for trained soldiers. No one will think badly if you give it a miss."

Quinn looked up, his finger marking a place in the file. "I've got a big stake in this. I'd like to get my money's worth."

Sanderson nodded. "You'll get value," he said. "I promise you that."

Hailey felt good, fit; felt like a new man. No pain now. Tristan had fixed that; talked to him while he rested in the darkness, and his head was fine now. Now he could work again, do what he had to do, what he *wanted* to do for Zeller and Tristan.

Hours ago he'd followed Quinn and Teal from the hotel to this Muswell Hill house and since then he'd stood across the road in the rain, waiting. His orders were specific. Kill them both. By whatever means necessary. Do it quickly and efficiently, within the next two weeks, then report back to *Shadow* when she docked in Ibiza. Something important was afoot; a big arms shipment to be delivered to the Italian Red Brigade. It would be run in from the Sardinian dump next month. Hailey would find a boat, make the run, collect payment on the spot—gold—and rendezvous with *Shadow* at sea to deliver the bullion. But that was the next job. First there was this job.

He'd seen the girl leave half an hour ago. She'd pulled her duffle-coat hood over her head and walked slowly down the street through the rain. She didn't interest Hailey. She had nothing to do with the job. He had briefly considered who she might be and why Quinn and Teal were visiting the suburban house, and concluded they were visiting friends and that the girl and whoever else lived in the house represented no danger to his mission.

Hailey tossed a cigarette butt among the soggy leaves on the pavement and moved from one foot to another to keep his blood circulating. He thrust his hands deep into his pockets for warmth. His right hand touched the gun butt. His friend. *You always have a friend. You always have a friend.*

The door of the house opened again, casting a rectangle of warm light onto the cold garden path. Hailey stopped moving and took one pace backwards to place himself deeper within the shadows of the trees. The silhouette of a man appeared in the frame. Hailey was just close enough to recognize a beard as the man's profile turned toward him an instant before the closing door swallowed the light. Teal!

Teal walked fast down the street in the direction of the shopping center, hunching forward against the rain. Hailey hesitated for perhaps ten seconds, considering whether to follow Teal or wait for Quinn. He decided to follow Teal. The two were never apart for long. Stick with Teal and Quinn would eventually appear. Besides, he needed to walk again after hours of immobility in the freezing English weather.

Hailey kept to the shadows a hundred yards behind Teal. A pity he couldn't kill him here and now. It'd be so easy. But it wasn't the place. You didn't make a hit unless you had a planned exit, and there was no exit when you were on foot in a suburban street.

But the time would come. Hailey would stick close and pick his moment.

* * *

Quinn read the file on Zeller once and decided to work through it again.

Sanderson's biography of the arms dealer was not sequential, but a compilation of hundreds of disjointed facts which, combined, presented a rough sketch of the man rather than a portrait. As Sanderson had explained, the facts came from dozens of sources: policemen, criminals, insurance companies, the press, Interpol, the United Nations, Dutch registry offices, misplaced persons organizations, German concentration camp records, captured terrorists and terrorist organization correspondence, shipping records, private statements from harbor and customs officials around the Mediterranean and, finally, from Quinn himself.

The facts showed what Zeller had done, but told little about who he was. Quinn hoped that a careful second reading might supply some insight into that essential riddle.

Quinn had scarcely settled back to his reading before he heard a key in the front door. For a split second he felt fear, then, just as quickly, realized Lena had returned from her walk. As she closed and bolted the door behind her, Quinn was acutely aware of the pleasure he felt at the fact that she was back and that they would be alone for a few minutes.

He heard the rustle of cloth as she removed her coat and hung it on the hooks beside the door and then she stepped into the room. She looked like a little girl, with her hands clasped in front of her. "Oh," she said, "I expected my father."

"He's gone to bed, and Teal's gone back to the hotel. I've been invited to stay, to read these." He tapped the files on his lap. "I hope you don't mind."

She shook her head. "I'm glad," she said, and then, embarrassed, "I mean, it's a change, having a house guest."

They smiled awkwardly at each other.

"Can I offer you something? Coffee, tea?"

Quinn shook his head.

"Beer? Wine? A brandy, perhaps? A nightcap?"

"A brandy, then."

Quinn watched her walk through the door which connected with the kitchen and heard the clink of glasses. She returned, handed him a glass, then touched hers to his. "Cheers," she said.

"Cheers," Quinn said, and sipped, feeling a glow of warmth as the spirit coursed down to his stomach.

Lena sat on the couch. "You must think me a child," she said. "Leaving like that when the conversation became serious."

Quinn placed the files on he floor, walked across the room and sat beside her on the couch. He shook his head. "The other night you explained yourself quite clearly. Who can blame you? People's lives are at stake. Your father's life."

"And yours," she said.

She glanced at him, started to say something else, then seemed to think better of it.

"I found the money," Quinn said. "I guess you wish I hadn't. I hope you understand."

"Oh yes," she said. "I understand. I've never *not* understood why people want to kill this man. I suppose I want to kill him, too. For what he did to my mother, and God knows how many other people, for what he is. It won't help, but it should be done because no one else will do it . . ." She tailed off, confused. "I'm not making sense." She glanced at him once, then looked away, embarrassed again, and ran a finger around the rim of her brandy balloon.

For five, ten seconds, they sat in awkward silence, then Quinn spoke softly, soothingly, trying to show her that he understood her confusion, wondering at himself all the while that he already cared enough about her to make the effort. "I know how you feel," he said. "I don't want to be involved in all this either. It goes against everything I've ever been taught. On the other hand, I *want* to do it, not from any sense of revenge for Jenny's death—though I first thought it was because of that—but from a sense of rage that this bastard actually gets away with what he does."

Quinn sipped his brandy and then, still not looking at Lena, leaned forward with his elbows resting on his knees, both hands clasping the glass. "There's something else," he said, "something it took me time to admit to myself. I want to hunt Zeller because no one *does* this sort of thing anymore. This is legitimate adventure, and there are no adventures left for the ordinary man. Most men don't get this one chance in all their lives." Quinn glanced at her and smiled. "So there's childishness for you," he said. "Educated, sophisticated New Yorkers aren't supposed to think like that. Such thoughts don't reflect proper liberal attitudes."

"You're honest," she said. "I'll give that." She glanced at him, then away. "Tell me about Jenny."

Quinn felt himself flush and changed his position, not wanting to look at her. "There's not much to tell."

"Were you in love with her?"

"We were involved with each other. We hit it off together and we declared ourselves engaged and talked of getting married. But well before her murder I knew our relationship was heading downhill. I wanted to break with her after the cruise was over. I wanted to find a way of doing it without hurting her."

Quinn took a deep breath and let it out slowly, a protracted sigh. "When she got killed I was confused. I blamed myself. I guess I still do."

"You shouldn't."

"I suppose not."

"It wasn't your fault. It's that simple."

"I feel that I let her down. I don't think she'd reached the point of understanding that we would never make it together. I hadn't said anything to her about going our own ways. So, when she died . . ." Quinn stopped talking and shrugged.

Lena rested her hand on Quinn's wrist. "So, when she died," she said, softly, "she still thought you were in love with her. That's not so bad."

On the Mediterranean's great, dark plain, illuminated only by the feeble light of an overcast moon, *Shadow* slid westwards, her two escorts clinging to port and starboard, just clear of the churning, phosphorescent turbulence of her fan-shaped wake.

Shadow's captain, Ronald Blake, knew the course like the back of his hand. He'd guided *Shadow* thirteen times over the same route, with only occasional diversions. But still, out of habit, as he walked behind the helmsman, he glanced at the dimly lit chart table and felt himself drawn to it like a moth to light.

Shadow cruised a hundred miles northwest of Malta. Forty miles to starboard lay Sicily, and forty miles to port, the tiny, little known Italian island of Pantelleria with its eight and a half thousand citizens and handful of convicts clustered on only thirty-two square miles of volcanic rock. Blake remembered Pantelleria. Once he'd anchored *Shadow* in the island's only port to complete a small but urgent electrical repair—while Zeller had fumed aboard one of the escorts which wallowed uncomfortably two miles out at sea. Not that Blake cared if Zeller fumed, seethed or roared. He was charged with and well paid to keep *Shadow* in first class condition and he would do so, regardless of what that despicable old freak said or did. Zeller owned *Shadow*, but Ronald Blake captained her and he'd damn well look after her.

Blake had no family. Blake had boats. His life revolved around boats. Ten thousand ton coal carriers, thirty thousand ton cargo boats, eighty thousand ton oil tankers, he'd captained them all. And, later, when he'd left the merchant navy he'd captained his share of rich men's toys. But never a vessel as beautiful as *Shadow*.

Shadow was a sailor's dream. Built by a Swedish yard in 1974, her steel hull measured one hundred twenty-eight feet, her beam twenty-five feet and her draft twelve feet six inches. Her twin 342 Caterpillar diesels drove a single control shaft to a variable pitch propeller which, if Zeller ever wanted, could cruise the one hundred eighty-five ton vessel at a steady nine knots. At this cruising speed *Shadow*'s forty ton capacity fuel tanks gave her a range of over 5000 miles. Four spare five ton tanks especially added to her capacious hold guaranteed that *Stingray 1* and *Stingray 2*—her twin thirty-two foot escorts, capable of top speeds exceeding thirty knots—could stay with *Shadow* for over 3000 miles without coming into port.

Shadow's fresh water tanks held twenty-five tons, and her desalination plant could produce another six hundred gallons daily. Her galleys held food for forty men for six months. Her dual voltage electrical system supplied power even for air conditioning. A twelve foot by ten foot workshop built into the hold, and containing everything from electric drills to lathes, guaranteed that *Shadow*'s crew could maintain her—and the Stingrays—in top condition.

On the boat deck, aft of the bridge, were three cabins for Zeller, Tristan and the occasional visitor. Each of these cabins boasted a double bed, its own private bathroom and toilet. Further aft was a full width stateroom, a dining-sitting area, enclosed at the stern by polarized glass, and containing quadrophonic stereo, television with video cassette system and a collection of over 500 taped films, a 1000-volume library and an upright piano.

Aft of the hold, A deck, directly below the boat deck, contained quarters for Blake and Young, his first mate—private cabins with individual bathrooms—the galley and crew dining-room. Forward lay the crew's recreation room, with bar, billiards table and table-tennis, and also equipped with stereo and a video cassette system, plus storage areas. Blake and Young commanded eighteen men on *Shadow*, six men each working an eight hour shift. As well, each Stingray carried six men, three men each working twelve hours. Each week twelve men from *Shadow* interchanged with the Stingray crews to relieve them of the boredom of manning the smaller craft. Blake and Young each worked twelve hour shifts, each man during his shift in absolute command of the tiny armada and responsible only to Zeller and each other.

B deck, forward of the hold, contained refrigerated cold rooms, air conditioning equipment, stores and supplies. Aft was an area to which crew were forbidden entry on pain of death. The death sentence had been carried out only once during Blake's seven years aboard *Shadow* and was performed on Zeller's command by Blake himself. A curious crewman had entered the forbidden area and been caught snooping by Tristan. Blake shot the man in the back of the neck and threw him overboard. Blake had been in the area only once, during his inspection tour when he first took command of the ship. He'd seen two private cabins used as offices by Tristan and Zeller, a communications room and what looked like a medical laboratory with a huge steel box in the center. No one had explained to him what purpose the box served. When Zeller's ground agents visited the ship—he had six of them and each visited, on average, twice a year—they were escorted to this part of B deck and left waiting in the tiny ante-room beside the laboratory. Only Selby, *Shadow*'s radio officer, visited this private area regularly. He adjusted Zeller's highly complicated electronic communications equipment.

C deck was devoted to the engine room, paint lockers, anchor and chain lockers, fuel and water tanks, a small room containing scuba gear, a diving suit and an air compressor, and the desalination plant. The area of the hold not covered by the workshop remained empty on Zeller's orders. It was used for arms shipments too large to be handled by the Stingrays or whatever other methods Zeller used to deliver. Perhaps once a year *Shadow* met a ship at sea and took aboard several tons of arms. Zeller would then order Blake to change course and head for a rendezvous off Libya, Albania, Greece, Cyprus or perhaps Italy, and the arms would be transferred again.

C deck contained one other room, a small one, less than three meters long by two and a half wide, cunningly built into the superstructure to conceal it from casual customs inspection. *Shadow* was rarely inspected, because her captain was known in official circles around the Mediterranean for his hospitality and generosity. Blake estimated he gave away $50,000 of Zeller's money annually in "presents." Not that *Shadow* ever smuggled anything into the ports she visited. Zeller was adamant about that. Her transactions—when she was directly involved—were always completed on the high seas. The "presents" were awarded, in the form of interest-free personal cash "loans" on the understanding that *Shadow*, on her part, would never smuggle dutiable goods through the ports she visited for refueling, and that customs men would avoid searching *Shadow* when she docked, or, if they were obliged to because of the presence of senior officials, would avoid asking questions or repeating possibly embarrassing information about what they may have seen aboard the boat. *Shadow*, Blake assured them, was owned by an international company registered in Liberia and used as a tax-deductable floating hotel for company executives. Certainly, *Shadow* flew the Liberian flag.

The small room contained a selection of pistols, assault rifles, submachine guns and ammunition, hand-grenades and grenade launchers; enough weaponry to arm everyone aboard *Shadow*. Both Stingrays contained similar lockers. Each escort also mounted a heavy machine gun and carried portable ground to air missiles—the American Redeye anti-aircraft guided missile system weighing only thirty pounds but with an effective range, at supersonic speed, of over a mile. When either Stingray needed to enter port, all armaments were transferred to *Shadow*.

All of the thirty-two men who crewed Zeller's private navy knew how to use the weapons at their disposal. Some had learned their skills in the armed services, others had been mercenaries. All, Blake included, had at one time or another been professional criminals or smugglers—adventurers who operated outside society's accepted framework and welcomed the chance to sign on with Zeller. All were unmarried. Each man employed by Zeller was introduced to the organization by another already working for it. Each signed on for two years minimum, two years without vacation, but with a guaranteed $50,000 paid in any currency anywhere in the world at the end of that time. $50,000 clean, because Zeller paid all clothing, food, accommodation and entertainment costs from the moment a man joined him. Entertainment included brief shore leave when *Shadow* came into port, usually once a month, and visits to local brothels. At the end of two years a man who wished to sign on again was entitled to three months paid vacation before beginning his next contract.

Blake had figured it out once. To pay the thirty-two crewmen—eighteen on *Shadow*, six on each Stingray, the first mate and himself—to feed and clothe them, to cruise the boats and maintain them, cost Zeller $800,000 in wages, $175,000 in food, clothing and facilities, $400,000 in maintenance and updating of electronic equipment and $300,000 in fuel. In round figures, $1,700,000 annually. And that figure didn't include salaries to his land-based staff, nor rents and maintenance on his real estate. The arms business, Blake concluded, was *big* business!

Blake leaned over the chart table and redirected the

moveable light to illuminate the overall map of the Mediterranean which lay on top of the current area chart. Soon they would steer north for the Tyrrhenian Sea, round the tip of Sicily and sail for the most northeastern of the Lipari Islands, Stromboli, a still active volcano, jutting out of the sea. It was Zeller's particular pleasure to cruise at night around the island waiting for one of its frequent and spectacular puffs, when great smudges of deep red flame and smoke painted the indigo night sky.

Then it would be northwest again, trudging the length of the Tyrrhenian into the Tuscan Arch between Corsica and Elba and west into the Ligurian Sea and southwest toward the Balearics, avoiding as much as possible the great rolling waves which built up in the Gulf of Lions. In Ibiza, with any luck he'd get ashore long enough to enjoy a meal in one of the quayside fish restaurants and perhaps find himself a girl for a couple of hours. Blake straightened and stretched, trying to ignore the almost instant contraction of his testicles at the thought of naked female flesh beneath him.

He yawned and glanced around the wheelhouse. The helmsman stood steady, conscious he was being watched, both hands on the wheel, one eye on the compass. Blake had never worked in a better equipped bridge, even in his merchant navy days. Zeller spared no expense. Among *Shadow*'s array of electronic marvels—all duplicated in case of breakdown—were satellite navigation systems, alone worth over $100,000 for the pair, sixty-mile range radars, echo sounders and depth recorders, auto-pilots, multi-channel transmitters and receivers, more decoders, and two computer controlled panels allowing every engine room system to be monitored from the bridge. Blake estimated that if *Shadow* was ever placed on the market she would fetch over $12,000,000.

Blake glanced at the master compass and nodded to the helmsman. "Hold her steady. I'm taking a walk around deck then rustling up coffee and a snack for both of us."

"Good idea, sir."

"Call me if there's a problem."

Blake slid open the weather-proofed wheelhouse door and stepped out into the night. He breathed the chilly air in deeply, tasting the salt in his throat. A fresh wind swept down from the north, whipping cones of spray off the choppy sea. He'd forgotten the helmsman's name. He was a new man who'd joined them in Malta; a good sailor, competent, polite. And dangerous. He was on the run after killing a policeman with a sawed-off shotgun during a raid on a London bank.

Blake leaned on the railing and stared out at *Stingray 1* on their starboard. If the sea kicked up any further—and the barometer was dropping fast—then the boys were in for a rough ride. Boats like that weren't made to wallow around at five knots. They were designed to get up on their haunches and go like the powers of hell. Blake smiled to himself. He'd ridden a few of those babies in his day, running booze into England from the Continent, cameras into Spain from Morocco, drugs into Greece from Turkey. That's how he and Zeller had found each other. The Greek cops were after him in Piraeus, searched his boat when he was ashore, found five kilos of heroin and arrested his partner. Someone told the girl he was with and she hid him. Then Tristan appeared out of nowhere, like a miracle, and next thing he was aboard one of the Stingrays that was in port picking up fresh vegetables and on his way to *Shadow*.

Blake turned up his collar. It'd worked out well, but Tristan and Zeller, Christ, what a pair they were. That creepy old bastard, snooping around the ship like a ghost, looking, checking, never speaking to anyone except him, Blake, or the first mate. Not even talking to Tristan now. Something had happened between those two. They avoided each other. Ate in their cabins, never sat together in the salon, locked themselves in their offices. And Tristan, well Tristan was just a fucking freak, and nothing more to be said.

Blake leaned into the freshening wind and walked toward the bow with its spider-like landing pad bolted into the deck and protruding three feet either side of the railing. Atop it the three seater Bell helicopter stood poised, a great, ungainly silhouette against the starless sky. If Zeller ever wanted to sell *Shadow* he'd have to dismantle that damned ugly pad. It destroyed the ship's line, made her look like a cross between an aircraft carrier and a pregnant sow instead of the sleek beauty she was.

Blake checked the cables and slings holding down the chopper and satisfied that all was secure strolled aft down the port side, glancing over at *Stringray 2*. He saw her uncomfortable roll. *Shadow* was still steady because of her stabilizers. A storm was brewing, he could smell it, and he continued on down the deck, deciding he'd check that the three twenty-four man life rafts, the two twenty foot Boston whalers and Zeller's speedboat were properly battened down.

Zeller was leaning on the stern railing staring at *Shadow's* white, bubbling wake. He turned, somehow hearing Blake's approach, even above the wind. Blake inwardly cursed, more interested in coffee and sandwiches than talking with his employer, this thin, weird old man with his wheezing, stinking breath and white skin stretched tight over his skull. How old was the old bugger, anyway? Eighty? Older? Zeller stared as Blake approached. He wore that ancient black overcoat which made him look like a beggar on a Soho street. His shoulders hunched against the cold wind. The coat melted into the near blackness of the overcast sky, only his white face shining from the glow of the stern deck light.

"Ah, Captain Blake."

"Evening, Mr. Zeller."

Blake watched Zeller's head nod up and down. He leaned on the rail beside Zeller waiting for him to speak, and noted with disgust the faint odor of decay which even the salt laden wind couldn't disguise.

"The dollar dropped two points today, Mr. Blake."

"Really, sir."

Zeller turned back to face where they had come from, and Blake saw him staring in the direction of Sicily.

"Will we have a storm, Mr. Blake?"

"Very probably, sir. I would say, yes."

Zeller sighed. "I can't tell you, Mr. Blake, how much I despise the sea."

Blake said nothing, waiting, hoping Zeller would leave or dismiss him.

"I have based my whole business practice on the philosophy that a commodity is better than cash. A commodity holds an intrinsic value, Mr. Blake, which is dependant upon its practical use at a given moment. If one can create circumstances to raise the value of the commodity one holds . . ."

"Yes, sir."

"The dollar dropped two points, did I mention that?"

"Yes, sir."

"But gold rose twenty-five cents per ounce. So if yesterday one bought a commodity with dollars and today one sold it for gold . . ."

A sudden squall chased *Shadow*, caught her and flicked a sheet of spray against the stern. Blake sensed the growing movement of the ship beneath his feet. The sea ran stronger now, could kick up into a hell of a blow.

"If one trains oneself to anticipate which commodities the world needs, and can buy those commodities with a . . ." Zeller coughed, reached into his pocket for a handkerchief and wiped the salty dampness from his face.

". . . one despises the sea. All acts of nature. Irrevocable. Uncontrollable. Unprofitable. When do we see Stromboli again, captain?"

"Two nights from now, sir."

"People live on Stromboli, Mr. Blake."

"Yes, sir."

"And tourists visit. People *live* on a live volcano. They cannot control it, not anticipate its action. They are playing with God, like children. Trusting Him not to turn the game into a practical joke. Do you believe in God, Mr. Blake?"

"Haven't thought too much about it, sir."

"God is a thief, Mr. Blake."

Black clouds descended, and with them came rain, sudden torrential sheets, and on the horizon spider's webs of lightning seared the sky. Another squall, vicious, swept spray high over *Shadow*.

Zeller wiped his face again and moved unsteadily from the rail. Blake took his arm to support him and led him toward the salon door.

"Death is a nonprofit enterprise," Zeller said. He coughed again, wheezed, and leaned against Blake.

Blake slid open the salon door and helped Zeller over the storm step, then stood waiting to see if Zeller wanted anything.

"Did I tell you, Mr. Blake? The dollar dropped two points today!"

Outside it still rained, and wind gusts swept down the street, slamming into the houses, rattling windows. Quinn didn't notice.

"We'd been on holiday in London," Lena said. "My mother and I. We were happy to be home again. I couldn't wait to leave the airport and catch the bus from Tel Aviv to Jerusalem. We were waiting for our luggage, talking with some Puerto Ricans who had arrived on another flight. They were pilgrims, they'd been saving for years to make the trip. My mother spoke some Spanish. They were asking her about Israel and she was suggesting where they could go and what they could do."

Lena sipped her brandy and took a cigarette from her pack. Quinn leaned forward and flicked his lighter for her. Her hand gently touched his to steady the flame in front of her cigarette and she stared into Quinn's eyes, through them, beyond them, as she sorted and censored her memories of that day, choosing the images with which she would describe the horror to him.

"I was very young," she said, "so for long moments I didn't understand what was happening. Suddenly there was noise, and it didn't make sense. Talking with these people one moment, then this noise the next. Grenade explosions, bursts of automatic fire, people screaming. My mother pushed me to the floor. I fell into a pool of blood, beside one of the Puerto Ricans. The side of his face was ripped away. He clutched at me when I fell beside him, babbling in agony and shock. I think I screamed, he looked so monstrous, but I remember I kept staring at him. My mother yelled at me to take cover behind a row of luggage trolleys. My mother was pushing me, sliding me across the floor through the blood. I got up and ran and reached the trolleys. I turned to look for my mother."

Lena drew on her cigarette and then very carefully knocked the burned ash into the ashtray. She drained her brandy glass and ran her finger around its rim.

"It was so strange," she said, quietly, "that I should have turned at that exact moment. And it was so strange the way my mind analyzed what I saw, because it must have taken less than a second, but I turned, with the screaming and the shouting and the shooting roaring in my head, and I saw my mother on her hands and knees scrambling toward me and then, at the edge of my vision, I saw a man come to his feet and sprint toward an exit door and a line of bullets exploded across the floor toward him, blasting chunks of the floor as they impacted, and this man was hit in the knees and somersaulted and landed on his back screaming, screaming, and I saw the same line of bullets bursting across the floor toward my mother and when she was only meters from me they caught her and one knocked her legs from under her and two more hit her in the chest and she lay on her side in her own blood with her hand stretched out toward me and I crawled out from behind the trolleys and grabbed her and somehow pulled her behind cover, thinking she was safe.''

Lena took a deep breath, steeling herself to tell the climax of her terrible story. Quinn stared straight into his glass, his head bowed, unable to meet her eyes, shocked at the intensity with which she related the dark events of a day which had marked the end of childhood for a little girl.

"Then she opened her mouth to speak to me, but no words came, only blood, and she died, and at the moment she died the shooting stopped and there was only the screaming left.''

Lena drew on her cigarette again and still speaking quietly, said, ''That's how my mother died. May 30, 1972. One of twenty-eight dead and seventy wounded. Three Japanese members of the Red Army killed all those people. They used Kalachnikov carbines and hand grenades. Two of the Japanese died during the attack, but the survivor, Nozo Okamoto, told Israeli intelligence that he'd been trained in Europe by a man called Hector Hippodikon. It was later established that Hippodikon was an alias for Carlos, the 'Jackal.' My father was able to prove that Zeller provided Carlos with weapons from 1971 through to 1973.''

Lena stubbed her cigarette into the ashtray, doubling the butt, grinding the tip into the base. "Zeller was as responsible as anyone for turning my mother into a statistic.''

Zeller sat at the desk in his communications room on ''B'' deck and brooded. In front of him lay the two inches thick master inventory for the six arms dumps he had spent the last fifteen years establishing around the Mediterranean. Zeller boasted to his customers that at any time he could supply them with enough light and medium weapons to equip an army of up to 20,000 men. So far such a large order hadn't materialized but there had been, for instance, the recent Cuban order for 2500 self-loading rifles, 1500 sidearms and three million rounds of ammunition which Zeller had successfully delivered to representatives of the El Salvadoran guerrillas. A cargo boat had landed them in Puerto Barrios in Guatamala and the guerrillas' intelligence service had made their own arrangements for delivery from there. The invoice on that order, including shipment and bribes to customs officials in Morocco—from where the shipment originated—and Guatamala, had totaled $1,650,000. Zeller's profit totaled over half a million dollars. The sum had been paid in gold.

Crumbling regimes provided Zeller with an almost inexhaustable supply of first class weapons. Procurement was risky, but the rewards immense. For instance, during the first months of 1975, as the North Vietnamese swept through the south to take Saigon, Zeller and half a dozen other dealers negotiated with corrupt South Vietnamese army officials to buy thousands of tons of ammunition, military equipment and unused weapons which the Americans had left in huge arsenals during their withdrawal. Zeller paid over five million dollars in gold for a boatload of material which was now distributed between his six dumps. He estimated that he would eventually realize $23,000,000 profit on the purchase.

But Zeller considered the everyday weapons bought from these kind of stockpiles—handguns, rifles, light automatic weapons, grenades—as the bread and butter of his trade. All dealers held warehouses full of such material and pricing was competitive. There was simply too much of it about. For instance, the AK-47 Soviet assault rifle—named after its designer Mikhail Timofeevitch Kalachnikov—had been in service somewhere in the world since 1951 and built in a dozen versions in as many countries. The advantages of the weapon —instantly recognizably by its distinctive thirty round banana-shaped magazine—were simplicity of design and dependabil-

ity. Under the toughest conditions and in the most inexperienc-
ed hands the gun simply kept on firing. So, apart from being a
superb weapon in the hands of experts, it became the ideal
weapon for revolutionary armies fighting wars with partially
trained soldiers who paid little attention to the maintenance of
their hardware. But for Zeller, the AK-47 offered one big
disadvantage. Over 30,000,000 of them had been produced.
They were literally a dime a dozen. It was impossible to corner
the market. And it was when you had a corner on the market
that you made the *real* money!

For Zeller, specialization was the key to successful business
because there were simply too many merchants in the business
and not enough money to go around. The world currently spent
one hundred and twenty billion dollars annually on weapons,
but dealers, between them, had to share less than one percent
of that sum.

True, the casualty rate among dealers was high—over forty
had been assassinated since the Second World War, mostly by
government agencies or pro-government organizations desperate to halt the arms flow to insurgent forces. "The Red Hand,"
the French Right Wing organization, had killed eight dealers
supplying rebels during the Algerian conflict; the Israelis had
killed two supplying the Palestinians; Zeller knew of two the
KGB had assassinated who had sold weapons to the Afghan
rebels. From Zeller's point of view, the more dead dealers the
better. Their demise left a greater share of trade to the survivors
who were able to edge prices upward. On the other hand
continual attacks on dealers were instrumental in forcing
Zeller's decision to live on *Shadow* and protect himself with the
Stingrays. Too many people on both sides of the political fence
wanted him dead. There'd been three attempts before he'd
condemned himself to *Shadow*, a narrow moveable front,
easily defended.

Specialization though, that was the key. And during the last
few years Zeller had concentrated on procuring weapons no
other dealers had. Weapons terrorists and guerrillas wanted,
weapons they'd pay anything to get with money they had in
abundance supplied by outside forces intent on destabilizing or
re-establishing the status quo. Russian money channeled to the
Italian terrorists; Libyan money supplied to the Palestinians;

Cuban money given to the guerrillas of El Salvador; American money given to the Afghan rebels.

Among Zeller's best-selling items:

Liquid Explosive poured or sprayed on any substance and detonated remotely or by pressure. If poured on the ground the liquid self-neutralizes within four days. Though designed primarily for use against tanks, terrorists had successfully used it against trains and police vehicles. ETA assassination units in Spain's Basquelands were studying the possibility of applying it to door handles and automobile foot pedals used by their intended victims;

Riot Control Munitions traditionally used by police to disperse riots or potentially riotous crowds, were now being used by urban terrorists to create panic among peacefully gathered congregations at meetings and rallies, among spectators at football matches, even on crowded city streets during rush-hour. Among the most popular items: a 38mm multi-purpose gun capable of firing hard rubber balls or the more dangerous 135 gramme rubber baton round which leaves the gun at one hundred meters per second and causes severe bruising, and a wide selection of gas grenades. Zeller's best-selling gas grenades, all capable of being hand thrown as well as fired, were the CN's which triggered a powerful lachrymal effect, irritated respiratory passages, caused coughing, difficulty in breathing, tightness in the chest and often nausea and vomiting as well. Also popular was the slightly less powerful CS gas which came in a handy aerosol can and was regularly used to stupify kidnap victims;

Incendiary Hand Grenades containing a thermite mixture which burns for forty-five seconds and generates heat to over 2200 degrees centigrade and prized by terrorist groups as a fast-acting and effective arson weapon;

M21 7.62mm Sniping Rifles capable of laying a ten round group within a six-inch circle at 300 meters range and fitted with a muzzle suppressor which, without affecting bullet velocity, successfully reduced velocity of emerging gases to below the speed of sound thus making location of riflemen difficult to estimate. Also fitted with zoom telescopic sights which, when adjusted for range automatically, apply correct tangent elevation. Coveted by IRA snipers for use against British troops in Belfast street ambushes;

Electronic Sights, sought after by guerrilla armies to improve shooting accuracy of hurriedly trained recruits. Infinitely more effective than traditional open iron sights, electronic sights—for example, the Swedish designed Aim-point—are battery operated optical units which clamp on the rifle like telescopic sights and project a red dot within the optics which exactly coincide with the weapon's point of aim. When this red dot coincides with what the firer is aiming at, the rifle is on target. Rapid fire accuracy, particularly in low light levels, is enchanced by several hundred percent;

Portable Missile and Rocket Systems, either anti-tank or anti-aircraft were the most wanted items in Zeller's arsenals. They were also the hardest to get and, thus, the most expensive. Typical of the systems Zeller occasionally supplied: the French SARPAC anti-tank rocket-launcher weighing only three to four kilos (depending on ammunition used) and capable of being fired from the shoulder and piercing 300 mm of armor at 200 meters; the American Stinger Anti-Aircraft Guided Missile system, an optically aimed, rocket propelled, infra-red homing missile weighing 13.4 kilos and fired by one man from the shoulder to a range of over 1000 meters. Many missile systems of this type could be used for tasks other than they were designed for. Some anti-aircraft missiles could be used—though with little accuracy—as artillery pieces. Most anti-tank systems could be employed against other road vehicles and trains and also against fortifications or buildings. Most portable systems could be vehicle-mounted. Also, Zeller was carefully monitoring, through his spy network, develop-ments in the United States and Britain of portable systems capable of launching rockets armed with miniature nuclear warheads. How he could ever buy or steal such weapons he did not know, but he had three clients who had offered him one million dollars in gold for nuclear warheads capable of one man delivery against an airfield. These clients knew that having such a capacity would allow them to recoup their investment many times over in publicity and ransom.

Zeller flicked through the inventory then pushed it to the

back of his desk. He knew, just about to the last round of ammunition, what he had in the six dumps, each of them opened in a strategic location to serve particular areas. Tangier for Saharan and Mauritanian insurgents and the terrorist factions in Northern Ireland and northwest Spain. Barcelona as a staging dump handling repairs and modifications. Naples, specifically handling trade with the burgeoning Italian militants. Cyprus, the perfect midway point for supply to the trigger-happy Lebanese, to the Palestinians and Turkey's beleagured Kurdish guerrillas. The small dump on the Greek island of Corfu had been established in anticipation of renewed trouble by Croatian separatists in Yugoslavia and of coming guerrilla activity in Albania; in the meantime, it proved useful as an alternative supply for Italy and occasional deliveries to various Central African rebel groups sponsored by Libya— Libya allowing the arms to move across her territory, but preferring to pay for weapons untraceable to her own arsenal. The newly opened Marseille dump would supply French Basque separatists, West German militants and, Zeller hoped, eventually prove a profitable demonstration and display warehouse for the growing number of South and Central American revolutionary factions searching Europe for regular supplies of up-to-date hardware.

Zeller dealt not only with revolutionaries, terrorists and sponsoring regimes like Libya, Cuba, America and Russia who paid for weapons to aid dissidents, but also with outcast nations in need of arms but unable to buy them because of political and economic embargos.

Common—and not so common—criminals were also a source of income to Zeller. His agents, all working on a retainer, expenses and commission basis, were chosen as much for their ability to move comfortably in the higher stratas of diplomatic society where they could discover who wanted to sell, who wanted to buy and who was open to bribes should certain documents be needed, as they were for their considerable practical knowledge of small arms. But these agents—twenty-four of them, both men and women, and all multi-lingual—all knew how to work with equal facility in the underworld of European crime and terrorism.

Nowadays murder attempts were made at night with sniping rifles fitted with infra-red nightscopes, with FF 028 anti-tanks mines which not only blew up cars but disintegrated them, or with shotguns loaded with flechettes, or miniature darts, within a twelve gauge shell, which left the barrel at 1800 feet per second and literally tore a man in half. Bank robbers were habitually armed with submachine guns capable of spewing out bullets at the rate of seven hundred per minute, house-breakers considered cannon-sized Magnum revolvers an essential tool of their trade, kidnappers armed themselves with military gas masks and CS grenades and even everyday muggers felt undressed without a service automatic tucked in their waist-band. Zeller's agents sold all these items and more. With some satisfaction, Zeller had estimated that during the previous twelve months his sales for criminal activity had risen three percent to now total twelve percent of all sales. For the rest, terrorist and guerrilla organizations accounted for seventy-one percent of his turnover while international deals to govern-ments accounted for the other seventeen percent.

Zeller opened another folder and glanced at the top page, at the long list of arms he had supplied to all sources during the previous twelve months. The list gratified him, demonstrating a significant upward sales trend.

Operating costs were high; Zeller realized that, but he considered the costs acceptable because he was preparing for a future filled with the enormous promise of expanding political chaos.

The great ebb and flow of fortune and circumstance battered the ramparts of both the world's principal ideologies. Russia promoted the decline of the West by supporting worldwide terrorism and revolution, apparently ignoring that her own back was to the wall as her hostage satellites experimentally flexed their nationalistic muscles with strikes and symbolic declarations of intent against Moscow. In the Middle East, Jews and Arabs probed each other warily, never sure of the amount of support they could expect from Moscow or Washington, but both knowing that eventually the cauldron would overflow again with either an all-out war against each other, or—better from Zeller's point of view—an all-out war among the Arabs themselves.

In Africa, the blacks crouched poised to wipe out the whites, and in the meantime practiced on each other. In Afghanistan, the Russians found themselves sucked deeper and deeper into the quagmire of guerrilla warfare. In Iraq, the Kurdish minority fought a belligerent government for their very existence. In Iran, a revolution within a revolution had dragged the population through victory against a political dictatorship, into a religious dictatorship, through a war and, now, into complete social confusion and despondancy. Pakistan poised herself warily, expecting a Russian invasion from the west, half expecting an Indian invasion from the south. India herself sought an impossible task, national unity in a land of 670,000,000 people, who comprised three different ethnic types and spoke fifteen languages. Southeast Asia continued ripping itself apart, those countries not yet defeated by communist invasion fighting pitched battles against communist guerrillas within their national boundaries. Taiwan pointed her guns uselessly at China, knowing she was a mere pawn in East-West relations. China patrolled her borders with Russia, each country knowing that the other waited only a favorable mesh of international events before escalating border clashes into full-scale war. North and South Korea continued to peck at each other. Japan policed her revolutionaries; the Philippines engaged hers in jungle warfare. America, the guardian of the west, spent billions annually, frantically trying to knit the mess into a coherent front, matching dollar for dollar and deterrent for deterrent Russia's equally frantic attempts at disruption.

And all this without even considering the maelstrom of Central and South America, a continent so riddled with social unrest, political dissatisfaction, ambition and sedition that in some capitals—so the joke went—presidents left the palace gates open to save the country the expense of replacing them when the next contender rolled his tanks into the courtyard for his coup.

But Zeller considered South America a market for the future. He'd made sales there and would make more. For now, though, the Mediterranean basin and Europe were his special territories. Fully eighty-five percent of his sales originated there—some twelve million dollars—and he knew he had only scratched the surface. Zeller felt that between North Africa and Europe he could double his sales within five years.

If he could live that long.

If Tristan would *allow* him to.

Zeller sighed and wearily pushed himself from his desk. He felt the movement of the boat beneath his feet. The stabilizers had held her fairly steady so far, but now she was beginning to pitch and the stabilizers couldn't do anything about that.

Still wearing his old, black coat, Zeller walked carefully across the cabin and stared out into the blackness through a porthole. Water, like black oil, smeared itself across the glass and fell away, then sloshed up again as *Shadow* pitched into another trough. Zeller couldn't see further than the glass, only sensed rather than saw the black, sloshing water against the demon black of the night.

He turned from the porthole and looked around the small cabin which served as the fulcrum of his empire, at the powerful transmitting and receiving equipment and the banks of filing cabinets which contained political analysis and carefully gathered information about opposing forces in each of the world's countries. Somewhere in each file lay the key to introducing illegal arms into every nation in the world. Every nation had its Achilles' heel and Zeller knew them all.

But there wasn't time to conquer the world. Tristan was forsaking him.

Zeller's shoulders slumped as he thought about Tristan.

Zeller had left the safe open, the man-high strong room. He glanced once at it contents then swung the heavy, well-oiled door closed, switched out the light, locked his office door and walked up the gangway to his private cabin. He kicked off his shoes and lay in the darkness on his double bed, hating the movement of *Shadow*, hating Tristan, willing himself to fall into the precious hour of slumber which was the nightly ration his body allowed him. How long since he'd slept a full night's sleep? Forty years? Since the day he'd entered the camp. Never slept more than an hour a night since then. How he hated the sleeplessness, the laying awake in the dark waiting for dawn.

Awake and listening to the sounds of the bastard sea, the creaks and groans of shifting bulkheads, feeling *Shadow* pitch and roll. And forty years of this treacherous body denying him escape into the bottomless black depths of sweet sleep. No one could ever understand the subtle torture of a body denying sleep it didn't need, of forcing a mind to live with itself twenty-three hours a day. Working sixteen hours a day, watching films seen over and over again, just to pass the day and the night until finally it was time again for that one precious hour of escape from the self. And the release gone in a flash, replaced again by the demands of the seething, tumultuous mind. Contracts, payments, deliveries, purchases, bribes, assassinations, information, collation, anticipation, end certificates, military missions, testing reports, daily bulletins.

And Tristan. Denying him. Locked in that laboratory, theorizing about the tank, writing a thesis on sensory deprivation to awaken the medical world to his genius. The fool. What was he doing for Zeller, the man who had given him everything? Nothing. Tristan was denying him, taking instead of giving, hoarding instead of sharing, denying instead of affirming. Not acting as a son should act.

Dollar down, gold up, francs an advantage over marks, diamonds performing better than silver. Contact Cyprus tomorrow re PLO request for anti-aircraft missiles; the Swedish contact could supply, ship direct to Israel, intercept boat and remove. Hailey would do that. Has Hailey solved the problem of those two snoopers? Must close the Paris apartment. Find another. Just in case. Probably not important. And that idiot in Rome. A drunkard, unsavory, uncouth, like Gloster in Málaga. Not performing . . .

Zeller closed his eyes and tried to relax his mind, tried desperately to sleep, to cheat the unreasonable demands of his body, to escape the hailstorm of thoughts and ideas that pelted him day and night.

He concentrated on the one thing in the world he loved. The contents of his strong room. The fruit of his labors.

Over one thousand pounds weight in pure gold. Worth ten million dollars.

* * *

Quinn didn't know how it happened. He certainly hadn't planned it. They talked for hours together in the cocoon of the house, deep into the stormy, wind-blown night, talked about how Lena's mother died, what had happened that day on *Destry*, the events which had led him to her father, the wild, crazy adventure which now confronted him. And of his fears, and of hers. And of his father's fear and generosity, and what he must do in the future to repay him. And she said that she understood what Peter and her father were about to do and would not try to stop them. And paused, and added quietly, that when her father came back—if her father came back—she would make him promise never to touch a gun again.

Then suddenly she was crying. This tough girl. Scared out of her mind because of what was about to happen. And, unknowingly, Quinn had his arm about her, comforting her, quieting her like a child, hushing her, shushing her, consoling her, promising her that everything would be O.K., that nothing would happen to her father.

Then she nuzzled her face against his neck, sobbing, and he stroked her hair, then kissed the top of her head, and she raised her face and he kissed her forehead, whispering to her all the time, then brushed his lips against hers, still whispering, pleading with her not to cry, and Lena kissed him back, lightly, and their hands met and clenched and they stared at each other, then kissed again, mysterious urgency commanding this physical reply, forcing lips to press and mouths to open, tongues to caress and breath to mingle and hands to move in silent exploration over unfamiliar bodies. And to Quinn and Lena came a strange emotional release, a mutual laying of the ghosts of the past, a salve easing the tensions of the present and a soft, uncomplicated promise for the future. And they broke the kiss and drew each other close, feeling tensions fall away. They accepted each other.

"I want you to make love to me," she whispered.

He didn't answer, but kissed her forehead and let his hand wander over her breasts.

She took his hand gently, pulling it away, squeezing it. "But not here."

Still not speaking, his hand fought hers gently, wresting

itself away and finding her breast again, weighing lovingly the soft mound of it, tempting the nipple through the fabric of covering clothing, unable to stop.

She didn't refuse him, but surrendered to the caress, gasped as his softly pinching fingers pulled at the core of her and her hands moved over his thighs, pushing between his legs and she felt the growing swell and she squeezed and he mumbled to her, begging, lovingly pleading.

"Not here," she whispered again, and smoothly broke from him, determined, standing, reaching down with both hands to take his. "Come." And she led him silently through the silent house, upstairs to her bedroom.

She closed the door, took three steps through the darkness and switched on her bedside lamp. It lit the small, cosy room with a warm glow. They stood quietly beside the bed staring at each other in childish wonder, as if neither believed what was happening. Outside, gusting wind blew sheets of rain against the house. It spurted rhythmically against the windows, then stopped as the wind momentarily faded.

She smiled, then turned her back to him as she began to undress. He sat on the bed staring, unable to wrench his eyes away, mesmerized by the sliding slip of cloth against her skin, each movement revealing more of her slender, strong, olive-tanned body. Naked, she turned, suddenly embarrassed, arms across her breasts to conceal them, and with eyes averted she smiled, stepped quickly to the bed and slipped under the covers.

Still sitting on the narrow, single bed, Quinn kicked off his shoes, then stood, pulled off his clothes, turned and looked down at her. She reached up one hand and traced her fingers down his chest to his stomach.

Then she lifted the covers for him and her eyes beckoned and he lowered himself over her, down between her open legs, and she pulled the covers up over their shoulders and gripped her legs around his waist.

He nuzzled her neck, kissed the curves there, savored the taste of her, resting himself on one elbow, his free hand stroking the long, black hair, whispering to her, telling her she was beautiful, playing out the ritual of seduction where none was needed. Then ran his hand down through her hair and softly over her face, down her body and under her buttocks, squeezing them, and his mouth trailed down her neck to her two small, firm breasts, nipples erect and hard, and seized them first one, then the other between his lips and teased them, tempted them, sucked them until they swelled even further and she groaned and gripped him harder with her legs, arching up against him, trapping his erection between their stomachs and, thus contorted, he reached between them, took his cock in his hand and rubbed the swollen head against the entrance to her vagina.

"Be careful," she whispepred.

"I'll come outside you."

"Not that." She buried her head in under his chin. "Be careful. Be gentle."

She kissed him, her tongue fighting desperately with his, her eyes clenched tightly closed, and Quinn sensed a desperation in her, a tenseness, a fear, a stiffening, and interpreted it as lust and slipped into her and almost immediately felt her hips twitch as if in self defense and heard her gasp within the deepness of their kiss and he held his own hips steady, unwilling to push in further.

"Did I hurt you?"

"It's nothing."

"Are you moist enough?"

"I don't know."

"I'll help you."

He disengaged himself from her, slid down her body and twisted so his head rested on her thighs, his chin on the silky black triangle of her pubic hair. He felt her tensing, kissed her firm, warm thighs and as she relaxed pushed her legs further apart, gently tongued the lips of her cunt, darting here and there, playfully teasing her into enjoyment, letting saliva moisten her entrance, making her own juices flow.

Suddenly her hands sought him, commanding him to right himself again, and as he buried his face first into her stomach, then between her breasts and finally found her neck again, she reached down and almost tentatively grasped his penis, spread her legs so he could lay comfortably between them, and guided him into her.

This time, excited by her touch, he pushed recklessly inwards, but encountered an elasticity as if her muscles were clenched against his desperate probing. She jerked away from him, this time with a tiny, hurt cry, and her legs stiffened.

He lifted himself off her and eased down beside her, troubled and confused, his breathing hard and short, aching with the need to come. She turned quickly from him, her buttocks pushing in against his groin. He pressed in against her, his erection hard and uncomfortable. He trailed light fingers up the curve of her hips, down the valley of her waist and gently held her breast.

"What's wrong?" he whispered.

"It's not working," she said.

"I'm hurting you."

She turned her face further into the pillow, unable to look at him. She made a strange sound. Quinn didn't know if she was laughing or crying. "God," she said, "I must be the only twenty-two-year-old virgin in London."

Quinn sat up suddenly, rolled her over on her back and straddled her. She smiled up at him through embarrassed tears. "Why the hell didn't you tell me?" he demanded.

"I'm sorry. I thought it'd be easy." Then she giggled. "Would it have made any difference? I mean, are you an experienced breaker-in of twenty-two-year-old Anglo-Israeli virgins?"

Quinn placed two fingers over her mouth to symbolically seal her lips. "That's not funny," he said.

Lena opened her mouth and playfully chewed his fingers. "It *is* funny," she said. "It's *very* funny." She giggled again. "When I asked you to make love to me I was trying to be so sophisticated, so urbane . . ."

"Quiet," Quinn whispered. "You'll wake your father."

"Don't worry. He might carry a .45, but he doesn't own a shotgun." She stopped talking and looked at him steadily, her brown eyes still moist. "I'm sorry," she said. "I guess I'm scared."

"Don't be scared."

Quinn lay down beside her again and she lifted her head so he could put his arm around her, and she turned her face so she could look at him, and she smiled. "Can we try again?"

"You sure you want to?"

She nodded.

He kissed her nose. "Then it will be my pleasure."

"Will it hurt much? Will I bleed?"

"If we're careful it won't hurt. And you'll only bleed a few drops.

"So you *are* experienced!"

"Not with Anglo-Israelis."

"Then who with?"

He kissed her gently on the lips. "Don't make a joke of it," he said. "I want us to do this properly."

He'd wanted the girl all during their long conversation in the downstairs room, but thought little of the urge. He liked her, found her intelligent and beautiful, a unique and warm person, but hadn't seriously considered taking her to bed, discounting the impulse as the simple result of that maverick male imperative which conjures up visions of conquest after only the merest glance at an attractive female.

And there was more. When they'd touched each other and she'd said she wanted him to make love to her (the first time a woman had told him *that*) he'd experienced conflicting emotions of guilt and fear: guilt that only weeks after Jenny's death he was even contemplating taking another woman to bed; fear that once in bed he would be unable to perform.

But it hadn't happened like that. Jenny had never entered his mind, and now, as he lay in the dark, Lena soundly asleep, her head on his shoulder, her limbs entwined with his, he knew that he had finally convinced himself of the truth: he had never loved Jenny in any deep emotional sense and her death was not connected in any way with their relationship. They had professed their love for each other and he'd realized his mistake but hadn't told her before she'd died. He had liked Jenny and shared her bed and she'd been murdered. And now he was hunting the man ultimately responsible for her death. Hunting him for revenge, because the authorities wouldn't or couldn't touch him, and for adventure, to prove himself, to just once pit himself against the forces of evil. Those were the facts. The simple yet complicated truths.

And Lena. He'd admitted to himself when he first met her that there was something special about Lena and now after having taken her to bed his sense of her had heightened. He wanted to see a lot of this girl. Cautious now, after his experience with Jenny, he would not call it love. Not yet. Perhaps never. But he wanted to be with her and, because of her, for the first time since the events of *Destry*, he could imagine a future stretching beyond the destruction of Zeller.

Lena stirred, muttered something, then, still asleep, disentangled herself from Quinn and turned over. Carefully, Quinn slid his arm from beneath her head. The arm felt numb; she'd lain on it since they'd fallen asleep. Quinn looked at the luminous dial on his watch. Six o'clock. They'd slept only two hours, but he felt refreshed, ready to go. Slowly, quietly, so as not to wake her, he pushed back the covers and swung his feet to the floor. He searched in the dark for his clothing, dressed himself and crept downstairs. Better to leave her bedroom now while he was wide awake than risk falling asleep and perhaps cause Lena embarrassment with her father later on. As quietly as possible, he made his way into the front room, closed the door and turned on the light. He sat himself in the easy-chair and lit a cigarette.

Outside, the storm had raged itself into oblivion. Quinn sat in perfect peace and quiet. He picked up the file on Zeller, deciding to absorb each of the hundreds of facts Red Sanderson had so painstakingly gathered since his wife had been cut down that day so long ago.

Sanderson had recorded nothing of Zeller's childhood except the date and place of his birth, those facts contained within a photostated copy of a birth certificate Sanderson had bought from the Amsterdam public registry office. Sanderson had appended a translation of the certificate. Vincent Johan Zeller had been born in a suburb of the city January 23, 1901. Those were the first facts in the file and, from Quinn's point of view, among the most unsavory. They meant that he, Teal, Sanderson and the rest were setting out to destroy a man over eighty years old. Quickly, he corrected himself. They would destroy an old man, yes, and hopefully a young one, too, that fair haired bastard, but more, they would be destroying an organization that had no right to exist, an organization that traded in the means of death without even taking a patriotic, moral or philosophical stand on who could buy their weapons. They would be destroying a form of cancer which grew fat and strong by exploiting the decaying body of a sick society.

Quinn turned the page.

Zeller's precious hour of sleep had long since passed. The storm had not. With diabolical fury, great hammer-heads of water punched at *Shadow*, shuddering her with every blow. Half an hour ago he had heard Blake piping up extra hands, and he knew that among their tasks they would have to lash down tarpaulines over the helicopter and open boats. From his cabin compass, Zeller saw they had changed course. Blake had headed *Shadow* into the storm to let her ride against the sea rather than having her wallow in the troughs.

The sea. Oh God, how he hated it. The sea and the insomnia.

Zeller lay on his double bed and pulled the old black coat tight across his chest. He stared at the light fitting on the wall and tried to imagine himself in a hotel room in Cannes or Sorrento, away from this thrashing storm, but his concentration was wrecked by the crashing slap of *Shadow*'s bows as she smashed against yet another attacking monster wave.

The camp. That was when the insomnia started. He, a Jew, but in name only, betrayed by neighbors, dragged from his bed by Gestapo, prodded at gunpoint into a car and dumped at a railway siding with hundreds of other ensnared in the roundup. Luckily he was only in his early forties, strong still, and useful. So while most of the rest—old man, women and children—were packed like animals into cattle-vans and transported to extermination camps, he and six or seven score other younger, fitter men were jammed into two goods vans at the end of another train and taken on a three day and two night long journey into the heart of Germany where they were interned in a work camp.

It'd been summer when he'd been arrested and throughout

the sixty hour journey the seventy-two men in Zeller's van had only half a loaf of coarse, black bread each to sustain them. No water. They were packed shoulder to shoulder with scarcely room to move. They slept standing. They defecated at their own feet while standing. Daytime temperatures in the van exceeded eighty degrees fahrenheit. Eventually the tortures of dehydration and thirst forced some men to piss into their handkerchiefs so they could suck the acrid urine into their parched mouths.

After twenty-seven hours of being packed shoulder to shoulder with no more fresh air than that which wafted through one or two knotholes in the van walls, or under the iron-reinforced sliding door, one man went mad from claustrophobia. First he plended reasonably that someone should call the guard to stop the train and open the door so they could have fresh air, then he began weeping, then became angry and strident, and when his self-control finally and irrevocably snapped, he began to shout and scream and ram his elbows and knees into his neighbors and that soon started a chain reaction, bringing other men in the stinking, jolting, airless truck close to breaking point, and finally, in mad desperation, the man closest to the screaming man kneed him in the testicles and he slid down choking among the legs of his fellows and never regained his feet. At the end of the trip, when the train finally halted at the work camp siding six men were dead, two fallen and trampled to death, four still standing, cadavers, packed shoulder to shoulder with the living.

The nightmarish journey represented the turning point in Zeller's life, not because he was in any way used to such mindless brutality, but, curiously, because it awakened a latent response in him. He realized that he was a survivor, capable of applying a strength of will he never dreamed existed within him.

Obviously, he reasoned later, nothing that had happened in his life previous to his arrest by the Gestapo had been potenially destructive enough to trigger that response. He was the only child of a well-to-do Amsterdam merchant, and the simultaneous death of his parents in an automobile accident had left him sole heir to his family's modest fortune when he was only twenty-two years old. Though his inheritance made him a highly eligible bachelor and guaranteed him the attentions of many lovely girls, Zeller showed no interest in any of them, nor, regardless of suburban gossip, in any man. Zeller was his own man; business his mistress and profit his pleasure.

Until the German occupation had severed Holland from the outside world in 1940, Zeller had made his living carefully, profitably and cunningly in the complicated field of international commerce, importing fine cloth, carpets, hand-crafted artesania, antiques and curiosities from Holland's far eastern colonies and exporting European luxuries to homesick colonials both there and in Africa. The occasional gentlemanly smuggling arrangement—gold and diamonds into Holland, paintings out of Holland—added a spicy touch to an otherwise predictable existence and had allowed Zeller to hoard a useful amount of gold and rare postage stamps in a Swiss bank strong box far from the prying eyes of Dutch tax officials. That would be the only one of Zeller's assets to survive the war. It would set him on the road to becoming the most powerful arms dealer in the Mediterranean.

On reflection, Zeller realized his first survival response triggered itself at the moment of his arrest. He had half expected the betrayal—all Jews could expect that—but when he heard the door burst open and saw the Gestapo gunmen he felt no fear. He resigned himself immediately to the idea that he faced an alternative: survive within the system he was about to be thrust into, or escape from it. His acceptance of these simple facts determined his attitude to everything during the following four, long years.

At the railway siding he looked for the means of escape and saw none. After the sorting, when he and the other fit men were prodded toward the goods vans and he realized they were destined for forced labor, he coldly analyzed probabilities. When the guards issued each man with a half loaf of bread and sneeringly told them to "make it last," Zeller realized the trip would be long and excrutiatingly uncomfortable. He maneuvered himself close to the van door and looked inside. When guards shouted the order to board he vaulted inside, rushed straight to a far corner and claimed that as his position. The corner offered two advantages: he could lean and thus enjoy some measure of rest, and there was a small crack in the wood paneling against which he could lay his face for a breath of fresh air. Zeller finished the nightmarish journey in better shape than most, but throughout it he never closed his eyes once, never fell asleep for even ten seconds, fearful he would lose his advantageous position. During his first night in camp he thought he would sleep like a dead man. He slept only an hour and woke refreshed. He had never slept a full night since.

The camp was nestled in a chestnut forest twenty miles from Ulm, in southern Germany, beside a munitions factory. Four hundred and fifty prisoners lived in the camp, all but fifty working shifts of twelve hours each in the factory. The remainder ran the camp under the guards' supervision: digging latrines, growing produce, cutting wood, cleaning guards quarters, running the camp laundry, working in the kitchens.

Conditions were tolerable compared to those experienced by hundreds of thousands of prisoners in other forced labor camps across the Reich. Food provided enough calories for a reasonably fit man to survive; beding was adequate except in the freezing months of December and January; because of the forest, fuel was always available for the small, pot-bellied stove in each of the fifty-man huts. The guards, though rough and uneducated, were more intersted in the *fräuleins* and beer halls in Ulm than in practising overt acts of cruelty on their prisoners. Scherrer, the dough-faced Commandant, a Hamburg accountant in peacetime, was interested only in the efficient running of his camp and in assuring himself of good relationships with the munitions factory manager by organizing the clockwork arrival of each work shift. Scherrer rewarded cooperation by leaving the prisoners alone and permitting a degree of autonomy, even down to the organization of concerts and football games. Non-cooperation—pilfering, attacks on guards, escape attempts—brought retribution: short rations, solitary confinement, even death.

Zeller soon realized he could lead a more comfortable life working with the camp detail rather than in the factory. Camp detail men rarely worked more than ten hours a day and enjoyed the advantage of being able to scrounge extra food from the kitchens or produce gardens. More importantly, camp detail men could beg or buy cigarettes, pencils, paper, chocolate and other luxury items from guards and the goods could be traded with fellow prisoners for a hundred times their value. After maneuvering to have himself changed from a factory shift to the camp detail Zeller was, in effect, back in business.

His immediate problem was collateral. What did a prisoner with only a prisoner's possessions own which could be traded with the guards so that profitable commerce could be begun among his fellows? Zeller set his merchant mind to work and quickly concluded that he owned only one negotiable commodity—his body.

To Zeller, sex meant nothing. It aroused no passion in him. He found it merely curious that human beings spent so much time in the pursuit of orgasm and, even here in the camp, in talking about the act. As a youth he had learned to masturbate and had continued to do so throughout his adult life whenever physical tension demanded release. But it was only that—a release. He did not enjoy an orgasm to any greater degree than the voiding of his bowels. Masturbation was simple and did not require emotional participation or the sharing of secrets. Above all, masturbation offered a considerable saving of time over the ridiculous formalized ritual involved in taking a woman to bed.

Zeller had been to bed with only two women by the time he arrived at the camp—and none in the forty years since. The first time, merely for the experience, he had bought himself the services of a Montmartre streetwalker while in Paris on a business trip. He'd been twenty-five years old. He'd performed mechanically, climaxed, paid, and walked back into the street with absolutely no feelings about his first sexual experience with a woman. The second time, when he was thirty-three, had been in different circumstances—to help close a business deal. An elderly merchant with whom he was negotiating the sale of several thousand guilders worth of Indonesian batik had hinted that his young wife was lonely for the company of a younger man. Would Mr. Zeller be kind enough to escort her to dinner? One could, after all, trust the discretion of a fellow businessman. Zeller took the hint and, without excitement, disgust, or any other recognizable emotion, wined and dined the young wife, took her to the theater and thence to bed. Again, he performed mechanically and, if he was to judge from the woman's ludicrous moans and painfully scratching nails, adequately. The batik deal went through.

One of the three soldiers who guarded the kitchen detail to which Zeller had managed to have himself posted was a young private whom Zeller quickly recognized as homosexual. Zeller had watched the way his eyes followed the younger prisoners, seen him giving cigarettes to them, whisper to them, seen them rebuff him, noted his angry reaction, heard him suddenly shriek orders at them, watched several times his rifle butt cracking into their backs.

Zeller waited his moment. Finally one day the guard escorted Zeller to the store to carry back a sack of turnips and they were alone.

"It must be lonely being a guard," Zeller said, softly. He turned as he spoke so his back was to the private and he bent to pick up the sack. The soldier didn't answer. "I know how it is being a prisoner," Zeller said. "A man misses the company of—of his kind." He turned and smiled at the guard.

"There're plenty more Jews here."

"That's not what I meant."

"I know what you mean. I know what you Jew-boys do in the huts after lights out."

Zeller shook his head. "Brutes," he said, "heterosexuals who do not truly understand the subtleties. Not a real man among them." He paused, then added in a near whisper, "Not a real man like you."

It took Zeller less than two minutes to seduce the guard. For his five minutes work Zeller received twenty cigarettes, and each day for the next week Zeller performed the same service for the same reward, accomplishing the act with less emotion than if he was adding a column of figures. At the end of that time, just when Zeller had convinced himself he had found a gold mine, the guard was posted to another camp. But the one hundred and sixty cigarettes Zeller now owned were, by prisoner standards, a fortune, and Zeller cunningly parleyed them into a larger fortune.

After a year in the camp Zeller owned five hundred cigarettes, twenty cans of preserved fruits, several pairs of socks, four razor blades, six cakes of soap, nearly half a pint of brandy, a fork, a pocket knife, six pencils, thirty sheets of paper, ten envelopes and an eighteen carat gold ring—a wedding ring which a prisoner had smuggled into the camp up his anal passage and finally traded after Zeller had tempted him with sixty cigarettes.

As the average prisoner owned only the clothes he stood in, one or two small things he had smuggled into the camp, utensils, made from scrap with his own hands, or stolen at great risk from the factory or the guards, Zeller found himself the object of jealousy and, subsequently the victim of theft. Thus he was forced to employ other prisoners to protect both himself and his goods. These four men became the foundation members of a gang which eventually numbered over twenty and, under Zeller's supervision, controlled the economic and social life of every prisoner in the camp.

Toward the end of the second year, one of Zeller's spies reported that four men sleeping at the other end of the hut, only thirty yards from the barbed wire, were planning to dig a tunnel, starting beneath the floor and ending in the undergrowth twenty yards beyond the wire. From there they would dash into the forest and try to make their way across the Swiss border. Zeller nodded, paid the spy with two cigarettes, then lay on his straw mattress and stared upward at the filthy, cobwebbed rafters which bisected the hut.

An escape attempt, and from his own hut. That could only mean trouble. When the Germans discovered the breakout they would tear the hut apart and Zeller's carefully hoarded fortune would be discovered and confiscated. The work of over a year would be lost, but worse, such a discovery might even put his life in jeopardy if the guards considered the hoard a cache against yet another escape attempt.

Zeller sighed. The would-be escapees must be discouraged. For an hour he sifted actions, alternatives and consequences and, his plan finally made, considered who among the men he trusted could most efficiently do what had to be done. He settled on a young Frenchman, a boy really, no more than sixteen, but tall, and even after a year of camp life, stronger than most men.

The French boy's name was Tristan. He'd worked for Zeller for six months, running errands, reporting tid-bits of information he overheard from the prisoners, garnering war news from the guards. Zeller paid him with chocolate. Tristan spoke fluent French, German, English and Spanish. He'd taught himself German in the camp. He doted on Zeller, gravitated toward him as if Zeller was his surrogate father, a replacement for his own family which had been shot in the streets of Paris.

Zeller sent for him.

"I have something I want you to do for me."

Tristan nodded.

"You must do it well."

"What?" the boy asked eagerly.

"You must kill someone so that to the Germans the death appears as an accident."

"Murder," Tristan breathed.

"Self protection," Zeller said. "For us both. If you don't kill this man we will both suffer."

"But *murder*. The Germans hang murderers from piano wire."

"They'd hang both of us," Zeller said. "We're accomplices." Zeller smiled. "If you do it," he said softly, "we would always be accomplices."

The next day the leader of the would-be escapees, a Pole named Lasvlo Kochininski, slipped and fell into a vat of molten brass used to make casings for high explosive cannon shells. He was dragged screaming from the vat by Tristan who burned his arm in the process. Kochininski died screaming ten minutes later, never in that time uttering an intelligible word. The incident passed without investigation from the Germans who simply noted that another prisoner—number such and such—had died. Even the prisoners themselves hardly mentioned the death. Death on the factory floor was too common to merit unusual comment. Many men purposefully committed suicide there, preferring a relatively quick death, even if agonizing one, to more tedious years of coldness, half-starvation and a relentless work schedule which sapped the body of strength and the mind of purpose. But three prisoners had reason to comment among themselves about Kochiniski's death. They were his three partners in the escape plan. Each received an anonymous note threatening a death equally as garish as Kochininski's if they pursued their plan. They didn't.

Zeller was well pleased with Tristan's performance. He rewarded the boy well. Zeller gave him a half pound block of chocolate, a prize worth a fortune on the camp black market. And in the future he trusted the boy with further important missions, all of them designed to solidify Zeller's economic position within the sub-society of camp life. Tristan negotiated for Zeller, lied for him, cheated, and when necessary, used violence on his behalf. He made loans for Zeller and collected debts. He found other inmates who, like Zeller, used cunning, force and ruthlessness to survive on a higher plane than, and at the expense of, their common fellows, and brought them and Zeller together to forge what in terms of camp life were grand alliances.

Zeller and Tristan worked together like the two torn halves of a thousand dollar bill. They became so essential to each other, that neither could operate effectively alone. The death of Kochininski was the fortuitous blood pact which had thrown them together. It kept them together more than forty years.

And now after all I have done for him he is forsaking me. God, there is no justice within the machinations of the human mind. I gave him a decent life in the camp; when the Allies over-ran Ulm I dragged him through the forests with me and used my own gold and jewels to bribe border guards to let us into their precious Switzerland. And what is my reward . . . ?

The sea. Oh God, how he hated it. The sea and the insomnia.

Zeller slowly swung his feet to the cabin floor. He held his ̄d in his hands, feeling faintly nauseous from the violent ̄ding of the boat. Every fitting in his cabin creaked as pile- ̄g waves crashed over *Shadow*'s bow, sending colossal, shuddering vibrations pulsing through the steel hull like an electric current.

Zeller pushed his feet into a worn pair of carpet slippers, shrugged the old black coat higher up on his thin shoulders. Even through the sound-proofing of his cabin and above the hum of the ship's machinery, he could hear a faint, piercing whistle which was the wild, uncontrolable wind, stepbrother of that terrible sea which lashed his nerves.

Zeller reached for the telephone hand-set beside his double bunk which connected him directly to the bridge.

"Bridge, sir. Blake speaking." The noise of the storm on the more exposed bridge was magnified into the speaker Zeller held to his ear.

"How long more?"

"I think it's peaked, Mr. Zeller. A couple of hours may see it through. Wind's dropped a little."

A couple of hours. Zeller replaced the hand-set. Two, three hours more. Well, if that was how it was, that was how it would be. He would persevere as he had always persevered and as he would do in the future. He was strong, stronger than any of them and he was in control, of himself, of everything.

His hands held out slightly from his sides to balance himself against *Shadow*'s ceaseless pitch and roll, Zeller walked carefully from his cabin and aft to the state-room. The curtains on the huge picture window which ran the whole width of the stern were open, and through the smoked polarized glass and against the darkness of the moonless night Zeller saw nebulas of silver spray exploding in the ebony vacuum, and sheets of dark water hitting and sliding down the window like the black breath of the devil. Zeller pressed a button and the heavy, brocade curtains slid across, blocking the hateful view from his sight.

He doesn't care about me anymore, after all I've done for him he doesn't care.

Talking to himself, muttering, murmuring, petulant, Zeller randomly pulled a video cassette from the library and slipped it into the machine. Distorted, bizarrely colored shapes criss-crossed the thirty-six inch TV screen as the picture settled. Zeller sat in an easy chair staring at the screen. With his remote control console he turned up the sound so that music swelled through the state-room, smothering the background noise of the storm. The film was a western. A group of wild-eyed riders galloped through clouds of dust toward an unsuspecting town which sat on the horizon beneath a pure, blue sky.

I ask you, is it fair after what I have done for him? I gave him education. I sent him to America to take his medical degree. I gave him facilities to pursue his research. I gave him money. I gave him power. I gave him a future—my future. He knows that when I die he will have all that is mine.

Zeller chuckled to himself and shook his head. *Is it fair?* The riders had reached the town. They were shooting. A child was trampled under horses' hooves. A mother screamed. She fell, shot.

What did I ask of him in return? Do you think it was unreasonable? I asked him to use his skill and knowledge to protect me from sickness. And what does he do now when I approach him and ask him to use this expertise which I bought him with my own money? He laughs. He laughs at me and tells me I am an old man and that I must face the one true fact of existence which is that all men are mortal. He has betrayed me.

Zeller turned down the sound. The faint hissing noise of the storm returned again; the faint sound of the rising and the falling wind. On the screen a man held a gun at the head of another. The picture changed to a close-up of the man who had the gun at his head. He looked inestimably sad. Zeller stood, and with his hands outstretched appealed to him.

It is betrayal, is it not?

The man holding the gun pulled the trigger. The victim's head exploded into a mask of blood. The sadness in his eyes changed to shock and then to nothingness as he fell to the floor.

Zeller sat down heavily. He held his head in his hands. His frail body shook beneath the worn black overcoat.

Out in the night the wild sea still snapped hungrily at *Shadow*'s writhing bows. In the stateroom a phantom eddy of wind came from nowhere, blowing a silent breath through the room. Zeller shivered, looked up in fright.

All life is a betrayal, is it not?
He wept.

At 8:10 the next evening, Hailey watched Quinn and Teal dash
through the rain from the cover of the hotel entrance and climb
into a red Ford Escort. Before the Escort turned left into the
Strand, Hailey was running for the hotel taxi rank.

Fifteen minutes later he watched the red compact park
outside an apartment block half way down a quiet street in the
Bayswater area. He ordered the cabbie to drop him a hundred
yards further on. He watched the three men enter the building,
wondering who the driver had been and who they were
visiting.

He crossed the road and walked slowly back along the street
observing the apartment block. He waited five minutes then
crossed the road, intending to check nameplates above letter
boxes in the lobby, when through a slightly open curtain on the
window of the ground level flat on his right, Hailey saw Quinn.
He stood, sipping from a wine glass, talking to Teal. The
driver—tall, slightly stooped, red-haired, vaguely military-
looking—pointed to papers laid on a table, explaining something to a short, tough-looking character who nodded as he
fiddled with a wine glass.

Hailey edged as close to the window as he dared, straining to
hear even a word of the conversation, but the double red-brick
walls muted every sound from within the building.

Hailey shivered, sleeked rain from his golden hair and ran
his eye along the street. Empty, except for half a dozen cars
parked outside apartment blocks. The red Escort was the only
vehicle parked in front of this building. Hailey glanced again
through the crack in the curtain and saw the short man who
obviously owned the flat corkscrew open two bottles of wine
and, still talking with the red-headed man, walk to Quinn and
Teal and top up their glasses. The short man then walked out of
the room and returned a minute later carrying a tray laden with
four plates of spaghetti and a mountain of bread.

How long? Hailey wondered. How long would it take me?
He quickly estimated the feasibility of his plan. Perhaps fifteen
minutes to taxi over to Notting Hill and gather what he needed

from the London man. Ten minutes back. He glanced at they Escort. Less than ten minutes to do the job. Thirty or forty minutes in all, maximum.

Hailey turned and walked fast back toward Bayswater Road to find a cab. He smiled as he walked because he knew that now, at last, luck had touched him. He'd kill two birds with one stone. Three, if he included the red-haired one who'd be driving. But you couldn't count him. He'd been ordered to eliminate Quinn and Teal. The other was simply in the wrong place at the wrong time. Too bad. Too bad.

Teal forked the last of the spaghetti into his mouth 'and nodded his approval as he munched. "Not bad," he said, "not bad."

"Bloody wonderful if you'll excuse the French," Johnny said. He pointed to his bookcase. "Fifty-some cookbooks there. I decided that if a chap was determined to stay a bachelor he owed it to himself to learn the odd things in the kitchen."

"Wish I could say the same," Teal said, "but all I ever learned in a kitchen was how to open a can."

Johnny laughed and made the rounds puring wine. The second bottle was nearly empty. "Have to dash out a little later and find some more."

Quinn knew enough about English licensing laws to raise a dubious eyebrow.

"No trouble, old man," Johnny said. "Chap has a bottle shop five minutes from here. Lives at the back. Always comes through in times of crisis."

Sanderson shuffled the paperwork on the desk. "What do you think of it, Johnny?"

"Seems a bit hairy to me, old man."

"It is hairy, but it can work."

"Nothing else up your sleeve?"

Sanderson shook his head. "Because of the way Zeller lives there are no alternatives."

Johnny shrugged. "So be it. But let's go over that budget again. Marine Insurance has already placed the money at your disposal. It's yours to use as you see fit. But they do love their paperwork. If the figures look business-like then they'll puff their pipes and assume the operation will go like clock-work."

"My God," Sanderson sighed. "If life was so simple!"

"Oh it is," Johnny said, "if you happen to be an accountant."

Half an hour later, Sanderson pushed aside the budget file and dug into his briefcase for notes he'd made on the training schedule.

"My mercs are here in London now," he explained. "Tomorrow morning we drive up to Dartmoor to start ten days training."

"I thought chaps like these would know their weapons backwards," Johnny said.

"It's not weapons familiarity I'm worried about. These gentlemen tend to over-indulge between projects. The course is designed to make them sweat, bring them back toward combat fitness."

Sanderson stood and paced the comfortable sitting-room. He leaned against the mantelpiece above the fireplace. "Look, Johnny, excuse me for saying this, but you're not obliged to accompany us. I think it's going to be a nasty one."

"Been in the odd tight spot before, old chap. Police-force and all that. Company watchdog, too, you know. Must keep an eye on all that cash."

Sanderson smiled and shook his head. "Didn't think I could talk you out of it, Johnny, but I felt obliged to try."

"Company released me from the office to stay with you on this thing as from five o'clock this afternoon."

Sanderson nodded. "So we'll pick you up at ten tomorrow morning." He walked back to the table, sat down and flicked through the training schedule. "Let's go over victualling needs for the next ten days."

Johnny held up an empty bottle. "Let's replace this first. If you'll trust me with that fine vehicle of yours I'll be back in five minutes."

Sanderson nodded and tossed him the keys. Johnny walked out of the flat, through the lobby and paused at the entrance. Damned rain! He turned his collar up around his neck, dashed to the red Escort, fumbled with the unfamiliar keys, opened the door and eased himself into the driver's seat. He found the ignition key, inserted and turned it in the one movement and then the world turned blaring, melting white, then orange, then a terrible ripping weight tore into Johnny's chest and then he was floating and then he was dead.

A half mile away, in Kensington Gardens, Hailey walked slowly through the rain. The sound of the explosion reached him, a dull *woomp!* that lasted less than a tenth of a second. He didn't stop walking. He'd done his job. Zeller and Tristan would be pleased. And now there was another job, money to be carried to Holland, and after that Berlin, where instructions would be waiting for him. Then back to Ibiza to meet *Shadow* and receive a special briefing about the shipment to the Italian Red Brigade. Hailey kept walking, ignoring the soaking rain, sensing deep within himself the beginnings of another headache. He hoped it wouldn't be a bad one. He had no chance of seeing Tristan for another two weeks. And so much work to do. Back to the hotel, must get back to the hotel, he told himself, get to sleep, get to sleep . . .

The darkness of the park enveloped him like a womb. Vaguely, on the edge of his mind, he heard sirens and bells.

Sanderson, Quinn and Teal didn't sleep that night. When the police came the three of them were taken to the Bayswater station where they made independent statements. Sanderson phoned a friend, a retired General, who contacted someone on the Prime Minister's personal staff, who telephoned someone very high in the Police department. At three o'clock in the morning they taxied back to the Roberts Road house with an assurance that news of the bombing wouldn't appear in the media. Lena slept, not knowing what had happened to Johnny James in her father's car. Quinn and Teal, with a .45 apiece sat by windows downstairs watching the front and back gardens. Sanderson loaded a repeating shotgun and sat in his upstairs bedroom staring into the street, thinking of the tough little investigator and wondering who had planted the bomb and if that person knew he had killed Johnny instead of himself and Quinn and Teal. Was this something to do with Operation Flying Dutchman? Or was this someone trying to settle another old score? Sanderson shifted the shotgun on his lap and listened to the night.

Fourteen of them—the ten mercenaries, Quinn, Teal, Sanderson and Lena—drove in two microbuses, to a farmhouse on the edge of Dartmoor. The farm consisted of a three-roomed house, a barn and a small concrete block of more recent construction which contained four cold-water showers and four toilets.

Sanderson stood, hands on hips, staring at the ramshackle buildings.

"Yours?" Quinn asked.

Sanderson nodded. "Used it perhaps eight times in twelve years. It's no palace, but then again, we haven't come for a tea party."

Suddenly he pushed by Quinn, strode into the barn where the men were laying out sleeping bags and blankets and yelled, "Right. Five minutes to get this place ship-shape, then I want every man out front dressed in pullover, long trousers and runners and carrying a frame pack. We're taking a stroll, gentlemen."

He turned back to Quinn. "You, Teal and Lena, unload food from the trucks, stow it in the kitchen. Lena, we'll be back in two hours. Have tea and coffee ready. Quinn, Teal when you've finished helping Lena, climb into your gear. You're coming for a stroll, too."

Five minutes later the ten mercenaries and Quinn and Teal were lined up in two ranks in front of Sanderson, who strode up and down in front of them. All vestiges of his professional air had gone. Wearing an old army pullover with leather shoulders Sanderson looked like a soldier, and sounded like one.

"First time I've had a chance to speak to you all together. Thanks for responding so quickly to my telegrams. The job in front of us is a short one, but if half of us come out in one piece we'll be lucky." He turned his back to the group and spread his hands to indicate to them the boring, rocky, bleakness of the moor. "That's why I've brought you on this short holiday into the heart of beautiful England." He turned back smiling in response to the hisses and hoots of derision coming from the men. Then his smile faded. "To toughen you up, to sweat the booze out of you. To give you a better chance of survival."

Sanderson started pacing again, hands clenched behind his back, his eyes searching the faces of the men in front of him. "We'll train eight hours daily. After each evening meal, we'll spend several hours studying and perfecting every aspect of our operation. Every man must understand every other man's job. That's another way of improving our survival chances.

"All duties to be shared. Draw up rosters. We need cooks and dish washers to assist my daughter in the kitchen, wood-cutters, latrine-cleaners, sweepers etcetera. You'll have half a day free next week for clothes washing. No letter writing until the operation is finished, for obvious security reasons. With one exception . . ."

Sanderson paused for effect. "To your bank managers. Once we've reached our destination, and the day before the operation starts, each of you will be given checks for the full agreed amount payable against a Swiss bank."

Sanderson held up his hands to quiet the cheers. "If there's any questions about financial arrangements, I'll answer them tonight after dinner. Follow me!"

Sanderson turned and trotted gently down the path leading from the farm toward the open moor, ignoring the theatrical groans of the men following him. After running one hundred yards he held up his hand for the men to slow down and led them walking for fifty yards. Then he sprinted them for twenty, followed by fifty yards walking to recover their wind. Then the cycle started again: run a hundred, walk fifty, sprint twenty, walk fifty. And again: run, walk, sprint, walk.

After the first mile Quinn was pleased he was still staying with the leaders. By the end of the second mile he'd dropped half way back in the field, behind the Corsicans, the Scot and two of the Englishmen. Sanderson still led, losing a couple of yards on each sprint, but regaining them with his long-legged stride during the walks and holding his own on the runs. Half way through the third mile, with the sweat sliding down his face, Quinn felt he'd be content merely to finish whatever

Sanderson had in mind. He'd dropped even further back, now, while Sanderson still held his lead.

And it was then Quinn suddenly realized that not one of the men leading him was less than ten years older than him, and that Sanderson was more than double his age.

Quinn hissed breath out between his teeth and with a burst of energy dragged up from the depths of his pride he launched himself after the leaders, ignoring the heaviness of his legs and the nagging stitch biting into his side.

Suddenly the run-walk-sprint routine was forgotten. As Quinn overhauled the first of the men ahead of him and started after the next, the whole group surged after him.

Sanderson glanced behind, saw what was happening and without breaking his stride pointed to a high-standing group of rocks three hundred yards away.

"The rocks! Go! Go!"

Quinn heard a man behind him curse as he stumbled on the soft ground, then felt an elbow in his ribs as someone else shoved him aside as he passed. Quinn lifted his knees high, drove his feet into the ground, propelled himself after his aggressor, and saw through sweat-blurred eyes as he grabbed at his collar that it was Teal. He hauled backwards, swung him off balance and then like an automaton plunged forward after a group of three men a few yards ahead of them. As he approached to pass them, the one on Quinn's inside, one of the Corsicans, half turned and slammed his shoulder into Quinn. Quinn stumbled, regained his balance and charged straight at the whole group, downing the Corsican and managing to catch the leg of one of the others, flipping him into the mud. Quinn rolled, pushed himself to his feet, caught the third man in the group in half a dozen strides, passed him, then set his sights on Sanderson who had now slowed badly into third place. He drew level, hearing the older man's gasping breath. He glanced sideways, caught a wicked gleam in Sanderson's eye and saw Red's big fist launching itself at him. With a tenth of a second to spare Quinn ducked, sprinted forward to escape, then risked a look over his shoulder to see Sanderson crashing to his knees, exhausted.

Now there were only two men ahead of Quinn, an

Englishman and, five yards ahead of him, the Scot. With breath like steam searing his lungs, and thigh muscles that felt like dough, Quinn plunged after the Englishman overhauling him step by step so that one hundred and fifty yards from the rocks he was level, but giving him a yard's berth to avoid an elbow, fist or shoulder.

Still at full pent, and now two feet behind Quinn, the Englishman slipped the rucksack from his shoulders and swung it at Quinn. The bag caught Quinn in the small of the back. His mouth wide open gasping for oxygen, Quinn twisted as he ran, hands ready to ward off the next blow which he knew was coming. He slowed fractionally as he twisted. The Englishman came level with him, swinging the bag. Quinn snatched as it whipped down at him, got a handful of canvas and jerked with all his strength, ripping the bag free and sending the Englishman sprawling facedown into a puddle.

Quinn dropped the bag, regained his stride and started after the Scott who was now a good seven yards ahead but slowing on the heavy ground. With a hundred yards to go Quinn had picked up two yards on the tough little Scott. Leaning forward into his stride, trying to dig his toes into the soft ground, he remembered that only a few short years past he had gone out for track and run four hundred and forty yards in under forty-five seconds. He'd once broken ten seconds for the hundred yards in full football rig. And now, on this three hundred yard human obstacle course he felt he was hardly moving.

His vision blurred by sweat and effort, Quinn saw that the Scot, too, was in a bad way. Less than two yards separated them with fifty to go. Calling on the last of his reserves, Quinn made the supreme effort and with twenty yards to go came even with his man. The Scot let fly with a backhander that caught Quinn across the chest. Quinn lashed back with an elbow which exploded against the Scot's ribs. The Scot fell back half a pace, and now, with less than ten yards to go, Quinn sprang toward victory. Then, to Quinn's amazement, the Scot launched himself in a rugby tackle, caught Quinn around the waist and slammed him to the ground, landing on top of him, winding them both. For a fraction of a second neither man moved, then simultaneously they tried to regain their feet, failed because of the muddy ground and instead scrambled on hands and knees like two giant crabs toward the rocks.

They reached them together, fell against each other, then rolled onto their backs fighting desperately to force oxygen into their tortured lungs; and then started laughing at the sheer stupidity of the thing—chuckles at first, then, later, as they caught their breath, great roars of laughter.

"Jesus," the Scot gasped, "You're a serious laddie!"

As the others staggered in, Quinn counted two eyes already blackening, one bloodied nose and three split lips.

Sanderson came in last. In the finaly, mad dash for the rocks his age had betrayed him, but he seemed pleased with himself. He slumped to the ground a few yards from the rest and looked at each man in turn. As a squad of combat soldiers they were impossibly old, mostly in their late thirties and early forties. But they had spirit, they were fighters at heart. They weren't there *only* for the money. And spirit was the mystical ingredient that tipped the scales in any physical encounter between men.

Spirit and firepower, Sanderson thought wryly.

They walked the three miles back to the farm each carrying forty pounds of rocks in their knapsacks. They walked slowly, each successive step harder than the last. The sweat sprang from every pore in their bodies. But as their aching backs and legs settled to the task the men split into groups, chatting and joking to spur each other on. Quinn and Teal struggled along with the little Scot who had introduced himself as Jock Culloden. Jock helped them put names to the mens' faces and supplied identifying gossip about each of them.

"Now the two Corsicans," Jock said. "Rene and Victor. Very quiet pair. Been working together for about ten years. Met in the Foreign Legion, got discharged the same day and haven't been separated since. They're explosives experts. Nasty job that. But they've got the right temperament. Calm and thorough and very, very tough. You pick a fight with one of them you have to fight them both. I've seen them lay out seven men in a fist fight."

Jock pointed to the two Americans who were striding along

beside Sanderson who was quietly explaining something to them.

"Charley Tripp and Hank Selby," Jock said. "Sanderson hasn't told us too much about this operation yet, but I'll bet my eye teeth helicopters are involved. Charley's a pilot and Hank's a gunner. They went through Vietnam together. Since then they've been government advisors in the Middle East and Central America."

He nodded to the five Englishmen who were sticking together. "All ex-SAS, all seen action in northern Ireland, all were mercenaries in Angola. The big fellow is Roberts. They call him the Gentle Giant. Nice fellow as long as you stay on the right side of him. Reed and Field stick together like glue. In Angola an MPLA patrol captured Reed. Five of them. They staked him to the ground and started cutting him with bayonets. The grand finale would have been his castration. Field came looking for Reed. He gunned down three of the patrol and killed the other two with a knife and his bare hands."

Jock spat on the ground. "Nice place Angola." Quinn looked at him and Jock looked away. "The other two worked in Angola with Roberts. Their names are Amos and Zachery. Some smartass journalist once called them 'the A–Z of death and destruction'." Jock hauled his pack higher onto his shoulders trying to find a more comfortable position. "They've caused their share of both."

"And what about you, Jock?" Teal asked.

Jock plodded on in silence for half a minute. "Same background as the rest. Saw my first action in Suez. Then the army sent me off with my popgun to Aden, Malaya and Cyprus. Got my papers in 1964 and tried to settle down. Found a job in a London sports store selling fine shotguns to fine gentlemen. Drove me bonkers so I became a merc." Jock looked at the ground as he strode forward, his brow creased as if trying to understand something. "Hard to explain," he said, "but if a man's been in action long enough with good men around him it's hard to take civilians. Different breed." He pursed his lips, "So I became a merc," he repeated. "I was with the Colonel in the Congo, and other places. Red

Sanderson's my sort of man. He wants me for a shooting match he's just got to pick up the phone."

"Suez was 1956," Teal said. "How the hell old are you, Jock?"

"Forty-bloody-eight." He dug a none too gentle elbow into Quinn's ribs. "And whipper-snapper athletes like your friend here make me feel every year of it."

"You got family?" Quinn asked.

Jock grinned. "That I have laddie. A sweet and beautiful wife. A bonnie lass. Married her two months ago. This is my last show. I promised her. With the money from this and the loot I've stashed away, I'll be leasing a pub in Glasgow. You'll be welcome to visit." He chuckled. "I'll be inviting all the lads up. Bit of luck there'll be the odd brawl to relieve the boredom."

They stole half an hour in the back of a microbus while the kitchen detail cleaned up after the evening meal. Then Lena's father would give the men their first full explanation of Operation Flying Dutchman. They had lowered the seat backs, and were lying in each other's arms under a blanket.

"We haven't got much time," Lena whispered.

Quinn grunted and kissed her neck.

"And if we don't do it now we won't be able to do it. We can't go sneaking around after lights out."

Quinn kissed her neck again.

Lena took his hand and placed it in a strategic position. Quinn didn't move.

"Come *on*, darling, we've only got a few minutes." She started moving her hands around on him.

Quinn moaned.

"You like that?"

"Lena . . ."

"You want me now?" She leaned over him, smothering his face with kisses. "Make the most of it." She kissed him a dozen times more. "A recently deflowered virgin completely at your disposal." She kissed him again.

"Lena . . ."

She nibbled his neck, then his ear. "You keep saying that,

but you don't *do* anything. I'm not supposed to initiate proceedings you know." She pulled his shirt from his trousers and scraped her nails across his stomach. "It's not ladylike."

Quinn flinched.

"You don't like that?" She nibbled his neck again. "What *would* you like?"

Quinn rolled onto his stomach. "I just carried half a ton of rocks half way around the world. What I'd really like is for you to massage my back."

"Jesus," Lena sighed. "After all these years I've finally found romance."

Each day began at six-thirty with a quiet breakfast of coffee or tea, eggs, and homemade bread which Lena and Charley Tripp baked the previous evening. By eight o'clock, when the red ball of the sun broke through the thin mist over the moors, the men started their six mile hike. Three miles out using Sanderson's grueling run-walk-sprint-walk plan, then three miles back with knapsacks full of stones. During the second five days they carried sixty pounds.

After the hike came the calisthenics program, a half hour of sit-ups, push-ups and squats designed to reinforce stomach, shoulder and thigh muscles.

At eleven o'clock, and after a fifteen minute coffee break, Sanderson led the men in an hour long unarmed combat refresher course. For Quinn this part of the day was an eye-opener. All of the men, including Teal, were truly dangerous, scientific brawlers. Sanderson was only helping them brush-up techniques they had known and practised for years: the devasting Karate snap kick known as *mae-geri* which could drive an opponent two yards backwards; four basic Karate blocks which even though defensive in character could actually break a man's arm or leg if applied efficiently; three judo throws designed to turn attacks from the front, side or back to the defender's advantage; attacks to vital points capable of incapacitating, crippling or killing an adversary; knife-fighting and stick-fighting techniques; disarming techniques. At the end of the hour, after being thrown a dozen times and punched twenty, Quinn felt bruised to the core. His only consolation was that no one else in the group was in visibly better shape than him.

During the last three days Lena joined the unarmed combat sessions. It was then that Quinn saw another side of his lady-love. She held her own with most of the mercenaries, including Roberts. In a free-for-all sparring session against the Gentle Giant, she threw him twice before he finally captured her in a neck-lock from which escape was impossible. That night Quinn learned from her that she held a black belt in Karate and a brown in Judo.

A light lunch followed unarmed combat practice and in its way this break was the cruelest part of the daily program. After eating, the men sat around chatting and smoking for half an hour. Slowly, they relaxed. Some would doze off. But, at two o'clock exactly Sanderson would call them to order and tightening muscles would once again have to obey the unreasonable demands of the training program.

It was on the fourth day that they began to play Sanderson's little game called Pass-the-Rocks.

Each day for the first five days the men had carried home over 500 pounds weight of rocks. During each of the last five days they carried home nearly 800 pounds. On day four the rock pile in the farmyard weighed over 2000 pounds.

Sanderson kicked at it and glanced at the line of expectant men. "Hope you didn't think I had you carrying these home just for the sake of carrying them." He picked up an average sized rock. "Weighs about three pounds." He turned and hurled it with the over-arm action of a grenade thrower. It landed fifty feet away. "Very light. After all, I don't want to over-exert you. That's why I only asked you to carry small rocks home."

"Come on," Hank Selby drawled. "Cut the shit. Wadda we do with the goddamned rocks?"

"The American contingent is eager," Sanderson said, "That's good." He picked up another rock, walked by the line of men and dropped it on the other side of the yard. "That's all we have to do, gentlemen. Move the pile of rocks from one side of the yard to the other."

That afternoon it took them twenty-three minutes to move

the 2000 pounds of rock. But by the tenth day when the rock-pile weighed around 6500 pounds it took them one hour and fifty-seven minutes. One hundred and seventeen minutes of back-breaking labor which left them breathless, with their necks, arms, back and legs screaming for respite. Every rock seemed heavier than the last; each chipped a fingernail or took its toll in skin. They counted the rocks as they went; eighteen hundred and twenty nine of them.

After Pass-the-Rocks, Sanderson led them in a game called British Bulldog. They played in an open space fifty yards wide. One man, the Bulldog, stood in the center. The others had to run from one end of the field to the other without being caught. The Bulldog had to catch anyone he could by dumping him bodily on the ground. The runners could attack the Bulldog to stop him downing one of their own. Any man the Bulldog caught became a Bulldog himself. In the end, one man had to run the gauntlet of twelve Bulldogs. The only rule forbade attacks to the head or genitals. The Gentle Giant was the only lone runner who successfully ran the gauntlet. On the first day, three men were knocked unconscious by flying tackles.

Each night after dinner Sanderson patiently explained each phase of Operation Flying Dutchman.

The group would be divided into two teams. Quinn, Sanderson, Charley Tripp, Hank Selby, Amos and Zachery, Jock Culloden and Roberts would be Team A. Team B, led by Teal, would include Reed and Field and the two Corsicans, Rene and Victor.

Teal's task was to fly with his men to Marseilles and buy a cruiser, gather weapons, then sail for Ibiza.

Team A, under Sanderson, would board *Shadow* in Ibiza harbor, overpower the crew, capture her captain and set sail to rendezvous with Teal outside the harbor. Then, with Teal sailing close to *Shadow* to avoid radar detection, the two teams would head for the strike against the two Stringrays. Two miles from the Stringrays Tripp and Selby would take up *Shadow*'s helicopter. The three battle units—the helicopter, the cruiser and *Shadow*—would then attack the Stringrays as near to simultaneously as possible.

On the last night, Sanderson leaned on the kitchen table

looking at each of his men in turn. In the warm glow of the two gas camping lanterns he saw that they were fit, aware of their bodies again, confident of their toughness.

"Any questions?" he asked.

Teal raised a finger. "My group is to procure weapons. You got special contacts in Marseilles?"

Sanderson smiled. "I'll talk to you about that on the way back to London. Any other questions?"

He waited ten seconds. No one spoke. "That's it, then. We head back to London tonight, to our destinations tomorrow afternoon. One thing to remember. The object of this exercise is the complete destruction of *Shadow* and the two escort boats. But the name of the operation is Flying Dutchman. If there's a foul-up and we can't destroy the boats, that doesn't matter. What matters is Zeller. I want him dead."

They drove through the night to London. By unspoken agreement the men in their van left Quinn and Lena alone on the last of the three rows of seats. Lena snuggled in close to Peter, her head resting on his shoulder. They slept together like that until close to London, then awoke and watched bleary-eyed as the van made its way through the endless, grubby suburbs.

In Bayswater, where Sanderson had arranged lodgings in hotels and boarding houses, the men went their different ways. Lena took the wheel of the microbus. Quinn climbed in beside her. With Sanderson and Teal in the second van, she led the way to Muswell Hill, driving fast and expertly through the light post-midnight traffic.

"Guess it's the couch for me tonight," Quinn said.

Lena eased off the accelerator as they approached a red light, then picked up speed again as it changed to green. "I don't think my father minds if you sleep in my room."

"I'd rather not confront him on the issue."

Quinn watched her smile. "You can always sneak upstairs when the house is quiet."

Half an hour later, in Roberts Road, the four of them relished the first whisky they'd had in ten days. When she'd finished, Lena said goodnight and went upstairs.

"Bob and I have to go over the Marseilles details," Sanderson said. "You might as well turn in."

Still nursing half a tumbler of whisky and water, Teal wandered out of the room toward Sanderson's study. Quinn started arranging sheets and blankets on the couch. Sanderson watched him with amusement.

"What the devil are you doing, lad? Making Teal's bed for him?"

Quinn looked at Sanderson.

"You think I'm a fool?" the Colonel asked gruffly. "Get on upstairs with her."

Quinn nodded, felt himself blushing and turned for the door.

"Peter." The Colonel's voice was soft. "You're two fine young people. You deserve each other."

Later, it must have been five o'clock, they awoke from an hour of deep sleep. They made love slowly in the warmth and the darkness, and when they'd finished, lay relaxed and happy in each other's arms.

"Are you scared, Peter?" she asked.

"Yes," he whispered.

"I don't want to lose you," she said.

He kissed her on the forehead and stroked her hair. "It'll be over soon. In four or five days we'll be back together again."

For a long time she didn't speak. Then she said something, muttered it against the warm skin of his neck. For a moment what she had said didn't register with him. Then he pushed away from her and raised himself on one elbow to peer down at her through the darkness.

"No!" he said. "No, Lena, no! That's not possible."

She reached up and pulled him down close to her again. "Oh yes," she said. "No matter what you say, or what my father says. I've as much right as either of you. I'm going after Zeller, too!"

From Tristan's diaries, found in the laboratory aboard Shadow

July 15

I see now that when Zeller is gone all will be possible. When my endless arguments with him have ended I will be free to pursue my own way. I know I am ahead of anyone else in the world in my field.

I owe a lot to Zeller, but my debt of gratitude cannot support the basic stupidity of the man. No—those words are too harsh. Zeller is not inherently stupid. Zeller is senile. He is eighty years old. He no longer fully understsands what is happening about him. He sells his guns, makes his accounts, collects his money and thinks that is the extent of the world. He doesn't see that the age of technology, in the accepted definition of that phrase, is coming to an end. Technology is all well and good. We need communications systems; we need computers and all the rest of it. But they are mere toys of convenience which give us the time and skills to devote ourselves to more pressing matters.

The future rests in the manipulation of the human mind—in what I choose to call "psychotronics."

Zeller's reaction to my theories is one of obstinate negation. He is well pleased with my experiments with Hailey, but he cannot see the broader application of my ideas.

True, Hailey, at the moment, is only a test case, but he is performing more or less as planned. And the simple truth is this: if one man can be psycho-manipulated to obey my every whim, then ten, twenty, one hundred men can be manipulated in the same way. And one hundred psychotrons acting in accord with one man's will could begin to change the world.

That is what I want to do.

I think the concept is too big for Zeller to digest. But he's an old, old man, and soon he will die.

November 19

Zeller called me in the middle of the night. We were running through a high sea. That was probably what disturbed him. I know how much he hates the sea. He complained about his heart and I examined him, but it was only the old angina problem. I told him to take the same pills whenever he had pain and tried to leave him so I could get back to the laboratory and my work. But he started to cry. Accused me of not looking after him, of not preserving his health. How do you preserve the health of an eighty-year old man? He reminded me of the camp, as he always does in these difficult moments. Of how he took me under his wing. And how he paid the bribe to get me into Switzerland. And how he paid my way through medical school. And all the rest of it. Ad infinitum. He won't let me forget what he considers my debts to him. But he conveniently forgets some of the things I've done for *him*. To mention the least of them, I've killed for him. *Murdered* is the precise words. My debts were paid long ago.

December 29

If business is to expand after Zeller's death, then a new method is needed, and psychotronics will be the basis of that method. Zeller waits for a customer to come to him and then he sells that customer what he asks for. Like a shopkeeper selling eggs. Ridiculous. My application of psychotronics can triple or even quadruple business over a three year period.

Weapons sell primarily as a result of political strife. The

more political strife, then the more demand there is for weapons. That is elementary.

So, isn't it also elementary that a weapons dealer interested in expanding sales should encourage political strife?

What better way to accomplish this than to send in psychologically manipulated men to *cause* that strife?

How many times have I tried to explain this rudimentary idea to Zeller?

December 30

Hailey came in on the helicopter today. He needed an immediate session in the tank. I'm worried about Hailey. Of my six test persons he's the only one I would consider to be completely and dependably programmed (I consider his dependability proven by the actions he has performed for me). But something is desperately wrong with Hailey. I'm worried about him.

I tried to raise the subject with Zeller over dinner. Purely out of politeness. He wasn't interested. He didn't even care to discuss the matter. He considers my ideas so much hogwash. When I pointed out to him that my "hogwash" has given him six absolutely dependable field agents who daily perform tasks no normal hired agent would contemplate, he shouted at me, saying that he wished I would spend as much time looking after *him* as I did my precious psychotrons. I'm afraid I responded hastily, calling him "a stupid old man." He left the table and retired to his cabin.

But Hailey worries me. There's something desperately wrong. I just hope the error isn't in his program!

February 28

Soon, I suppose, I must write a substantial paper for the medical world in which I shall outline my researches in, and practical applications of, psychotronics. The great problem, of course, will be to disguise the *actual* application of the subject.

Probably, when Zeller dies, and after I have processed a suitable lieutenant who can control the business in my absence, I shall seek a formal university appointment and retrace my work using properly selected volunteers. Perhaps convicted criminals. Regeneration of the criminal mind is one obvious field of psychotronics likely to appeal to the establishment, one which certainly will win press acclaim. The paper will steal time from more profitable projects, but I do believe that in all fairness to myself I am obliged to seek recognition for my original work.

I shall, I know, be accused by my peers of derivation. (But isn't this part of the art of science? To derive from the past and thus forge the future?) The problem is that the CIA MKULTRA so-called mind-bending experiments of the 1950s and 1960s are well documented. But the origin of these experiments— Chinese mind-manipulating techniques used against American captives during the Korean War—are laughably naïve. And their object equally so: "to investigate the development of a chemical material which causes a reversible non-toxic abberant mental state, the specific nature of which can be reasonably well predicted for each individual. This material could potentially aid in discrediting individuals, eliciting information and implanting suggestions and other forms of mental control." (Helms to Dulles in a 1953 memorandum.)

Well, perhaps in the medical-historical perspective, not so naïve. But chemicals! They, too, are part of the dying Age of Technology. The entire human experience is in the mind. And the mind can be controlled by simple hypnotism aided by sensory deprivation.

Take Hailey. He was assigned as my patient in the Veteran's Hospital after being wounded in Vietnam because it was thought I could cure his recurring headaches with hypnotism, headaches which had started after his evacuation from the war zone where he received shrapnel in the head and stomach. At first his original doctors thought the headaches resulted from the head wound. Later they suspected psychosomatic origins and placed him in my care.

I hypnotized Hailey and psychoanalyzed him. I quickly discovered that the wound was not the direct cause of the headaches, rather that the wound had been the catalyst which had triggered the attempted emergence of a sublimated and highly unstable "secondary" character resident in his subconscious. The wound was incidental. Any sharp blow to the head could have triggered the same reaction. The headaches resulted from a "personality war"—the secondary Hailey trying to emerge, the primary Hailey battling to retain his status.

When Hailey was released from hospital and agreed to work with me I used hypnotism along with sensory deprivation techniques and, over a period of several weeks, turned his mind topsy-turvy so that the secondary character surfaced into his consciousness and his true character submerged into his subconscious.

Having effectively created the "new" Hailey I completely control him, and the point is, I gained control and I retain control *without the use of drugs* apart from mild sedatives which assist his relaxation and acceptance of my dominance.

Here is where the future lies; in the manipulation of the human mind. The possible applications are endless. On the factory floor, for instance, psychotrons would be more efficient than mechanical robots. Soldiers, policemen, firemen, could be programmed not to experience fear. Astronauts could be programmed to withstand the rigors of decade-long exploration flights. Children's learning potential could be enhanced several hundred percent, thus giving us genius made to order in specifically chosen fields. Criminal minds, as I have suggested elsewhere, could be regenerated. And with the most mundane application of psychotronics, sportsmen could be programmed to perform even to the point of death—an idea which would be wholeheartedly embraced by the masses. In the mind of every human being is the key to manipulation and change. The psychotronic scientist has only to find the key and turn it.

The application of psychotronics on any grand scale will, of course, change the face of society. Society will, eventually, to put it crudely, divide itself into The Manipulators and The Manipulated, these divisions being the modern equivalents of the "haves" and "havenots." The actual heirarchy of power in the world will not change, merely become more efficient.

March 13

Hailey back again. Intense headaches. It took two hours in the tank to calm him. I see now what is happening. His original personality is "leaking" back into his conscious mind. A session in the tank is the only way of plugging the leak. This represents failure on my part, but I am not despondent. Hailey ·is my first psychotron. I will learn from the mistakes I have made with his program, apply what I learn to the others. I may yet be able to salvage Hailey. Time will tell.

March 15

Zeller is becoming more childlike, and like a child he is obstinante, petty, irresponsible and untrustworthy. Our every conversation deteriorates into argument. He says he does not trust me anymore. When I explained to him what I was doing with Hailey and the other five psychotrons, he accused me of creating an independent force which would eventually rebel and overthrow him! I found his analogy of himself as some form of dictator awaiting a *coup d' etat* most amusing!!! But for all that sort of talk he likes Hailey, and apart from using him as an assassin, entrusts him with the most delicate financial negotiations. When I mentioned this to Zeller and pointed out that not only Hailey but also the other five operate faithfully on his behalf, he just laughed and asked me did I think he didn't know what was going on!!

Zeller is an impediment to himself, to me and to the entire future of the business.

March 17

Tonight I walked by Zeller's study. The door was open. Zeller was sitting in front of his open safe, staring at his gold.

March 23

I took two hours in the tank today. It's several years since I've done that. I adjusted the saline solution to my exact body temperature. I removed my clothes. I found the first moments after I closed the lid uncomfortable. It took me several minutes to relax enough to float. I found that the deprivation of my surroundings troubled me. In the darkness, in the silence, I could find no relation with myself. Then, slowly, I allowed the experience to overwhelm me. I emptied my mind of conscious thought. The tank became a womb, then an egg with me at the center. I felt myself drifting, an astral body loose in the dark and furthest reaches of the universe. I could hear nothing, see nothing, feel nothing. Then, as absolute peace suffused me I could see in the darkness images from my own subconscious mind, visual projections from the deepest, most private part of me. A dream state bursting into the dimension of reality. The jet-black walls of the tank became a cinema of myself. Like a drowning man I saw the story of my life unfold before me, with me the leading actor.

My childhood in Paris, my parents, my schooldays, my friends. The Germans came again to my house and herded us into the street. Again I saw the trudging group of us Parisian Jews herded along cobbled streets toward the Gare du Nord, my father with one arm around me, the other around mother. My mother stumbling. The SS guard clubbing her with his rifle butt. Heard my mother scream in pain. I saw again as if being there my father leaping on the guard. Heard again as if being there the burst of submachine gun fire which killed them both. Saw again blood leaving their bodies and dribbling between the stones. And the train, the aimless wandering of the train. A week of purgatory, with scarcely any food or water. First north, then south, then east. Forty out of ninety-six of us in our car dead. And the camp, and the factory and Zeller.

Then after the Allies liberated the camp I saw Zeller and me fleeing through the forests around Ulm, hitching rides from sympathetic American soldiers, begging food, and I saw again my first view of the Alps and again watched Zeller's masterly bribing of the two Swiss border guards with gold and jewels accumulated in the camp. I saw us kiss the man and his wife at the isolated farm and exchange our camp rags for new suits from the farmer's wardrobe. I saw us find his hidden cache of francs, enough to buy us train tickets and respectability on our journey to Zurich. And in Zeller's safe deposit box I saw again the treasure which would launch us into a new life. Money, gold, rare postage stamps, precious stones.

. . . Zeller is buzzing me. No doubt he thinks he is dying again. Given he doesn't trust my ministrations, why does he bother to call?

. . . He can't sleep, he told me. He hasn't slept for forty years. There's nothing I can do about that. Pills don't work except to make him even more depressed and you certainly can't give a man that age anything stronger. When I left him he was on his way to the bridge. Blake can put up with him for a few hours. They deserve each other.

I'm tired, and I haven't written up my laboratory notes yet. I must give myself more time in the tank. The effect it had on me this time was most remarkable. Total memory recall. A phenomenon usually only experienced under hypnotism. One contemplates the extent to which the tank offers the chance for accelerated learning techniques. None of our psychotrons, for instance, speaks Arabic. Could they be taught while in the tank?

March 24

Blake came to see me. He wonders if there's some way Zeller can be kept off the bridge. He touches things. Talks all the time about money, comes out with the most inane philosophical mumbo-jumbo. I laughed at Blake and suggested he might learn something if he bothers to listen. Blake left in a fine rage. I don't think he likes me.

March 27

I now know how to use the psychotrons politically. I've always had an inkling of an idea, but now I've formulated a concept, and like all grand schemes it really is devastating in its simplicity.

I consider Italy the most unstable country in Western Europe and thus I have chosen Italy as my target. I shall choose subjects, zealots from university political clubs, lower echelon labor union members, common criminals, ex-soldiers. I shall pay them well to assist in simple medical experiments. Under hypnosis I will decide which of the subjects are useful, which not. The unsuitable shall be eliminated, the rest reconstructed to the necessary specifications. Initially I shall build a group of twenty. After psychotronization they will be the deadliest force of urban guerrillas in the world. I shall set them loose in Italian cities to recruit and control terrorist cells. The most susceptible recruit in each cell will, in turn, be reconstructed and he will be sent forth to create his own cell. Within a year I estimate I can have one hundred cells operating throughout six or eight major Italian cities. Proceeds from robberies committed by these cells will more than pay for the cost of their initiation. Each group will also be paying for its own weaponry. When each group is fully armed and correctly motivated by its psychotronized leader—half of the groups motivated toward the far left, the other half toward the far right—I shall launch them against each other. During this initial action stage I shall continue recruiting, expanding the number of cells, both leftist and rightist. At this point I shall probably need the assistance of several more doctors who shall join me on a partnership basis. Now, also, I shall be seeking to enlist military men, civil servants, extremist politicians, et cetera. They will be programmed to cause further trouble within the rank and file of their fellows. After a second action stage of controlled violence I shall attempt to polarize the church. The press, by now, shall have chosen their individual stances. One more wave of violence should push the country toward street war. The politicians and military will now step in with their big sticks. No matter whether left or right gains control I should have representatives among them, albeit on the first rungs of the ladder of power. This could come to pass within five years. I should have my first psychotrons at cabinet level in government and at board level in defence within ten years. I shall, in effect, be a controlling member of the Italian government. The business possibilities in the arms trade at this point are staggering.

PART FIVE

Teal grinned as he felt *Charger* heel and pitch beneath his feet, momentarily forgetting the terrifying moment of truth he and his team would face when they rendezvoused with Sanderson off Ibiza and, instead, exalted in the feel of a boat wheel in his hands again. He glanced astern. A mile behind his wake he saw thousands of lights cascading down Marseilles' hills to Vieux Port, the harbor which had served the city for 500 years. Behind, and to port, he could recognize the low black silhouette of the Château d'If, the island immortalized by Alexandre Dumas as the prison of the Count of Monte Cristo.

Teal looked forward again and watched spray creasing off the point of his bow. He'd held the thirty foot cruiser on twenty knots since clearing port. Now he slowly adjusted the throttles and listened keenly to the changing note as the twin General Motors diesels gathered power. He let *Charger* nudge twenty-three knots and left her there. At that speed they would reach Ibiza comfortably within twenty hours. *Charger* was no *Destry*. She was old and badly in need of a complete overhaul, but Teal knew from the brief sea trial he'd given her before parting with $135,000 cash, that she could hold a respectable twenty-seven knots and that she had guts. He felt a sailor's twinge of remorse that this should be her last voyage, that within seventy-two hours she'd be on the bottom.

He heard footsteps thumping up the gangway behind him. Field appeared. He glanced once at Teal, nodded, then headed for the stern rail. Teal heard him retch. A moment later, Reed joined him to offer a sympathetic supporting arm. Teal grinned as he heard hearty oaths against ships, sailors and the sea drifting astern across the Mediterranean. But he sympathized.

The Gulf of Leon was a notoriously choppy puddle and Teal guessed there'd be more upset stomachs before the night was through.

"You O.K.?" he asked when Field came back into the cabin.

The mercenary's nod of assent wasn't convincing.

"Get yourself a double brandy, then come back up here," Teal ordered.

Field nodded and, supported by Reed, made his way below. Teal watched them, then set his eyes back to their task of scanning 180 degrees from port to starboard, assuring himself that no other ships were dangerously close. A mile or two to starboard he could see two clusters of lights which he guessed to be a fishing fleet on its way out for the night, and further south he could pick four more sets of lights at intervals: probably merchantmen on the Barcelona-Marseilles run.

Five minutes later Field came back up top. Teal clapped him on the shoulder. "Best way of fighting sea sickness is to look at the sea. Take the wheel." He quickly explained the steering characteristics of the boat and warned Field to keep her close to her course and to keep a good eye for other shipping, then left him to it and went below.

In the small cabin Teal flicked the cap off a beer and looked with satisfaction at the proceeds of their visit to Marseilles. Reed, Rene and Victor were cleaning weapons. They were surrounded by weapons: grenades, sub-machine guns, automatic pistols, and six spare magazines for each gun. They sat on ammunition boxes. Against a bulkhead leaned three long crates, each containing a rocket launcher.

"How is it?" Teal asked.

Victor grinned. "*Bon.* Very good."

Teal picked up an Ingram sub-machine gun and weighed it in his hand. Sanderson would be well pleased with their haul. The weapons hadn't cost a cent. They'd stolen them from Zeller.

"We'll destroy Zeller with his own weapons," Sanderson had told Teal as they drove back to London. "The idea appeals to my sense of justice."

Acting on the coded telex Quinn and Teal had brought back

from Paris, Sanderson had commissioned Rene and Victor to make a discreet reconaissance of the Rue des Cascades arms dump before they joined him in England. During a night-time inspection they discovered that the property was guarded by four men who worked in pairs—one pair sleeping inside while the other pair patrolled outside.

"Kill the guards, take what we need and blow the place," Sanderson had instructed. "If we foul up the attack on Zeller at least we'll have cost him a few hundred thousand dollars."

The dump lay concealed behind the walls of a warehouse which boasted it was the biggest scrap-metal yard in southern France. The building sat in the middle of a four acre lot surrounded by a chain fence. The lot was piled with rusting cars and farm machinery.

Teal and his team reached the dump two hours after having bought *Charger*, just twelve hours after landing in Marseilles. They arrived in a van Rene had rented for an exorbitant three thousand francs from a crony who owned a café on the notorious La Canebière. It was ten o'clock at night, pitch-black, thick cloud obscuring the stars and the moon.

Reed and Field handled the guards with a cold-blooded efficiency which left Teal faintly ill in the stomach. Reed quietly scaled the fence with a ladder brought for the purpose, dropped catlike to the ground, then worked his way towards the main gate, concealing himself behind piles of scrap. With Teal, Rene and Victor concealed in the back, Field drove the van to the main gate, got out and hailed the guard working that side of the building.

"Eh, matey, this the road to Paris?" he demanded in English.

The guard, his flashlight lighting the ground in front of him, one hand in his pocket clutching an automatic, walked warily to the gate.

"Paris," Field said. "This the road to Paris?"

"Ah, you go Paris," the guard said, breaking out his rusty English. "You go *auto route*. You go Marseilles, to *Arc de Triomphe*. You go . . ."

He never got any further. Reed appeared behind him, a black, ghostly shadow holding a length of piano wire with a wooden peg handle at either end. The guard didn't get a chance to react; the wire sliced halfway through his neck. At the instant of Reed's attack, Field took three steps backward, then ran and leaped for the top of the gate and hauled himself over. With a thumbs up signal to each other Reed and Field sprinted into the darkness, one in either direction, Field drawing a thin stiletto as he ran. Field reached the second guard first. He came up behind him, rammed the stiletto into his kidneys and then jabbed it into his eye as the man turned, his mouth opened to scream. The scream never reached the night. The stiletto pierced the guard's brain, killing him instantly. Two minutes later the guards inside were dead, too, their skulls smashed with iron bars.

They found the keys to the compound on the guard Reed had killed by the gate. Teal backed the van in against the warehouse door, and the four mercenaries began a flashlight search for the weapons they needed. As they found the crates they jimmied the lids off and checked that each piece they chose was in perfect working order. It took two hours before the mercenaries were satisfied with their choice of weapons and then, while Teal, Field and Reed loaded the van, Rene and Victor set about the destruction of the dump.

The Corsicans unpacked and fused twenty high-explosive grenades, then tied each activating handle to the grenade bodies with thin string. Then they snuggled each grenade into a nest of high explosives or ammunition and linked each of them with a one hundred yard reel of demolition fuse. That done, they carefully eased the pins from the grenades. The burning fuse would burn the string, thus releasing the activating handles.

As Teal, Field and Reed loaded the last of the crates, Rene and Victor rolled the fuse outside the warehouse door. Victor flicked a cigarette lighter and touched it to the fuse.

Teal swallowed the rest of his beer, then picked up a rag and wiped grease from the sub-machine gun. They were nearly a mile away when the dump blew. He'd felt an evil wind stroke the van, pushing it slightly off course, just seconds after the horizon glowed briefly from the explosion. Five minutes later fire brigades were hurtling past them in the direction of the warehouse.

"Good stuff, this," Reed said appreciatively, as he pushed home a magazine. "Be a pleasure to work with this stuff."

Rene shrugged. "For me a gun is a gun," he said. "If it shoots straight, doesn't jam and there is plenty of ammunition, this is the only thing that matters."

"Me, I take my guns more seriously," Reed said.

Teal grinned, made his way back up top and relieved Field of the wheel. He checked the compass. "Not bad," he said. "We'll make a sailor of you yet."

Field snorted. "No bloody way."

"Try and get some sleep."

Field stumbled as *Charger* dipped into a trough, then emerged with her bow streaming water. "You've got to be joking."

When Field had gone below, Teal stood at the wheel, his feet spread wide. He adjusted the throttles a touch, checked their bearing, scanned the horizon. They'd done well with the weapons, better than they'd expected: Ingram assault submachine guns with box mags taking thirty-two rounds of 9mm ammunition and with a cyclic rate of fire in excess of 1000 rounds a minute; 9mm Colt automatic handguns with fifteen shot mags; German M-DN 11 hand grenades. But best of all were the rocket launchers, American made Cobras; "super-bazookas" the mercs had called them. The 3.5 inch motorized rockets had a maximum range of over 1200 yards and could pierce tank armor at 100 yards. They'd be devastating if they could bring them to bear against Zeller's escort boats. One man could handle them. A complete unit, fully loaded, weighed under thirty pounds.

Teal shivered. It wasn't the wind coming off the sea; it was fear of the unknown. He was going to war. He'd never been to war before. He'd been too young for Korea, too old for Vietnam. And now, at forty-five years of age, in just two or three days time, he was going into battle.

At three o'clock in the afternoon of the day after Teal sailed from Marseilles, Quinn and Sanderson stood on the high ramparts of Dalt Vila, the ancient quarter crowning Ibiza town. High above them soared the incongruously named *Cathedral of Our Lady of the Snows*. Below them stretched the panorama of the modern town—narrow alleys, crumbling white-washed walls, sagging rooftops with tiles turned orange and green from lichen and the ravages of time. From their vantage point they commanded a view over Ibiza's port, and, to the south, ten miles away, the smaller island of Formentera. Sanderson lifted binoculars and scanned the horizon.

"You sure he'll come?" Quinn asked.

"He'll come," Sanderson said. "Zeller's operation runs like clockwork. *Shadow* will dock before dark."

They'd seen *Shadow* just three hours before. Immediately after landing in Ibiza, Sanderson and Quinn had hired a Cessna from the aero-club and flown a zig-zag pattern across the sea south-east of the island. And they'd seen *Shadow* sixty miles off-shore, cruising like a great, gray whale, the two Stingrays flanking her like pilot fish. Sanderson was satisfied with just one glimpse. He continued on course, then banked to the west and made his way back to the airport. He hadn't wanted to arouse any suspicions down there. And now they waited.

Sanderson lowered the binoculars and sat on the wide wall. His eyes never left the horizon. He's a man possessed now, Quinn thought; he's locked into this thing; he won't let it go until Zeller's dead or we're dead.

Quinn walked twenty paces along the battlements. He lit a cigarette, staring unseeing across the sea, beyond Formentera to where the great dome of the sky dipped into the sea—to where, somewhere, *Shadow* cruised inexorably toward them.

After all the activity of the last two weeks, Johnny James' death, the grinding slog of the training camp, he suddenly felt confused and deflated. He'd played the battle in his mind a dozen times trying to convince himself that soon, he, Peter Quinn, would stand with a gun in his hand, fighting for his life. But his defenses surrounded him every time. He didn't really believe what was about to happen or the part he was to play. He felt as if there were a veil between himself and reality. And he felt frightened.

Sanderson had sent an agent to Ibiza during the training

period who had hired beds in three different hotels and rented a secluded villa on the eastern side of the island which would serve as a hospital. A doctor and two male nurses—ex-mercs known personally by Sanderson—were at the villa now, rigging an emergency operating theater. They had a van at their disposal. They'd be waiting with it at the remote beach Sanderson had chosen as their return destination ready to shuttle the wounded back to the villa. Quinn had involved himself as deeply as possible with the planning and details of the operation. But now the planning was over, the details decided. All that remained was the fighting. When he'd checked into the hotel he'd finally realized that.

Compounding his fear was Lena's insistence that she come on the operation. When she'd told him that night in bed, he'd agreed, and suggested that her help would be invaluable at the hospital. "Help me convince my father," she'd said. The next morning Quinn had done so, and, reluctantly, Sanderson had approved. But now she'd told them both she was joining the attack. When both men had exploded at the idea, she had calmly demanded their reasons. Of course, there were none. She knew weapons as well as any man and could handle herself physically. She was a woman, and where she had been born women bore the brunt of battle beside their men. Sanderson retired from the argument. He knew his daughter and her inflexibility when it came to matters touching on the equal prowess of the sexes.

Quinn, too, had surrendered. But he was scared. For himself and for her. The great adventure he'd embarked upon didn't seem such a good idea anymore. If it hadn't been for the lingering, deep-seated hatred for the man who had hurled Jenny's body into the sea, Quinn may seriously have considered taking Lena—by force if necessary—and finding his way back to the States, turning his back completely on this mad enterprise of destroying an eighty-year old man and his evil empire. But on *Shadow*, or on one of the escort boats, he might find the man with the golden hair. And he would kill him.

* * *

Hailey stood in front of the immigration desk at Ibiza airport. His handsome face looked sallow and haggard beneath a three day growth of beard. His blue eyes were circled by dark shadows. The hand holding his American passport trembled.

The immigration officer flicked through the passport, glancing from the photograph to Hailey. The hand holding the stamp above a blank page hesitated.

"Excuse me, *señor*," the official said in Spanish, "but you look ill. Do you require assistance?"

Hailey tried to smile. He shook his head, concentrated on what he had to say. "*Muchas gracias*. I have been ill. My doctor ordered me to take a week's vacation. Soon I will be better."

The official grunted, let his hand holding the stamp thump onto the passport.

His holdall in his hand, Hailey walked through customs and out to the taxi stand. He had to will himself to walk firmly and steadily, and not to stumble. He found a free cab and told the driver to drop him at the Montesol Bar at the end of the Vera del Rey promenade, just a five minute walk from Ibiza port.

He sank back thankfully into the seat of the Renault 12. *Shadow* would dock soon, perhaps in three or four hours time. He had only to hang on until he could go down to where the tank was. Even being in the same room as the tank helped. The sight of it calmed him. And twelve hours later after *Shadow* went to sea and Tristan and Zeller came back on board off the Stingrays, he'd be able to enter the tank and everything would be alright. All he had to do was wait a little longer. He could do that. He felt ill, but not like yesterday, in Hamburg, before he caught the plane, when the hammer-blow headaches nearly drove him mad and he lay writhing on the hotel bed with a handkerchief stuffed in his mouth in case he started screaming. The headaches had built during the previous two weeks, ever since he set the bomb in the car belonging to that pair from *Destry*. Well, they were dead now; he'd done his job, but it'd nearly cost him his sanity. His friend, that feeling, that ghost within him—he couldn't explain it to himself—but that being, darting in and out of his brain, had started *talking* to him, like a real person, telling him no, no, no, no, no, but he had to do what Tristan and Zeller wanted him to do; he *had* to, and doing it was like driving a cactus spike through his mind and ever since he'd done it that ghost in his brain had surrounded him with confusion and pain, driven the spike deeper, and he'd vomited he didn't know how many times and when he'd gone to Hamburg to arrange the sale of self-loading rifles to the Urban Freedom Army such waves of pain had engulfed him that he thought he was going mad. It was like an animal trying to claw its way out of him.

   two hundred and fifty pesetas, señor

a wild animal eating through his brain

   señor, two hundred and fifty pesetas

Hailey realized they were parked outside the Montesol and that the driver was staring at him.

"You feeling well, *señor*?"

Hailey nodded, gave the man three hundred pesetas, told him to keep the change and walked inside, into the cool, cavernous interior of the bar. He'd order coffee and brandy and close his eyes and let himself drift, let the hours between now and the arrival of *Shadow* pass as calmly as possible. He would not think. Of anything. If he did not think, then the other one within him could not hurt him.

At four-thirty Teal recognized Ibiza on the horizon. They'd made good time and completed their tasks. The weapons were cleaned and oiled. The mercs had loaded four thousand rounds into magazines. They'd primed the grenades. And everyone had managed to snatch a few hours sleep, himself included. When the sea settled, Field had suddenly found an interest in boats and happily taken the wheel for four hours.

An hour later *Charger* was half a mile outside Ibiza harbor. Teal throttled down and steered the cruiser through two slow, lazy figures of eight. That was his arrival signal to Sanderson who he knew was keeping watch high on the walls of the old city. The signal completed, he put on power again and steered for an islet two kilometers outside the harbor. He anchored there and posted Rene and Victor with binoculars to keep watch on port traffic. If a police launch came toward them he'd head for the open sea. With the lethal cargo he carried Teal couldn't risk the chance of a search.

Two hours later, soon after seven-thirty, after Teal, Field and Reed had refilled *Charger*'s tanks from six forty-four-gallon drums they'd lashed onto the deck at Marseilles, they saw *Shadow*.

"She's coming now," Sanderson said, softly. He passed the binoculars to Quinn.

Quinn focused, scanned. He caught her superstructure on the horizon and watched for five minutes as, imperceptibly, she became larger. He tried to analyze what he felt. It didn't take long. He felt only fear. A weakness in his legs and his stomach, as if his body would betray him.

Sanderson snapped his fingers and Quinn returned the binoculars. Quinn stared at the horizon; he could hardly see *Shadow* now, she was only as long as a matchstick out there.

"It'll take her another hour to dock," Sanderson said. "We've got plenty of time. Let's join the others."

They made their way off the walls and onto the street and walked quickly downhill through a tangle of alleys toward the Avenida Andenes where they'd left Lena and the rest of Team A drinking coffee in *El Corsario*, a waterfront bar from which they had a good view of the port and the fuel bunkers. The sun hung low in the sky now. Rich orange light seeped through the streets, backlighting the cobbles, painting ancient whitewash with a subtle golden brush.

"This may be the hardest part of the operation," Sanderson said. "No weapons apart from bare hands, knives and garrots." He glanced around the peaceful street. Children bounced a ball. Two old ladies in black shawls sat on rickety chairs in their doorways. "It will be messy. How do you feel?"

"Scared," Quinn said.

"That sums up my feelings exactly."

Quinn flicked a look at him.

Sanderson smiled and put an arm around Quinn. "Peter, at a moment like this no man could feel any other way. No sane man."

* * *

"I'm going mad," Hailey told himself.

"You are," he told himself.

"Something going on in my head."

"Been something going on in your head for a long time, fella."

"Things were O.K. until you came along."

"What's with come along? I didn't come along, fella, I been here all the fucking time."

"Weren't here before. Not here after Tristan fixes things."

"Bullshit."

"Cut the language."

"Bullshit is an essential part of the American vocabulary."

"Shut up."

"Who, me, man?"

"Shut up!"

"Why don't *you* shut the fuck up?"

"SHUT UP!"

Hailey opened his eyes. Stared at the empty coffee cup in front of him. At the brandy glass. *Click-Clack. Click. Click. Click. Click. Clack-Click.* In front of him four old Spaniards played a noisy game of dominoes. At another table a foreigner read the *Herald-Tribune*. To his right a group of six youths drank Cokes. Two of the girls wore skin-tight tee-shirts. Hailey saw the outlines of their breasts etched beneath the thin cotton. Out on the terrace, under the awning, the tables were filling as tourists and office workers gathered for the evening drink. *Click-Clack. Click. Click-Click-Click.* Hailey picked up his glass and downed the brandy at a gulp.

Hailey closed his eyes and listened deep into his mind. He'd gone. The headache was still there, but he'd gone. He'd discovered that during the last week. If he yelled at him he went. But he'd come back. He'd returned six, eight, ten times a day since he'd arrived in Hamburg and even when *he* wasn't there the headaches were.

He opened his eyes and tried to think calmly and logically above and beyond the pulsing ache that expanded and contracted in his head. He wiped his hand over his forehead. It came away wet with perspiration.

I'll think calmly and logically, he told himself. Logically and

calmly. Have another coffee and think it out and then walk
down to the harbor and when *Shadow* docks I'll go aboard and
wait down by the tank. They'll sail tomorrow. Let the crew
loose in town tonight. That's what Tristan told me. You just go
down and wait by the tank, and if your head starts hurting too
badly you take the sedatives I've left with the captain and you
sleep, and the next day at midday I'll be with you, I promise
you Hailey, at midday the next day I'll be with you Hailey, I
promise you Hailey at midday the next day.

Hailey reached for his brandy glass and raised it to his lips.
His hand shook. He tipped up the glass. It was empty. He'd
forgotten he'd already drunk it.

He heard a chuckle.

He lit a cigarette, his hand shaking, making it hard to guide
the flame.

The chuckling echoed in his head.

"Hey, man, why don't you just relax. I mean, all this agro,
and for what? We were never like this before. Jesus Christ, just
let it go, man."

Hailey didn't answer.

"I mean, fella, you tell me, just what the fuck you gonna do
if Tristan doesn't turn up?"

"Tristan is always there when he says he'll be there."

"So far, man, so far. But one day he won't be there, fella.
Then you and me both we're in big trouble, you and me both;
we're in the original, patented and copyrighted deep shit. Just
let it go away, man."

"Tristan's my friend."

No answer.

"Tristan knows how to fix things."

No answer.

"Tristan never lets me down."

"Yeah, go on . . ."

"And I owe it to Tristan and to Zeller, for fixing me, for
looking after me."

No answer.

Nothing.

Gone again.

So order another coffee and brandy and wait a bit and think

things over and be very calm because it's only another fifteen hours. And this time I'll get him to fix things properly. I'll explain how bad it's been these last two weeks. How difficult to work when my head's like this . . .

"You don't remember what Tristan told you, do you fella."

Back again. Five, six times today already.

"Don't you remember the last session, Hailey? Your big friend, Tristan. Friend my royal ass. Tristan couldn't give a donkey fuck about you. Tristan never lets you down; you owe it to Tristan and to Zeller. While you're listening to all that crap they feed you, man, I'm *watching* them. You're a *machine* that they're frigging around with, man. They got you all wired up and everytime you visit them and they put you in the tank, all they do is solder your circuits, change the transistors and recharge your batteries. Jesus Holy Christ, can't you *remember* what Tristan told you last time?"

"To be calm, to remember his voice. Always."

"And what did he say?"

"I JUST TOLD YOU. To be calm . . ."

"Don't shout, mother fucker; that shouting doesn't work with me anymore and you should thank God for that because I'm going to tell you the *truth*. And . . ."

"SHUT UP!"

"And you're gonna listen."

"SHUT UP!"

"Sure man, that's one of the things Tristan told you. To *dominate* me when I appear. Well, Tristan's fucked things up, because I'm stronger than you, and I'm stronger than Tristan. I'm back, man. Been away a while, but I'm *back*, and I'm *staying*. Dig?"

Hailey refused to listen. He opened his eyes wide and stared out through the windows to the *Vara del Rey*, to the statue on the promenade. If he could stare hard enough, concentrate on nothing but the statue, then perhaps he could dominate that monster in his head. Tristan had told him that. If it won't go away when you command it too, Hailey, then you must use this technique. You must choose an object and stare at it until that object fuses with your very being; you must stare until you *understand* that object, and if you do that then the thing in your head will dissipate like a cloud; it'll be gone, and you'll be free. It can't beat you Hailey becaue you are strong in your mind and because you owe it to Zeller and me to stay strong, so when it happens, you concentrate Hailey, for me and for Zeller . . .

He stared at the statue, opening his eyes wider and wider, breathing in deeply and out until his lungs were empty, then in again and out, forcing oxygen deep into his stomach, hyperventilating himself, forcing the concentration.

Then, like a piece of spring steel which finally reaches breaking point, something in his mind snapped and the concentration was gone, replaced by inhuman pain which contracted and expanded like a red-hot universe, pressing against his skull until his head felt as big as a basketball, then, between the throbs, reducing to a pea that had the mass and weight of a locomotive. Hailey's hands went to his ears and his mouth opened in a silent scream. He slipped one hand over his mouth in a gesture of pure anguish, and in his mind he begged:

"Please. *Please. PLEASE!*"

"You ready to hear the good news, man?"

"Anything. Please stop."

"How's that? I hardly hear you."

"Stop the pain! Please, I beg you! Please stop the pain!"

"That's better. We're working together very nicely now. Perhaps we can sort this thing out after all."

Slowly, over maybe a minute, a minute and a half, the pain in Hailey's head lessened until first it was tolerable and finally gone. Hailey experienced the sensation of a spring being ever so slowly unwound inside his brain. When the pain stopped completely tears of gratitude sprang to his eyes; he felt light-headed; he wanted to laugh; he loved his friend.

"You happy now? You see what I can do for you?"

In his mind, Hailey nodded.

"O.K. then fella, you listen well. This is what your big buddy Tristan told you. He told you that if you get in a bad fix on my account, you're to kill yourself."

When *Shadow* docked the sun had gone and the sky was a canopy of deepest indigo punctuated by clear golden stars. A crystal moon illuminated the tired old city, pouring romance and dreams into the warren of streets, silhouetting palm trees, etching roofs and crooked buildings in hard relief.

At *El Corsario*, the waterfront bar, Team A still sat around a cluster of tables. To an observer they were simply a quiet group of friends enjoying the sweet, Ibizan night air.

Sanderson leaned forward and spoke softly. "There's eighteen crew, plus the captain and mate. Half the crew goes ashore now and returns at midnight. Then the other half go off to return at four a.m. That makes it easier for us." He glanced at his watch. "We'll board at ten, take over, then knock out the rest when they return at midnight.

"We work in pairs. Quinn and I. Charley and Hank. Amos and Zachery. Jock Culloden and Roberts. Watch out for each other! And remember, no noise. Any questions?"

"Yes," Lena said. "What about me? What do I do?"

Sanderson shot Quinn a glance and raised an eyebrow.

"You stay here," Sanderson said.

Lena shook her head. "No way."

"Peter will come and get you after we've taken over."

"I'm coming!"

Quinn started to say something, but Jack Culloden held up a hand to quieten him. "Look, lassie, you come on this part of the picnic you're liable to cause trouble. You want to join the attack tomorrow, that's your business. Personally I'd rather you didn't, but it's your business; you can't cause trouble for any of us. But tonight you can. This could be a nasty piece of fighting. If one of us makes a mistake, then one of us will get killed. You're not up to this, lassie, believe me."

"He's right," Roberts growled. "You bloody stay here. No amateurs on this ride."

"Listen, lady," Zachery said. "Put it this way. If you don't do what the Colonel says, I'm going to personally clobber you."

"Bastards!" Lena looked away from them as she said it, her face a mask of petulant anger. But Quinn detected more relief than outrage in her outburst.

*   *   *

In the *Montesol*, Hailey slept, his head on his arms, his body slumped across the table. When "he" had told Hailey what Tristan wanted him to do if he got in trouble Hailey had waited, listening for more. But "he" had gone, flown from him, left him. The disappearance of both "him" and the pain had left Hailey with a sense of emptiness, of euphoric well being. He had fallen asleep almost immediately. His body and mind had demanded it of him. He had not slept properly for over two weeks.

When a waiter noticed Hailey creased over the table, he moved toward him to wake him and ask him to leave. But the owner had a memory for faces, and this foreigner had been a customer over the years. He had never caused trouble. And tonight he looked ill. Leave him, he instructed the waiter, he is not drunk and he does us no harm.

At eight-thirty, the first group of nine sailors disembarked from *Shadow* and in talkative clusters wandered toward the bars. Two prostitutes latched onto them immediately and walked toward a *pension* with four of them. Two more sailors settled behind a table at the bar next to *El Corsario* and ordered drinks. The other three headed uphill into the backstreets.

Sanderson told Jock and Roberts to stroll down to the end of the quay by *Shadow* to check how many sentries were posted. They returned within fifteen minutes.

"One at the bottom of the gangway," Roberts reported. "Another at the top."

"None on deck?"

Roberts lowered his bulk into a chair and drank from a beer bottle. His huge hand made the bottle look like a doll-house toy. "None that we could see. At least two men on the bridge. Forward on A deck there's a cabin with lights on. Portholes were open. Heard TV. English voices. Video system, I guess."

"Guards armed?"

Roberts spread his hands. "Couldn't tell. Probably."

The two crewmen at the next bar paid their bill and wandered away laughing and joking with each other.

Sanderson looked at his watch. "One hour to go. Give those guards plenty of time to get bored."

Quinn reached over and took Lena's hand and squeezed. She squeezed back. Her hand felt cold. Quinn stared at *Shadow*. Her sleek gray body lay low in the water. She reminded Quinn of an animal about to spring. Only the clumsy platform with the helicopter lashed to it spoiled the illusion of movement at rest.

Shadow, Quinn mused. From her emanated the orders which resulted in Jenny's death.

With a start he realized exactly what he was doing and suddenly the dull fear which had nagged at him since arriving on the island dissipated, to be replaced by an excitement at what he was about to become involved in.

He squeezed Lena's hand again, hard, so that she flinched and looked at him with questioning eyes. She saw what he was staring at and the look in his face. Then she looked at her father and saw an identical expression.

She wanted them both away from this place.

Hailey awoke. He looked at his watch. A few minutes before ten. He felt good. He'd only slept two hours but was as refreshed as if he'd slept between cool sheets for a night. No headache. And no "him"—though Hailey didn't know that. Hailey had forgotten "him." Sleep had cleansed his mind. There lingered only the vaguest memory of some conversation, faintly unpleasant, but almost forgotten, a transparent cloak of remembrance which recalled the rhythms of dialogue. Nothing more.

God, he felt so good. He stretched, looked at his watch again. No great hurry now. Perhaps a snack and a stroll. Perhaps—and why not—a visit to Maria-Dolores and her girls in the bordello up in Dalt Vila. He hadn't been there in two years. He hoped the police hadn't closed her down. He guessed not. She always had a good understanding with the police. Some familiar faces would be there, for sure, some of the crew from *Shadow*. A tumble, two tumbles, drinks, then to the ship. A good night out. He'd earned it.

He signaled the waiter and ordered a toasted cheese and ham sandwich, and a beer. The waiter made no comment about his having been asleep.

* * *

The guard leaning on the gangway stanchion looked at the time. Five after ten. O.K., he was halfway through the watch. His name was Jenkins. He'd been with Zeller two years now. Jesus, when you broke it down, two years of boredom. But well paid boredom, oh yes, indeed. Man worked for Zeller he got some money in the bank. But the boredom, Jesus. He stamped his feet on the ground. Christ, he hadn't touched solid ground in how long . . . ?

Jenkins saw the two men walking toward him. Lurching was more like it. Drink. The lucky buggers. He looked at his watch again. *Six* minutes past ten. Shit. A match flared. He looked up at the top of the gangway. Brown had lit a cigarette. He raised a thumb to Brown. In two hours he and Brown would be on their way, straight to that brothel Brown kept talking about. Jenkins put his hand into his pocket and surreptitiously rubbed himself. Not that he needed any rubbing. He'd been thinking about the brothel for two hours now. Bloody hell, the thing was *throbbing*. Bit of luck he'd get three off tonight before he had to be back at four a.m. Jenkins removed his hand from his pocket and rested it on the butt of the .45 that nestled in his belt under his jacket. The two drunks had cigarettes in their mouths. They were walking by him just six feet away. One of them turned toward him. Jesus Christ, you could smell the booze on him a mile away. He was flicking his fingers in front of his cigarette.

"Gish a light, pal."

Jenkins smiled. "Fuck off, mate, I'm working."

"Me too," the drunk said.

Jenkins eyes opened wide as he felt something slide off the butt of his .45 and dig itself into his stomach, something very sharp, being pressed with just enough force that if another ounce of strength was applied it would split the skin and sink straight into his gut.

"One move," Amos said, "and you'll never work again."

"What the fuck you want?" Jenkins croaked. The other drunk was beside him now, frisking him. He felt his jacket pulled up and the .45 slid out from his belt.

"We're drunks," Zachary said. "Got it? We're causing you

a little strife. You call your mate down to help you." Zachery chuckled drunkenly. "Call him, fuck-face!"

Amos slapped Jenkins on the shoulder, hard, then he chuckled, too. "Call him," Amos said under his breath. "Say, Hey, come and help me with these pricks." He lowered the knife and jammed it into Jenkins' privates, which suddenly weren't throbbing any more. "Do it," Amos smiled, "or I'll cut your balls off."

Jenkins resisted for two seconds more, then turned slightly and whistled to Brown. Amos put his arm around Jenkins.

"What gives?" Brown asked.

"These bastards . . ."

"What?"

"Tell him," Amos giggled.

"I said, come and help me get rid of these bastards."

Brown flicked his cigarette over the side, then, holding the ropes on either side of the gangway, came down toward the group. "O.K., mateys, piss off. This is private property."

"Only want a light. Gish a light," Amos said.

"O.K., Jenkins, give him a light," Brown said, "then you two get moving. Bars are over there, along the quay."

Then he saw the confusion and fear in Jenkins's eyes and knew something was wrong, but he was too late to do anything. As he grabbed for the automatic in his waistband, Amos's knifehand streaked toward his belly.

"Nice and easy," Amos grinned. "That's it."

Brown's mouth flapped without a sound, like a fish's under water, and when Amos's hand yanked the automatic free it opened and closed, silently, twice more.

"What's the captain's name?" Amos demanded.

"Blake," Brown said.

"Where is he?"

Brown glanced nervously toward the bridge.

Amos shoved the automatic's barrel into Brown's solar plexus just enough to hurt. "Lead the way. We want to meet Captain Blake."

From where Sanderson and Quinn sat, thirty yards along the quay from *Shadow*, they saw everything that happened. Tripp, Selby, Jack Culloden and Roberts still sat at a table outside *El*

Corsario with Lena. When Sanderson stood and stretched, that would be their signal to join them.

Sanderson tossed a rusted nail into the harbor and saw shadows of fish darting away.

"Another couple of minutes," he said. He nodded toward *Shadow.* "We'll see them when they enter the bridge, then we move."

Quinn nodded, watching four silhouettes moving slowly up the gangway onto *Shadow*, climbing in pairs, each pair separated by three yards. Every part of the operation would be tricky and dangerous, but this first move was the one that worried Sanderson most. They'd arrived on the island without firearms, not able to risk baggage X-ray or body searches at London's Gatwick Airport, nor a possible customs search at Ibiza Airport. Hunting knives they'd bought at an Ibizan sports shop. Garrotes they'd brought with them. They were poor weapons to use against professionals armed with guns. If Amos and Zachery made one mistake the operation could be wrecked in the ensuing chaos before it even got started. But it looked good. Amos and Zachery were playing their gambit beautifully. They now had weapons, and in minutes they'd have *Shadow*'s bridge under control. Then it was the responsibility of the rest of them to take control of the entire yacht.

Quinn watched the four figures disappear into the interior of the ship, then, a moment later appear behind the big, curved storm window of the bridge.

"They're in!" Quinn said.

"Then let's join them," Sanderson said, casually.

Both men stood from where they'd been sitting with their feet dangling over the side of the quay and stretched. Then they lit cigarettes and stood, ostensibly chatting, and watched as four figures rose from a table outside *El Corsario* and strolled unhurriedly across to join them.

"Very well, gentlemen," Sanderson said. "No hurry, keep together and straight up the gangway. Anyone who sees us will think we're crew returning to the ship."

A few yards from the gangway Quinn looked back once. He could recognize Lena, sitting under the bar's outside lights. He knew she'd be staring at *Shadow*, trying to pierce the darkness and her steel hull in an effort to see what was happening. He'd be going back for her within half an hour.

If nothing went wrong.

Blake was entering the day's events into his log, and Young, his first mate, was checking charts when Amos and Zachery burst into the bridge with the two crewmen.

"On the floor, face down," Zachery commanded, and at the same moment, both he and Amos tripped and shoved Jenkins and Brown so they sprawled onto the deck. Young took a step forward. Zachery shoved the automatic out toward him. "I fucking mean it!"

"Do what he says," Blake said.

Both Blake and Young lowered themselves face down onto the deck.

"You want money?" Blake asked.

"Shut up," Amos said.

"The ship's safe is in my quarters. I'll give you the combination."

Amos took two steps forward and booted Blake in the thigh. "Another word and I break your nose."

Zachery frisked Young and found an automatic. Amos found another handgun in the chart table drawer. Good, that was four guns they had, enough to hold things down until they met up with Teal the next day.

Two minutes later they heard footsteps mounting the short gangway up to the bridge. Zachery and Amos swung their guns onto the door.

"Hold fire," they heard Sanderson say. It was the pre-arranged signal. They covered the four bodies on the floor again while Sanderson, Quinn and the four others entered.

"Which is the captain?" Sanderson demanded.

Zachery indicated with a wave of the automatic. "His name's Blake."

"Roll over on your back, Blake. How many more men aboard?"

"Six. Look, I've told your friend, you can have the cash."

"How much?"

"At least one hundred thousand dollars."

Sanderson grinned at Teal. "That should help offset expenses." Then, to Blake. "Where is it?"

"In the safe in my quarters."

"Combination safe," Zachery said.

"What's the code?" Sanderson asked.

"You'll leave when you've got the cash?"

"I don't make bargains. You give me the combination. You don't give it to me correctly the first time, I'll take you down into the hold and shoot you."

Blake glanced at the eight men in front of him and then at his own three men laying face down on the floor. "Seventy-two, eighty-four, ninety-six."

"Where are your other six men?"

"Crew quarters probably, watching TV."

"Zeller?"

Blake's brow creased as he suddenly realized this was no simple robbery. "Zeller's on *Stingray One*," he said softly.

"Tristan?"

"Same place."

"Those six men down below. Are they armed?"

Blake shook his head. "On this ship only the Captain and First Mate are armed. And sentries when we're in port."

"Where do you keep weapons and ammunition?"

"A locker in my cabin. Couple of shotguns and automatic rifles. For emergencies."

"Keys?"

"My pocket."

Sanderson nodded. "Slowly."

Blake withdrew a key ring from his trousers pocket with thumb and forefinger. Sanderson slipped them into his pocket. "Right, Amos and Zachery, stay here with these four. Charley, keep yourself concealed and keep an eye on the quay and the gangway." He turned to Blake. "What time do the shore-leave crew get back?"

"Midnight."

"Charley, if one comes back early, kill him. If two or more come back early come for help."

Charley nodded and left the bridge.

"Quinn and I, Culloden and Roberts will fix the crew. We'll

take two handguns. Hank, you take a third and stay in the corridor behind us acting as a rear guard. That leaves one gun in here to hold these four down. Let's go." Sanderson paused at the door. "Anyone moves, kill him. No warnings."

Zachery had his automatic trained on Blake; Amos weighed the big hunting knife in his hand. "Yes, sir, Colonel," he said. "My pleasure."

Sanderson and Jock Culloden led Quinn and Roberts down the gangway and along the short passage toward the crews' recreation room. Both were armed with automatics. Quinn and Roberts carried hunting knives. Hank, with a third firearm, stayed well behind the group, walking slowly backwards, ready for any unforeseen emergency.

Quinn felt alert but breathles. The knife in his hand felt heavy. He remembered the last time he'd held a knife. Remembered Block. Plunging the knife into Block's chest and ripping it downwards. A long time ago.

The door to the crew's recreation room stood half open. Sanderson saw the TV in front of him and to the right. The crew had their backs to him, engrossed in *Raiders of the Lost Ark*. Sanderson signaled to Jock to move to the right while he took the left. Jock nodded.

Sanderson eased open the door, moved behind the seated crewmen to where he saw the TV was plugged into an electrical outlet. Jock moved right. Quinn and Roberts stood directly behind the cluster of chairs around the TV.

Sanderson reached down and yanked the cord. The TV image died immediately, retreating to a tiny pinpoint of light on the screen.

"Bloody hell!"

"Fucking power's gone!"

One man came directly to his feet and took a step toward the video machine.

"Hold it!" Sanderson said, softly. "On your feet, all of you."

Glancing over their shoulders, the men slowly stood. Two pushed their hands into the air. One of them held a beer can.

"On the floor. Face down," Sanderson ordered.

Five of the men immediately did as they were told, dropping

to the floor between the chairs and coffee tables. The sixth man, the one with the beer can, hesitated a moment, then hurled the can at Sanderson and charged straight toward Quinn and Roberts. Roberts' arm whooshed by Quinn's ear. Quinn's eye retained an impression of a silver blur, then he heard a terrific *thump* as the knife hit, its six inch blade burying itself in the sailor's chest. The man fell five feet from Roberts. Roberts took one bound forward, stamped down onto the man's temple, killing him instantly, retrieved the knife and was ready for the next hero. There were none. One sailor had half come to his feet. Jock clocked him on the ear with his automatic so that he fell stunned.

"Any more for any more?" Jock asked politely. "Next stupid bastard gets the same."

Sanderson was coming to his feet from the floor, a wet stain spreading over his jacket.

"You O.K.?" Quinn asked.

"Ducked and slipped," Sanderson said in disgust. The can had missed him, smashing against the wall behind, but had sprayed him with beer. "Smell like an east-end brewery." He flicked beer froth from his clothes. "Search this lot, then search the hold and shove them all in there. All except Blake. I want to question him."

Roberts indicated his handiwork, laying on the floor. "What about the dead one?"

"Leave him. We'll put him overboard tomorrow."

He clapped Roberts on the shoulder. "That's first blood to us."

Teal sat on *Charger*'s deck staring at the lights of Ibiza two kilometers away. He glanced at his watch. Ten-thirty. Shouldn't be much longer. By midnight at the latest Sanderson said. And if he'd heard nothing by eight tomorrow morning he was to ditch the weapons overboard and get the hell away from the island. If he'd heard nothing by eight it would mean one of two things: they'd failed in their attempt to takeover *Shadow* or the police had somehow been alerted to what was happening on their quiet little island.

Teal flicked a cigarette butt overboard and lit another.

Waiting. He hated waiting. When the action was on that was fine. But the waiting was a bitch. It demoralized a man. Left him ragged. Idly, he wondered how Quinn was going. Christ, how the kid's life had changed these last few weeks.

Charger moved suddenly on her anchor chain as someone walked up to the bow toward him. It was Field, grinning from ear to ear; a rare occurrence.

"It's O.K.," he said. "They found our frequency."

"What did they say man, for Chrissake!"

Field spread his hands. "Jesus, Teal, calm down. Like I said, it's O.K. Here . . ." He handed Teal a sheet of scribble pad."

Teal held it so that moonlight reflected from the surface. The message from Sanderson read, "ACT ONE FINE/ACT TWO CURTAINS SOON AFTER MIDNIGHT. STANDBY FOR CRITIQUE."

"When do you refuel?"

Blake looked at Sanderson and Quinn and at the giant they called Roberts who stood beside them. He still didn't know what was happening, but he knew tough men when he saw them. He wasn't sure about this kid, Quinn, but the rest were professionals, and you didn't fuck around professionals.

"Seven tomorrow morning," he said.

"How long does it take?"

"I'm taking forty tons this trip. Two hours, give or take ten minutes."

"What time do you sail?"

"Ten."

"Seven plus two is nine. Why don't you sail at nine?"

Blake decided to push just a little bit to see what would happen. "Jesus, that's a stupid question."

Sanderson nodded to Roberts. Roberts stepped forward and backhanded Blake so he fell off his chair. Then Roberts picked up the chair, grabbed Blake by his collar and hauled him back onto it.

"Answer the question," Sanderson said.

Blake wiped blood from his mouth. "Supplies. Food. Bits and pieces."

Sanderson paced up and down the bridge. "What armaments are on *Shadow*?"

"Only the handguns you took off us and the stuff in my cabin." Blake felt his mouth. At least two teeth were loose. He'd have that fucker Roberts if he got the chance. In the meantime he'd be damned if he'd tell this Colonel, or whoever he was, about the secret room on C deck which contained *Shadow*'s real armory—the rifles, SMG's, grenades and launchers. Who knew, there might be a way of getting at them. The key was hidden in the paint locker.

"How are the escorts armed?"

"Same as *Shadow*," Blake said. "Handguns, one shotgun, couple of rifles on each boat."

Sanderson nodded again, and again Roberts launched a mighty slap at Blake's face.

"Try again," Sanderson said.

"You got it the first time," Blake said.

Roberts moved forward again, but Sanderson stopped him. "Listen Blake, I've done my homework." He stepped forward, grabbed Blake's chin and lifted his face so he could see the bleeding mouth and great bruise already darkening under Blake's eye. "Next time, I'll ask Roberts to punch you, not just slap you." He stepped back again. "Now give me some answers."

"Heavy machine gun each. Portable ground to air missiles. Redeyes. Usual collection of small arms."

"How many men on each escort?"

"Six."

"What time do you rendezvous with them tomorrow?"

"As close to midday as possible."

"And then?"

"Zeller and Tristan come back aboard *Shadow*; the crews on *Shadow* and the escorts interchange."

'Your destination?"

"Zeller never tells us until the last moment. Probably Sardinia."

Sanderson nodded to Jock and Roberts. "Take him to the hold. Lock him up with the others."

He glanced at his watch. "Another hour before the rest of the crew's due back. Peter, why don't you go and get Lena."

From the bridge he watched Quinn walk quickly along the quay toward the line of waterfront bars. He scratched his chin. His intelligence, gathered so painstakingly over all those years, had been good. Nearly perfect. But that didn't console him. Those ground-to-air missiles would make life hard. They would be used against the helicopter. Over short distances they could be fired on a parallel trajectory. Which meant they could be used against *Shadow*, too.

Hailey felt as light-hearted as a child. When had he last felt so good? He couldn't remember. Hailey couldn't remember much at all prior to his first meetings with Tristan. It wasn't that there were no memories. They were there, but they were hazy, soft. His mind was like a long tunnel, with light at the entrance. He could see everything at the front of the tunnel but deeper in the light faded until finally it went to deepest black. He was aware that memories existed in the deep, dark part of his mind, but he couldn't recognize them. They were black, amorphous shapes, wraiths of the past that refused to reveal themselves. But Hailey felt good, that was the important thing. He wasn't struggling to look back into himself. That was one of the things that gave him headaches.

He didn't have a headache now. Right now he was concentrating on the more pleasurable sensations of the body. He was between the legs of a very short Spanish girl who was arching her back so that her ample breasts were offered to his lips. Her nipples were as hard and erect as Hailey's penis. Hailey and the girl rolled onto their sides so that they were still able to copulate and it was easier for him to pay appropriate homage to those marvelous breasts.

He pushed his face into them, kissed them, licked them. The girl sighed. She liked this one with the golden hair. He was beautiful, different only as an *extranjero* could be. It was a pleasure working with a customer like this. She made little sounds and twisted her shoulders slightly to bring her nipples closer to his lips.

Hailey took up the offer, drawing a nipple into his mouth,

sucking gently on it, feeling it become even harder between his lips. He liked breasts, particularly nipples. The thought of them, the actual act of kissing them, sucking on them, sparked a tiny flash of light way down in the deepest darkness of that tunnel and revealed for the briefest instant a shadow which became a face and then melted into darkness again before he could recognize its features.

That is what happened as he caressed this girl's breasts with his lips. With his eyes tightly closed he drew her nipples into his mouth, first one, then the other, and he saw that mysterious face illuminated for the minutest fraction of a second in his mind. It disturbed him. The idea that there was something down there in his mind which he couldn't bring to the surface made him feel that he was not whole. So as he sucked, he fought to retain the image which would flash every so often, tantalizing him with its briefness, and he concentrated, forced himself into alertness, ignored the sensations of the copulation and used the girl, or more specifically, her breasts, as a trigger to illuminate the image.

And the more Hailey struggled to recognize what was buried and lost within him the more he came to feel that some indefinable chasm existed in his mind.

And as he struggled, the headache started again. Ever so faintly. Nothing serious. An ache. Pulsing. There. In his head.

"There's a lot you don't know, fella. Helluva lot."

The girl suddenly screamed. She shoved Hailey aside and leaped off the bed. *"Hijo de la puta!"* she yelled. She ran from the room, naked, shouting for Maria-Dolores, holding her left breast in both hands. A thin smear of blood seeped through her fingers.

That golden haired son-of-a-bitch had bitten her!

Tristan tried to make himself as comfortable as possible within the confines of the tiny twin-bunked master cabin of *Stingray One*. Oh, how he hated this refuelling business, transferring to this tiny boat with its perpetual rolling and pitching, its minimal facilities, the forced proximity to those rough crewmen and worst of all, having to sleep in the same room as Zeller.

He glanced across at Zeller who lay on his bunk staring at the ceiling, wrapped in that filthy rag of a black overcoat, his lips moving soundlessly, silently repeating some insane litany to himself.

Tristan fluffed up the pillows behind him and tried to concentrate on his work. He wrote three lines in his notebook and scratched his nose with his pen. So much work to do with this Italian thing. What short weeks ago had been a broad idea was now, slowly, becoming a minutely detailed plan. Tristan had already made over one hundred pages of notes, but he had a long way to go yet. As he worked, options opened. For instance, perhaps he could forego much of the violence he had originally envisaged. Perhaps one highly trained guerrilla group could kidnap a string of politicians, and perhaps those politicians could be processed, released, and robotic, working at the highest levels of government policy-making, provide the first stepping stones for the eventual takeover.

For he was thinking in terms of complete takeover now, not just partial control so he could sell arms. His ambitions were expanding. The real riches of life lay in power, not in money.

Tristan closed his eyes, reviewing images of the future. It was not impossible, not at all. Look at the great dictators of the 20th century. Hitler, Mussolini, Stalin, Tito, Franco. They had scrambled to power in morally and economically sick countries by the balanced use of violence and charisma. He, Tristan, could do the same through psychotronics.

If he could perfect the processing of his psychotrons!

Hailey. Dear, oh dear, what a disappointment. Only short weeks ago he had considered Hailey a living monument to his intellect, to his application of a compendium of the scientific arts. But now—and he accepted the fact with all humility—he knew that he could consider Hailey a mere guinea pig. Soon, he knew, he would be obliged to take Hailey out of the field. Sad. Sad. Sad. Instead of an agent, Hailey would become a species of laboratory animal, existing only to be observed, mentally dissected, mutated and grafted in the hope that his complicated, unbalanced mind would offer up the key to his, Tristan's, errors in the application of psychotronic processing.

But—and here Tristan congratulated himself—Hailey could

be safely utilized in the field until Tristan found the time necessary to perform the analysis. Hailey may suffer conflict within himself, but he would never leak that conflict to anyone except Tristan. If Hailey ever found himself in an inescapable situation he would take his own life. During the last minutes of every tank session Tristan reinforced that idea in Hailey's mind.

Tristan sighed. Hailey was a disappointment, no doubt about that, but no one could expect the perfection of momentous techniques in a flash. Not even a man of genius. The important thing was to keep working, and to keep the source of money which funded the research.

Tristan glanced at Zeller. Zeller was the source, but he, Tristan, was now the force behind the success of Zeller's empire. During these last weeks Zeller's senility had advanced at a gallop. It was hard to believe that a man could deteriorate so far in such a short time.

Thank God he would be gone soon. Old men smell, he thought; old men are dirty. This one even dribbles. Another year, eighteen months at the most. It could be sooner, Tristan often reminded himself, but he knew he no longer had the courage to kill Zeller, or anyone else. The idea of confronting death face to face frightened him. One thing to order a man's death a thousand miles away, another to cause a death with your own hands. Tristan still recalled with a shudder those terrifying weeks, months, of dissecting cadavers at medical school. The sheer, crawling horror of those blank, dead faces. And when he worked in the hospital. Blood, vomit, excretia, pain and, eventually, inevitably, death in so many horrifying forms that the diabolic vision of mortality would never be scrubbed from his mind.

No, Tristan's days of murder were over. They finished a year after the war. He still saw the face of the men he had killed in the concentration camp, the farmer and his wife in Switzerland, and others, too. Those murders had been acts of desperation committed by someone else in another time. That person, that youth, was gone now. A miraculous act of metamorphosis had taken place. The power of desperation had

been transmuted into a force of will, and that will would
conquer the world.

The dollar is on its way up now, Zeller thought, and that's
good, but prudence is everything, and prudence dictates that it
may be best to place a certain amount in German marks. Or
Swiss francs? No, not Swiss francs. My holding in francs is too
high. Too many people place too much confidence in the
stability of a tiny country with an exaggerated financial
reputation which is not dictated by the facts of modern
economic life but which exists as a species of historical
curiosity. What I must do . . .

Zeller pulled the lapels of his old black overcoat higher
around his neck. He tried to ignore the ceaseless movement of
the small boat. He tried to ignore the ceaseless scratching of
pen on paper coming from Tristan's bunk. He tried to ignore
the sounds of the crew. He tried to ignore his own mind, that
mind which denied him the one thing which all his money
could not buy. He tried to ignore his need to sleep.

—gold is still strong, but it has slipped several cents to the
ounce and it will slip further, I know that, so now the question
is whether to sell before it slips further and reinvest into
another commodity and gamble on a short-term profit, or
to stay with my gold and define the holding as a simple,
easily managed long-term investment which will inevitably
strengthen magnificently over the next decade . . .

 . . . decade . . .
 . . . long-term . . .
. . . .

Zeller wiped his hand over his eyes. He blinked to clear
them of tears. He slowly turned his head to look at Tristan.
Dear, dear, Tristan, his son, who was now a traitor, who now
hated him, who didn't understand . . . *anything*. Who understood *nothing* about a poor, old man who only wanted to live
and mind his own business. And that boy could do it.
Could save him. Give him years more of life. Hadn't he, with
his own money, paid the boy's way through school? Given him
the means to turn himself into a doctor? And there he was,
laying there, scribbling in those hateful notebooks. Presenting

strange, illogical ideas. Doing nothing to save the old man who once saved him, who gave him *everything*. *Nothing* in return.

Despicable.

Hateful.

Ungrateful.

Zeller wept out loud. Deep, racking sobs like those of a child who hated the world and all those around him.

Tristan glanced once at him in disgust, then returned to his work. Ignoring him.

While Charley stood guard against the unlikely event of a crewman arriving back on *Shadow* early from his shore leave, the rest of Team A searched the yacht.

In the safe in Blake's cabin, Quinn, Sanderson and Lena found $107,000 and a further two million pesetas.

"We'll leave the pesetas aboard," Sanderson said. "They'll pay for the fuel. Peter, as soon as we've caught the rest of the crew, I want you to take the dollars back to the hotel."

"Why not take the pesetas, too?" Lena asked. "They're worth over $20,000. We don't need much fuel for what we intend doing."

Sanderson shook his head. "*Shadow* must follow the same routine she always does, just in case someone around here's on Zeller's payroll." He took stacks of dollars from the safe and shoved them into a plastic bag he found under Blake's bunk. "Tomorrow we follow normal refuelling procedure, with Blake on the bridge. Two of us will go to the market, buy a vanload of foodstuffs and have them loaded aboard. We'll leave port at exactly ten o'clock and approach the *Stingrays* as close to midday as possible. *Shadow* will follow her exact schedule, except she'll stop for ten minutes to take aboard weapons from Teal."

Amos entered the cabin. "Hey, Colonel, you better come along here. Found masses of paperwork. Think you're going to like it."

Now why had he done it? Why? Because of the headache? The headache had come back and he'd actually bitten her! Hailey shuddered. And the headache was still there. Not bad yet, but there, and it would get worse.

He looked around him. He was in a dirty fisherman's bar, the white-washed walls cracked and smeared with the grime of decades. Pin-ups of girls with their legs open covered the worst cracks. They stared down at Hailey with wide, inviting smiles and impenetratable eyes that offered and refused and taunted all at once. A huge black and white television set blared from one corner. The two other customers in the bar weren't watching it; they were deep in conversation with the owner who leaned against the back of the bar with his arms folded. Behind him, on greasy shelves, stood lines of dusty bottles with faded labels.

Hailey poured himself another double brandy and drank it back in one go. He couldn't remember coming to the bar. The last thing he remembered clearly was Maria-Dolores, the madam, swearing at him, screaming that she'd call the police and have him thrown off the island. Screaming that he was a pig, a monster, a pervert. And he remembered taking two five thousand peseta notes from his pocket, and the girl he'd bitten who was being comforted by two others stopped crying at the sight of the money and the matter was settled. He'd left. He didn't remember anything else.

Hailey felt a sudden, sharp stab of pain in his head.

"You're fucked up, fella. That's what I'm trying to tell you."

Hailey tried to ignore the voice.

"They've really done a job on you."

Hailey listened, but didn't answer.

"Your only chance is to step out. Believe me, fella, I've thought this through."

Hailey hesitated. Another thud of pain creased his forehead.

"You listening to me?"

And again, another needle of pain.

"You listening?"

"Stop it. Yes, I'm listening."

"O.K., you heard what I said. You gotta step out! That's your only chance."

"Step out?"

"Yep. Dead simple. Just step out and keep on listening to

me. I'll tell you what to do. Shit man, I know what to do. Done it all before, haven't I? I used to be you, right?"

"*Used to be me?*"

"*Used to be you, man.*"

Hailey gritted his teeth. He half filled a water tumbler from the brandy bottle and tipped it back, letting it burn down his throat and into his stomach.

I'm going crazy, Hailey thought, I can't stand it anymore, I'm going crazy, I'm not going to listen anymore, I can't stand it.

He was sweating now, the perspiration streaming down his forehead. He gripped his glass hard, stared at the stained table, eyes bulging, fighting to get that mad thing out of his head, struggling to crush it, destroy it, to become whole again, sane and ordinary the way Tristan wanted him to be. Tristan. Just twelve, thirteen hours more and he'd be in the tank and Tristan would be talking to him and everything would be alright.

A sudden, lightning streak of pain flashed through his head, imbedding its jagged outline on his brain, so that the agony lingered like the burn of a brand. He opened his mouth to scream, strangled the cry in his throat before it burst from his lips and with one final, tremendous effort willed the devil in him to leave him in peace.

And it was gone again, gone, and he felt he was floating toward the ceiling with the relief of it and all that was left was a dull echo softly whispering in the back of his mind: *Used to be you, used to be you, man, used to be you, I used to be you, man, I used to be you.*

Amos and Zachery found over two hundred files in Zeller's study. Quinn swiftly divided them into four piles: operations and plans; agents and sales; purchasing and stock; political/economical/military profiles and cooperating entities.

"Cooperating entities?" Lena asked.

"Bribed politicians and officials," Quinn explained. He turned to Sanderson who was rapidly flicking through page after page of the thick, dog-earned reports. "Some of this stuff is dynamite. Look, Zeller's been dealing with just about every rat-bag terrorist outfit in Europe. He's a major supplier to these people."

Sanderson nodded, moved on to another file. He scanned the first few pages, then tossed it to one side. "That one we keep. Location of all his arms dumps with complete inventories."

"You better take this one, too," Lena said.

She passed an open file to her father.

"What is it?" Quinn asked.

Sanderson was silent a moment then, slowly, he said. "Big trouble for a lot of people. English members of parliament sympathetic to the IRA helping launder funds through private corporations. Spanish ultra-right-wingers diverting public funds for ETA arms purchases. And here'a a juicy bit; an Italian politician is Zeller's go-between to the Red Army Brigade."

Sanderson snapped the file shut. "Not only names, but code-names, addresses, telephone numbers, secret rendezvous points, bank account numbers and most significantly, the amount each subject receives as a retainer from Zeller. All of these fine, upstanding citizens are in Zeller's employ."

"Can we use the information?" Lena asked.

"If we're careful," Sanderson said. "Give it to the wrong people and we stand a good chance of being murdered in our beds. Governments don't want scandals as big as the ones these documents will cause." He smiled. "But they're damned well going to be stuck with them, I'll make sure of that. I'm going to cross-pollinate this information. Stuff incriminating Italians I'll drop around Germany. Stuff incriminating Englishmen we'll spread in France. The Spanish stuff we'll drop in England, and so on. Some to intelligence agencies, some to police departments, some to government bodies and photo-copies of *everything* to journalists."

They rifled every drawer and cupboard in the study, but the office was strangely bare. There was no suggestion that a human being actually worked in the room. No books, magazines, newspapers, personal mementos, photographs, clothing, cigarettes or pipes. Just a bare desk with a pen stand and notepad, a covered typewriter on a stand, and in drawers several reams of paper, boxes of carbon and envelopes. Zeller's

entire being seemed to be contained in the two bulging filing
cabinets, neatly indexed for instant reference. And there was
the man-high strongroom.

Quinn, Sanderson and Lena contemplated it. Each in turn
touched its massive steel door, its locking wheel and combination lock.

"We've got the files," Quinn said, "and we've got the
money. So what's in here?"

Sanderson shrugged. "I'd like to find out."

"Didn't you say that Roberts . . . ?"

Sanderson snapped his fingers, rushed out of the cabin and
returned a moment later with Roberts.

"Roberts, I hear you had a little trouble with the police a few
years back. Something to do with safe-busting?"

Roberts said nothing, eyed Sanderson cautiously, the safe
with somewhat more enthusiasm.

"Don't be coy, Roberts," Sanderson grinned. "Can you bust
safes or not?"

"Done a few, Colonel."

"Could you do this one?"

Roberts ran a sharp, professional eye over the strongroom.
"Sure," he said. "if I had a lot of time and a lot of expensive
equipment."

"Haven't got either."

"So, in that case, I'd just blow the fucker open." He
glanced at Lena. "Sorry miss."

"That's O.K.," Lena said, sweetly. "You just go ahead and
blow the fucker whenever you want."

"But not now," Sanderson said. "Tomorrow, when we're
out of port."

Blake lit his second-to-last cigarette and looked at his watch.
Quarter of an hour off midnight. They'd been in here an hour
and a half already. Bastards had left them in the stinking hold
with no light except their matches and cigarette lighters. He
still didn't know what was happening, but whatever it was, it
was bad. That old bastard would have his balls for this. One
cushy job right out the window. Who the hell were those

pricks? They knew what they were doing, they'd planned it right down to the last detail.

Mainly to give his men something to do Blake had the crew feel all around the steel walls of the hold in the slim hope they'd find some way out. But Blake knew the only exit was twenty feet straight up to the cargo hatch. When he'd been locked in he'd gone straight to the toolshop in the corner of the hold. In there were the means to escape. Then he'd cursed his own efficiency. The door was double-locked, and the implements he'd need to get in were *inside*.

If there was just *some* way to reach the weapons locker!

"What do we do, Captain?" Young asked.

"We've got one chance left," Blake said. "In fifteen minutes the shore-leave crew come home."

"Forget it. That lot'll be so pissed they won't have a leg between them."

"Then we've got no chance," Blake said. And then, maliciously, "So don't ask any more stupid questions."

Young sighed in the dark. "Can you give me a fag?"

Blake instinctively covered his breast pocket which contained the packet with its one remaining cigarette. "That," he said, "is classified as a stupid, fucking question."

Young sighed again, sat tiredly on the floor and leaned against the cold, steel wall. He stared into the pitch-thick blackness. He listened to the murmuring, slightly hysterical conversation of the other men and dreamed of the bright lights back home.

Teal read the message for the third time and stared through the night to the distant lights of Ibiza. "WHOLE SHOW COMPLETE SUCCESS. ETA 11:00 A.M."

So, they'd done it! Preparatory stages of the operation had been completed without a hitch. Team B had brought arms and a boat and Team A had successfully captured *Shadow* and all her crew.

Teal suddenly felt dog-tired, and he knew the others were the same. No one had enjoyed more than four or five hours sleep since they'd left England. He looked at his watch. Twelve-fifty-seven. Enough time for them all to take some shut-eye before the fun and games started. He went below. Rene and Victor were stretched out on the bunks in the forward cabin. Rene snored softly. Victor tossed and turned. Reed sat at the chart table playing solitaire by the soft glow of the chart light. Field slouched on the narrow settee in the dining area polishing his stiletto with a piece of oily rag. The weapons were stacked in their crates around the cabin.

"We better get some sleep," Teal said, quietly. "We'll do two hour watches. I'll take the first."

Field slid the stiletto into a sheath attached to his wrist. "You two bed down. I'll take the watch." He slipped a packet of cigarettes and a lighter into his pocket, took a can of beer from the table and clambored up the low gangway to the deck.

"Wake me in two hours," Teal softly called after him.

"He won't," Reed said. "Field won't sleep until this is over."

Teel and Reed squeezed by crates into the stern cabin. They made themselves comfortable on the narrow bunks.

"Field never sleeps during an operation," Reed explained. "When there's a fight on he can go a week without sleep. He's got this trick. He sort of dozes with his eyes open. But he's still alert."

"He should sleep," Teal said. "Body needs it."

Reed said nothing for a minute, then, quietly, he spoke. "Three of us used to soldier together. Field, me and Barney Jackson. We were doing a stint in Angola, infiltrating an MPLA stronghold. Twenty-eight of us. Bastards infiltrated *us* one night. Next morning we found four sentries with their throats cut. Six more men dead, too. Barney was sleeping between Field and me. They'd cut off his head and sat it on his chest."

Teal waited, listening to Reed's breathing.

"I started screaming. Sort of went crazy for a few minutes. I liked Barney. Field slapped me until I got control. I was O.K. after that. But Field . . . Well, Field has never slept on an operation since then."

"Jesus Christ," Teal whispered.

"Yeah, well that's the way it goes," Reed said. He chuckled. "Sleep tight, Teal."

* * *

Sanderson stared at the steel tank in the middle of the room. He glanced at Jock, who shrugged.

"Don't ask me, Colonel. Haven't the faintest."

They opened the heavy, steel lid. Jock dipped a fingertip in the water, then tasted it. "Salty. Some sort of fancy bath?"

"Maybe."

Sanderson examined the two-way communication system built into the tank beside the headrest. He traced the wires to the book and paper-covered desk, to the microphone and speaker and tape recorder. He shuffled through the strewn papers, trying to make sense of them. Some sort of thesis, but on what? He shuffled further and found twenty or thirty papers clipped together, faced by a cover sheet:

PSYCHOTRONIC TECHNIQUE

Sensory Deprivation, Suggestion,
and Emotional Exchange.
(A Non-Chemical Application of
Mental Manipulation.)
By Dr. Francois Tristan

Tristan? Sanderson mentally reviewed his scores of pages of research on Zeller. Tristan. Of course. The boy Zeller had met in the concentration camp. The doctor who'd attended him during all these years of isolation from society. But, *Psychotronic Technique*? What the hell was that?

Sensory deprivation?

Sanderson watched as Jock closed the lid to the tank, and suddenly understood what the strange, enclosed, bath-like object was.

But on an arms dealer's ship?

He started to read and continued for over an hour. When he'd understood enough of the medical and psychiatric jargon he knew that these papers, too, had to be passed to the authorities.

Then he thought, no, no one gets these. These papers went down with *Shadow*. The world didn't need them. The world had enough problems already with men who *consciously* chose evil as a way of life. Why should he pass on information which would give man the chance to create more?

Sanderson pushed the papers from him, sat back in the chair and stared at them.

"What you got there, Colonel?" Jock asked.

"The scribblings of a madman," Sanderson said.

Quinn and Lena walked slowly along the waterfront. They'd hired a safety deposit box in the hotel for the bundles of dollars. Now, almost reluctantly, they were returning to *Shadow*, to complete what they had voluntarily decided to do. Lena clung to Quinn's arm, purposefully slowing them so that they could stretch these last moments of peace and privacy.

"How's your eye?"

"Guess I'll survive."

Quinn tenderly patted his right cheekbone where he'd taken a solid, straight right during a quick brawl outside the hold. As expected, the crewmen had returned from shore leave drunk and had been easily captured. But outside the hold, one of the crew started swinging and Quinn had taken the punch. He'd responded with a knee into his aggressor's stomach and a fast backhand to the face, a no-nonsense counter-attack which simultaneously surprised Quinn by its effectiveness, quashed any rebellious ideas in the rest of the crew and won Quinn a measure of respect from the mercs who, until now, had considered him something of a curiosity—a mere civilian, a money-man along for a lark.

They walked in silence, hardly noticing the late-night revelry spilling from the waterfront bars. Groups of tourists sat around tables outside the cafes laughing, joking, dancing to piped music and slugging back round after round of drink as if their lives depended on it. They'd be there until three o'clock or later, until the presence of the municipal police reminded bar owners that they risked their licenses if they didn't close.

"This time tomorrow it'll be over," Lena said.

Quinn nodded and put his arm around her.

"I don't care about Zeller," she said. "I know what he's done to us, but I don't care. I just want us to be away from here."

Quinn turned her to face him, then put his arms around her and pulled her tightly to him. He whispered to her, urgently, the words tumbling from him. "I've only known you two, three weeks, and perhaps I don't have the right to say this, but I love you, and because I love you and because it was me who brought you and your father here, because I feel responsible for you, I'm going to ask you something . . ."

He stroked her hair. Over her shoulder he could see the long, sleek lines of *Shadow* at her moorings, her lights reflecting like dancing, golden imps in the harbor waters.

"Lena, don't come with us. Please wait for us here on the island." Even as he said it he knew he'd uttered a useless plea.

She pulled back from him and cupped his face in her hands. She reached up and kissed the bruise under his eye.

"I'll stay if you stay," she said.

Then she took his arm and, wordlessly, they walked toward the silent ship.

Hailey descended from the warren of streets of Dalt Vila and into the Calle Montgri which led to the waterfront. He walked along by the ferry terminal, his eyes glued to *Shadow*. The mere sight of her shed some of the drunkeness from him. Tristan was just a few short miles, a few short hours away. The headache had gone but he knew it would return soon. Tristan was the only one who could cure the headaches.

He felt vaguely ill in the stomach. He'd drunk a third of a bottle of brandy in the fishermen's bar. He'd never drunk like that since he'd worked for Zeller and Tristan. Tristan had told him not to. You drank like that and your judgment was impaired and you could get killed. But he'd had to drink, had to do something to rid himself of . . . of . . .

Hailey squeezed the bridge of his nose tightly between thumb and forefinger, trying to remember what had driven him to those sudden, fast glasses of brandy. Something . . . Voices? A voice? A voice wouldn't make him do that. A voice . . . ?

Hailey took three or four deep breaths to clear his head and walked on. A couple walked arm in arm in front of him, whispering to each other. They stopped as he passed them and the man pulled the girl close to him.

He decided black coffee and mineral water would settle his stomach and walked across to one of the quieter bars and sat at a vacant table. A waiter took his order. He sat staring at *Shadow*, vaguely wondering about the feeling somewhere in him that there'd been a voice.

The waiter served his drinks. Hailey poured the mineral water. It was icy cold. He drank it thirstily, knowing it would be a good antidote to the dehydrating effect of the brandy.

He saw the couple he'd passed turning onto the quay, strolling toward *Shadow*. He watched them idly, not interested in them one way or another, and then watched them turn onto *Shadow*'s gangway and board the yacht.

Suddenly Hailey was on his feet!

He pulled a note from his pocket, dropped it on the table and walked swiftly down the length of the waterfront.

He knew that man! As he'd walked by the table not ten yards from him his face had turned toward the bar, his features caught in the glow of the terrace lights. He knew that man! He hadn't remembered when he'd seen him, hadn't even *realized* he knew him. But as he and the girl climbed *Shadow*'s gangway the latent image his mind had received from that brief glimpse suddenly exploded into a tangible shock of remembrance.

That man was supposed to be dead, blown to pieces in a booby-trapped car!

That man was Quinn, the man from *Destry*!

. . . *holding the girl high in the air and throwing her into the sea* . . .

And Quinn had boarded *Shadow*, casually, with a girl on his arm, as if he owned the yacht. That meant . . . What?

Walking swiftly, Hailey approached the quay, keeping to the deep shadows of the harbor wall. Fifty yards away he stopped and slipped between two giant containers and, concealed, studied every inch of *Shadow* and her deck. No guard on the quay by the gangway. That was the first thing wrong. No guard on deck. Wait, yes, one, but not in the usual place. He looked at the lighted bridge. Three men in there. He squinted his eyes, concentrating. Quinn was one of them. The other two he didn't recognize. Not Blake. Not Young. Strangers. Blake never permitted strangers to enter his bridge.

Hailey closed his eyes and slumped against the cold metal of the container. Something terribly wrong. The worst thing possible. *Shadow* captured. And the headache. Ever so slight. Pumping away deep inside his skull.

"Big problems here, fella."

"No *Shadow*, no Tristan. No Tristan, no tank."

"Good time to step out, fella. Just turn around and go home."

And the headache.

Hailey walked back to the cafés ignoring the headache and the probing, nasty little voice. He needed two things: the tank and Tristan. The tank was on *Shadow*; Tristan was on *Stingray One*. Each was useless to him without the other. So he had to take the tank to Tristan. But *Shadow* had been captured. How many strangers were aboard? At least four men and one woman. Probably more.

"Could be a whole army of them, fella."

Shadow's crew would be aboard somewhere. Unless they'd been killed. No, not killed, too risky, too much noise. If they were to be killed that would come later, out of port, on the high seas. When Quinn and his friends sailed to . . . to . . .

Hailey took a deep breath. His fingers stroked the handle of his coffee cup. He stared at *Shadow*. Sailed to . . .

"When Quinn and his friends sail to attack Zeller and Tristan, right, fella? Right. Right on. Like the man said, this is a fine time to step out."

"Crew'll be locked up somewhere. Hold probably. If I could get aboard . . ."

"Whoa there, fella. Let's not be hasty . . ."

". . . release them . . ."

"Fella, I'm giving you due warning . . ."

". . . arm them . . ."

"You do that there's gonna be one hell of a firefight, man, and a lot of people gonna get hurt. Like you maybe, like me. Cut your losses, step out. You and me we can make it together."

". . . key to the armory should be where it always is . . ."

"You're ignoring me, man. You want me to lay a number one goddamned headache on you?"

Hailey ignored the voice. He knew now what he would do, wait until the right time, when the bars closed and the port area was empty of people and *Shadow*'s guards were tired and lulled by the quietness into a sense of security.

"Hey! Hey, fuck-face!"

A ragged sheet of pain slashed through Hailey's head. His hand flew to his mouth and he retched. Then, as quickly as it came the pain was gone, a fading stencil of fear on his memory.

"You get that, fella? More where that came from. Now, you want to talk with me?"

"O.K.," Hailey said, "I'll talk."

"Good fella. You know, I don't like to hurt you. It's all for your own good. Got a big stake in keeping you alive. Like, man, you go, I go, right?"

"I go, you go."

"Now you get the idea. You go on that yacht, fella, and you're a fucked duck."

"Cut the language."

"Cut the language, oh Jesus precious Christ, aren't we cutey-pie. You don't get it, man, do you. We were talking about it before, before you cut me off, before you went and stuck your fangs in that sweet little pussy's tits. Whatever I say it's you saying it, fella. Whatever you say, it's me. We're like yin-yan, fella, two separate parts of the whole, except we don't quite gel anymore. And you can thank your pal Tristan for that. He's cut us apart. But I'm squeezing back through the cracks, man."

"You don't make sense."

"You don't remember me? The way you used to be? Before Tristan got you?"

"I don't know what you're talking about."

"I'm *you*, man, and you're me, the worst part of me, put under a magnifying glass and blown up into the biggest, nastiest son of a bitch I ever heard of in my whole life. Jesus, sometimes I'm ashamed of you, things you do . . ."

"You don't make sense."

"Well, smartass, I ask you. Who do *you* think I am?"

"The part of me that tries to stop me accomplishing what I have to do for . . . for . . ."

"For Tristan?"

"Yes."

"For Zeller?"

"Yes."

"They've fucked you over man, turned you inside out. They *use* you, man."

"They don't *use* me. We work together."

"That's the way you see it."

"That's the way it is."

"What about what I told you? Your head gets too screwed up on my account you're going to kill yourself."

"Tristan never told me that."

"He sure did, fella. The message is down here, man, all mixed up between us way down here."

"I don't believe you."

"Turn around, step out. Go aboard that yacht and you're finished."

"Tristan will fix me at midday."

"Tristan ain't *there*, you dummy. Tristan's on one of the escorts, and someone else got the yacht and they're going out after Tristan and Zeller."

"I won't let them. I'm taking *Shadow* back to Tristan and Zeller."

"You'll be killed. And me, too, goddamn it."

"Not if I do it right."

"I won't let you. I'll blow up your fucking head, man."

"I'm going."

Hailey stood, took two short, experimental steps away from the table. The pain punched him like an electric shock. He staggered, tripped, fell to his knees grasping his head. A waiter rushed over.

"Señor, you O.K.?" He reached for Hailey.

Hailey came to his feet, weaving, holding his head. People at nearby tables looked at him. A girl giggled and whispered to her companion.

"I'm O.K.," Hailey said.

The waiter helped him back to his chair.

"You sick, *señor*? We call taxi to take you to doctor."

"I'm O.K.," Hailey said, "leave me now. Thanks. I'm O.K."

The waiter backed off, unsure, then finally turned to answer a call from another table.

"That was just a little job, fella, and I knocked you right off your feet. Next time I haul out the old haymaker."

Hailey didn't answer. The pain still lingered. He breathed deeply, willing control back into his body.

"Not just doing it for you, doing it for me, too. Like we said, you go, I go; I go, you go. Shitty situation, man."

Hailey closed his eyes. Red doodles danced against his lids. He waited until they disappeared and only blackness remained. Then:

"I'm going aboard Shadow."

"I'm warning you : . ."

"It's my duty to Tristan and to Zeller. And I need Tristan. At midday he'll be there by the tank, talking to me, and everything will be alright. I'll be well again and you'll be gone."

"I won't let you."

"You can't stop me."

"You move towards that yacht and I'll lay you out on the cobbles."

"I'll get up and I'll keep going."

"I'll make your ears bleed, man."

"I'll keep going."

"I could kill you!"

"Kill me, kill me. I don't care about dying. Dying doesn't matter. All that matters is doing."

"That's so much bullshit!"

"Kill me, kill you."

"I'll do it, fella."

"It's the only way you can stop me. Stop me, stop you. I'm walking away from here and in one hour I'm boarding Shadow."

"You're fucking crazy!"

Crazy me, crazy you, Hailey thought, and got up and walked away from the table.

Nothing stopped him, but this time he remained aware of the conversation and as he walked he replayed it in his head, testing it, listening to the nuances of that other one's speech, the style of language. The patterns stirred deeply buried memories which disturbed him. He knew the rhythms, *remembered* them somehow, understood them. But within minutes, before he had wandered two hundred yards from the bar, as he struggled with himself to give image to those sounds, they floated away from him and there was only a blank smear in his mind and the vague, vague idea that something, something was wrong . . .

By three in the morning the last customers had gone. By three fifteen the bars had closed. By three thirty the last of the owners and waiters had left, the shattering roar of their motorbikes wrecking the silence of the calm, cool night. At three forty-five a cruising police car turned at the far end of the waterfront and slowly rolled back toward the silent town. It wouldn't return for another half hour.

High up in Dalt Vila the spotlights illuminating the walls and the flat tower of the cathedral had been turned off, so that the massive stone structure, reflecting only star and moonlight, merged darkly with a darker sky.

Hailey slipped into the cold, dirty waters of the harbor and with a slow breast-stroke which only rippled the still surface, glided like a giant, slow fish toward *Shadow* a hundred yards away.

Shadow's bridge lights still shone, and on B deck in Zeller and Tristan's work quarters more lights were visible.

Fifty yards from the yacht, Hailey stopped swimming and tred water to take his bearings and get his breath. He shivered, then silently began swimming again. He'd taken to the water because the guard was watching the quay. The guard wouldn't expect a single man to board *Shadow* from the sea side.

Shadow loomed above him. Hailey grabbed the thick links of the anchor chain. With just his face out of the water he scanned the quay, then, for fully three minutes he listened, channeling all the sensitivity of his hearing to *Shadow*'s boat deck, straining to detect the faintest scuff of a shoe on the bleached wood. He heard nothing except the soft slap of water against the yacht's steel hull.

Swiftly, silently Hailey hauled himself hand over hand up the chain until he could reach for the waist-high deck railing at the bow. He swung himself over the rail and lay on the deck, listening. He heard only the sound of his own heartbeat.

Hailey came to his knees. He pushed his wet, golden hair from his eyes then ran, cat-like, and crouched, for the passageway which contained stairs leading up to the bridge and down to the lower decks. This was the most dangerous part of his plan; no concealment here. Straight in, straight down.

As he passed the closed bridge door, Hailey heard voices. He didn't pause, but with his hands sliding on the metal bannisters swung himself down to A deck in two agile leaps. Then B deck where, again, he heard voices, and the door in Zeller's office closing.

At the bottom of the stairs on C deck he paused, listening. Nothing. No guards down here. He padded along the narrow corridor between fuel tanks and lockers, through the engine room to the steel hold door. The pivoting locking levers sat snugly in their locks.

Hailey put an ear to the cold steel and listened. From inside he heard muttering voices. He recognized Blake's among them. His hands moved instinctively to the levers to unlock them, but then he paused.

Wait, he told himself, wait until they make their move, wait until they sail and clear Spanish waters. Start a fight in port and the *Guardia Civil* will be swarming over the yacht within minutes. And if you let these guys out now someone will maybe do something stupid.

Hailey crept back silently through the engine room. He opened the door to the paint locker, cursing a rusty hinge which momentarily squeaked when the door moved. Inside, Hailey moved a two gallon can of leaded rust proofing paint and felt around on the tin shelf beneath. He found a key.

He closed the paint locker door and walked back to the hold. On the far right of the bulkhead, at a point always hidden in deep shadow, was a narrow flush-fitted door. Hailey used the key, entered and quickly closed the door behind him.

He felt for the switch inside the door and turned on the light. The feeble glow from the low wattage bulb revealed a room about ten feet long and perhaps eight feet wide. It protruded into the workshop, which itself was in the hold. It wasn't a secret room. A serious customs officer would quickly notice the irregularity in shape of the workshop and work his way around the outside of the hold bulkhead until he had found the door, but with the money Blake paid on Zeller's behalf in "presents," *Shadow* had never been inspected so thoroughly.

In the unlikely event of it happening there would e big trouble.

Hailey pursed his lips as he looked at the racks and shelves lining the perimeter of the room. There were enough weapons here to take over the entire island: assault rifles, SMGs, grenades and launchers, handguns, flares, gas grenades, masks.

Hailey chose himself a Colt .45 automatic. He released the magazine from the butt and checked it. Loaded. He pushed it home again and laid the weapon to one side. The Colt would be his special friend when the action started.

He lifted a heavy wooden box from a shelf. It was one of three filled with magazines for the SMGS, Israeli Uzis. The magazines were loaded. He checked a box of grenades. They were primed.

Satisfied that the weapons were ready for when he needed them, he stripped off his clothes and wrung them as tightly as he could, then spread them on a shelf to dry. He found a pile of sacking that had once covered weapons crates, spread one on the floor against the chill of the steel deck, then turned out the light and pulled the other pieces over him to serve as blankets.

He closed his eyes. Almost instantly he was asleep. But just before unconsciousness came he heard the voice:

"You're doing it. You're actually goddamned well *doing* it, you dummy.

"I'm doing it," Hailey thought, "you're doing it. We're doing it."

And oblivion claimed them both.

* * *

Slowly, majestically, *Shadow* sailed from Ibiza harbor, her twin 342 Catepillar diesels grumbling in unison as if slighted at only being permitted to push the 185 ton tacht at 2 knots.

On the bridge, Quinn sweated, but it wasn't the mid-morning sun that caused him to do so. It was concentration as he guided *Shadow* toward the open sea. He'd never been at the wheel of so large a vessel. The experience was a lot different from steering tiny *Destry*. He thanked his lucky stars he'd had such a good teacher in Teal, but even so he knew he would never have successfully cleared port if *Shadow*'s bow had not been pointing out of harbor.

They had planned to force Blake, at gunpoint, to take *Shadow* from her berth and clear of the harbor; from there Quinn would have taken over. But guns didn't scare Blake. Sanderson had held an automatic against his spine during the refueling procedure with the warning that he'd pull the trigger if Blake tried anything. Half an hour into refueling, Quinn noticed that the bridge radio had been flicked to "transmit." Blake thought the band was still tuned to the Stingrays and that they would receive the bridge conversation and be warned that *Shadow* had been pirated. The only people who received the transmission were Teal and Group B on *Charger*—Hank Selby hadn't retuned the band after contacting Teal with news of the successful kidnapping of the shore-leave crew. After that incident Sanderson wasn't willing to risk having Blake at the wheel as *Shadow* left harbor. He might purposefully do something to damage the yacht so it couldn't sail. Blake had been returned to the hold.

Quinn breathed a sigh of relief and relaxed.

"Clear," he said.

"Good work," Sanderson said. "Take her up to about five knots and we'll rendezvous with Teal within half an hour."

Sanderson turned to Selby and Tripp who had patiently watched Quinn maneuver the big yacht.

"You want to check the chopper?"

The pair of them nodded in unison and headed out to the landing platform on the boat deck. They'd do a quick safety check and top up the tanks from five gallon jerry cans of high-octane aviation fuel stored on C deck.

Lena entered balancing a tray laden with sandwiches and cups of coffee. "Last chance for a snack," she said. "By the way, Roberts has been snooping around that safe and he says he can open it without explosives."

"How?"

"Says he can cut through the bulkhead behind with the oxy-acetylene equipment he's found."

Sanderson hurried down to B deck. Safe-breaking wasn't part of his operational plans, but if Zeller's safe contained what he thought it might, then it would be worth the trouble.

He found Roberts in the communications room which separated Zeller's office and Tristan's laboratory. He was moving equipment into place.

"The big door is all front," Roberts said. "Look." He patted two six foot high, three-feet wide walls which protruded back into the communications room. "These are the back and one side of the safe. The other side is the actual wall. No need to play around with combinations and explosives." His big hands slapped the side of an oxy tank. "I can cut through the fucker like butter with this beauty."

Sanderson nodded. "You've only got an hour."

"Half an hour's enough. But I'll have to move a lot of this radio equipment to make room."

"Smash it if you have to," Sanderson said. "This tub'll be on the bottom in three hours anyway."

From his secret hiding place in the armory Hailey listened intently for any sounds which would give him a clue as to what was happening.

Four times there'd been movement on C deck, and each time he had cocked the Colt .45 and patted his pocket into which he'd slipped a grenade. Twice, at an hour's interval, he'd heard Blake's voice and the sharp clang of the hold door being opened and shut. Once he'd heard someone muttering something about fuel, and the fourth time he'd heard two men grunting as if they were struggling up the gangway to B deck with something heavy. And *Shadow* was under way now.

Still he had no clue as to what actually was happening, and instinct told him to wait. He hoped that instinct was correct, because instinct also told him that when he did move there would be only one chance of success. That, or death.

Blake glanced at his watch. In the darkness the luminous dial told him it was 11:05. He knew what was happening. That bastard they called the Colonel was taking *Shadow* out to attack the escorts. Which left him where? If they succeeded in the attack what would happen to *Shadow* and to him and the crew? Not that the fate of the crew worried him. In these situations it was yours truly first and only. One of those bastards back there in the darkness of the hold was actually crying. And the stink, Jesus Christ Almighty. Those drunken pricks had been vomiting during the night. He'd told Sanderson that when he'd been taken up to the bridge to supervise refuelling. Sanderson said he'd see about opening the boat deck cargo hatch. Then he'd tried that stunt with the radio and the result had been a backhander from that big bastard who'd escorted him back down below . . . and no fresh air. No food. No coffee. No sanitary arrangements either. Jesus, what he'd give to get out of there, with a gun in his hand. Sanderson and that big bastard, they were the two he wanted. He'd have them, nice and slow. One in the guts and leave them to work it out for themselves.

Suddenly, in the darkness, Blake cocked his head to one side. No, he wasn't mistaken. *Shadow*'s engines were winding down. Then they stopped.

With *Charger* secured alongside *Shadow*, Teal clambored up a rope ladder and swung himself over the railing onto deck. He grabbed Quinn around the neck in a bearhug and pumped Sanderson's outstretched hand.

"Got the goods for you, Colonel."

Sanderson signalled to Jock. "You, Amos and Zachery help get the weapons aboard." he took Teal's arm. "There's coffee on the bridge. Peter, you join us, too."

Over hot coffee and a cigarette, Teal told Sanderson what he'd brought from the Marseilles arms dump.

"No machine guns?" Sanderson said.

Teal shook his head. "Sorry, there weren't any. But we found three Cobras with four rounds each."

"Good weapon. But God, what I'd give for a couple of light machine guns. With those we could open the attack from five hundred yards."

"Reed told me the Cobras have a range of over a thousand yards."

"Sure, but I wouldn't count on accuracy over two hundred. Teal, I've got bad news for you. Those escorts are mounted with heavy machine guns. Worse, they both carry Redeye ground to air missiles. They're portable units, fired from the shoulder, and incorporate infra-red tracking systems. They're supersonic."

"What's it all mean?" Teal asked.

"It means the bloody things wipe you out before you even know they're coming."

Quinn poured himself another half cup of coffee. "Do IR systems function if there's no heat source, like a jet exhaust, for them to lock onto?"

"In the case of the chopper, heat from the engine will be enough. At short range these things can be manually aimed; and *Shadow* is a hell of a big target. If there's any fire, then the IR system will work. The only answer is get as close as possible as fast as possible and spray their decks with small arms fire to keep their heads down. Then, by whatever means, destroy their craft."

Teal shook his head. "Christ."

"Zeller's on *Stingray One*. Whatever happens, that boat goes down."

Teal nodded.

"Both you and I are attacking Zeller. Charley Tripp and Hank Selby will try for *Stingray Two*."

"Do they know about the missiles?"

"They know. But with luck they'll get in first strike."

Lena rushed into the bridge. "You better come below. Roberts has cut through the back of the safe."

They crammed into the tiny communications room, staring through the blackened, peeled-back mess of steel which had been the safe's rear wall. Roberts, sweating from his labors, stood shaking his head. "I don't believe it," he said. "I don't believe it. Best crack of my life, right in the middle of the bloody ocean!"

Teal whistled. "Holy Christ."

Quinn reached into the safe and lifted out a gold ingot. He passed it to Sanderson. "Must be half a ton of the stuff."

"Maybe eight or ten million dollars worth," Sanderson said.

Roberts took the ingot from him and stroked it reverently.

"Teal," Sanderson said, "take a couple of hundred-weight and stow it in *Charger*. Then, if either of us goes down we still have a chance to get some ashore. Spread the word among the men. If we get some home, whatever is left after the operation is paid for will be split as booty."

Sanderson grinned. "That should perk up their fighting spirit."

Ten minutes later *Shadow* was under way with *Charger* hugging close to her side. Sanderson noted with satisfaction that scarcely a ripple broke the even surface of the sea. He glanced astern. Ibiza was well behind them, Formentera only a low hump on the misty horizon. The men had already taken their positions, Jock Culloden and Roberts at the bow with the Cobra, Amos and Zachery beside them with Ingrams and grenades. Hank Selby was making a last check on the helicopter, while Charley Tripp loaded it with weapons: a Cobra, submachine guns and grenades. Sanderson would direct the battle from the bridge while Quinn steered. Lena, armed like the rest of the men with an Ingrams and a Colt, would do what she could for anyone wounded.

On *Charger*, Teal had split his men in a similar manner; Reed and Field handling the Cobra, while Rene and Victor flanked them with small arms. He would steer, taking Sanderson's orders by radio.

Mentally, Sanderson reviewed his forces and what had to be done. Doubt began to seep into his mind. It always did before he commanded men in action. Had he done everything possible to ensure the success of his operation? Given the circumstances, did his men have the best possible chance to survive the coming fight? He felt a chill go through him. No machine guns. And they had those damned missiles. How many of them would survive, he wondered.

Sanderson stepped down from the bridge to the boat deck and walked forward to the four men at the bow. The mercs had dragged thirty or forty cases of canned goods up from the store and built a defensive position. Behind these they'd stacked sacks of flour and sugar. The crude fortification wouldn't be much use against machine gun fire, but it would absorb grenade shrapnel and bursts from small arms.

He gave the four mercs the same instructions he'd given Teal and the men on *Charger*.

"At two hundred yards, try a shot with the Cobra. Then hold the rest until one hundred and fifty and under. Aim just above the waterline and slightly rear of center. Bit of luck you'll damage their engines. Amos and Zachery, don't open up with the SMGs until one hundred yards, then pour it on. Any questions?

Roberts leaned back against a sack of flour. "Yeah, Colonel," he said, "what's the price of gold today?"

Sanderson grinned, then touched his forehead in a casual salute. "Good luck."

As he walked back toward the helicopter pad, Hank Selby was wiping dirty hands on his jeans. "Loaded and ready to go, Colonel."

Sanderson nodded with satisfaction. "O.K. Plan of action's the same. We'll catch them on radar eight or nine miles away. That's roughly an hour's sailing. You take off half an hour before contact, head due south at sea level to avoid being picked up by their radar, then climb as high as possible so they'll read you as a light plane. You attack from the rear, with the sun behind you. Try and judge your strike so you hit when we're about two hundred and fifty yards from them. You go for *Stingray Two*. They're numbered on the bow. If you sink *Two* try for *One*, but be careful of us, by then we should be just about alongside."

"Colonel, listen," Selby said "we came up against some pretty rough shit in Vietnam, but I never struck one of these missile systems. What's our chances?"

Sanderson rested his hand on the holstered automatic on his hip. "If they get one in the air, your chances are zero."

"That's what I thought."

"If it's any consolation, you won't see it coming."

Selby smiled. "That makes me feel a whole lot better."

Sanderson looked away, scanning the horizon. "You see any of those bastards pointing a tube at you, you know you've got maybe ten or fifteen seconds to kill the operator. It takes that long to aim and activate the missile."

"But you can't run from it?"

"No. The rocket flies for fifteen seconds. If it hasn't hit something by then it destroys itself. But it flies at *Mach 1*, plus, so that doesn't happen until it's traveled at least two or three miles."

Selby shrugged, spread his hands and pulled a face. "So, that's the way it is. One other question . . ."

Sanderson waited.

"Colonel, what's gold worth an ounce today?"

Sanderson clapped Selby on the shoulder and led him toward the bridge. "The clever bugger who named mercenaries certainly picked the right word."

Ten minutes later Lena identified two blips on the radar screen. "That'll be them," Quinn said. "Nothing else on the screen. Better get your father, Lena."

Lena grabbed him from behind, hugging her face into his back. "That can wait a few seconds."

Quinn half turned, keeping one hand on the wheel, pulling her into his chest with the other. He kissed her on the top of her head, then, when she lifted her face, kissed her on the lips.

"You O.K.?" he whispered.

She nodded.

He looked down at her, at the wide, webbing belt holding the .45 in its holster sitting heavily on her slim hips. On the floor behind her lay the Ingrams with a pouch of spare magazines, and beside them, a selection of medical supplies she'd found in the laboratory which she'd laid out for easy access. He felt proud of her. She was facing her task with the same courage and calmness as the professionals surrounding them. But then, he thought, she is her father's daughter, and he's the ultimate professional.

He kissed her again.

"Let's get this over with," he said. "Then we can go home."

Half an hour later, in the darkness of the claustrophobic armory, Hailey heard the helicopter take off, its distinctive sharp popping whirr pitched high above the deep-throated chug of *Shadow*'s powerful diesels.

Still he wasn't sure what was happening. He'd analyzed every sound and movement he'd heard, but couldn't put sense to them. For instance, when *Shadow* had stopped an hour ago what had that meant? Something had brushed several times against the yacht's starboard side. Another boat? Had they been loading or off-loading? He knew Zeller had gold aboard. Had they managed to blow the safe? Were they stealing the gold? Was that all that was happening? Had Quinn simply come for the gold?

Too many questions.

And now the helicopter, taking off an hour and a half out to sea.

An attack against the escorts? That was most likely, but he had no actual proof that an attack was planned, and he couldn't move until he knew *exactly* what he was moving against.

Hailey waited.

Alert.

In the hold Blake, too, had heard the helicopter taking off. So, the chopper was being used in the attack. That explained why *Shadow* had run to a stop a while back, and the noises of another boat scraping her sides. Those bastards had rendez-voused with someone who had supplied them with weapons.

Blake cursed the darkness and the heavy, sickening stink of the foul air. Panic and desperation suffocated him. He wanted a weapon in his hands, a gun, an axe, an iron bar, anything. He wanted a chance to live and the way things stood now there was no chance. If the Stingray sank *Shadow* he'd go down with her, locked in the metal tomb of the hold. If the effing Colonel and his men sank the Stingray he'd be shot, or at best set adrift to take his chances in the sea.

In frustration, Blake punched a clenched fist against the heavy steel door of his prison.

The escorts were in sight, perhaps ten minutes sailing away. Sanderson examined them yet again through the powerful Zeiss binoculars. He could read the numbers on their bows. *Two* on his right, *One* on his left. Teal sailed astern of him now, navigating *Charger* in the bumpy trail of *Shadow*'s wake in an attempt to stay concealed from the escorts as long as possible.

Sanderson scanned the escorts once more. They drifted peacefully on the idyllically calm sea. He saw no weapons, no suggestion that anyone aboard was suspicious of *Shadow*'s approach. Men lolled around the decks catching the midday sun. A sailor on *One* was looking them over through binoculars. As long as *Charger* managed to ride their wake he would see nothing suspicious. The man behind the binoculars would note the pile of food crates in the bow but couldn't guess what they concealed. He would note the absence of the helicopter but perhaps wouldn't find the fact significant enough to dash below and report to Zeller. The pilot was among the captured crew in the hold. Perhaps the man behind the binoculars would simply conclude that the pilot had taken the machine aloft on a test flight.

Sanderson lowered the binoculars, and flicked the transmit switch on the two way radio with which he stayed in contact with Teal on *Charger.*

"*Stingray One* dead ahead, but bearing to port. Come under our starboard side."

Sanderson watched Quinn gently turn the big yacht so it slipped a few points further to starboard than the course which would take them directly toward *Stingray One*. That way Teal would remain completely concealed from both escorts until the moment he put on power and made his dash around *Shadow*'s bow to start his attack.

Sanderson looked at his daughter. Her hand rested lightly on Quinn's shoulder as she watched him make the maneuver. He wished she wasn't here, feared for her safety, but somehow it seemed natural that she should stand beside Quinn as they crept toward battle. They are a pair, these two, he thought, they belong together. And how much like his wife she looked. The slim figure, the dark hair, those eyes and, God Almighty, that unbendable will.

Sanderson snapped himself out of his reverie and lifted the binoculars once more. He scanned *Stingray Two*, saw no change in the attitude of the men on deck. *Shadow* was only minutes away now. He lifted the binoculars and searched either side of the sun and thought he saw a black dot which could be the helicopter. He swung the binoculars across to *Stingray One*, refocused and saw a figure stepping out of the steering house. He turned the focusing wheel minutely and the figure snapped into sharp definition.

A man in a black coat.

An old man.

Zeller!

Zeller stared at *Shadow*. He dug his hands deep into the pockets of the old black coat. There she was. He hated the sea, but he loved *Shadow*. *Shadow* was his only home and more than that, *Shadow* housed everything that was important to him. *Shadow* was the heart of his empire, the nerve center of the business he had so painstakingly built since that day in 1947 when he had bought 3000 Lee-Enfield .303 rifles for five shillings each from a corrupt British Army stores sergeant in southern Germany. Zeller's thin lips creased in a sad imitation of a smile as he recalled that first transaction. He'd sold the rifles in South America and even after paying for shipping still turned a profit of twelve hundred pounds. He'd never looked back. He felt proud of that.

He'd be aboard soon, perhaps fifteen minutes. He'd go straight to his study and lock the door. He'd open the safe and look at the gold. A small pleasure for an old man, to look at his gold. The color and the texture, the weight, the sheen, the very *being* of it. Gold was God's gift to old men.

Zeller sensed someone beside him. He turned. Tristan. He took a step to one side. He could hardly stand being with that thankless boy now.

"Where's the helicopter?" Tristan asked.

"Call them," he heard Tristan say. "Find out where the helicopter is."

Gold should rise next month, Zeller thought. If the Germans want that next shipment I shall insist on full payment in gold. Perhaps I shall allow a small percentage to be paid in Deutschmarks, but there's a risk of devaluation there . . .

"They don't respond, Doctor Tristan."

Tristan stared at *Shadow*, the faintest idea forming in his mind that something could be wrong. The helicopter should be aboard. The helicopter was under Tristan's personal orders. He'd not told the pilot to take it up today.

"I think something's wrong," he said in a half whisper. He snatched binoculars from a sailor lolling against the cabin.

"Wrong? Nothing's wrong," Zeller said to no one in particular. He pulled the collar of is old black coat tightly around his neck as if the Mediterranean sun offered him no warmth. "We'll be home in a minute or two. Nothing wrong."

Shadow was less than three hundred yards away. Tristan focused the binoculars on her. He frowned as he observed the pile of crates and packing cases in her bow.

Then, huge in the frame of the binoculars a man stood up from behind the cases aiming a metal tube towards them. Tristan recognized what it was at the instant a flash of red flame leapt from the Cobra's exhaust, and threw himself to the deck yelling, "They're attacking! They're attacking!"

The Cobra rocket missed *Stingray One,* exploding on contact with the sea twenty yards behind its stern sending a thirty feet high column of water jarring into the sky.

"Weapons!" Tristan shouted. "Weapons!"

Already *Stingray One*'s captain had fired her huge, twin diesels, and the thirty-two foot escort was lifting on her haunches moving away from *Shadow* in a precautionary retreat until Tristan decided what to do.

Two men tore away the fiberglass cover of what appeared to be a life raft cannister forward of the wheelhouse. From under it appeared the chubby snout of a heavy machine gun.

"Back toward them!" Tristan screamed. "Fire! Fire!"

The *Stingray* heeled into a tight turn, her machine-gunners opening fire, strafing the defensive position high on *Shadow*'s bow.

Zeller hadn't moved. His frail hands tightly gripped *Stingray*'s railing as the powerful cruiser threw itself through the contortions of momentary retreat and sudden attack. His eyes had opened wide as the first noise of battle exploded and now they stayed that way as he hung on for dear life to the wooden rail. "Someone has my gold," he whispered. "Sweet Jesus, someone has my gold. Do something. Someone do something."

As *Stingray One* surged to within a hundred and fifty yards of *Shadow*, Tristan bellowed an order to prepare the missile launcher. At that moment two things happened: he saw *Charger* leap from behind the protective cover of *Shadow*'s steel side and, as he turned to shove a sailor down the gangway to help with the launcher, saw a helicopter swooping down to attack *Stingray Two*.

Five hundred feet up, dropping fast away from the sun's protective glare, Selby guided the helicopter toward the shining sea. Held secure by a trapeze, Charley Tripp leaned out the chopper trying to steady the thirty pound weight of the Cobra super-bazooka. He only had one shot with this thing then he had to ditch it. There was no way of reloading within the confines of the cabin.

Both men saw the configurations of the opening stages of the battle, the wake of *One* as it turned in a circle to the attack, the frothing trail of *Two* as she suddenly haunched up and threw herself after *Shadow*. Even above the roar of their engine they heard the fast, deadly thudding of *One*'s machine gun and saw great arcing sparks fly from *Shadow*'s bow as the huge slugs smashed against her metal skin. Then they saw *Charger* dashing from behind *Shadow* and cutting across her bows, swerving port to starboard and back in a weaving course to avoid the machine gun bursts.

"O.K.," Tripp yelled back into the cabin, "take her down Hank, let's get those fuckers."

Selby stuck a thumb into the air and grinned a sly combat grin as he dropped the chopper like a stone slightly to port of

Two's course so that Tripp could take the best possible shot. A bare ten feet above the sea he leveled out. Forty yards behind the racing cruiser he slowed to give Tripp his chance. He saw every detail on the deck below him: the captain, one hand on the wheel, his head out of the cabin screaming orders; two men ripping the cover from the forward mounted machine gun, another running forward with an assault rifle. No sign of that god-damned Redeye. Christ, the crew hadn't even seen them.

At the instant Selby fired, a great chunk of *Two*'s stern exploded as the rocket tore through the deck sending shards of wood and metal and a flash of flame skywards.

Tripp dropped the Cobra, pushed himself back inside, reaching for grenades on the floor beneath his feet. *"You see that, man, we got the bastard. Turn. Come on, man, turn!"* He grabbed the Ingrams from the passenger seat behind, cocked it, rested it on his lap, tore the pin from the grenade.

Selby hauled the chopper around in a sharp bank one hundred and fifty yards from *Two*. He came in low, chasing the cruiser from its stern again. He heard the vicious chatter of Tripp's Ingram, saw the bullets impacting like an exploding string of pearls along the length of the burning deck, heard Tripp whoop as he hurled the grenade.

He spun the chopper on a pin fifty yards beyond *Two*, and held her as Tripp changed magazines, slapped the new one home with the palm of his hand and raked the cruiser forward and aft in four fast bursts.

Tripp ripped the pins from two more grenades. "*O.K.*," he shouted, "*take her in!*"

Selby put on power. The crazy grin still twisted his face. *Two* was slowing now, pulling to starboard. Under all that smoke and flame the cruiser was badly damaged. Couple of grenades in the right place and her tanks'll go up, Selby thought. Whoo-ee, what a fucking bang!

As he raced the chopper in for the kill, the black, billowing smoke cleared for an instant. The crazy grin never left his face as he saw the man keying in on him with the Redeye.

Hailey heard the *thump!* of the first bazooka shot and moments later the distant stacatto chatter of a heavy machine gun. He knew now exactly what was happening. What he had feared all along, but now he *knew* and he reacted immediately, knowing intuitively that he had been correct to wait. With Quinn and his men engaged in battle against the escorts, their whole attention rivetted to their front and not aware of an armed third column within *Shadow*, Hailey, Blake and the crew could attack from their rear with devastating results. He opened the armory and rushed for the steel doors of the hold.

Teal pushed the hell out of *Charger*. He gave her full power as he dashed from the protective cover of *Shadow*'s steel flank. He hauled down on the throttles as if the power of his wrists could squeeze an extra revolution from the screaming engines. The game old lady rode high on her haunches, leaping the distance separating her from *Stingray One*. A knife of spray slashed the air either side of her racing bow.

Out the side of his eye Teal saw Tripp and Selby's surprise attack against *Two*; the sudden swoop from the rear, the sheet of flame as the bazooka rocket scored a hit. The four mercs in *Charger*'s bow saw too, and roared approval at the expertise and courage of the attack sequence. But then the men saw something which silenced the shouts on their lips and set their faces into grim masks of anger and fear.

Traveling at over six hundred miles per hour, the Redeye rocket took a fraction less than one-sixth of a second to leave its launcher, hurl itself fifty yards through the air and impact against the belly of the chopper. Tripp was killed instantly, decapitated by a two feet long lump of viciously spinning rotor-blade as he leaned out of the cabin preparing to drop his grenades. His lifeless body hung against the trapeze straps, half-in, half-out of the burning cabin, the arteries of his neck pumping gushes of blood into the sea below.

Selby's mind registered his friend's death, but his war-trained reflexes didn't permit shock or mourning. There was no time. He had only seconds to live and knew it. Fighting his shattered controls, ignoring the searing slash of pain that blanketed his back where a red-hot piece of shrapnel had penetrated behind his seat and ripped into his shoulder muscles, Selby fought not to live, but to die in the most useful way.

Screaming in anger against the gushing flames enveloping the cabin, Selby hauled on the jammed controls, fighting the nose down. He got it into position a split second before the heat of the fire melted metal and irrevocably denied further movement of any mechanical control in the helicopter.

"Here we go, Charley boy. Hang on!"

The crippled chopper plummeted directly toward the deck of *Stingray Two*. A moment before impact, Hank Selby closed his eyes and smiled.

From *Shadow*'s bridge Quinn, Sanderson and Lena saw the helicopter falling like a flaming meteor, saw it crash into the burning deck of *Stingray Two*. For a tenth of a second nothing seemed to happen, then, simultaneously two explosions sent shock waves across the sea, actually rocking the 185 ton yacht as fuel tanks and ammunition in the cruiser and the helicopter ignited in an orange-black fireball that bloomed against the blue sky like an evil flower.

Sanderson ignored Lena's cry of horror and snapped his attention back to *Charger*. Teal's launch was only sixty yards from *Stingray One*, the four mercs in the bow strafing with their Ingrams.

Sanderson grabbed the radio mike.

"Teal. Use your rockets."

"Can't," came the calm answer, "moving too fast. Too much movement, too much spray to aim."

"Try, damn it, try!"

"Will do."

Sanderson dropped the mike and snatched up his binoculars. Good God, between them they should be able to do it now. Selby and Tripp had taken out one escort. Now it was *Charger* and *Shadow* against *Stingray One*. They should be home and hosed, unless they got that damned missile into action.

Sanderson focused the binoculars just in time to see the two man crew behind the heavy machine gun on *Stingray* sweep the gun around to bear on *Charger*. He saw Reed and Field come to their feet, trying to hold their balance as they aimed the Cobra, and Rene and Victor pouring in fire from their SMGs. Then the machine gun on the escort opened fire from a bare thirty yards away and great chunks of *Charger*'s bow splintered and flew and Sanderson saw the four mercs jerk like rag dolls, one falling into the sea, the three others sprawling on the deck, rolling and slithering in blood and seaspray back toward the cabin. He saw Teal haul the cruiser sharply to port, trying to escape the deadly bursts, saw another line of bullets gouging great chunks from the deck.

"That's it," Sanderson breathed. "We're on our own."

He looked forward, saw Jock Culloden fire another round at *Stingray*, saw it miss, bludgeoning spray into the air five yards off target, cursed at the miss, then saw two men struggling out of the escort's cabin with a metal tube.

And saw Zeller still clinging to the railing, his mouth moving, as if screaming at *Shadow*.

Even on the glassy surface of a completely calm sea *Charger* bucked and leapt like a bronco as Teal came around full circle, cut his own wake and bore down on *Stingray*'s starboard side. The escort's machine gunners had turned their attention back to *Shadow* now as the huge yacht ploughed the sea toward them. Teal, too, had seen two men on the escort's deck with the deadly tube which he knew from Sanderson's description was the Redeye missile system.

Reed was dead, flung overboard as bullets from the heavy caliber machine gun smashed into the mercs fighting from the bow. The Cobra had gone overboard with them. Rene, Victor and Field were all wounded—he didn't know how badly— huddled against the window of the steering house. Teal's instinct was to stop *Charger* and haul the men below into the comparatively safety of the cabin, but a greater instinct told him to get back into the battle, that fighting *now* was the only road to self-preservation.

Teal picked up the Ingram, let the wheel go a moment to cock it, then steering with one hand and shooting out the open wheelhouse door with the other strafed the *Stingray* with one long burst as he ran even with her then outstripped her, seeing an old man in a black coat raising his hands in horror, the machine gunner slumping over his gun and the two men with the Redeye ducking for cover.

"Take her back again."

Teal looked behind him. Field limped into the cabin holding his arm.

"Sit down, man."

"Reed's dead."

"I saw."

"Take her back again. Real close. I'm boarding."

Teal looked again, saw the heavy Colt .45 pointed at him.

"You can't board, man, we're doing close to thirty knots."

"You do it, Teal."

Teal saw blood appear on Field's lips, and realized that the bullet he thought had caused only an arm wound had penetrated the chest cavity. Field was shot in the lung.

He nodded toward Field's chest. "We can fix that."

"Reed's dead and I've had it." Field coughed and more blood rimmed his lips then dribbled down his chin. "Hate to pull the trigger on you Teal. "You're O.K. . . ." he coughed again, the gun wavered, then straightened, ". . . but I'll do it."

Teal nodded once, hauled *Charger* around in a tight circle so that he was coming up on *Stingray*'s stern then poured on the power, letting the launch have her head.

Field dropped the .45 and picked up two grenades from the box behind Teal. He unpinned them, holding the levers shut under his clenched fingers then without a word to Teal or a look backward made his way forward along the sea-slippery deck. Half way he fell, and Teal involuntarily ducked, clenching his teeth, but Field kept his grip on the grenades and on knuckles and knees made his way to the bow.

Twenty yards behind *Stingray* Teal minutely adjusted course judging to miss her beam by no more than two or three feet. Field edged back a bit from the bow, ready to make his leap.

Ten yards away a *Stingray* crewman opened fire with assault rifle. Teal ducked, shards of broken glass stinging his face and hands as the rounds exploded through the weather glass and into the cabin. He came straight to his feet, hauled the wheel around to put them back on the same heading then saw Field's arm arcing as he loosed a grenade. The explosion killed the rifleman, sent chunks of railing and splintered deck hissing through the air.

Now, with only five feet separating him from the escort, Field slipped the stiletto out of his wrist sheath and leapt the short distance separating the two boats. He fell on his shoulder, the pain of it wracking a scream of agony from him which Teal heard above the roar of the high-powered motors.

Teal saw him roll to his feet, stabbing with the thin blade at a sailor who jumped at him, saw the sailor double and fall and then as another crewman leapt at him firing a handgun saw Field twist as the bullets smashed him into the steering house; and saw the grenade tumble from his hand.

The explosion killed Field and the escort's captain and wrecked the *Stingray*'s controls. She veered savagely to starboard cutting across Teal's bow, away from land, away from *Shadow* which was now less than thirty yards from *Charger*.

"What's your situation, Teal?"

Teal grabbed the mike. "Two dead, two wounded. I'm O.K., boat's O.K."

"Can you make another strafing run?"

"Will do."

"Keep them occupied. I'll try and ram."

Then through the crackle of the radio connection he heard Lena scream, *"Behind, look out!"* and the speaker erupted in a storm of submachine gun fire.

Teal stared up at *Shadow*, now only yards from him. He wrenched the wheel around and took *Charger* back fifty yards so he could see the entire length of the ship. He saw pin-pricks of fire on the bridge and saw Amos and Zachery running back along the deck toward a group of armed men who'd burst out of the bridge.

"Sanderson!" he yelled, *"what's happening?"*

His only answer was the disembodied stereo effect of machine gun fire drifting across the water and bursting from the radio speaker.

Lena saw them first and screamed the warning. *"Behind, look out!"* At the same time she lifted her Ingram and pulled the trigger, spraying the doorway leading to the bridge. She saw a figure lifted by the impact of her burst as if an invisible hand had snatched and thrown him aside. Another figure appeared. Lena's finger didn't leave the trigger. Her second target twisted sideways against the mahogany door jamb and crashed face downward two yards from her feet. A third man charged through the door wildly firing a handgun. Lena pulled the Ingram's trigger and in the instant she knew it was empty was saved as Quinn butted her aside with his shoulder and sprayed the doorway with his own SMG. The man's face exploded in a crimson veil of blood as he was blasted backward from the bridge.

Vaguely, above the booming of his gun, Quinn heard Sanderson grunt with pain. He didn't wait to see what had happened, but leapt through the door, gun ready.

A group of ten men had burst out of the passage onto deck. Quinn went after them, firing into their rear until his gun clicked empty. He slapped home a new mag, saw Amos and Zachery advancing at a run, their SMG's spitting short, controlled bursts. He saw men twist and fall, weapons wheeling in the air before crashing to the deck.

Six survivors rushed for cover behind a twenty foot Boston whaler. In unison, like a pair of puppets controlled by the same string, Amos and Zachery hefted grenades at the boat and threw themselves to the deck. The explosions wrecked the boat, killed two men and wounded the others. From the scant cover of the destroyed whaler the four wounded men engaged Amos and Zachery. The mercs rolled for cover behind a liferaft module returning fire. Culloden and Roberts were racing for cover from where they could engage the crew's flank.

Quinn left them to it, slipped back into the gangway leading down to A deck and up to the bridge. He heard movement on the stairs below him and flattened himself against the wall, gun at the ready. He counted to three, then pushed himself forward, crouched and fired in the one movement. One man screamed, a high-pitched woman's scream of shock, and crashed down the stairs on top of three others. Without thinking Quinn fired into the huddle of bodies until he saw smoke rising from the charred, bloody holes in their clothing. He took two tentative steps down the stairs, the Ingram thrust before him.

Then he saw him.

For maybe half a second he saw him.

The man with the golden hair! The man who'd stolen *Destry* and murdered Jenny! Here on Shadow! That half second expanded like a lifetime. Quinn's eyes widened, his mouth opened as he sucked in air, he felt his wrist swinging the Ingram's barrel onto target, felt the cushion of his finger flattening against the trigger, felt the gun kick just once, experienced an age-long frustration as he realized the magazine was empty and then an aeon of fear as the man with the golden hair jerked back a step, lifted his automatic, fired, then dived for cover.

Quinn hurled himself back against the stairs as the automatic leveled at him and simultaneously heard the booming explosion as the bullet smeared itself against the brass balustrade.

Quinn scrambled up the stairs to the bridge and over the bodies of the dead crewmen, fumbling for a fresh magazine as he ran.

Lena turned to him. She was at the wheel, guiding *Shadow* at full speed toward *Stingray One* which was now a good thousand yards away. "Peter . . ."

"I'm O.K."

Quinn tore his eyes from Lena and looked at Sanderson. He was on the radio to Teal, one hand holding the mike, the other an automatic. Blood streamed from the shoulder of his gun arm.

"The crew got out, armed themselves. We have it under control."

"Give me the mike," Quinn said quietly.

Sanderson creased his brow, handed Quinn the microphone.

"Teal? Quinn. That golden haired bastard's here."

Lena's eyes jerked toward Quinn.

Quinn listened to the radio crackle. Then, "You catch that, Teal?"

"I caught it, kid. You take it easy."

Staring at Quinn, Sanderson took the microphone from him. "Teal? Keep after the escort, but stay close to us. This ship can

survive one of those missiles, yours can't, and we need yours
to get home."

"It's wallowing out there. I think Field's grenade blew the
rudder controls to hell."

Sanderson nodded, his eyes still on Quinn. "How's Rene
and Victor?"

"Got them down below. You can't kill these Corsicans."

"Stick with us, Teal."

Sanderson replaced the mike. He looked away from Quinn
and over *Shadow*'s bow toward the crippled escort where Zeller
waited. The battle on the deck had finished, the crewmen dead
among the ruins of the wrecked whaler. Sanderson saw his four
mercs taking their positions again on the bow."

"Take Roberts," he said. "And come back."

Quinn started toward the door.

"Peter . . ."

"Ten minutes, Lena, that's all. I'll be back in ten minutes."

He dashed from the bridge, frightened that his courage
would desert him, that the dreamlike state which had carried
him through the action of the last five minutes would suddenly
dissipate and leave him like a blubbering useless child.

He ran full speed along the deck, called Roberts, and
quickly explained what he wanted him to do. Roberts nodded
and trotted back toward the bridge. Quinn lifted the hold hatch
cover, slung the Ingram over his shoulder, lowered himself over
the edge of the hold, hung a moment by his fingertips, then let
himself drop into the darkness.

Hailey fell down the stairs from A deck to B deck. He tried to
control himself, but the pain and the headache were both fusing
into one and when he'd tried to use his feet, his legs had given
out, just stopped working like they had nothing to do with him.
So he'd crashed down the stairs, and now he was crawling on
hands and knees toward where he had to go. Nearly twelve
o'clock. It was time and he had to get there.

It had all gone wrong. He'd heard the storm of submachine
gun fire from the bridge and up on deck and now the firing had
stopped and Quinn, that stupid kid from *Destry*, was still alive

and that meant the men he'd sent up to take the bridge and clear the decks were dead.

And he was wounded. He could hardly believe that. He was wounded, and it hurt, hurt like it was part of the hurt in his head. Quinn had loosed one shot at him, a snap-shot, a kid who'd probably never used a gun before in his life, and he'd snapped off a shot and hit him.

Right in the stomach.

From up on A deck he heard a ripping burst of fire and the crunch of a grenade which echoed within *Shadow*'s steel guts. The sound of it seemed to physically punch into his intestines.

"Keep moving . . ."

"O.K. fella, let's see what we can do . . ."

Hailey crawled on toward where he had to be.

Quinn emerged cautiously from the dark hold into the lighted passageway. He strained to hear above the din of the pounding engines. He would work his way up the ship; Roberts would work his way down. Three of them down here somewhere. He wanted them all, but particularly he wanted the man with the golden hair. He had to have that one.

Quinn glanced left down a narrow passage outside the hold door. Light gleamed at the end of it, spilling from an open door. He'd helped search this deck last night when they'd taken *Shadow*. He hadn't noticed any door then. He took three quick steps, paused, then swung around the frame ready to shoot.

He relaxed as he took in the scene before him. He saw sacking on the floor, SMG magazines and shells strewn around, two rifles and a shotgun standing in racks that had obviously held many more. So this was where the bastard had holed up last night. He'd been on board and come here, or got aboard somehow and hidden down here, then he'd released the crew from the hold and armed them.

Quinn continued his search along the deck, each door that he opened costing him another ounce of courage, each packing case he shoved his gun behind awarding him another ounce of fear. Three of them somewhere between him and Roberts.

Then he heard a burst of fire and the sound of the grenade. With a sudden lift of his spirits he hoped Roberts had surprised the three of them, killed them, that the big merc had blown the villains away with one well tossed grenade. Then he grabbed hold of himself, forced himself to concentrate on the search. With the sound of the explosion still reverberating in his ears he steeled himself to enter another dark room. Quinn took a deep breath, opened another door.

For all he knew they'd killed Roberts.

Roberts had done this before. It was street fighting, house to house stuff, except the streets were a ship's gangways and the houses cabins. When you cleared an area like this you moved fast and silently, without thinking of anything beyond surviving the next step.

Swiftly, expertly, he'd checked the crew recreation room; cupboards, corners, the bar, a small cold-storage room, every nook and cranny where a man with a gun could hide. Then, ghost-like on crêpe rubber soles, the giant mercenary had sprinted aft along the length of the narrow passage which skirted the hold's well to the galley and crew dining room. Nothing. That left the captain's private cabin where they'd found the one hundred thousand dollars, and the cabin beside it used by the first mate.

Blake's door was open, the way they'd left it after ransacking the safe. The light still burned. No danger there, Roberts told himself. He checked, found the cabin empty, checked his bathroom.

But the door of the first mate's cabin was shut. It hadn't been. He'd seen Amos and Zachery leaving after they'd opened Blake's safe. They hadn't shut the door.

Roberts waited and listened, his ear close to the heavy wooden door.

He frowned, strained to hear more closely. He'd got it the first time.

From inside he heard the sound of whimpering.

Young cowered on his bunk kneeling and huddled, jammed as far back into the corner as he could get, the submachine gun gripped tight in his hands, his eyes staring at the closed door. He'd heard noise in Blake's cabin. Not a loud noise, the merest scrape of a chair leg, or of a book slithering across the floor. But it wasn't Blake who'd been in there because Blake was supposed to be guarding C deck against any mercenaries who tried to penetrate back into *Shadow*'s bowels. It wasn't Blake. And it wasn't Hailey, who had released them from the hold, because he'd gone up to take over the bridge. Blake hadn't liked that. He'd argued. Hailey had smashed him over the face with the barrel of his automatic and ordered him to stay on C deck, saying that he had no right to step onto Zeller's bridge, that he'd thrown away the command of *Shadow* when he'd allowed her to be captured. No, it wasn't Hailey, because Hailey had left him, Young, in charge of A deck.

They'd been coming to get Young all his life. He was thirty years old and they'd been for him six times, the first when he'd been fifteen and he'd bashed the old codger for his wallet and they'd come and put him in reformatory.

Now someone was coming for Young again, and he was scared, and he had a submachine gun in his hands and he wasn't going to let anyone take him anywhere. The door handle moved.

He hauled back the cocking handle on the SMG, frightening himself with the hugeness of its metallic clatter in the tight confines of his cabin.

He saw the door handle spring back to its original position and pulled the trigger of the submachine gun, feeling it buck in his hands, hearing its incredible bark as bullets exploded from its muzzle and chopped jagged splinters from the heavy door. Then, surprisingly, the gun stopped jumping and the noise stopped and the door opened a few inches and a metal ball sailed gracefully through the air and landed on the bed exactly at his feet and Young looked at it kind of sadly as if he'd known it was coming all along and then the grenade exploded.

Stunned, hardly understanding anything except that someone had his gold, Zeller stared at the wreck of *Stingray One*; dead bodies, splintered wood, twisted metal; a thin cloud of smoke still hovering around the smashed wheelhouse, and in the wheelhouse a terrifying mangle of blood, bone and flesh, the result of that maniac's leap from the attacking boat. Aft, he saw

Tristan kneeling on the deck struggling with the Redeye launching tube, muttering to himself, tears of frustration streaming from his eyes. That stupid, stupid boy.

It was all so stupid, and it was so peaceful out here, so quiet, bright sun sparkling off the calm sea, gulls wheeling out of the blue sky, their squarking the only sound except for Tristan's ridiculous, childish noises and the soft slap of water on *Stingray*'s drifting hull. So quiet after all that terrible noise and fighting and screaming and shooting. And way over to the south, still more than five hundred yards away, he saw *Shadow* creeping toward him, the low punch of her powerful diesels reaching out across the sea to him.

Zeller smiled. "Ah," he said. "See?"

Tristan looked up from the launcher.

"You see? They're bringing her back to me."

Tristan looked over his shoulder at the approaching yacht. "What?"

"They're bringing back my gold."

"Fool," Tristan breathed, and turned back to the launcher.

"No need to *speak* to me like that. See with your own eyes."

Not looking up from his work Tristan said quietly. "We're going to sink *Shadow*."

"Sink *Shadow*?"

"Our only chance. Sink them. Get this escort moving again and try and reach France."

"You can't sink *Shadow*. The gold's aboard."

"The gold's no good to you now, you stupid old bastard. They're trying to kill us!"

Zeller smiled, choosing to ignore this childish outburst. He shrugged deeper into his old black coat, thrust his hands into its pockets and watched proudly as *Shadow*, laden with his beautiful gold, sailed toward him to take him to safety and comfort.

Lena felt sick to her stomach. Her heart pounded. Tears stained her face. She forced herself to concentrate, to keep *Shadow* on a direct course for *Stingray One*. Her mind was in turmoil. Peter down there somewhere in the bowels of the ship, moving from cabin to cabin ready to kill or be killed. If he died she could never live with his death. Peter. Oh Peter. Hysterical, she thought. Stop it! Concentrate! No one asked you to come. Oh Peter, please, please be alright . . .

"Calm down," Sanderson said, softly.

"I'm O.K."

"Peter's tougher than you think."

"But he doesn't know anything about fighting. You heard the gunfire, the grenade . . . He doesn't *know* . . ."

Sanderson held his bleeding arm. He'd refused to let her bandage it. Better let it hurt a bit, he'd said, keep me alert.

"You could've sent someone else down instead of him."

"I didn't send him. He went." He pointed with his good hand toward the drifting escort. "That one out there is mine. The one below is his. That's all there is to it."

"I'm scared."

Sanderson didn't look at his daughter. He could make out the figure of a man in black on the escort's deck. "I know, my darling," he said, "I know."

On *Shadow*'s bow Jack Culloden cradled the Cobra and stared at the crippled escort. He still had two rockets. And he had a sitting duck for a target. He'd fire one at one hundred yards, the second at point blank. Beside him, Amos and Zachery crouched, staring ahead, cigarettes dangling from their lips, silent as they always were in battle. He wondered about Roberts down below. He'd heard the machine gun fire, the grenade. He hoped the big brute survived. He'd be a fine customer for a new pub.

Roberts slid silently down the stairs to B deck. One down, two to go. He hoped that kid was O.K., that Quinn. Tough young bastard that, make a good merc except he thought too much. Good soldiers didn't think beyond what was twenty yards ahead of their gun barrels. The kid had guts though, volunteering to go down through the hold to the engine deck. Some bastard hiding down there would be hard to find.

Roberts saw blood on the floor, smeared down the length of the passageway. He followed it. It left a trail through Zeller's office and through the communications room where he'd burned open the safe to get the gold, and then it led behind a closed door, into that room with the weird metal box. Roberts took two deep breaths and listened from behind the closed door. He heard nothing. He glanced once at the ripped-open back of the safe and smiled as he caught a peek of the gold ingots still in it. He'd have those aboard *Charger* before they sank this fucker of a ship. Then he silently cursed as his gun barrel tapped against the metal wall.

Hailey sat crouched in the far corner of the laboratory staring at the closed door. His head ached, pulsed with an indescribable pain which chopped rhythmically into his brain in time with every heart beat. He wiped sweat from his face. The hand holding the automatic shook. He dropped the automatic and gripped his head in both hands, trying to control the great, gasping breaths that wracked his chest, breaths filled with the chemicals of fear, breaths that shook his body with their intensity but still left him sucking for precious oxygen.

"Control yourself!"

That's it, he thought, control, gotta control myself. Do what I have to do. Straighten out this mess, then Tristan will fix me, patch up this hole in my stomach, give me some peace and quiet, fix me, just gotta control myself.

Hailey closed his eyes, squeezed them tightly shut, forced himself to stop gulping in air, made himself relax his body, commanded himself to ignore the wound.

"I want to stop now . . ."

"Control yourself, you stupid son of a bitch!"

Control yourself, Hailey thought. He lifted his arm to look at his watch. His arm weighed more than anything he'd ever lifted before. Three minutes before midday. Tristan had said he'd see him at midday. Just three minutes to go and then he'd be with Tristan and Tristan would fix him, stop the pain.

"I want . . . I want . . ."

"What do you want you silly bastard? Three minutes . . . Just three minutes, then it's all gonna be alright . . ."

"Control myself."

"That's it, control yourself."

"Just three minutes."

"That's it."

Hailey stared at the black tank, the great, coffin shaped, black tank. He smiled at it, watched it shimmering and moving in front of his eyes and kept smiling as it softened. He opened his eyes wider and watched the steel rectangle take shape again.

Home, Hailey thought. He smiled. Home is where the heart is. I'm coming home.

Hailey felt a stab of pain in his stomach. He pressed his hand in against the wound. Blood oozed from between his fingers. Tristan would fix it. Just three minutes. Two minutes now. Maybe one. Maybe he was coming right now. Tristan was always punctual. The pain abated. Hailey held up his hand and stared at the blood.

"C-c-control mys-s-self . . ."

"Yes you prissy bastard, you do that . . ."

"Control yourself . . ."

"I'm doing O.K., fella, don't you worry about me. I'm doing O.K."

Hailey smiled again at the tank. Gonna take a little swim, he thought. Gonna take a nice, *long* swim. Fix me up. Me and Tristan gonna fix us up, get us together again, get us one hundred percent operative again, have a little talk, a little soothing conversation, get rid of all the aches and pains, any minute now, fix this head of ours, of mine, floating in that water and the voice talking to me, soon, soon . . .

Hailey heard something. Close. He tore his eyes from the friendly, soothing shape of the tank. Someone was coming. Someone on the same deck. Someone running.

"Tristan."

"Not Tristan."

"Tristan!"

No, not Tristan. Hailey reached for the automatic. It slipped in the blood in his hand. He changed the automatic into his other hand and wiped the bloodied hand on his trouser thigh.

No, not Tristan. Someone gulping great lungfuls of breath. Hailey heard a shallow metallic clang as something struck a bulkhead. A gun barrel. Not Tristan. One of them. Out to get him.

"*Get the gun!*"

"*I got it! I got it!*"

"*Shut up! He'll hear us.*"

"*Ready for that mother, fella.*"

Hailey clutched the automatic in his right hand. With his left he supported the intolerable weight of it which bore down on his right wrist. He gritted his teeth, trying to ignore the pulsing pain throbbing through his temples. Forced himself to keep the gun aimed at the wooden rectangle of the laboratory door.

Got my friend, he thought. *Got my little friend. Always got my friend. Never alone. Surrounded, outnumbered, how could you avoid capture? I would kill myself.*

"*How? By whatever means were at hand.*"

"*There may be no means. There are always means. There are always means. Always.*"

"*Zeller and I don't want you to suffer, Hailey, ever . . . I know that. I know.*"

Hailey saw a red mist descend in front of his eyes. The gun wavered, fell low from his point of aim. He breathed deeply, forced his eyes wide open, willed the haziness of tiredness and fear and pain to lift, commanded all his remaining strength toward this one last task. When it was done, Tristan would come with his reward. With peace. And quietness. And soft words.

The giant launched himself through the door behind a submachine gun that bucked and screeched and twanged and spat as a great hail of lead sprang from it, smashing instruments, exploding glass, tearing inch thich files, richoceting off steel walls, pulping chairs, ripping wires, upending a table as a slug splintered a leg.

Three bullets hit Hailey before he fired. One nicked the point of his right shoulder, another smashed his right foot, another ploughed into the inside of his right thigh with such force it slithered him sideways so he crashed onto his wounded right shoulder.

Hailey screamed in shock and pain. But he saw clearly now. No red mist. Everything in sharp focus. He screamed and pulled the trigger and from his sprawled position on the floor saw the figure in the doorway slammed against the frame, saw the machine gun fly through the air and crash onto Tristan's desk. He pulled the trigger again and saw a spray of blood leap from the figure's face, saw the feet kick out in the throes of death.

Hailey was still pulling the trigger after the magazine was empty.

Hailey let the gun fall from his grasp then let his face rest on the cool steel of the floor.

You see, he told himself, you did it. Now Tristan will come and everything will be alright.

He stared at the hole in his stomach. At the shiny, white intestinal lumps that rose from the blood.

"That's not so good, right?"

He shook his head.

"That's not too good, at all!"

He chuckled tiredly.

"Tristan'll have to sew me together."

If he can, he thought.

"He's late."

He'll get here, Hailey thought, *he'll get here*.

"I was really scared then."

Nothing to be scared of, Hailey told himself. *It's all worked out. Something goes wrong, it's all worked out*.

"This really hurts fella, this hurts like hell, I mean this hurts worse than anything, I mean we've got to stop this hurting, I'm getting, you know, nervous about this, I don't want this pain too much longer . . ."

"Not too much longer. Tristan'll come. Not too much longer."

'He better hurry. This is real bad."

Hailey forced himself up again into a sitting position with his back to the wall. He stared at the empty automatic with his blood smeared on the butt laying in front of him. He looked at his foot. It was numb. The bullet had gone in one side of the shoe and out of the other. Two neat red holes. Blood oozed out from between the laces. His leg was broken where the bullet hit him in the thigh. There was no pain there yet, but at the slightest move he could sense bone grinding deep within the flesh.

Hailey groaned.

Then he felt the bulge in his left pocket. He stared at the pocket trying to understand the hardness of the thing within it which pressed against his groin. His hand moved slowly. He took out the grenade.

Got one shot left, he told himself. They come down, I got this one shot left. Blow 'em away.

"Where's Tristan?"

"He'll come, fella."

"Getting worried."

"Yeah, I know. Gotta hang in there."

Hailey stared at the tank.

Get in the tank, he told himself, then when Tristan comes you'll be ready.

That's it, he told himself.

The tank was six feet away. Hailey reckoned it must have taken him an hour to get there. He couldn't understand why it took so long, or why it hurt so bad, or why the hell Tristan hadn't arrived to help him. He looked at his watch. Two minutes after midday . . . O.K., he'd be here soon. In the meantime . . .

Somehow Hailey opened the hinged, coffin-like lid of the tank. Then he forced himself upright, balancing all his weight on his left leg, his shattered right leg hanging uselessly.

Something was wrong. He stared inside the tank, trying to understand. He couldn't move. That was what was wrong. The edge of the tank was three feet off the ground and he had to get in there. That was what was wrong. He stared at the welcoming water, heavy with its saline and warmed to the temperature of blood and tried to figure how to get in there.

Slowly, he figured it out. He opened the air-supply valve and switched on the communications system. He lay the hand grenade on top of the control box in the tank. Then with one hand pressing in against the stomach wound he slowly let himself bend at the middle until his face was touching the blood-warm water. For one sharp, agonizing moment he nearly fainted with the pain of the contorted position. Then he let himself fall so he splashed into the water.

"That's it."

"That's it. Now close the lid."

Drenched, agonized, Hailey forced himself to stand inside the tank and reach for the lid. It took all his strength, but after he'd hauled it from the perpendicular the pneumatic hinges took the weight and inch by inch lowered the steel top, so the light inside faded gradually into absolute blackness.

"That's it. Now stretch out. Float."

"Leg . . ."

"Yeah, but you can do it, fella."

"Try it like this and . . ."

"That's fine. Jesus, that's better."

"Just wait for him now. Just a bit longer."

"I want to talk to you."

"Yes . . ."

"I've been wanting to talk to you for a long time."

"Yes . . ."

"Couple of things bothering me. About what we've been doing. And about the future . . ."

Hailey floated. The sound of submachine gun fire from the engine room never penetrated his dark universe.

Blake waited. He'd heard the sound of someone jumping down into the hold, a hollow echo of steel below the sound of the engines, and, dragging the bag of gold after him, had dashed into the paint locker and pulled the door to. He'd blast the living shit out of anyone crazy enough to open that door. He stood leaning against the steel wall of the yacht with the gold at his feet and the SMG in his hand, and he waited, listening.

His face ached. He carefully dabbed his cheek and his fingers came away wet with blood. That bastard Hailey had swiped him with his automatic. There was time for Hailey another day if someone else hadn't got him already. Been a lot of shooting and grenade throwing up there and he didn't see how the milk-sop of a crew could stand against those professionals. During the fireworks he'd made a dash to Zeller's office to see if he could rifle it for some cash and he'd found the safe open and something better than cash. He'd thrown half a dozen five pound ingots into a sack and headed below again. Maybe quarter of a million dollars worth of gold in that sack. All he had to figure was how to get himself and the sack off the effing yacht. But he'd do it; he'd find a way. When they'd finished with Zeller and the escorts they'd be taking *Shadow* into port somewhere—no one in his right mind sank a $12,000,000 yacht loaded with maybe another $8,000,000 worth of gold—and when they got into port he'd figure a way to get ashore.

All he had to do was use his nut and hang on.

He heard a noise close to the door, a sharp noise that rode above that of the twin diesels. That bastard was still creeping around out there like a baby elephant, opening doors, poking around.

Blake flexed his hand on the pistol grip of the SMG and waited.

His eyes now accustomed to the gloom of the engine deck, Quinn moved surely, even recklessly, as he checked every conceivable hiding place.

He'd heard the ripping chatter of the SMG interspersed with the deeper booming thud of an automatic handgun coming from directly above on B deck, and knew that Roberts had shot it out with the second of the three. What had happened? The handgun had been the second gun to fire and had kept firing after the SMG stopped, and Roberts would have used his SMG . . .

He snapped his mind back to the job in hand. Was there anywhere left down here where a man could hide?

One place he hadn't tried. He read the sign on the door. "PAINT." For a moment he considered forgetting the locker, getting up onto B deck to find out what had happened to Roberts. But he couldn't do that. One, perhaps two of them still hid somewhere on *Shadow*. If he went up to B deck and there was one down here, and that one followed . . .

His hand touched the handle of the paint locker door. He stopped himself in mid-action. Don't do it that way you silly bastard, remember what Roberts and Amos and Jock and the rest of them taught you.

It took him only a moment to find a mop by the engines. He flattened himself against the wall by the door and holding the mop by the head used the handle to shove the door open.

The gloom was rent by jagged flashes of lightning and a slashing burst of shots shrieked high above the rhythmic boom of the diesels. Quinn dropped the mop, a hand automatically raising itself to cover his face as he heard the cruel whining of the lead slugs ricocheting off engine mounts and steel walls and ribs.

Quinn waited three seconds then picked up the mop and rattled the handle on the floor. Another terrifying burst erupted from the locker and again Quinn couldn't stop himself covering his face as the ricochets slid whirring around the deck.

Quinn saw from the flashes which lit the door frame that both bursts had been fired chest high. It was something the mercs had taught him to look for in this kind of fighting; and they'd told him what to do.

He slid down the wall onto his stomach, slipped the Ingram around the door frame at floor level, pulled the trigger, and as the gun roared and jumped in his hand moved his wrist horizontally and vertically and kept shooting until the whole thirty-two shot magazine had emptied itself into the tiny room. Then he changed mags and did the same thing again.

He stood, pushed home a new magazine, reachd a hand inside for the light, flicked it on and took one quick glance around the door frame.

He stepped into the locker and looked down at his handiwork feeling strangely calm and detached. Blake. Quinn couldn't tell how many shots had hit him. The man sprawled back against the wall, eyes open, mouth moving, his clothes a rainbow of reds, greens, browns, blues, yellow and orange from the punctured paint cans which slewed their contents over him.

The moving lips tried to make words.

Blake died.

Quinn saw the bag, the hessian ripped, one paint splattered ingot propped against the man's ankle.

Quinn turned, ran to the gangway leading to B deck, mounted the stairs cautiously, gun at the ready. Deep inside him he knew that Roberts was dead and that the man with the golden hair had killed him.

Tristan glanced over his shoulder. *Shadow* steamed steadily toward them, less than two hundred yards away. Zeller stared at the yacht, talking to himself, hunched down in the old black coat. Tristan swore under his breath as he wrenched at the jammed safety actuator device on the launch tube. He felt sweat running down his face. He fumbled in his pocket for a coin, slipped it under the actuator and applied all his strength.

"Coming," Zeller said, "here she comes. Coming to get me."

Quinn stood at the open door of the laboratory and stared at Roberts' body. The giant merc's face had been torn away by a bullet; four or five others had impacted against his chest. Quinn lifted his eyes and scanned the wrecked room. The submachine-gun bursts had ripped it apart. He saw smears of blood against the far wall. So Roberts had wounded his man. But where was he? And *who* was he?

He stepped over Roberts' body and crept through the communications room. Then he heard the voice.

"Just want you to understand a thing or two, fella."

Quinn spun, his gun barrel searching the room for the source of the voice.

"Well you better say it fast. You know, I'm feeling, you know . . ."

The tank. Quinn stared at it.

"You've got to understand it wasn't my fault . . ."

That voice. Quinn would recognize it anywhere. That voice would be with him until the end of his days; cold, cruel, metallic.

"I'm not blaming you."

"When they did it, I mean when they turned us over and I got buried and they dug you up, I fought. Like I was drugged and I was in one of these things where we are now, but I fought. I held you down as long as I could. Not because I don't like you, fella, but I knew all about you and I figured you for being better off where you were . . . Christ, man, this *hurts* . . ."

"Can't take it much longer. Is Tristan coming?"

"What do you think, fella?"

"I guess not, right?"

"That's the way it goes."

"So it's over."

"That's what I want to talk to you about."

"No future, right?"

"Tristan told you what to do."

"Yeah . . ."

"Jesus, if you'd just stepped out when I asked you . . ."

"Sorry about that . . ."

"Could've been well away, fella. Could've sorted it out between us . . ."

"I couldn't. I *couldn't*."

"O.K., calm down, I know you couldn't. Tristan wouldn't let you . . . No blame, man, no blame . . . Too late for that . . ."

"Too late . . ."

Quinn listened to the disembodied voice drifting from the speaker on the desk. He'd moved toward the tank when he first heard it, ready to lift the lid, the anger and frustration flaring in him. He'd wanted to shoot, open the tank and rake it from end to end. Do what he'd promised to do. But he stood now, staring at the speaker, eyes wide, throat dry, listening, struggling to understand . . .

"Got to do something about this pain . . . getting worse."

"Tristan told you what to do."

"Better do it . . ."

"But not for him, fella."

"But he told me . . ."

"Sure, do it, but not for *him*. For *us*!"

"For us."

"Tristan screwed you. Me. Us. Turned us inside out. We were getting along . . . Jesus, it's worse every second . . . *Jesus!* . . . we were getting along O.K. I mean, when you started coming up I sort of put a wet blanket on you, kept you in check. We weren't good, but we were balanced. And now look at us. You and Tristan against me. Really screwed up . . . Tristan turned the key, fella, and you just burst up out of there, like a jack-in-the-box . . ."

"I'm sorry."

"No blame. But let's do it, eh?"

"Sure, sure . . ."

"But this time we'll screw Tristan. We're doing it for us, to stop the pain, not so we don't get captured."

"I . . ."

"Please. Just this once."

"It's hurting . . ."

"Please."

"I have to do it. Have to finish it now."

"For us?"

"Anything, anything . . ."

"Well say it . . . Say, fuck Tristan . . ."

"I . . . fuck Tristan!"

"*Fuck* Tristan!"

"*Fuck* him! *Fuck* him! God, Jesus Christ, I'm dying . . ."

"Good fella. First time you've ever cussed. Bit of profanity never hurt anyone. O.K., so do it . . ."

"Ready?"

"Ready."

"I'm sorry, I really am."

"So am I."

"See you next time."

"Sure, fella."

"*Ciao.*"

"*Adios.*"

"I'm doing it now."

"Go right ahead."

"For you and for me . . ."

Quinn heard a click over the speaker, then a metallic *twang!* His eyes snapped from the speaker to the metal box, back to the speaker, then in a flash realized he'd heard a grenade handle being released and threw himself to the floor, one arm covering his head.

He needn't have bothered. The steel box shuddered from the

forces released within it and lifted a full inch off the floor, but the thick, metal casting absorbed the explosion and ricocheted the grenade's diamond shaped shrapnel pieces through every angle within the dark space and blood-warm water within.

Quinn came to his feet, stared at the isolation tank, saw thin beads of liquid escaping from the lip where the lid joined the bottom of the box, pinkish water glistening on the gray, metal surface.

Quinn felt suddenly empty, tired, as if a great and terrible weight had suddenly been taken from him and he'd been told he could rest. He wanted to lie down, sleep, then wake and examine what had happened and when he understood take Lena and go with her to a distant country and not return for a long time.

Instead, he turned, stepped wearily over Roberts' body and walked slowly to the stairs leading up to A deck.

He was half way up when the Redeye missile exploded against *Shadow*'s bow.

One hundred and fifty yards from *Stingray* Jock Culloden saw a figure straighten, swing around and aim something toward *Shadow*. Jock shouted a warning to Amos and Zachery, lifted the Cobra to his shoulder and desperately tried to find his point of aim.

Before he could he saw a flash from *Stingray*, was vaguely aware of a ripping sound like a sheet being torn apart, and then *Shadow* seemed to rear up as an explosion jabbed at his eardrums. He slid across the deck, saw the Cobra go over the side into the sea and then he was falling too, hands flailing to grab something, anything, and then he was in the sea, *Shadow*'s beam only feet from his face. He kicked away, coughed water out, and then saw what the rocket had done.

Shadow's once sleek bow was wrecked, punched open by the explosion. The hole, a dozen feet around its jagged circumference, was sucking in hundredweights of water with every yard the yacht traveled. Already the bow angled down, and when the weight of water dragged the hole below sealevel, *Shadow* would inexorably nose herself to the bottom.

As Jock fought the yacht's frothing wake, Teal, who had

immediately responded to signals from Amos and Zachery, raced *Charger* around the *Shadow*'s stern and threw him a line. The wiry Scot hauled himself aboard, vomited sea water over the decks and then shoved Teal into the cabin.

"Get Sanderson on the radio, fast!"

Both Sanderson and Lena had been thrown to the floor by the force of the explosion. Now, with Lena back at the wheel, and *Shadow* only a hundred yards from *Stingray*, Sanderson listened to Jock's report and watched the bow, seeing, even as the Scot spoke, that it was dipping, degree by degree.

"Tell Teal to keep close by. We're ramming them and then we're . . ." He smiled at the microphone. "And then we're disembarking. Stand by to pick us up."

Teal's voice barked into the mike. "How many of you?"

"I don't know."

"Quinn alright?"

Sanderson looked at Lena. His daughter kept her eyes on the escort, adjusting the wheel, trying to compensate for the weight of water in the bow which dragged the yacht off course. "We don't know."

"We'll stand by. Good luck."

Sanderson replaced the mike, then gently pushed Lena aside and took the wheel from her. "This part of it is for me to do," he said.

He fixed his eyes on the man in black on the escort who stood staring at *Shadow*. Zeller! He had him now, but it didn't make him feel good. During all those years of spying, collating information and planning he'd thought that the final moment, if it ever came, would be one of wild and vengeful joy. Well, the moment was here. He was about to kill Zeller and he didn't feel anything. He just wanted it to be over. He just wanted the killing to stop.

As he concentrated on pushing the crippled yacht toward its destiny with its owner he didn't notice Lena slip out of the bridge nor hear her rush down the stairs to A deck to search for Quinn.

* * *

Zeller stood aghast as he watched the rocket rip a hole through his yacht's bow. He saw her shudder then list to starboard toward the hole which he knew was sucking in the sea.

On matchstick frail legs he turned to stare at Tristan, his son Tristan, who had done this despicable thing. Tristan was on his knees, pulling open another Redeye canister. He had the parts on the deck now, struggling to fit the battery/coolant unit to the launcher, fumbling, cursing, stealing glances at *Shadow*, which like a huge, crippled, predatory animal was lunging toward them in preparation for the kill.

Zeller's mouth opened and closed as he searched for the words with which to whip this contemptible, vile bastard of a traitor, but none would come, and like a cartoon robot he staggered toward Tristan with ancient clawed hands outstretched and with desperate strength latched them around his throat; long, old, yellow nails digging into the skin, brittle joints cracking as he applied every last ounce of pressure he could summon. And he found the words at last: "The gold! The gold! *The gold! The gold!*"

Tristan gasped. He dropped the missile coolant unit. His stronger hands grabbed at Zeller's wrists. He twisted, feeling the skin at his throat tearing. He tried to shout as he felt the mad fingers spearing into his flesh. He kicked, twisted, rammed his hip into the old man's stomach, punched back at Zeller's head, feeling his knuckles numbing on the ancient skull and with dimmed hearing heard him screaming: "*The gold! The gold! The gold!*" And as consciousness began to fade and golden sparks leaped in front of his bulging eyes he heard the old man crying and with every sob the mad fingers pulsed harder and then he felt himself falling, the old man falling with him and the sea embraced them, and they writhed and twisted and danced down, down below the surface, the old man still holding him, clutching at his neck and at the instant that he died Zeller released him and he floated, serene and weightless, directionless in the great depths, contained, hearing nothing, seeing nothing, drifting into oblivion and infinite isolation.

And Zeller drifted too, not far from dear Tristan, his face a frozen mask of hate, his arms outstretched, fingers still clawed in anger as if even in death he was ready to kill. And his old black coat billowed as deep sea currents filled it, and small fish flicked and flew from the strange and dark apparition.

Zeller slept at last.

Sanderson saw them go overboard and knew his work was done. The prey was gone, dead. No need to risk more lives. He hauled back on *Shadow*'s throttles, swung the wheel hard to port in an attempt to avoid the escort. But *Shadow* moved low in the water now, her bow burdened with hundreds of tons of water. She didn't respond.

He looked for Lena, saw she was missing, yelled her name. He saw Amos and Zachery sprinting up the slanting deck toward the highground of the bridge. Then, with only seconds to go before impact, Sanderson let go the wheel and jammed himself in a corner of the wheelhouse.

Shadow struck the *Stingray* broadside, her water-weighted bow driving the lighter boat abeam. The great crunch of first impact slid Sanderson across the bridge wrenching a cry of agony from him as he jarred his wounded arm against the wall. Above the screech of rending metal and fiber glass he heard Amos shouting to Zachery.

Dazed, Sanderson grabbed at the leg of the heavy chart table for support. *Shadow* reared, her wounded bow driving itself up and aboard the escort's hull, like a great sea monster emerging from the deep to devour all in its path, and the escort cracked in half like a chopped board, the bow and stern sections gliding aside, then sliding into the depths.

Shadow's bow crashed back down as the two halves of the destroyed escort slipped from beneath her, the weight of the fall ramming the hole made by the missile far below the surface so that the sea rushed in unchecked, racing through the bow section, cracking the walls of the hold, flooding all of C deck. Then, as the yacht settled, her bow dipped further and further until she was pointed at a thirty degree angle toward the seabed and sliding under foot by foot, second by second.

Sanderson hauled himself to his feet as Amos and Zachery burst through the bridge door. They grabbed him, one on each arm, ignoring his wound. They hustled him out onto the boat deck. Teal was circling *Charger* just thirty yards off the stricken yacht, ready to pick up anyone who jumped.

Sanderson struggled. "Quinn . . . and my daughter . . . they're below somewhere."

"No time, Colonel."

"We have to get them."

"This tub's sinking, Colonel. You know the rules. You made them."

Amos nodded to Zachery. They shoved Sanderson together, watched him plunge twenty feet into the sea, saw Teal edge *Charger* in closer and Jock lean over the side with a looped rope to pick him up.

"Got to give it a try," Amos said.

"Fucking heroes," Zachery said.

They dashed toward the stairway leading to A deck.

Shadow suddenly lurched, her bow dropping another five degrees. From beneath the sea the two mercs heard a deep-throated painful ripping sound as water pressure tore another place from *Shadow*'s weakened hull. Then, with terrible rapidity she slid another ten feet under water, so that all of her forward section was so far under her screws nearly cleared the water.

From *Charger*, Jock, Teal and Sanderson shouted for them to jump. As *Shadow* settled even further, Amos and Zachery hesitated, turned, scrambled along the slanting deck, and hurled themselves into the sea.

Sanderson, standing on *Charger*'s aft deck, saw the two mercs make their try and saw them jump. As they hit the sea he bowed his head and closed his eyes.

Quinn was halfway up the stairs leading to A deck when the missile struck. The force of the explosive warhead against *Shadow*'s bow rocked the ship. Quinn grabbed at the railing for support, missed it, fell backward, cracked his head on the steps and landed stunned at the bottom.

He struggled blearily to his feet, only half realizing what had happened, saw the crazy angle of the deck. He crawled toward the stairs, pounding waves of pain enveloping his fuzzy brain.

Then Lena was there, somewhere above him, calling his

name. He called back, shook his head, desperately trying to
clear the grogginess. Then she was beside him, pulling on his
arm, trying to force him to his feet.

"Oh, thank God, thank God," he heard her say, and he put
his arm around her for support and heaved himself up.

Using all the wiry strength in her slim body, Lena half lifted,
half pushed Quinn up the stairs.

Then the world went crazy as *Shadow* struck the escort, the
yacht changing its angle, the stern dipping as the punctured
bow climbed high aboard *Stingray*.

Quinn and Lena clung to the railing, she with one arm
around him, her fingers hooked into his belt. "Hang on!" she
breathed. "Hang on!"

As the escort broke in two *Shadow* crashed back into the sea.
Quinn tried to move, but Lena saw he was exhausted and let
him rest for five precious seconds before starting to crawl up
the stairs with him.

Those seconds could have killed them. They heard the deep
ripping sound of tearing metal and *Shadow* lurched to an even
greater angle as she began her unstoppable slide toward the sea
bed.

Lena looked behind them, saw sloshing water creeping up
the slant of B deck and knew that deep in the ship all bulkheads
and doors had been burst by the enormous water pressure.

She tried to force Quinn upward. He looked at her, shaking
his head as if he didn't recognize her. "*Peter*," she shouted,
"*you have to move! We're going to die!*"

He tried to force himself forward. With her help he mounted
two more stairs. Then he stopped, his face resting against the
cold steel of the stairwell, unable to move.

Behind them the water was gaining, deepening inch by inch
as the sea forced its way through the smashed bow.

Lena pushed Quinn, pulled at him. He wouldn't move.
Finally, in desperation she hit him, slapped him, punched at
him, bruising her knuckles on his head and face, screamed at
him. "*Damn you, I don't want to die here with you. Goddamn
it, get us out of here. Coward! Bastard! Help me get us out of
here!*" And she punched and slapped and kicked at him,
screamed and ranted at him and slowly her rage penetrated the

veil of tiredness and pain which enveloped his brain and he nodded and forced himself up, finding just enough strength to help her too and slowly they crawled toward the light of day and out of *Shadow*'s steel womb and the encroaching, deadly waters.

On deck they stood together, sucking the safe, fresh, clean air, neither one hearing the cheers and shouts of relief and encouragement from *Charger*.

Then, hand in hand, Quinn and Lena jumped into the sea just seconds before *Shadow* released one great sigh of trapped air and gave up life and slid from sight—plunging, twisting and turning into the depths in search of her master.

Epilogue

Quinn had suffered a concussion from his fall down the stairs after the missle hit *Shadow*, but a week in bed in the Roberts house under the gentle and very personal ministrations of Lena sped him quickly on the road to recovery. Ten days after flying back from Ibiza he drove himself in a hired car to Heathrow Airport to greet his father.

Feisty old James P. greeted his son with open affection. He threw his arms around him, and hugged him and kissed him on both cheeks. The truth was that he'd never expected to see Peter again. But he should've known better than that, he told himself, the boy was the son of an Irishman, wasn't he? And you couldn't get rid of an Irishman just like that. Bejesus no!

As he drove through the rain back into London Peter outlined for his father everything that had happened since he'd last seen him, right from Johnny James' murder to the scuttling of *Charger* off a deserted Ibizan beach to cover the last traces of the battle.

James P. Quinn listened in silence, nodding from time to time, knowing, finally, as he listened to the horrifying details, the truth of the saying that "no father ever knows his son."

"Couple more things, too," Quinn said. "We got enough gold home to pay off the operation and split a bonus between the surviving mercenaries. I have your two hundred thousand."

360

James P. Quinn grunted, waiting for the next "couple of things."

Quinn drove half a mile in silence, trying to find the words to say it properly. In the end he just blurted it out. "Look Dad, if it's O.K. I'd like to start working with you next month."

"It's not O.K."

Quinn's eyes snapped around to meet his father's.

"I thought that was what you wanted?"

"It is. But not now. I want you when you're ready to come."

"I'm ready."

"Rubbish!" Quinn Sr. growled an incomprehensible sound deep in his throat. "That's an Irishman's polite way of saying bullshit."

"I don't understand you."

"And bullshit to that, too. Talk to me in twelve months. In the meantime enjoy your trip."

"What trip?"

James P. Quinn chuckled. "Teal and I have been plotting while you've been recuperating. Teal, you, me, your lady and her father, are going down to Poole the day after tomorrow to paint the name on *Destry II*. He's captaining you and Lena on an around-the-Med cruise."

Quinn ran the car into a parking bay and braked to a halt. He turned and looked at his father, shaking his head. "You crazy old bastard."

Quinn Sr. spread his hands in mock horror. "A father buys his son a thirty-eight foot cruiser for a wedding present and the son calls him a crazy old bastard. Jesus and Mary, what's the world coming to?"

Sanderson felt tired and he felt old. The wound in the arm seemed to have robbed him of more than a lump of flesh; he felt as if he'd aged ten years since they'd left London for Ibiza. But he knew he'd get over it. He always did. Battle did this to him. Deaths in his command weighed on him, always had. Tripp, Selby, Reed, Field, Roberts, and dear old Johnny James. All good men and gone forever. And Rene and Victor still on Ibiza recovering from their wounds. Out of ten hired men only three had emerged unscathed. Amos and Zachery had disappeared into the London fleshpots. Jock had flown straight to Scotland to present his new wife with the cash to open their pub. And good luck to him. Like himself, the little Scot had finally laid down his arms.

Sanderson sighed wearily, shuffled files that he'd brought off *Shadow*, then pushed them to one side of his desk. He'd finish his new book soon, after he'd used Zeller's meticulous documentation to wipe out the last vestiges of the arms dealing empire.

He went to his filing cabinet, pulled open the bottom drawer and took out a bottle of whisky and a glass. He poured himself a good shot and slugged it back in one gulp. Snap out of it, he ordered himself. Can't be an old grump. You're on parade tomorrow, Sanderson, father of the bride.

He heard a tap on the door and turned as it opened. Lena stood there smiling, the long white wedding dress a perfect fit, almost as if it had been designed for her in the first place. He stared at her, his memory cast back to another time, to another girl who had worn the same dress. Tears flooded his eyes and he compressed his lips into a thin line to hold them back. He shook his head, trying to smile.

"You look so beautiful, Lena."

"It fits."

"Perfectly." He walked forward and took his daughter in his arms. "The week you were born your mother boxed it for you." He kissed her on the forehead then hugged her to him. The tears dried in his eyes and he kissed her again.

"Right," he said, "a quick drink, a toast to the bride-to-be."

He found another glass, poured them both a tot, then toasted her, admiring her beauty and her softness, and felt the weight of battle lifting from his soul.

The killing was over.

And life went on.